DEADLY DIVISIONS

PAUL
FERRIS

REG
McKAY

DEADLY DIVISIONS
The Spectre Chronicles

MAINSTREAM
PUBLISHING
EDINBURGH AND LONDON

First published in Great Britain in 2002 by
MAINSTREAM PUBLISHING COMPANY (EDINBURGH) LTD
7 Albany Street
Edinburgh EH1 3UG

ISBN 1 84018 601 1

A catalogue record for this book is available from the British Library

Typeset in Allise, Trixie, Bembo and Van Dijck
Printed and bound in Great Britain by
Cox & Wyman Ltd

CONTENTS

1 APRIL 1989

It started as a joke. A good joke. Not sensible but it's what we did when we were kids. How we lived. Like the chicken runs — knocking off a motor, something a bit tasty, and searching out the polis. Aggravating the buggers then you're off with them on your tail. Not smart but funny as fuck when you lost them miles off their patch. Jokes like that were useful, toning up the driving skills — unless you ended up in the jail or frying in some burned-out wreck. A kids' game but lessons well learned for future years, whatever happened. Besides, everyone did it. Everyone I knew.

But this, this was a joke, that's all it was. Someone else's joke. Until things changed. First it turned useful then it turned serious. Now it's my secret. And it's going to stay that way.

A

FOND FAREWELL

The razor blade zipped through her white flesh and she was glad. Just a few more zigzags to add to the crooked white tramlines running down her forearm. Pain would cleanse her, flush out her degradation, awaken her real self. Cathy Brodie turned on the cold tap, drenching her arm till the water turned red and looked up to stare out of the window above the sink. She would watch him leave and hurt herself.

This one room was her world and it stank of cooked lard, dampness, sour milk, stale cigarette smoke. And him. She knew the cramped room so well she could describe it without turning to look. A crazy angled wardrobe, its door gaping open like a slavering drunk's mouth. The skinny-legged, canary-yellow kitchen table, fag-end scarred and littered with her entire food supply. The ragged-edged, faded Paisley pattern carpet that had been pillaged from a smaller room and didn't fit. Stuffed black plastic bags lining one wall, her worldly belongings from a better time and another place.

'Double, in case you need it, doll,' the landlord had wheezed with a grin and a wink, nodding at the metal-framed bed. The mattress dipped deeply in the middle, wearing a collage of stains, a legacy from long-gone strangers. Old springs creaked when she lay on it and when he, when they . . .

Scrubbity Screech
Scrubitty Screech
Scrubbity Screech

The bed's lament mocked and tormented her. Haunted her still. She wanted to leave the window, cross the room and turn on the radio, blotting out the grating echo with loud, trashy pop music. But she couldn't. She must stay at her post making certain he had gone before she could take up the shreds of her existence once again. The room didn't bother her but that stench did. Cooked lard, dampness, sour milk, stale cigarette smoke. And him. Human mulch. It reeked of desperation. She sliced her arm again.

The top of his greasy head appeared as he slowly waltzed out of the close mouth directly below. She could still smell that dank, sweat-sour hair and it made her retch. He was whistling through his teeth, some tuneless, self-congratulatory mess. A big man, so broad across the shoulders people were forced to step into the gutter to let him pass. Tall, he was a giant in this city of underfed runts. Flat feet made him waddle, adding a comic grace that threatened to spoil his menace, but no one laughed apart from strangers and the suicidal.

In the middle of the street he stopped and stretched his arms out. The cat who'd scoffed the kipper. A happy man satisfied with his lot, at home in his own territory; safe, sound, confident. Stooping to light one of his small cheap cigars, cupping his hands against a non-existent breeze, he exhaled a trailing blue cloud and went on his way, crossing to the pavement at the other side of the road. Walking his walk. Moving on to his next victim.

Cathy Brodie opened her dressing gown and splashed freezing water between her legs. The cold shocked and stung, punching the breath from her lungs as she knew it would. Watching him pad away, she scooped blood-pink water onto her body, rubbing at the filth between her legs, scrubbing at the folds of her sex with her fingernails. All the time watching him leave.

Farther up the street a young man came out of a tenement close. Small, dark haired and slightly built, he was dressed in denims, T-shirt, a shiny dark blouson and a baseball cap pulled low on his head. In that rig-out he had to be young and a stranger to that street of housebound, friendless oldies and working girls who only emerged at night to barter barely clothed bodies for that night's supply of smack. If the young guy had known the area he would've crossed the road, avoiding the man now padding his way. Cathy Brodie stayed stock still, watching and worrying for the stranger as he kept walking smartly, perkily towards trouble.

As the men drew near, the small one looked up smiling, saying something Cathy couldn't hear but which brought a sneer to that big slimy face that had lain on her pillow minutes before. She knew the look too well. It promised violence. The big man swivelled, reaching into his jacket for the long-bladed knife he kept there.

BANG

The young man pulled a pistol from the back of his jeans, swiftly reached up and shot the other in the face, buckling his knees and dumping him in a heap on the pavement. Crouching over the body the outsider stuck the gun barrel between those fat lips and shot him again.

BANG

Pocketing his pistol, he walked away as if nothing had happened. Two buildings down he hesitated, swiftly scanning the street and the windows, his blue-eyed stare arching past his silent audience before he turned abruptly and disappeared up a close.

A loud, steady beat thumped in Cathy's chest, her stomach fluttered and sea waves roared in her ears. Since her tormentor had hit the deck she hadn't been able to take her eyes off the crumpled mess of his body splayed on the ground. A trickle of blood ran from his skull across the paving stones.

The baby had been grumbling for food for the past hour, but only then did Cathy hear him. Going over to the old Moses basket wedged on the floor against the bed she picked up her son, shooshing and stroking his face, kissing his cheek. Cuddling her child in close to her breast, Cathy gently, rhythmically sashayed on the spot, smiling for the first time in a long while and softly sang her favourite reggae lullaby,

Everything gonna be all right
Everything gonna be all right . . . Tea
Everything gonna be all right

RESPECT

'ADDIE!'
　'Whiiit?'
　'IT WAS ADDIE DONE THE HIT!'
　'Eeeeehhh?'
　'JAMES – fucking – ADDISON!'
　'Cannae hear ye, man.'
　'Wee minute.'
　'Whiit . . .'

Joe ignored the last question, left his seat and wound his way through the mob of drinkers till he found the source of the racket. He smelled her before he saw her, standing in her own no-go zone, the hardened drinkers anxious not to get too close. Madge had drunkenly shit herself years before and never quite broken the habit. A ragged woollen coat hung open, revealing layers of cardigans and jumpers covering a pastel summer dress soiled grey as the Glasgow skies. On her feet, wellington boots – one green, one black. Naked legs akimbo, the skirt hiked high up short tartan thighs, her red-mottled face thrown back, a toothless mouth wide open.

　'*Awww hey, big shpenderrrr,*

　'*Shpeeend . . . a lissshle tiiime wi MEEEeeeee.*' She bawled more than sang, white gobs of spittle spraying the air in front of her.

　'*Zaaa minute yese waaaalked in the joint . . .*' and she flounced up and down, less sex symbol, more child bursting to pee.

　'Very nice, doll,' Joe smiled his most reassuring smile. These alky grannies could be lethal.

　'Helloooooo, darlin, want tae buy wee Madge a drink?' and the woman winked suggesting more might be on offer if he treated her well. 'Ah'm awfy thirsty, shon. Dae anything for a wee shwally. Anything at all.'

　'Course, hen. Here's a few bob for singing so sweet. Bet ye used tae be a professional.' Close up, Joe could see that Madge's matted grey hair was tobacco stained at the front and a green, lumpy stain ran down her temple.

'Been a profeshional at a few things, shon,' she replied with a leer.

'Ah'm sure, doll. Ah'm sure,' Joe turned and headed back to his table. Behind him Madge was already burrowing her way to the bar, the fiver clutched in her mitt.

'Right, that's better. Hear me now, wee man?'

'Sure, Joe. That was one fucking racket, eh?' Fergie pulled on his pint of export and lit another roll-up. 'Wee Madge aw right?'

'Aye, on good form.'

'Offer yese any extras?' Fergie's eyebrows were lifted high, his head tilted to the side. Without a word they both knew he was teasing his friend on his current lack of female companionship. Joe hadn't been laid in a month, an all-time record since his early teenage years.

'Whit dae you think?'

'Ah think ye might be tempted . . .' Fergie hadn't completed the sentence before his mate grabbed him in a headlock and was noisily kissing his forehead. 'Get aff, ye big poof. Christ sakes, oor secret's well oot noo.' Around them, nervous men backed off, uncertain and unsure if the scuffle between the known street faces was in fun or serious but taking no chances either way.

Order restored, the two slumped back in their seats till Joe gestured his friend to move in close.

'Addie. James Addison is getting the credit for the hit on that big slippery bastard,' Joe finally finished his sentence without shouting.

'Big cunt deserved it. Well, nae chance of the polis clearing up that crime then, eh?' Fergie was nodding as if he'd said something profound rather than something everyone already knew.

'Nae chance at aw,' replied Joe with the hint of a grin. 'They'll never track Addie down. Except . . .'

'Whit?'

'Word is somebody's grassed him tae the polis.'

'Yer kiddin?'

'Naw.'

'Shit. But how could they . . .'

'We'll have tae see whit we can dae.'

'Aye, course we will.'

'But they'll never catch Addie, man.'

'Never have . . .'

'Never will . . .'

'Never in a month of Sundays . . .'

18 AUGUST 1989

It used to be a joke but it's far from funny now. At times like this I get drunk - morose pissed. Hang around in company being sociable enough on the face of it but in truth buried deep in my own thoughts. Two sides of me - one public, one private - trying to work out the one that's really me. At these times I can't think of the now or even the recent. Instead I think back to the how and that joke that's become deadly serious.

It was an extension of the false name hoo-haa. You know, police stop you for speeding and you rhyme off someone else's name and details. Unless you had a serious grudge against some sod you gave them a false ID.

Trick is to be fluent in everything they ask. It got so I had invented various characters. Sammy Mackie, Joe McLean, Bertie Meldrum - I knew everything about them: jobs, football team, preferred drink, who they were shagging, their mothers' maiden names. In any given situation I chose a name at random, playing the part till the coppers let me go. From speeding to arrests on more serious matters. As long as I wasn't confronted by a familiar face I conned them along till they showed me the door.

It was a hoot and useful but I was denied the best part of the joke. I mean they went looking for Sammy Mackie, Joe McLean, Bertie Meldrum in fictitious houses in real streets and I wasn't there to witness them scratching their nuts.

Then I traced her, my mam, after all these years. Traced her too late. I didn't like what I found out. Didn't like it at all. Grew up that day. Starting thinking about right and wrong, acceptable and unacceptable. Felt responsible for what happened to her - guilty for not being there. Doing nothing wasn't an option. I had to act. That's when I turned the joke into a weapon and I've been tooled-up ever since.

SURVEILLANCE NOTES

Sean Ferguson (aka Fergie)

Mid to late 20s, small build, dark-brown hair. Ex Shamrock team. Fast on his feet and handy with a blade. Done a five stretch and lesser stints. Bit of a wisecracker, easily thrown, not the brightest bulb. Would be dead by now if it wasn't for his one friend, Joe Murphy. Weaknesses — too many to list.

Joe Murphy

Late 20s early 30s, small built, dark-red hair. Respected. Never part of a gang when young but known by them all. Street fighter and still handy with his fists. Smart, moved into rackets. No jail time worth talking about. Known by all the major players who leave him alone. Weakness — his friend Fergie.

A

MARATHON MOUSE

'Boss! Boss!' the call was accompanied by a timid knock on the door.

'Beat it, Shuggie. Ah'm busy.'

'But, Boss . . .'

'Dae Ah have tae come oot there an tell yese?' Andy Grimes wasn't used to having to give orders twice. He noted with satisfaction, though no surprise, that the interruption ceased and turned his full leer on his companion once again. The young woman smiled as his big podgy hand clumsily cupped her naked breast free from her dress. The tight neckline cut sharply into her soft white flesh but she knew that to complain or even wince would bring grief. 'Very nice, doll. Very nice.'

Andy Grimes stared down at the young woman where they stood in the middle of his office. Next door, staff busied themselves getting The Cat's Whiskers Club ready for the lunch-time crowd – scores of cowed, wan-faced men who'd soon be arriving for a pint, a sandwich and cheap thrill chasers from the lap dancers, strippers and scantily clad waitresses. 'Wee minute, hen.' Andy Grimes strode across the room, his customary ruddy complexion reddening even more from the effort, and pulled the door wide open, 'Here, Maggie, gonnae make sure there's plenty o sparkly white wine cooling – we got a civic party the day.' Grimes slammed the door shut and turned. 'Now, doll, where were we? Oh aye, let there be light.' As he snatched at a row of switches, strip lights overhead flickered, stuttered and burst into life, filling the room with a cold white glare. Automatically the young woman covered her breast with her arms. 'Naw, naw, hen. That's no the point. The point is we need tae see yese. Ah'll show ye.' Grimes reached down and roughly yanked the dress up and over her head, ripping seams and leaving her naked. 'Nice thought, darling, but ye'll have tae wear knickers for the show. Well, at the start o the night onyroads. Heh, heh, heh . . .'

'Boss! Boss!' called the same male voice, wee Shuggie Reid, known as 'The Mouse'. 'Ah'm sorry, boss, but it's urgent.' The knocking on the door was now more persistent.

'Ah'll fuckin show ye urgent, ye little bam,' Grimes turned and strode towards the door again, his fists clenched, his chin jutting forward. The door swung open and there to his surprise stood not Shuggie but Maggie Small, the only person in the club who he'd listen to – usually.

'Get oot o ma road, Maggie, Ah'm gonna gie that wee prick a good kickin.'

'Andy, you'd better listen.' Grimes turned and stared at her, eye to eye. Usually he softened whenever she was around, from that first time he'd spotted her dancing in that show. Tall, as tall as him, black hair, blue eyes, a full, voluptuous figure that turned heads wherever and whenever. She was beautiful but that wasn't all. Maggie had class. She spoke well. Didn't put out for a couple of free drinks like all the other girls. She kept secrets better than anyone he knew. Maggie Small held his respect and trust and for Andy Grimes that was a one-off. His furious glower transformed into his usual angry scowl and he nodded for her to speak on. 'There's been a shooting.'

'So, it's fuckin Glesca we live in no the Vatican fuckin City.'

'The boys think you should know right away.'

'The boys better be right,' he warned. Maggie turned and signalled to the small man hovering at a safe distance through the open door. Shuggie 'The Mouse' Reid was usually a cocky little man, always wisecracking, taking the piss. Today, his face was drained of colour, one hand constantly rubbing at a cheek as he stepped forward slowly.

'This better be good, Mouse.' Grimes spoke quietly, almost inaudibly, always a bad sign. Shuggie's lips moved but at first no words emerged. 'Christ sake get oan wi it.'

'It's yer bro,' Shuggie squeaked, much like the rodent of his nickname.

'Whit's ma brother?'

'He's been shot,' Shuggie stepped back as he murmured the words. 'Whit . . .'

'Shot, Boss, he's shot deid.' Shuggie's voice rose to a high-pitched squeal.

'Deid?' Grimes had a puzzled, contemptuous look on his face as if Shuggie had deliberately chosen to talk in a language he would not understand. 'Whit ye mean DEID? You fucking stupid or something?' Grimes looked around the room, searching out confirmation of the obvious madness of the little message bringer. Maggie Small caught his eye and gave him one curt nod of her head. Tears welled up in Grimes' eyes, his fat chins wobbled and his arms flailed out – an overgrown baby seeking comfort. Instead he found Shuggie's gullet. 'Ye filthy wee cunt. Ah'll fuckin massacre yese. Ah'll fuckin rip yese apart.' Shuggie's feet were hoisted off the ground as Grimes shook him from side to side by his throat.

'Andy! Let him go, Andy!' Maggie Small was having no luck in her pleas, a sure sign Grimes was fit to murder. Her voice was signal enough for the men who had been hovering outside the door waiting for Shuggie to pass on the news – a short straw he'd won by virtue of having failed to pay up his gambling debts from their regular three-card brag schools. The Mouse was always in debt, always being landed with the worst jobs.

The men teemed into the room and set about trying to prise Andy Grimes' fingers from Shuggie's throat. The task was complicated, requiring to be achieved without hurting or angering their boss in any way. They milled round him as he swung Shuggie to the edge of the room and proceeded to batter his head against the wall.

'Andy, come oan it wisnae Shug, man . . .'

'Let him be, Boss . . . please . . .'

'Oh, man, he's no breathin . . .'

Shuggie Reid had gone limp and was being thrashed against the wall like some dead rat in a terrier's jaw. Grimes' face was crimson, the colour of the blood now smearing his flock wallpaper. In the centre of the room, the naked young woman stood and stared, her jaw gaping loose and one knuckle rubbing against her lips and teeth.

'Come on, let's get you out of here,' Maggie Small said to the girl, scooping up her discarded dress from the floor.

'Whit's going oan?' she asked. Maggie looked over at the ruck of men and noticed that Shuggie's face had turned dark blue and his front teeth had been knocked out.

'It's just a misunderstanding. Nothing to worry about – they'll make sure he's OK.' Maggie pulled the dress over the woman's head and instructed her to slip her arms into the sleeves as she would with an infant. 'He'll be all right.'

'Naw, no him. Ah mean wi the job. Did Ah get the job?' the girl asked, her gaze unmoving from the battle.

'Oh that. Yes, you got the job all right.'

'Thank God. Ah thought that wee shite had blown it for me.'

Grimes had finally dropped Shuggie but was now stamping on his prone body as the other men pleaded his case.

'When can you start, eh . . . what do I call you?' Maggie Small asked.

'Ah've decided oan Suzie with a zed. Dead classy, eh? No doing anything the night. Right away if yese want.'

'Right away it is,' said Maggie, leading the woman out of the room, tugging against her persistent fascination with Shuggie's torment which was now reaching a finale as Andy Grimes ran out of steam but not temper.

'How dae ye think Ah'll get oan? Dae ye think Ah'll fit in aw right?' Suzie asked, hovering at the door as if reluctant to miss any of the stramash. Maggie stayed with her, straightening her dress and her hair, watching Grimes head to his desk and his phone.

'Who the fuck ye think this is? Get him oan the line NOW,' Grimes roared into the mouthpiece. Over by the wall, the group of men were trying to revive Shuggie, debating whether or not he was dead. 'Ah want tae know who did it,' bellowed Grimes, clenching the phone hard into his face. 'Listen, Ah need tae know . . . like now. You hearing me, ye cunt? Good, well sort it.' Grimes smashed the receiver onto the cradle. Snatching at a bottle of his favourite brandy he poured a large glassful. Two gulps later, 'Get that wee fuckin stiff oot o ma sight.' Suzie giggled nervously as the men lifted Shuggie Reid's still unconscious body. 'An you, doll, yer a smasher. Fix her up, Maggie.'

'Thank you, Mr Grimes,' Suzie replied with another nervous giggle and a half curtsy.

'You can call me Andy, pet.'

'Thank you, Mr . . . Andy,' and another girlish giggle.

'You'll fit in here very well, little Suzie with a zed,' Maggie reassured her, finally leading the new girl out of the room. 'Very well indeed.'

SURVEILLANCE NOTES

Andy Grimes
Mid 40s, about six foot, heavily built, balding with
a comb-over. Started as a doorman in city-centre pubs
before moving on to protection rackets against the
same pubs. Now he owns them as well as taxi firms,
building companies, demolition squads, scrap-metal
yards and a whole heap more. HQ - The Cat's Whiskers
Club in Clyde Street, Glasgow, officially a lap-
dancing dive but anything and anybody is available at
a price. Grimes likes to socialise with people in
power - has the money to do it. Done only minor time
in spite of his foul temper and vicious streak.
Carries a gun at all times. Weaknesses - greed and
young girls.

Maggie Small
Mid to late 20s, very tall, black hair, green eyes,
good body. From Coatbridge but you wouldn't know it
to hear her talk. Started as a topless dancer in a
club. Face of an angel but a gold-digger's heart.
Runs Grimes' girls, The Cat's Whiskers and a few
other businesses. No husband or boyfriend. A loner.
Very ambitious, likely to take over from Grimes.
Weaknesses - none identified.

Shuggie Reid (aka The Mouse)
Middle 50s, under five foot tall, thinning grey
hair. Dapper wee guy, always wisecracking. Worked
for Grimes for the last ten years but been a player
with every major team since he was a teenager. The
Mouse is just a loyal foot soldier,does whatever
he's told. Weaknesses - gambling debts.

A
August 1989

DEADLY DIVISIONS

HOUSE CALL

'OPEN UP.' Cathy Brodie was startled by the shout and turned just in time to watch her door splinter and crack.

'What the . . .' Two men came running into the room, pistols in their hands, sweeping round to all four corners. One started throwing cupboard doors open, under the sink, chest of drawers and that wardrobe falling open, terminally wounded. The other stooped and looked under the bed before kicking and shaking the black plastic bags. The pair of them were gibbering away, shouting stuff at her that wasn't registering with Cathy. She wondered if they'd bought their anoraks at the same shop and why, then questioned her own sanity for having the thought.

'PUT THAT DOWN NOW,' one crouched a few feet from her, his gun held in two hands pointing directly at her, flecks of spittle spraying her face from his shout.

'Put what down?' she asked in a little voice she didn't recognise as her own. She was sitting on the edge of the bed, her baby lying on one arm, the feeding bottle in her other hand.

'NOOOOW.'

'Don't go shouting at the lass, you. Can you no see she's feeding the wean?' The newcomer was known to Cathy, as he was to everyone in the city who read the local evening papers or watched crime reports on the television. DCI Alex Birse seemed to fill the room. It wasn't just his physical presence. Closer to seven than six foot, broad as brick shit house and with a huge head crowned with a shock of thick, white hair – he was unforgettable. But it was more than that. The two guys with the guns went from being in control to deferential monkeys the minute Birse appeared. Even Cathy ignored the pistol wavers and looked up at the florid face of Birse.

'Ah'm no in the mood for time wasting, Cathy, so you'll no be wanting tae see a warrant? Good.' Birse signalled behind him and two other men entered to join their colleagues in searching the room. 'Where the fuck's wee Jeannie? Tell her tae get her arse in here right noo. Get cracking. What yese think this is, a fucking knitting bee?' Into the room came a woman, the only one in police uniform. 'Take care o the wean, eh?' Birse barked. Jeannie Stirk approached Cathy holding out her arms.

'No way,' the power had returned to Cathy's voice and she was having none of it.

'C'moan,' said Birse, 'grab the kid for fuck's sake.' Cathy shied away, holding the child in tight, shaking her head and her body, lulling against her baby's frightened crying.

'It's a boy, isn't it?' Jeannie Stirk had moved in closer but not too close. 'A wee smasher too.' Cathy nodded and smiled against her better judgement. 'He's got his mammy's nose. Just a wee button nose, haven't you?' Jeannie stretched over and smiled down at the wee boy's face. 'A wee cracker, so you are. You're going to break an awful lot of hearts when you grow up.'

'For Christ's sake get a move oan wid yese?' Birse had no time for all this baby palaver. He didn't like babies. He didn't like people. He liked money and power and his football team and that was that.

'He'll be okay with me, Cathy,' Jeannie ignored her boss's grumbling. 'I'll take good care of him, promise.' Cathy looked Jeannie Stirk in the face, not at the uniform but straight into her brown eyes and decided she could trust the woman.

'He was in the middle of a feed,' Cathy explained. 'He'll get grumpy if . . .'

'No problem. His auntie Jeannie can take care of that, can't she, wee soldier.' Jeannie wrapped the baby and bundle up in her arms as Cathy handed over the half-full feeding bottle.

'Right you,' barked Birse, 'oot o here wi the wean. Get doon tae the car.'

'But I'm supposed to stay around,' Jeannie protested. 'You're supposed to have a female present . . .'

'You trying to tell me the rules? Want tae stay permanently in a uniform DC Stirk? Get that fuckin wean intae the motor and stay there till Ah tell yese.' Halfway to the door, Jeannie asked,

'What do I call him?'

'Tim,' replied Cathy.

'Aye, aifter his famous granddaddy,' sneered Birse. Giving Jeannie Stirk a few minutes to move away from the front door, Birse turned and looked down on Cathy Brodie. 'This'll no take long, Cathy, if yer smart.'

Around them the four policemen continued to ransack the bedsit. One was emptying the contents of a bag of sugar onto the tea leaves and instant coffee he'd already poured on the table. Another was pulling all the cleaning materials apart, leaving abstract patterns of soap powder, slimy washing-up liquid and now bleach all over the floor next to the sink. Another had scattered the baby's clothes around the room and moved on to tearing apart the paper nappies, shredding each one carefully and thoroughly. The last had ripped open the black bags and Cathy caught sight of outfits she'd worn in better times. Now all dated and useless, she couldn't bear to part with them, that would be to admit that her life could never be good again.

'Ye've been in aw day,' Birse's hand clasped Cathy by the chin, turning her face to look up at him.

'Aye,' she replied.

'It wisnae a question but a statement o fact.'

'Ah've been in all day.'

'Awfy wee place here, Cathy, must drive ye mad, eh?'

'No.'

'Jist you and the nipper and these four walls. Whit dae ye get up tae – tae pass the time like?'

'Tim takes up most o ma time.'

'Aye but no it aw, eh? Whit dae ye dae for a wee bit pleasure?' Cathy looked at him puzzled. 'Tae pass the time when the nipper's sleeping?'

'Nothing much. Jist read sometimes and listen tae music.'

'Oan the tranny?'

'Aye.' Birse turned and glowered at one of the policeman who immediately picked the transistor radio off a shelf, ceremoniously dropped it on the floor and stamped on it. 'He's an awfy clumsy bastard that one. Now let's cut the crap – whit happened this morning?'

'Nothing much, Ah just fed Tim and cleaned up the . . .'

'Nae shagging then? Mean they stains oan they sheets urny shagging stains? See's that sheet up.' One of the squad pulled on his leather gloves. With a sour look across his face, scooping the sheet off the bed he held it in front of him, as far away as possible, and started moving towards Birse. 'Fuck's sake, close enough, man. Can smell it frae here.' Birse turned sideways and gave an exaggerated show of examining the sheet carefully. 'Mmm, looks like a nooky stain tae me, hen.' Gripping the sheet he turned and rammed it into Cathy's face. 'Whit's it look like tae you, eh? Eh?' The woman wanted to be sick. She'd planned to strip those sheets after she'd fed her baby, make a trip to the launderette and wash that man out of her life forever. Now the smell of him was back in her head, wakening the memories and the disgust, wiping out her celebration of freedom. 'You oan the game, Cathy?'

'No.'

'Half this street is.'

'Well Ah'm no.'

'Oh for fuck sake,' the exclamation of horror came from one of the gun-toting cops now standing near the kitchen sink. Everyone turned to look at him with his hand stuck inside a small white bundle, his face twisted in disgust, his other hand flapping in the air. 'Shite,' he moaned. 'It's shite,' he looked like he was going to throw up. His three comrades in arms started to laugh at him but not Birse.

'Yer an incompetent wee wanker. Fuckin tolly so ye are. And they gie you a gun?'

'Jesus Christ.' As the policeman pulled the bundle off his paw it gave out a wet, smacking plop and the sweet smell of milky faeces. His fingers, wrist and anorak cuff were smeared in beige-coloured crap. Birse just shook his head and turned back to Cathy.

'Ah don't give a monkey's fuck whit ye get up tae but the DSS might, eh? Stop yer benefit cheques I reckon.' Cathy knew what he was saying was true, especially if the report came from the police, and she could ill afford it.

'Look, Ah wisnae up to anything this morning. You didnae come here to enquire after my love life did yese?'

'Smart lassie. Naw, yer right. It's that windae Ah'm more interested in.' Birse gripped her arm, leading her to the kitchen sink and the only window in the room. 'Shift, you,' Birse snapped at the cop still feebly rinsing baby shit off his hand and sleeve.

Cathy thought back to that morning, the cold water and the razor blade. She tugged at her sleeve and felt the wounds still raw in her arm. The view was the same but different. Now crowded with blue uniforms, police cars, yellow incident tape and a mêlée of onlookers. Just he wasn't there, lying there on the ground staring with dead eyes at the sky. But his blood and brains still smeared the wall and pavement and they made her happy in spite of her present company.

'You saw it all, didn't yese?' Birse looked out of the window as he spoke to her. 'Then ye phoned the polis. Except ye didnae leave yer name. Did yese?'

'It wisnae me that belled ye.'

'An ye telt us who did it. Didn't ye?'

'No, I . . .'

'But a call's no good enough tae us ye see. We need a name 'n' address. We need a body, a witness.'

'But it wisnae me . . .'

'How did you know it was James Addison?'

'Who?'

'Dinnae come the wise cunt wi me, Cathy.' Birse gripped her by the shoulders, his face pressed so close to hers she could feel the heat of his breath and the stink of stale whisky and last night's curry. 'Addie. Fucking James Addison — how did you know it was him?'

'Ah didn't. Ah mean, Ah don't know James Addison. Ah saw nothing.'

'Cos nae cunt in the polis knows whit he looks like,' Birse continued. 'Never had the pleasure o meeting the wee prick. Huv we?'

'Mr Birse, Ah saw nothing. Honest.'

'So, if ye recognised Addie ye must know the spooky wee bastard. Be familiar with him like.' Two other cops had moved in close to Cathy's sides, their body weight leaning against her, staring into her face.

'No.'

'Maybe that's his spunk clarted ower yer sheets.'

'No.'

'Maybe yer faither knew him.'

'No, Ah . . .' Birse pulled a pistol from his jacket and held it against Cathy's cheek.

'You got nothing tae say, Miss Catherine Brodie?' He nudged her lips with the barrel. 'Ye sure, hen?' He pushed the gun against her teeth. 'Certain?' Gun oil and metal against her tongue. 'Accidents can happen ye know. This is an awfy dangerous world. Especially for weans.'

'Please, don't . . .'

'We're jist looking for some cooperation.'

'Ah don't know anything.'

'Besides, maybe somebody else should be looking aifter that wean. Ah'm sure the welfare would be dead interested tae find oot you're oan the game.'

'Ah'm no.'

'An yer drug habit.'

'Whit? Whit dae ye mean?' One of the cops leaning into her side had reached into his inside pocket and was waving a small plastic bag full of brown powder in her face, smiling all the while.

'Maybe we should check her airms for tracks, boys?' Birse gripped her forearm and twisted, opening the fresh wounds under the cloth, sending fiery pain shivering through her body. 'Or are ye a bit secret wi yer habit? Shootin up in the veins, a bit lower down maybe?' Birse's big hand rubbed her thigh and pushed its way into her crotch. 'Whit the fuck?' A baby's cries drew him to a sudden halt.

'Sorry, boss, but we've had a shout.' Jeannie Stirk was standing in the room, baby Tim Brodie cradled in her arms.

'You takin the piss, Stirk?'

'No, the chief wants you back in for a press conference on the shooting.'

'Fuckin press. Bloody pariahs. But let's pander tae the bastards by all means. Dinnae want a bad press, dae we? No, no. Murderers walking the fuckin street but God save us frae a bad press.' Birse's colleagues were well aware that he had a special relationship with certain members of the media, passing out stories when it suited him and receiving payments in return. Most detectives did, just he was the worst. It was the official PR role he resented not the press. 'Right, boys, back tae the motor. Pronto.' Birse waited while the cops trotted out of the room and their footsteps could be heard echoing down the stone stairs of the close.

'Mr Birse, I really know nothin. I didnae make any phone call.' Cathy's voice was trembling in spite of her will, her face full of tears, her legs shaking, a slow crimson stain seeping through her sleeve. Birse moved in close, preventing her from backing away by wrapping one big paw round her buttocks.

'Ah'm coming back, doll, an next time Ah'll be oan ma oan. Savvy?' With that Birse turned and left the flat, roaring orders at the other cops as he strode down the stairs.

Jeannie Stirk looked at the devastation of the room and wondered why it had all been necessary. Handing the baby back to his mother, Jeannie and Cathy paused, holding the bundle together. They were about the same age, the same height, the same build. So much in common and so far apart. Two sides of some war that neither invented nor wanted. Caught up in the rules, play or get out – if you can. They looked at each other – one frightened and trembling, the other sad and mournful – till a persistent bleating car horn signalled Birse's impatience. As the cop made sure the baby was safely deposited in his mother's arms, her fingers stroked the back of the woman's hand. Soft, gentle, reassuring and swift, it was enough. Both women thought they knew what that touch meant, but were they talking the same language?

SURVEILLANCE NOTES

DCI Alex Birse

In his 50s, huge man, thick white hair, red complexion, eyes too small to notice colour. Wears expensive suits, heavy gold rings and bangle. Old-school detective for over 30 years. Almost sacked five or six times for extreme violence against prisoners or the public. Investigated twice for corruption — not proven. Lives well above his salary. Drinks heavily. Freemason. Season ticket holder at Ibrox — doesn't miss a game whatever is happening. High profile and unofficial press contacts. Always armed whether warrants issued or not. Well connected. Regular at Cat's Whiskers. Lives alone. Has no discernible sex life. Weakness — booze.

DC Jeannie Stirk

Looks about 30, black hair, around five foot six, full figure. Nothing much known. Not from here. Check origins. Check name. Married? One to watch?

A
August 1989

A VERY PRIVATE SHERRICKING

'Fuck it, we're too late, man.' Fergie backed up abruptly, pushing his mate Joe deeper into the close mouth.

'Jesus Christ, Fergie, cool it man. Ye'll blow our cover. Place is hoaching wi rozzers.'

'Sorry, Joe, Ah'm jist a bit edgy.'

'Edgy? Yer jittery enough tae get us hung.'

'Sorry, man.'

'Never mind that. Jist mind whit Ah telt ye. Cool. Stay cool. No feart. No worried. No wide. Cut the gallus swagger. Jist look as if yer oan yer way tae visit yer mammy.'

'Cathy Brodie's too young tae be ma mammy but.'

'Fuck sakes, Fergie, are you totally fuckin thick the day? Pretend it's yer ma. Think it in yer heid and yer body'll look like it's being dragged oan its way tae dae its duty.'

'Think so?'

'Look, ye either buckle doon or Ah'm oot o here.'

'It was your idea but.'

'Fuck, c'moan.' The two men staggered out into the daylight of the street. The forty-yard walk seemed endless in the babble of the police busying themselves around the scene of crime, the metallic whispering of their radios, the shouted jokes and orders. But they made it across the street, into the close, and were soon at Cathy Brodie's front door.

'That's a pure liberty, man.' Fergie was severely affronted by the battered-in door and wanted to debate the immorality of unnecessary police aggression right there in the close. Joe had other ideas and unceremoniously yanked him into Cathy Brodie's bedsit by the scruff of the neck. 'Hey, watch the good jacket, man.'

'Cathy? Cathy?' Joe was having a problem seeing if anyone was in the room in the middle of such a mess.

'The bastards. Whit are they like, man,' Fergie was off again.

'Whit dae you jokers want?' As Cathy spoke, so the two men saw her for the first time, sitting on the floor in a jumble of women's clothes.

'Jesus, Cathy, are you okay, hen?' Joe looked at the devastation and knew this was her world, all she had and she was far from all right.

'Whit's it look like tae you, Joe Murphy? Like Ah'm spring cleaning?'

'Was it Birse?'

'Naw, Santa bloody Claus and his fuckin elves had a party.' She turned her head away shaking it slowly, sadly, before turning to stare at him anger and scorn spread across her face. 'Aye. Birse. Who else?'

'Bastard.'

'Aye, bastard right enough.'

'Can we dae anything tae help ye?'

'Help? Now ye want tae help me?'

'Aye.'

'Better late than never I suppose.'

'Cathy . . .'

'Story o ma life, eh? The cavalry arrives ten minutes too late.'

'Cathy . . .'

'And who are you, Joe Murphy? Are you the John Wayne character?'

'Jist trying tae . . .'

'Whit? Help? That'll be a first.'

'Aye we are, Cathy. Jist came tae gie ye hauners annat.' Fergie decided Joe needed assistance in explaining but was rewarded by double-barrelled glares for his troubles.

'Ye want tae help as well, Sean Ferguson?'

'Aye,' Fergie replied, certain he wasn't going to enjoy what came next.

'Well, yese can clear up that lot for a start,' Cathy nodded towards the pine-smelling slush smearing the floor in front of the kitchen sink. Fergie's premonition had been spot on. One nod from Joe and he started to clear it up with a heavy heart. He'd rather have a knife with bad odds than do housework

'Need a word, Cathy.' Joe was counting their time in the flat. He reckoned ten minutes was the maximum before they ran the unacceptable risk of a visit from the police.

'There's a wee surprise then. So yese came tae help and just have a wee word while you're at it.' As Cathy clambered to her feet her skirt rode up her thighs. Joe caught himself admiring her and feeling guilty about it, an unusual combination in his experience. 'So give us yer news, Joe Murphy,' Cathy Brodie was now standing in front of Joe.

'The polis. What did they want?' Joe found himself having to clear his throat in the middle of the few words.

'Just popped by for a blether, the way they do.'

'Cathy?'

'Had a bit o a party while they were here.'

'Cathy, what did they want, hen?'

'Tae sell me a ticket for their next do at the Masonic lodge, whit dae ye think they fuckin wanted?'

'Was it about the shooting?'

'Naw, the weather.' With every response Cathy Brodie appeared harder, a small muscle in her jaw working more furiously – a determined look he knew so well. Joe remembered playground days when she would stand in the middle of them all, stamping her foot and they all backed off – every one of those self-proclaimed wild young team, himself included. He'd have to cut to the chase or she'd keep him there all day and not give an inch.

'We've heard tell that someone's been on tae the polis.'

'What, lost their tabby cat?' She raised her eyebrow in that impudent way that made Joe want to kiss her lips and slap her at the same time.

'Grassed up the shooter.'

'Folks these days, eh? What's the world coming tae?'

'We heard it was you.' Joe's throat gulped dry and sore, waiting for her response, but his body stayed stock still, his eyes staring into her face watching for a sign.

'Join the fucking queue and, by the way, you're last in line as ye might've noticed.' Cathy swung her arms around, displaying the room and the two turned to watch Fergie half-heartedly wiping at the sludge on the floor.

'Did yese?'

'Whit? Grass?'

'Say anything?'

'Naw.'

'Sure?'

'Certain.'

'Cathy?'

'Whit ye gonnae dae tae make me tell ye – trash ma room, threaten ma wean, plant smack oan me, grab ma fanny? Yer too fuckin late, buster. Ah've had the full repertoire already the day.'

'We've got something for you.' Joe pulled a fat envelope from his pocket, 'Just a wee helper.'

'A helper for what? Tae redecorate? Buy a pram? Or keep ma trap shut?'

'Just tae keep . . .'

'Aaaw, Jesus Christ.' Joe and Cathy turned in the direction of the exclamation. Fergie was standing by the sink, a white parcel stuck over his hand. 'Fuckin keech, man. Wean's shite all over my mitt.' Cathy watched the supposedly streetwise man parody the anorak-wearing copper of an hour before.

'Men,' Cathy said sadly. 'Big or wee. Gangsters or coppers. Right or wrong, ye're aw the same. Useless articles every single one of yese.' Joe glared at his pal and had to agree with the woman's sentiments. Cathy thought Joe looked a little embarrassed, a little sad and she felt almost sorry for him till he spoke.

'Just tae help, doll.' He placed the thick envelope on the draining board.

'Help is it? That word again. That's what ye're here to offer. Help?' Cathy swung her baby up into her arms and checked the blankets were away from his face. She said nothing, simply helped herself to a cigarette from the packet lying on the table, deftly lighting it one-handed before facing the two men across the room. Joe waited for her to say something but nothing was forthcoming – just her steady gaze and a too rapid puffing on her cigarette. He didn't like this at all.

'We'll just split then, Cathy,' he offered.

'So that's me being paid aff?' she started quietly. 'That's ma wages for holding ma tongue? Do you remember who ma daddy was? An ma big brother? Where Ah've lived aw ma life? You think Ah'm a grass?'

'Naw, Cathy.'

'Aye, Joe. Stick yer pieces o silver up yer arses, ye pair o insulting bastards.'

'It wisnae meant like that.' Joe's explanation arrived just in time for Cathy to snatch up the envelope and throw it at him. 'Jist trying tae help, Cathy.'

'Help?' She was crying again, this time without fear just fury and hurt. Joe felt like a louse and even Fergie realised they'd insulted the young woman.

'Please?' Joe couldn't think of anything else to say.

'Please yer fucking sell. Go oan, shift yer arses oot o here. Ye pair o wasters.' The two men needed no second bidding and were out of the door. Halfway down the stairs Joe ignored Fergie's prattling and turned back towards the flat. Cocking his head round the burst door jamb he saw her still standing there, the baby held tightly into her bosom, tears streaming down her face. It was how he remembered her that day they buried her father. In the old cemetery at Sighthill, standing by the grave, a wind that cut through you, her alone by the graveside the only one of her family left. Weeping but silent. And silent she'd remained ever since. Joe cleared his throat and she looked up to catch his eyes,

'Sorry, Cathy, wisnae called for. It's just these days everythin's money. Should've known better about you.'

'Aye, you should've known better, Joe Murphy. Especially you.'

'Aye, Cathy, Ah should've. Especially me.'

Fergie rushed to Joe's side at the close mouth bringing with him the smell of baby crap.

'Jesus she's mental, Joe. Aff her nut, man.' Joe strode across the road in silence, his friend half running to keep pace. 'Ah thought ma ex-missus was a bad witch but that one, she . . .'

'Fergie,' Joe interrupted.

'Aye?'

'Shut the fuck up, eh?' Joe stopped abruptly and turned to look up at the bedsit window. He could see her outline there, standing a few feet back from the glass so as not to be noticed.

'Joe, c'moan, man. The place is crawling wi bizzies.' Fergie tugged at his arm nervously, looking around with ferret eyes. Joe still stood and gazed up. 'Christ, they're looking at us.'

'Let them look. Fuck the polis. Fuck them all.'

'Joe, c'm . . .'

'This city belongs tae us, right?'

'Aye, eh . . . right.'

'These are our streets. Right?'

'Aye, course, but . . .'

Joe turned, heading towards a close mouth and their chosen route out, catching Fergie unawares and stranded in the middle of the road.

'C'moan you. Shift. We've goat work tae dae.'

Cathy Brodie

Thirty years old, dyed blonde hair, just over five foot, full figure, hazel eyes. Single parent. Baby – Tim, under a year. Baby's father – Chrissie Morton, smackhead, ex-Govan Team just started a 15 stretch for armed robbery. Relationship finished when Cathy was pregnant. Cathy's father – Tim Brodie, a major player of the old rules murdered. Word is it was an associate of her father's, cheating him out of money. Cathy believed to know about it – has never spoken out. Brother – Jamsie, stabbed to death in BarL while doing life for murder. Cathy down on her luck. Reliable. Trustworthy. Her father's daughter. Weaknesses – baby Tim. She's on her own.

A
August 1989

Thank you, Chief Constable Sharples. Good afternoon, ladies and gentlemen of the press. As the Chief Constable said, we have convened this conference today to make a statement on the distressing case of the murder of an innocent man in the streets of Glasgow this morning.

We need to put an end to speculation regarding this murder being carried out by a contract killer. Ladies and gentlemen, the days of 'No Mean City' are long gone. This dear green place has never been more peaceful or law abiding. The Chief Constable has followed in the path of his eminent predecessors and made certain there is no welcome for gangsters within the boundaries of this city.

Ladies and gentlemen, organised crime no longer exists in Glasgow. An innocent man we feel unable to name at this stage – I am sure you understand our priority is to apprehend the assailant – was shot down in cold blood as he went about his lawful business in the early hours of this morning. The victim, a law-abiding citizen, was en route to his place of work when the killer struck. Having examined all the available evidence we have reached the conclusion that the killing was an act of sporadic, unplanned and pointless violence. Ladies and gentlemen, it saddens me to say that it was a great waste of a useful life and it happened in the city I am charged to protect.

Given we are at the start of our investigation, I know you will understand that we are limited in the information we can release to the public. I can, however, announce that we have located one eyewitness and, through her assistance, we are searching for a man in his forties, tall, with grey hair receding at the forehead, wearing a dark overcoat.

Thank you ladies and gentlemen. We will take no questions at this time but assure you we will keep you informed on a regular basis.

DCI Alex Birse, Strathclyde Police

END . . .END . . . END . . . END . . .

I'd known about him for some time — the Fat Man. Why do I call him fat? He wasn't really, not physically. Just big with a soul full of blubber and grease and dog shit-smeared chip papers. If you could measure life in layers his would be below the basement and then some.

He ran working girls — the kind you see on the streets, flashing their tired fannies at you on a frosty winter's night, watching out for each other as they jag up away from the limp beam of the street lamps. He loaned money. Nothing fancy, just enough to let some poor sod pay their rent, some wrecked model dweller buy their carry-out for that day. He aimed low but, like them all, he hit big. A fiver to some homeless guy puts them in hock for life. Thirty pounds to somebody on welfare benefits with kids to feed does the same: puts them in bondage — to him.

Then he hit pay dirt. Bought a couple of run-down tenements, furnished them from bankruptcy auctions and let them out at fancy rates that folks with no other place to go couldn't afford . . . unless they borrowed some dough. Now he had them.

It started with my mam and someone just like the Fat Man. Too late for her. Then I learned of others. Good people driven to the depths. Like Cathy Brodie.

I chose the time and spot carefully. The weapon was bought for the job. The clothes I burned five minutes after the shooting. Ten minutes later I was in company, all legitimate people with good memories. I planned it all thoroughly. Especially the time and the place and who. If Cathy Brodie spotted me? Well, I couldn't think of anyone else in this city I would trust more. I chose her well. The Fat Bastard had it coming to him.

Now Birse is on the TV putting out a false ID. Does that mean he has no ID? A false lead? Or maybe someone did spot me and phoned in, and all his wee boy scouts are nodding their heads, assuming their

boss man is doing the old trick of laying a false
scent to put off the nutters who claim to see every
newsworthy crime and the masochists who want jailed
for everything. Maybe that is what he's up to. Then
again maybe he doesn't want me arrested at all.
Saving me up for a bullet from his bosom buddy
Grimes. Bastards will have to catch me first.

A

IT'S FOR YOU

'We've had a complaint you see,' explained Farquhar A. Farquhar in his most solicitous tones. 'Anonymous, of course.'

'Aye?' replied Sadie McElhone, who insisted her full title was Mrs Sadie McElhone in spite of her never having been married, not by formal or common law.

'About the children,' he continued.

'Aye?' Mrs Sadie McElhone was very accommodating, very polite in spite of having been caught out in her nightwear in the early afternoon.

'All of the children but particularly the boys.'

'Aye.'

'The most serious of allegations. I'm afraid we are obliged to investigate, eh, thoroughly.'

'Aye.' Mrs Sadie McElhone lifted the diaphanous nylon of her short negligee, scratched one podgy naked thigh then examined her overgrown nails for debris and wildlife.

'I am afraid that in the social work department we get such calls frequently. Often malicious but all must be investigated.'

'Aye.'

'Thoroughly.'

'Aye.'

'Let me run through the allegations with you, Mrs McElhone.' Farquhar A. Farquhar pulled a typist's spiral notepad from his coat pocket and flipped through the pages. Mrs Sadie McElhone preoccupied herself picking at a scab on the deep folds of flesh on her other thigh. 'Where are we now? Ah, yes. It is alleged that you frequently strike the children on their naked . . . buttocks . . . and genital area . . . while being under the influence of alcohol.' Farquhar A. Farquhar waited and looked but no response was forthcoming. He did worry about what Mrs Sadie McElhone had discovered under the nail of her left index finger. 'You do have children, Mrs McElhone?'

'Oh, aye. Aye,' she said, looking up from her left index finger.

'Boys and girls?'

The effort of thought was writ large across Mrs Sadie McElhone's face,

'Eh, aye.'

'How many exactly?'

'Eh?'

'How many boys and girls?'

'Aye. Aye.' Mrs Sadie McElhone was laboriously counting on the fingers of one hand. When she was done her lips flurried into speechless action, her brow furrowed and she started again at the beginning. Farquhar A. Farquhar didn't need this. After all, was he not Mr Farquharson, Senior Social Worker (Child Protection Team), Strathclyde Regional Council? Well, he was and he had the almost perfect identity card to prove it. At least that's who he was in here and the countless other houses he visited every week. Mr Farquharson, Senior Social Worker, not Farquhar A. Farquhar. Not the Angus some called him, choosing his middle name in preference to the mirrored perfection of his full name. Not Angie the Gopher . . . worse, much worse . . . that the boss and the boys at The Cat's Whiskers called him to his face, reflecting his role as the team's Go For and his facial likeness to a small worried rodent.

'Well, Mrs McElhone?'

'Eh?'

'I asked you how many boys and girls you had?'

'Aye. Eh, aye.' Mrs Sadie McElhone started counting her fingers again frantically. 'Four,' she shouted.

'Four children?'

'Naw.'

'You said four.'

'Aye.'

'Four what then?'

'Four boys.'

'Right. Good.'

'An four girls so Ah have.'

'Ah, eight children.'

'Naw.'

'Well what then?' Mrs Sadie McElhone looked puzzled for a long while and then said,

'Aye.'

'Aye what?' Angie the Gopher reminded himself not to get rattled.

Winning the client's confidence and trust was imperative. Like most of his kind he needed this hit, this bogus visit. Angie was the junkie trying to score a deal and he was close to his drug of preference – young boys.

'Four boys,' whined Mrs Sadie McElhone insistently.

'Yes, yes,' muttered Angie the Gopher sympathetically, his temper appeased at the prospect of four lithe bodies.

'An four lassies.'

'So, four of each.'

'Naw.'

Angie the Gopher sighed and reflected on whether this particular visit was going to be fruitful. He wrenched at his shirt collar, loosening it unnecessarily since it was already two sizes too big. Not tall, his skinny, almost emaciated build and habit of wearing over-large, dark, old-fashioned suits and coats gave him a haunted refugee look – oddball, misfit, recently released from institutional care. Which usually fitted the bill in the form of Her Majesty's Barlinnie Prison, or Shotts, or Greenock or Peterhead or Saughton or wherever the beak had put him. He decided that Mrs Sadie McElhone had two redeeming features – four glorious boys and she was far too dense to realise what he was getting up to. He would persist.

'Perhaps, Mrs McElhone, we could start with the lads.' Angie the Gopher's seconds of reflective silence had been too much for the woman. Easily distracted, she had raised her short nightgown and was concentrating hard on picking something out of her thick, greasy pubic hair. The sight of the woman's sex made Angie's stomach turn, never mind the thought of her being infected with crabs. 'Mrs McElhone,' he tried his best to sound severe and in control but the acid welling in his stomach made his already high voice vibrate. 'Mrs McElhone,' he tried again.

'Aye?' She looked up but omitted to cover her modesty.

'Will we start with the boys?'

'Eh?'

'I have to examine them, Mrs McElhone. Physically.' Her jaw dropped further while her brow wrinkled and her fat cheeks pushed up, narrowing her piggy eyes to almost invisible dots. 'Their buttocks and their . . . genitals . . . I have to look at their . . . genitals and . . .'

Mrs Sadie McElhone's face broke into a beamer of a smile. At last he'd said something she understood. Puffing and panting, raising herself to her feet she stepped forward. Jiggling up and down, holding the hem of her baby-doll negligee, she threw her head back and laughed. Angie was beginning to panic. Had the woman taken leave of her few senses entirely? With an ease belying her build, in one clean movement Mrs Sadie McElhone whipped her nightdress up and over her head, casting it casually behind her, eyes focused on Angie the Gopher. One glimpse was enough for him. She was obese, her thighs folding against her distended stomach, flaccid breasts flopping halfway down her torso, their large brown nipples erect and pointing at him. Dark pubic hair spread up her belly and down the tops of her thighs which she opened slowly. She was not the perfect size ten but Angie couldn't care less. She was a woman and it horrified him.

Slowly, in an open-legged gait, Mrs Sadie McElhone staggered towards him. He looked around him, anywhere but at her. The living-room of the old tenement flat was the usual scene of post-riot deluge. The only bright colours were bits of cheap children's toys, broken and discarded over the floor. Half-filled cups and empty lager cans marked the edge of furniture and filled every flat surface. On the floor, a ghostly carpet's pattern was discernible through layers of grime, crumbs and unidentifiable articles of clothing. The woodchip wallpaper had been ripped off in random, irregular shapes allowing the dull grey of damp-infested plaster to glower at the room. Three out of four panes in the curtain-free windows had been replaced by thin, warped chipboard. Below the window ledge, glass shards lay scattered and ignored. On one wall hung a faded poster of an angelic small boy, one crystal tear running down his cheek. Angie the Gopher had the exact same picture at home. In fact, he had the full set. In spite of the warm weather, a rickety, ancient gas fire burped and farted into the sweltering room.

Mrs Sadie McElhone was certainly feeling the heat. She moved slowly towards Angie the Gopher – one hand fondling her breasts, the other stroking her protruding vaginal lips – a smile on her face. Angie jumped to his feet, trying to remember where the door was. She was almost on him. It was too late. Angie would almost certainly lose any wrestling match, being far outweighed by Mrs Sadie McElhone. She was so close now he could smell her sweat mingling with that terrible fishy smell he associated with every woman. Angie the Gopher was done for.

When the klaxon howled it stopped Mrs Sadie McElhone in her

tracks, planting a puzzled twist on her phizog. For long seconds Angie the Gopher stood stock still, appearing equally flummoxed as to the source of the deafening blast. Then he jumped into action, snatching at the khaki-coloured briefcase he had carried in with him and planted between his legs throughout his visit. Snapping open the metal catches he reached into the case and pulled out a large, rectangular-shaped block of dull black plastic trailing wires. It was an ex-Army field phone, the latest experiment in team communications and it was proving to be an embarrassing failure. Angie the Gopher clicked some switch bringing a blessed end to the deafening whoop of the klaxon.

'Hello,' he muttered nervously into the mouthpiece. 'Boss! Right, boss.' On the other end of the line Andy Grimes was shouting his orders,

'Stop whit yer doin and get yer arse in here.'

'OK, boss.'

'Ah mean fuckin now, Angie.'

'Course, boss.'

'No fuckin about at yer games.'

'Naw, Ah'll get there right away.'

'An none o yer sick tricks, Angie.'

'Naw, boss, Ah'm no up tae anythin.'

'Better no be oan ma time.'

'Right, boss. Jist leaving.'

Angie didn't wait to tidy the field phone away. Lugging the gaping case under his arm he was heading for the door dangling a tangle of cables and assorted technical paraphernalia.

'Sorry, Mrs McElhone, I've got to go. Emergency call,' he shouted. Mrs Sadie McElhone stood in the middle of her living-room wearing nothing but a hurt hound-dog expression. She didn't understand. All men wanted one thing, didn't they? Wasn't that what he'd asked for?

Angie made the close and sprinted for the road. As he emerged from the tenement something hard and fast slapped him on the back, knocking the wind from his lungs and causing his legs to go wobbly. He turned in time to see a pack of kids come running after him, hurling stones, carrying sticks and lobbing paper missiles containing secret weapons of dog turds. Angie had met the McElhone children at last – all eight of them and none older than twelve. Dropping the field phone he took to his heels, holding his wig on his head, galloping down the middle of the road, the kids in pursuit. Terror drove his legs and he left his tiny pursuers behind, their shouts and threats disappearing behind him into silence.

Only when absolutely certain he had reached safety did Angie pull to a halt, wheezing like an asthmatic donkey pulling a full load. Reaching into his pocket he pulled out cigarettes, his shaking hands struggling with the mechanics of getting a fag into his mouth and lighting the damn thing. Several long drags and one fierce coughing fit later, Angie the Gopher leaned against the wall, heaving deeply but slowly and contemplated his day. He hated failure in his little expeditions. If he'd got his hands on one child, even a girl, his mind would be at peace and he'd get on with business. Now he was left with that ache, stronger than ever, and knew it wouldn't go away till it was satisfied. It would weigh on him, a monkey on his back, till he fed it. As he smoked and mourned his predicament, across the street an old woman dithered at the end of her close mouth, sweeping the dust-laden stone paving. The windows of her ground-floor flat shone out, glass in a montage of stone and rusting corrugated iron, the only inhabited house in a street which was obviously soon to be demolished, or ought to be.

'Oldies aren't weans,' thought Angie the Gopher aloud, 'but they'll do.' As a smackhead would reluctantly settle for Temazepam in a heroin famine, Angie too had his fall back hits. For Angie's little weakness he preferred boys. If he couldn't get boys he would accept flat-chested, hairless pre-pubescent girls. If he couldn't get children he would visit anyone, just anyone, simply to quell the urge. He crossed the road murmuring to himself, 'In and out in ten minutes. The dottled old dear will have forgotten I've been and the boss'll no notice. A one-off. Aye, this is a safe one right enough. Boss'll never know. No problem at all.'

27 AUGUST 1989

Grimes is a tight-fisted fucker. He splashes the cash on himself and his chosen few of top players but that's it. As a result, most of his team is made up of a hotchpotch of oddballs. Blokes who'd struggle to get work elsewhere, whose talents are hard to spot and sometimes invisible. Grimes employs a couple of specialists but with the rest he applies the principle of life is cheap.

There was a time he hired junkies to carry out hit jobs. Well, they were cheap and desperate. When they kept shooting the wrong targets or buggered off with the down payments without doing the job he eventually got the point. Now all he wants is strict obedience and he hires this crew of misfits who nobody else would employ. His crew are banned from doing anything without his express say-so. They obey, usually. Grimes' men fear him more than anything else - and with good reason. Terrified men with nowhere else to go are dangerous.

SURVEILLANCE NOTES

Farquhar A. Farquhar (aka Angie the Gopher)

Early 50s, just over five foot tall, skinny, wears a really daft wig and old-fashioned suits. Works for Andy Grimes. Weirdo. Brought up in a family that lived on a big country estate, his father being a gardener for Lord or Lady something. The family had pretensions (thus the unfortunate name) that old Farquhar couldn't meet. Black sheep of the family.

Got into a bit of trouble back home and was thrown off the estate. Made his way to Glasgow and tried to get into the teams. As an outsider he had to start at the bottom - Going For this, Going For that. It was this digging about, what he found from time to time and his rat-like expressions that changed his name from GoFor to Gopher. Whatever they call him he's

still low status and can't whistle without Grimes'
permission.

He has two addictions. Pretending he's a social
worker, sometimes a doctor. He's hooked – can't
resist an opportunity. He also pays for young male
prostitutes, thus his other nickname, Angie.
Weaknesses – a coward and a weirdo. Strengths – he'd
cheat his own mother.

A

STICK TO SNAP

'You know it's no right, Andy.' Joe muttered the words slouching over the table towards Grimes, sheltering his words from the people behind him. Business was slow at The Cat's Whiskers Club during that Glasgow afternoon siesta time when the customers went to work, hung out at the bookies or reported to wives and kids to prove they did actually exist. Three or four hardened drinkers sat at the bar silently addressing their gods who could only be found at the bottom of a glass. To one side, on the slightly raised platform that served as a stage, a bored and naked sloe-eyed brunette shook her hips and breasts too slowly and out of beat to Simple Minds' 'Belfast Child'. She looked as if she were there, across the water, far away, troubles or no troubles. These were the people Joe didn't care two hoots about. The worrisome crew gathered directly behind him spread out around a table drinking lager tops, smoking and chatting as if they cared about each other. He knew Grimes' mob would be listening to his every word. Planting Fergie amongst them would offer him little protection save serving up a minor distraction as they slagged him off in their usual style.

'Whit ye talking about, man?' Grimes leaned back in his chair, eyeing Joe suspiciously and speaking in his usual booming tones.

'Pull yer pals off Cathy Brodie.'

'Cathy who?'

'Don't come the wise cunt wi me, Andy.' Joe's capacity for quiet diplomacy was celebrated on the streets but was also limited. He could feel a steam of rage building pressure inside his chest. Behind him, sitting among the team, Gerry Kirkpatrick, the quiet but dangerous member of Grimes' mob, pretended not to hear and slipped his hand inside his jacket to rest on the handle of his pistol.

'Cool it, Joe, right?' As much as Grimes was unwilling to concede anything, he knew Joe Murphy's capacity for violence when called for and he could do without that, especially in The Cat's Whiskers, his space and HQ.

'Cathy Brodie . . . daughter of Tim Brodie. Remember him? Ye was at his fuckin funeral and some say . . .'

'Aye, Tim Brodie, right,' Grimes interrupted loudly. 'That his lassie's name, Cathy, eh?'

'You owe her, Andy.'

'Me? Owe the lassie? Whit for?' Grimes' face had the look of a troubled though innocent child.

'Want me tae spell it oot for ye?'

'Och, Joe, they rumours werenae true, pal. Ah get blamed for jist aboot everything – ye know that.'

'You owe her . . .'

'Murdering this one, killing that one, bribing the government, hiding Bible John, World War Three and, aye, the fuckin Berlin Wall as well Ah wouldnae be surprised.' Grimes answered Joe's puzzled look by nodding in the direction of a large television set flickering silently in the corner. The news was on and the BBC crew were broadcasting from Berlin, predicting the imminent unification of East and West Germany. 'Ach, ye know whit Ah mean.'

'Aye, an you know whit Ah mean.'

'Aye, Cathy Brodie, Tim's daughter. Now you mention it . . .'

'Cry the polis aff.'

'Whit?'

'Yer pals, the blue coats – tell them tae drop it.'

'Ah huv no influence oan the polis, Joe.'

'Andy, it's me yer speaking tae, no yer daft boys in the corner.'

'Ye come fannying in here asking for a meet jist tae insult me,' Grimes roared.

Behind him Gerry Kirkpatrick looked up and fidgeted. They called him 'Deadeye' though the origin of the name was long lost. Some said it was because he was never known to smile, others because he was a crack shot. One tabloid journalist had claimed he was called Deadeye because if he looked in your direction you were a dead man. Kirkpatrick secretly enjoyed the description, though it didn't stop him one dark night telling the hack to stop writing about him or he'd meet a slow and painful end. Fergie leaned over to Deadeye Kirkpatrick brandishing a pack of cards and asked, 'Want a game, Gerry?'

'Whit?'

'Game o cards, eh? Heard ye were a right dab hand at the three-card brag.' Around him, Grimes' team smirked and nudged each other.

'Yese play a lot, Fergie?' It was Shuggie, The Mouse, who had survived the assault by Grimes the day before but not well. Purple bruising to his eye and nose, red bald patches in his scalp where his hair had been yanked out and a crusty grey scar running the length of one ear all bordered by a white surgical collar reaching halfway up his chin all testified to his narrow escape. The doctors had ordered him to stay in hospital but he'd limped out that same night. More than serious injury, The Mouse feared missing out on the action. If you weren't there you didn't exist as far as Andy Grimes was concerned.

'Naw, Ah'm no a card hand,' Fergie replied. 'In fact Ah never play, Shuggie. Thought we could just pass the time like.'

'Fiver post, pound minimum stake.' Shuggie was pulling in his chair, unable to resist a rare chance to exploit a patsy. 'C'moan, boys, jist me an Fergie, eh? So's he can get the hang o the game, eh?' The rest of the mob, even Deadeye Kirkpatrick, felt sorry for The Mouse and the injuries he had suffered, all because he was such a poor gambler. They'd known the beating he'd get from Grimes for passing on the bad news about his brother and decided to allow him a respite by staying out of the card game. Surely even he could beat a novice, especially daft Fergie. In good humour and with sly winks they pulled their chairs closer to the table to watch The Mouse win at cards for a change.

'Right, Ah'll deal,' announced Fergie. 'How many cards is it again?'

'Three! It's three-card brag, ya stupid wanker.' The men howled with laughter at Deadeye Kirkpatrick's pronouncement. Deadeye didn't often crack jokes and raised a laugh even less frequently. He was going to enjoy commentating on this game. Pulling his hand out of his jacket, he swivelled round and joined the gamblers at their table.

'So whit's it tae be?' Joe demanded of Grimes.

'Look, Joe, ye know the score. It was my brother. My BROTHER, man.'

'Ye didna spend much time the gether when he was alive an kicking.'

'Aye. Aye, but aw the same he was ma bro.'

'So what are you gonnae achieve by leaning on Cathy Brodie?'

'She saw it all.'

'How d'ye know?'

'There was a phone call.'

'Tae the polis?'

'Aye, the polis.'

'An she'd phone the polis wid she?'

'It was a woman's voice and, well, she could see the whole shebang – frae her flat.'

'An she'd phone the polis, eh? Like she phoned the polis afore?'

'Well . . .'

'When she watched her old man get hit, eh?'

'It's jist that . . .'

'Like she has grassed tae the polis every day since her faither was killed?'

'Joe, this is no her faither.'

'Naw, it's your bastarding brother. Like she'd care about him all of a sudden.'

'Naw. Naw, of course no.'

'Well then, for Christ's sake, Andy.'

'But maybe she didnae like the shooter.'

'Oh aye, and who was that then?' asked Joe, not expecting an answer. Grimes pushed his chair back and stared at Joe, contemplating his next move. Then he noticed Maggie Small, his Maggie, behind the bar with the club's books spread in front of her, as his so-called gang laughed and chortled, totally engrossed in some daft game of cards. What he'd give for a team of Maggies. No need for muscle with such brains, discipline and loyalty.

'Wee minute, Joe, Ah'll just fetch us another drink.'

'Don't want a bevvy. Ah want a fuckin answer.'

'Ye'll get it – but let me get a drink. Ah'm in mourning remember?'

As Grimes waddled towards the bar, Joe thought, 'Mourning? Whit happened, ya big bastard? Lose yer wallet?'

'You hear aw that, Maggie?' Grimes was helping himself to a bottle of brandy from the gantry.

'Yes, of course,' Maggie replied while keeping her head down, still pretending to work on the club's accounts ledger spread out on the bar.

'Whit ya reckon? Dae Ah tell him anything?'

'I think he's fly fishing, Andy. I don't think Cathy Brodie's good name and dignity is the issue here.'

'Naw. It's whit Ah thought tae.' Grimes caught a nose full of Maggie Small's perfume. Always the same one. Classy, sexy, sensuous. She smelled like she looked. Long ago he'd given up any hopes of bedding her. She'd made it plain from the start – no mixing business with pleasure. Grimes wondered what pleasure was for Maggie. After all these years of working together he had no clue what she did for fun. But business, now that he knew about, and she was good. The best. The perfume also smelled of the Maggie he did know – sharp, ruthless, hard headed. He'd settle for that any day.

'He'll have heard the rumours like everyone else, Andy.'

'Aye, suppose so, he . . .' Grimes caught himself in time. Years before Maggie Small had told him that if he called her hen one more time she was quitting. He wondered why she'd made such a big fuss about such a small thing but wasn't about to take a risk.

'Tell him as much as you know,' she continued.

'Whit?'

'About Addison's name coming up. He'll know that already. Promise him you'll back off Cathy Brodie.'

'Ah'm no kowtowing tae that bastard. Ah'll lose face.'

'Nobody will know. Tell him. Shake hands on it and . . .'

'Fuck sakes, Maggie.'

' . . . when he's gone, you make a phone call.'

'Whit, tae the speaking clock?'

'To a friend from out of town.' At last Grimes was catching the drift.

'Go on.'

'Someone handy. No local ties. Give him a list.'

'Like it. Go on.'

'If it works out with Addison, add Joe Murphy's name to the list if you want,' said Maggie.

'Just below that cunt Addison's name, eh?' At that there was a howl from the card game. Fergie was on his feet, whooping with delight and throwing his cards on the table with a flourish, only to discover that he was beaten yet again by Shuggie, the smirking Mouse. 'An that daft fucker Fergie's name as well for definite.'

'If he's marking Joe Murphy he'll be marking Fergie.'

'Course he will. Whit aboot Birse and the bizzies?'

'Get them to have a look at Murphy's business. Maybe rattle his cage. By the time Murphy twigs . . .'

'Aye. Right. Aye. Shower a useless cretins anyhow.'

'More the merrier.'

'You're a class act, Maggie. You and me are gonnae speak aboot a rise later.' Without looking up from the ledger, Maggie Small smiled at the prospect of something Grimes did know brought her pleasure – more money.

Grimes and Joe went back into conference, talking quietly in confidence as the men continued with their game and Maggie Small went off to berate the brunette for her lacklustre performance. Eventually the two men stood up, shaking hands vigorously, and Joe called for Fergie to join him.

'Wee minute, Joe, one more haun, eh?' Fergie pleaded.

'One more then we're gone, right?' Joe and Grimes wandered over to the card table to watch the last game. Deadeye Kirkpatrick had taken over the dealing and flicked the cards out in a series of fast snaps. On the table in front of Shuggie the Mouse lay neat bundles of fivers, tenners and columns of silver. In front of Fergie lay a few lonely crumpled pound notes and a small pile of brown coins.

'Seeing how it's the last haun Ah'll dae yese a favour an play blind.' The Mouse's smile peeked unevenly over his surgical mask.

'Blind? Blind? What the fuck's that mean? You gonnae pull that bandage ower yer phizog?' Fergie was learning a new trick that the onlookers, aside from Joe, found hilarious.

'Naw. Naw. Ah'll no look at ma cards but bet oan them onyroads.'

'Whit, but that's fuckin crazy.'

'Catch is youse have tae pay double ma bets.' Fergie gave the prospect some thought and the effort was written all over his wrinkled brow.

'Right yese are,' he concluded with a smile. 'Dae yer worst, wee man.' A pair of threes in his hand had given him cause for optimism. 'It's you tae open the bidding. Fire away.' The Mouse's smile had disappeared as he contemplated his next move, fingering the thick wad of money at his side. Flicking through the notes he lifted a handful of fivers and ceremoniously counted four out into the pot.

'Bid ye twenty knicker.'

'Twenty ponds? Twenty fuckin quid?'

'That's forty ye've goat tae go,' offered Deadeye Kirkpatrick, his face threatening to break a lifetime's habit with the flicker of a grin.

'Ah can count, ye cunt,' Fergie exploded. 'It's just Ah've no got forty pounds. Yese can see that.' Around the table the men were laughing loud, with even The Mouse giggling with glee in contravention of the usual protocol of card gambling. Fergie looked over his shoulder at Joe who shook his head, drew out his wallet and handed over four crisp ten pound notes. 'See yese, ye bastard,' Fergie declared, confident of a win, throwing his own hand on the table first.

Slowly, one by one, Shuggie turned over his cards. Jack of Hearts, eight of Clubs and . . .

'Jack of Diamonds, ya beauty!' The Mouse was on his feet clawing the pot towards him, being slapped on the back by his team members.

Joe huckled the crestfallen Fergie to his feet and led him out of the club to the echoes of laughter and self-congratulations behind them.

'How much did ye lose?' Joe asked.

'A hunner an twenty notes.'

'Counting mine?'

'Shite. A hunner an sixty.' Fergie looked humiliated, cowed, walking with his shoulders stooped, both hands deep in his pockets. His friend couldn't stand the pain across his usually smiling mug.

'S'pose ye'll be needing a tap?'

'Naw, naw. Thanks, Joe.'

'How ye gonnae get through the week?'

'Ah'll get by, so Ah will.' Joe's hand was in his inside pocket. Without looking at Fergie he slipped his fist across.

'Here's a half ton.'

'Naw, Joe, it's aw . . .'

'Take it. Consider it a payment for services rendered.'

'Joe, Ah . . .'

'Shut yer gob. But dae us a favour, eh?'

'Anythin, man.'

'Don't go gambling ever again.'

'Right, naw. No way.'

'Specially wi they cunts.'

'Aye. Mean naw, Joe. Promise, man. Ah'm sticking tae snap in future.'

As the two men walked to their car a familiar figure ran into Fergie and Joe, jostling against them. Farquhar A. Farquhar, aka Angie the Gopher, stooped to scoop up his jet black wig from the pavement and took off again. Angie the Gopher was in a hurry. He was late but it was more than that. He had something for the boss. Something that would get him back into the good books. Something that couldn't wait.

30 AUGUST 1989

My alter ego has become a legend of the streets. While the police have punted my name about as an evil bastard; Joe Ordinary, anyone who knows anything about anyone I've seen to, knows better. Mass murderer of innocents or protector of the weak? That's how they see me – the police and the public – with no middle ground. Me, I know I'm neither. All I am is a spectre with attitude. When I act I do so for me, on my decision and my decision alone. I do so in the full knowledge that the police will hunt me – it's one of the prices I pay. And as much as it was never part of my designs, the adulation is useful as protection. Few of the public would think of grassing James Addison – well, not the citizens of the world I inhabit.

Other street players above all know most about who I target. They see me as the rat-catcher and are grateful that I take on the task. Well, most of them are grateful, apart from other rats.

Grimes is out to get me, that's for sure. While his police allies always need watching there's only one of his actual team with the wit and the mettle to threaten me.

SURVEILLANCE NOTES

Gerry Kirkpatrick (aka Deadeye)

Early 30s, tall, well built, short black hair. Works for Grimes as his local hitman. Done a five stretch for his part in a post office robbery. No convictions since he teamed up with Grimes. Always carries a shooter. Will hurt someone just for the hell of it. He's a cold killer, always alert, works alone. Weaknesses – smokes too much hash at times, thinks he's unbeatable.

A

BETTER LATE?

'How's it hanging, ma man?' Grimes was sitting at his office desk talking on the phone to a business associate in Manchester. The only other person in the room was Maggie Small. She was sitting across from him, her posture straight in spite of the chair's invitation to slouch, long legs crossed neat and demure. With that demeanour, she could've been a good-looking schoolteacher or a young vicar's wife. 'Haa, Ah'll bet ye are ye old rogue. Ah've been hearing things about yese. He he he.'

Out in the club a row had broken out. Now that the men had had their laugh at Fergie they were demanding that The Mouse repay some of his debts to them. Trouble was that the hundred and sixty pounds he'd won wasn't enough to pay off one obligation, never mind them all. So they were fighting about who should get what and roaring at The Mouse who was trying to slink away with his ill-gotten loot.

'A wee favour,' Grimes' tone changed to solicitous. 'Aye, a local difficulty. Oh, ye've heard. Thank you. That's very decent o yese. We werenae close but he was ma brother. Family – that's right. So Ah need a wee hander. Somebody that knows the city but has no ties here.' The row from the club had grown louder and Grimes put his hand over the mouthpiece and hissed at Maggie, 'Gonnae go tell they cunts tae shut the fuck up or Ah'll be oot tae them.' Even as Grimes made the threat he acknowledged to himself that one quiet word from Maggie would be more effective in restoring peace among the men and cause much less grief to himself. 'Aye, where was Ah . . . oh aye, somebody that's a bit useful. That's right. No feart tae carry a weight. Good man, Ah knew Ah could rely on yese. Help me sort this business oot an Ah'll owe yese big time. Of course Ah will, aw the best.'

As Grimes returned the handset to its cradle he noted with satisfaction that the racket from the club had calmed down. Maggie Small walked back into the office and from behind her shadow out popped the emaciated figure of Angie the Gopher. Grimes suddenly remembered that he'd called Angie over an hour ago ordering him back to The Cat's Whiskers. All that business with Joe Murphy had distracted him – another reason for his increasing irritation with that man's attitude. He intended to take it out on Angie,

'Where the fuck have you been, ye wee sicko?' Head bowed, Angie stood meekly in front of the desk – a schoolboy about to be belted by the headmaster. 'Ah fuckin warned ye, Angie, none o yer sick games oan ma time. So where the fuck have ye been?' Angie went to speak but was interrupted, 'An this better be really fuckin good, Angie, cos Ah've had a shit o a day.' Angie fidgeted with his wig, now clasped in both his hands rather than balancing precariously on top of his skull, and went to speak. 'So let's hear it then,' Grimes bawled, 'and hurry up.'

'Ah paid . . .' Angie the Gopher began.

'Have you been up tae yer tricks, ye wee shite? Aifter everything Ah telt yese? Ah'll fucking kill yese.'

'Boss, Ah've found . . .'

'See if Ah have tae get aff this seat yer a dead man. Get it? Dog food.'

'Boss, Ah've found something.'

'Aye, the end o ma fucking tether.'

'Something useful.'

'Like a noose for yer scrawny neck.'

'Naw. Really. Ah think it might be worth a few quid.'

'If yer just spinning me a line to cover yer filthy tracks . . .'

'Really, Boss, Ah think it could be worth a lot o brass.'

As much as Andy Grimes wanted to wring Angie the Gopher's neck, money was a bigger draw on his priorities. The little man had on occasions unearthed a good few earners and this might be yet another one. He had his bad habits, but now and again they paid dividends.

'Maggie, shut the door and pull up a pew.' Angie the Gopher went to take a seat too, 'No you, ye fucking weirdo, jury's aye oot oan you.' Angie jumped and stood back up, his head lowered from Grimes' gaze, hands pulling black hairs out of his ruined wig. As he tried to speak his dry mouth struggled, his lump of an Adam's apple wobbling up and down his neck. While Grimes took pleasure in his employee's discomfort, Maggie Small solved the problem by handing Angie her drink. Two swallows later his voice was restored and he started, 'Well, Ah went into this house like . . .'

BLUE BLUES

Detective Constable Jeannie Stirk hated to admit it but she was feeling sorry for herself. The fifty-mile flit from Edinburgh to Glasgow didn't seem much on the map but socially, professionally, she might as well have moved to a different planet. What was it her DCI at Lothian and Borders Police had said?

'Aye, Jeannie, you're moving to a hostile place.'

'I like the Glasgow folk,' she had replied, thinking that the kindly old copper was referring to the ancient myth of fierce competition and fiercer battles between Edinburgh and Glasgow.

'I don't mean the folk – they're much the same all over. I mean the bobbies. The force.' He'd turned away then to buy another round at the bar. It had been her last night, her going-away party and the place was crowded out with her colleagues. She didn't get another chance to speak with the old DCI alone that night. As soon as the karaoke started, drunkenness moved up a gear and everybody seemed to be leaning on everyone else. But it had troubled her for days till she expelled it from her mind – an old habit won hard as she had confronted life's tragedies in every mundane job the police could throw at her. She'd taken it all and more. She'd won through to detective constable. Her father was so proud, and him a beat copper all his working life. It made up for the son he never had, that and more. She owed him that and, besides, she loved the job. Well, she had, till now.

Two weeks in Glasgow and Birse had her back in uniform for the day using some excuse about showing a police presence at Cathy Brodie's house. So why couldn't they just get a uniform to tag along? Were they hiding something? Maybe, but he had to choose her – the newcomer and the only female in his section – just to put her in her place. Working with Birse was going to be a problem.

'The same again, please,' she leaned across the bar waving a ten pound note at the slim, blonde-haired man serving.

'Pardon?' The loud disco music had drowned out her order. As the young man moved closer she could smell his sweet flowery aroma like women's scent. He was good looking in a boyish way, girlish even, and fitted in with the majority of customers at Bennett's disco. She shouldn't have come here, Glasgow's main gay nightspot, even with the effort she'd taken to dress differently from her usual plain-clothes gear. The homophobic police were sure to pay this venue close and regular attention.

'Double vodka and lemonade. Plenty of ice.' She spelled it out, moving her lips in the exaggerated mouth exercises she imagined opera singers or newscasters went through before every performance, every broadcast. This was her third large drink and would have to be her last. She was on early shift the next day and would need to be on good form to cope with DCI Birse and his bunch of chauvinistic misogynists.

Jeannie Stirk should have stayed in, had a decent meal, a long soak in the bath and gone to bed early with a good book. She knew she should have. But that ran the risk of the phone going and Birse handing out instructions, or worse, a call from the other – the reason she left Edinburgh. She wasn't in the right frame of mind for a lengthy emotional tirade tonight. Couldn't cope with the crying and the pleading. But Jeannie was lonely, craving the power of intimacy. That strength that carries you through the tribulations of every day knowing of the comfort of the night before and the night to come. She felt weak and vulnerable and if the call came she'd grab it for want of anything else. No, she couldn't allow that to happen. She wasn't going back and that was that. She'd fought too hard for this job, suffered too much to give it up now for what? A relationship? Friendship? Sex and comfort? It was all that but it wasn't love, whatever that was. Later, when she'd sorted out this work situation, she would travel through and be a friend. Not now though. Later, when she sorted out Birse . . . if she sorted out Birse.

What had she walked in on at Cathy Brodie's? Those threats and the sexual bullying? Did Birse treat all women like that? Was there some special reason why they were leaning so hard on Cathy Brodie? Okay, so it was a murder investigation but still that didn't merit breaking the rules, picking on someone you didn't even know was involved. On the basis of what? An anonymous phone call. But was that all?

None of her colleagues would explain anything to her. She felt adrift from the knowledge she'd built up on the streets of Edinburgh over her eleven years in the police. Here in Glasgow there was a whole separate history, street dynasties and alliances – complicated enough to learn and keep up to date without being thrown into the middle of it with no clues, no lifebelt. Maybe Glasgow really was a different planet from Edinburgh. Maybe the myth of suspicion and hate between the cities was perpetrated by mutual ignorance. Scottish bigotry at its worst. Whatever, she felt sorry for Cathy Brodie and her baby.

'Love your headscarf.' The remark was spoken so close to her ear that it sent shivers down her neck and shook Jeannie from her reverie. It was a young woman she'd noticed come into the club with a group of female friends earlier, all dressed smartly, in suits and heels. She'd marked them down as an office night out, choosing Bennett's because it would be free of the usual hassle of predatory men, that and the good music and the absence of sporadic outbursts of gang violence.

'Eh, thanks.' Jeannie blushed at the unexpected compliment. 'Thank you.'

'It's very individualistic,' offered her uninvited companion. 'Gypsy-ish tied back like that, especially with your long dress.' The woman was in her early twenties, her red hair worn long in a wild mess of curls. She wore full make-up and smiled a great deal, showing small, white, even teeth and setting almost opaque blue eyes twinkling. 'My friends and I have had an argument. Some reckon you're a designer and others think you're a university lecturer. I've been sent over to settle the row.'

'So you drew the short straw,' Jeannie replied laughing.

'Yeah, and that's the one I was looking for.' The woman was leaning in close so they could be heard over the music. Jeannie could feel her breasts soft against her arm.

'And is there a bet on this?'

'Of course.' There was that smile again and aniseed breath. She must be drinking absinthe – a recent trend in the Glasgow clubs.

'And what do you think I do?'

'Everything.' The woman's smile was now a slow burning, cheeky grin and one hand had found its way against Jeannie's back. 'And beautifully.' Jeannie's turn to giggle and blush.

'That's an undeserved compliment.'

'So prove me wrong.' Her hand stroked Jeannie's back slowly, warm on her skin through the thin fabric of her dress, 'Or right.' Jeannie felt that familiar flush of anticipation running hot and cold over her limbs and down her neck. She looked away, watching the blonde barman preen himself for a dusky, leather-clad guy smiling at the end of the bar. It must have been the drinks and the loneliness, but she was tempted and she shouldn't really. She should be careful, take no chances.

'I'm Jeannie.'

'Amanda-Jane.'

'Pleased to meet you, Amanda-Jane.'

'Likewise, Jeannie. Want to dance?' The overhead lights had dulled as the DJ introduced Dusty Springfield's 'You Don't Have to Say You Love Me'. Across the floor of studded, flashing lights men embraced men, moving slowly and rhythmically to the music. By the far wall, two women stood locked in each other's arms, kissing long and deep. Men on their own circled the room eyeing up the talent. Some would be Vice Squad searching out under-age young twinks and clocking the others. She was breaking no laws, but her reputation, her profession, had to be protected. Any excuse, any rumour and Birse would be happy to use it against her.

Amanda-Jane moved towards the dance floor holding Jeannie's hand, gently pulling her arm her eyes smiling and inviting.

'Noooo,' Jeanie heard her voice say as if by its own will. 'No,' and she shook her head sadly. The look of hurt on her new friend's face was immediate.

'Why not? Just a dance.'

'I'd rather go back to your place.' There, she'd said it and hadn't even known she was going to. The smile again. Broad, beaming and open.

'All right,' smiled Amanda-Jane, 'this way.'

Out in the damp chill of the Glasgow night, they headed towards the lights of Clyde Street and a taxi. Jeannie Stirk no longer felt sorry for herself.

2 SEPTEMBER 1989

I watch them arrive one by one. Grimes really ought to choose a more difficult place to observe. Down at the bottom of the steps leading from Central Station to Union Street. Just there beside the *Evening Times* seller. Always drunks leaning against the wall, old homeless jakies trying to tap a couple of bob, young folks waiting for mates to head off on a Saturday night jaunt. So, I stood among them watching.

The main players were easy.

Grimes arrived early minded by his brains - that Maggie Small. Needs watching carefully that one.

One councillor I recognised from the papers, looking all serious with his arse licker running alongside him. The councillor's called Scully, a big shot on the planning committee and with the most greased palm of all the political hypocrites and that's saying something. Scully turns up to all of Grimes' social occasions. He's been around so long in the council that he's a dab hand at drawing in the others not yet corrupted. Scully's sidekick is some pen pusher called Benson. He's in charge of planning applications and some of the urban renewal projects round the city. The pair of them are useful to Grimes' semi-legit building company, Oxford Street Properties. No wonder Glasgow is full of wasteland and damp houses. In return for their favours Scully gets wads of greenbacks and Benson his pick of Maggie's girls.

Another face - also council. Think he was that guy hauled up in public for the roads being a disaster last winter. Kept his job though. Must be smart - or connected.

Spotted Councillor Wiley, vice-convener of the finance committee, going in. That was a shocker. He's an old guy, well known from his days as a radical shop steward before the shipyards shut down. Thought he was painfully honest - the kind of guy who did without wages on strike for months just on a principle of workers' rights. What can they have on Wiley? Can't believe he's part of Grimes' crew — but better keep my ear to the ground.

Grimes is no one's fool. At these social dinners he always invites a mixture of honest and bent individuals. At least half of the men are just there to meet with their equals — influential types in politics, law, C-grade TV personalities, a couple of football players or managers, sometimes the odd journalist. Grimes pays for the evenings — which must cost a few bob. But he gets good returns for his cash — a veneer of respectability, a cover for his crooked negotiations and some filth on the straight types that go all the way with Maggie's girls.

Maggie's girls stood out a mile. Looking classy, expensive compared to the normal customers with their fresh perms and Sunday coats. She trains them well.

There could have been more, would have been but that's one drawback of the venue — too many bodies. Had to leave when I spotted Birse. He might be a bastard but he's a para bastard — eyes in the back of his nut. Besides, I'd other fish to fry. Wish I had someone on the inside. Wrong religion and no contacts — see to it.

A

CIVIC DUTY

'Gies a smile, hen,' he drawled, wavering on bendy hips, his legs wide, rigid, unmoving. She continued staring straight ahead, anywhere but at him and his friends. Slightly built, shivering in her thin, short dress she appeared vulnerable and doe eyed standing there alone on the busy city-centre pavements of night-time Glasgow. Especially there on the Boots corner, at that time of night when all the other blind dates had long since realised they'd been stood up. It was brass-neck corner, reserved for the naive or the optimistically desperate. Maybe she didn't realise she was too pretty to be that tragic.

'Aw come oan, darlin. It'll never happen.' It was his mate. This one was eating chips and was drunker than most. He sashayed in front of her, shovelling vinegar-nippy, greasy handfuls into his gob and eyeing her up and down. The three young men were drunk, having started their usual pub crawl in the early afternoon.

'Whit's the matter, doll, he get you in the pudding club or sumfin?' All around them young people hurried on their way, dressed in their best, smelling sweet, laughing, in the company of friends, heading for the late-night Saturday venues.

'You're no a bad-looking wee tart really. Ah'd go wi yese.' To him she looked just right: young, frightened and alone. Her short dress was not quite in fashion but showed her figure off to good effect, an effect he could appreciate, bevvied or not. Sniffing and lowering her face she fumbled in her big shoulder bag.

'Aw dinnae greet, hen. C'moan tae Jamesie,' spraying the air with small white blobs of soft potato. She fumbled on searching, for what? A tissue to wipe her tears? 'Aw, doll, cheer up, ye've got a lumber noo.' Head down, still searching in the handbag. 'Christ, quit the weeping, ye sad bitch.' She looked up, straight in his eye for the first time. For a second he thought he recognised her then her arm flipped up, slicing his face open with the Stanley knife. He could feel damp on his cheek but felt no pain, yet.

'That's for ma wee sister,' she said quietly. He did recognise her, he thought he had. 'And that's frae me.' The blade struck out again into his eye socket. 'Govan Team,' she screamed and raised her arm. He couldn't see but he heard the call.

'Govan Team, ya bass,' the call rumbled behind them followed by rushing footsteps, scores of rubber-soled Doc Martins thumping against the kerbstones. The three young drunks turned to look and she slashed him again behind the ear. He pushed her away with one arm and took to his heels in pursuit of his mates, only yards ahead of the gang.

Up Union Street, a packed mêlée of bodies at pub closing time as drunken crowds queued to catch late-night buses. The girl lifted her handbag, hiked up her dress and joined in the chase. The pavements were too crowded so the three men took to the road, a nose-to-tail jam of buses, taxis and cars the length of Union Street. Before they reached the entrance of Central Station and the safety of bright lights and patrolling police they were caught.

The Govan Team set about them with fists and boots right there in the middle of the street. It was no contest. The ruckus ground the rows of buses to a halt, their headlights illuminating the action, passengers and pedestrians screaming with terror or moving closer, gawking.

She caught up with the group, 'That's the fucker. Him there. That bastard,' she screamed, pointing to one bundle huddled on the ground, his arms wrapped round his skull, knees pulled up over his stomach, blood seeping onto the road. Where were the police when they were needed?

High above the fight, in the Delta Club, DCI Alex Birse was taking a smoke break from the dinner table. He'd joined his father's lodge at the earliest opportunity but how he hated this freemason attachment to loyalty or, should he say, royalty. No smoking till the Queen was toasted, well he couldn't wait that long. A small cigar at the window watching the Irn Bru advert go through its mechanical paces high above Central Station. Birse remembered how as a child, from the street he thought Ba Bru was so real and the lemonade he poured so tasty, yet from where he was standing now it looked all too much like the series of strip lights that it was.

'All a con, just like fucking life,' he thought to himself. Then he spotted the fight down below – much more to his taste. 'Go oan, kill the fucker. Go oan, stick him.' Although he was too far away to recognise any of the combatants, Birse knew that they'd just be troublemakers anyway. It didn't matter to him why or how the enemy went down, or even who did it, as long as they went down. When the uniforms turned up on the street scattering the Govan Team in four directions, Birse noted that their target was left lying awkwardly on the ground, one arm twisted against the play of the joint and his head at a crazed angle. With satisfaction he stubbed out his cigar and headed back to the table.

'The Celtic have lost their way now – they'll never catch up.'

'Oh, I wish, but they're too big to slide.'

'Naw, too old fashioned – need to get modern, break ties with their old papist routines. Forget about winning the European Cup – it's history. Look forward . . .'

Sitting between the football commentators, Maggie Small smiled and looked intrigued in a topic that bored her rigid, always had, always would. Around the table the men were all dressed as if to a formula, in identical suits, some black though mostly grey. She had a theory that they all bought their suits from Ralph Slater's, the biggest single collection of men's gear in the world, all under one roof in the crumbling east end of the city centre. Some wise old salesman there had these guys sold on the notion of style and a good bargain. Instead he just palmed them off with the same suits in either black or grey.

The company was mixed. At the head of the table sat Grimes on his best behaviour, looking almost suave and calm for a change. She admired his capacity to discipline his moods where business took priority. And this was business. On either side of Grimes were two councillors, both Labour Party of course, since they were the undisputed municipal power in the city. These weren't just ordinary councillors but were influential members of the planning and finance committees. Their interests coincided with one of Grimes' commercial ploys – demolition. Another night it would have been councillors from the licensing board to hear his pleas on extending some of the opening hours of the numerous pubs he owned. Or maybe housing, to cater for the squads of subcontractors who paid him a cut of their income.

Maggie's girls were scattered around the table, seated between the men in black or grey suits, either the councillors or their favoured officers they'd brought along for the freebie night out. She was pleased to note the girls were behaving themselves, sitting demurely and smiling when spoken to. 'Deaf Decorations' she called them. Looking good, hearing the mundane chat-up lines but never catching a word of any of the business talk, or pretending not to. But these young women were tried and tested, all, that is, except Suzie with a zed.

'But we're boring the girls, lads, and we shouldn't really ramble on about football,' said the guy from the planning office. Short legged and overweight, his neck seemed on the point of bursting out of his collar, his red face carried a constant sheen of grease and sweat. Robert Benson was the name on his business cards but the girls called him Bent Bob behind his back. 'Sorry, Maggie, we'll change the subject.'

'No need, Robert, we don't mind. Truly. Football in this city is like a religion, except more important.'

'Phaaaaa.' Morsels of half-chewed food flew from his greasy lips as he laughed too enthusiastically at what was an old line, long past being a joke. 'You kill me, Maggie, so you do. But please, call me Bob. My friends call me Bob.' Across the table Suzie with a zed barely managed to smother a giggle. One cold stare from Maggie and her face straightened. The young woman was rough round the edges and lacked class. At least she'd learned not to cross Maggie Small in even the most trivial way, or had she?

The Delta was a club run by an association of Freemason lodges. Most nights it was cheap food and an even cheaper cabaret, but Grimes had avoided all that tat by hiring a private room and bringing in his own caterers – strictly against club rules but he was a generous contributor to the club's welfare fund. The Delta had no official bar on religion, unlike many other places in Glasgow. Catch was that the membership came via Masonic lodges and members only was the rule. Grimes had signed in his guests. Mind you, most of his guests were affiliated to Masonic lodges or the Orange Order, even some who officially batted for the other side.

'Business is business,' Bob Benson had once told Grimes, flashing his Masonic penny, 'and the Pope would never forgive this good Catholic boy if I failed to see that.'

'Aye, Bob, but he might excommunicate us both if he found out, eh?' Grimes had replied with a conspiratorial glimmer of humour on his lips. It was the least of the secrets the two shared.

'Whit about the sheep-shaggers?' Suzie with a zed had decided to join in the football chat. 'They no winning aw the time?'

'Don't you mention those Aberdeen fuckers,' DCI Birse had rejoined the company. 'Bunch a fouling, leg-breaking cunts so they are.' Maggie Small was trying to catch Suzie's eye, warn her never to mention football in front of Birse. 'Yon fucking Neil Simpson – cynical bastard . . .'

'Oh come on, Alex, she didn't mean harm by it. Did you, sugar,' Bob Benson smiled his greasy beamer across at Suzie who seemed to be enjoying Birse's angry outburst.

'Cunts come doon here wi their fucking Casuals slashing folk and pishing oan the Union Jack. Tell ye they should put me on stadium duty they Saturdays . . . Ah'd fucking show them.' Benson was still smiling at Suzie who was still grinning at Birse's rant. Maggie Small noticed, as she noticed everything, and she made a decision that had been bothering her all day. She looked round the room, at her other girls spread among the company. All were beautiful and well turned out – she saw to that. Most of them hadn't an active brain cell in their heads – or pretended they hadn't – and that suited Maggie just fine. Nor did they have a spark of attitude.

'Ah think he's dead handsome.' Suzie hadn't taken the hint. 'That one . . . what's his face? Eoin . . . smashing name. Young boy and . . .'

'Fucking Rangers reject that wee cunt. It was us he wanted tae play for.' Birse was still raving, falling for Suzie's jibes. She'd found his one weak spot and was going for it full steam ahead. It was a characteristic of Suzie that really worried Maggie.

At the other end of the table, Grimes didn't seem worried at all.

'Business has been booming this past year. Obviously a mark of the council's progressive urban planning.'

'Kind of you to say so, Andy. We like to think we put people's needs first,' replied Councillor Scully, convener of the planning committee and a regular attendee at Grimes' little soirées. A small, rotund, white-haired man, he had the countenance of a benign Santa Claus. A face you could trust, as the electorate had in voting him in for the last twenty years.

'Well, I have to thank you for your confidence in Oxford Street Properties,' Grimes said, raising his wine glass in a toast.

'You are the most reliable,' said Scully.

'And cost effective,' added Councillor Wiley, vice-convener of the finance committee. Wiley was a newcomer to these evenings, eventually persuaded along by his long-time comrade Scully. A long-jawed man, dour and unsmiling with a gravel-washed voice, Wiley had been a leading player in the trade union movement for the last thirty years. He was a familiar face on news broadcasts, pontificating sourly on the struggle of the workers against exploitation. On two occasions he had failed to gain a seat in Parliament in spite of sponsorship by one of the country's most powerful unions. The question on Grimes' mind was would Wiley accept his offer of sponsorship?

'We do our best,' Grimes replied in the closest he could get to a modest tone. 'Scuse me, gents. Alex, is it no time for the Queen?' Alex Birse was slapping the table to emphasise every point on the virtues of his team, sending the crystal tingling and the cutlery chattering. 'Will you oblige us, Alex?' Grimes lifted one eye and stared at Birse who caught and comprehended the look. If he was a child it would've been a parental signal of one last chance and he was being sent to bed. Normally he would've met any challenge head on. Normally.

'Eh, aye, great,' Birse mumbled apologetically, then continued unnecessarily, 'Huv Ah been rabitting oan a bit? Sorry annat, folks. It's the fitba, more . . .'

'. . . important than religion,' Suzie with a zed finished off his sentence, getting a glower from Birse. If Suzie had known Maggie Small's ways she would have noticed a much worse sign from her. Tiny white teeth nibbled quickly and gently at a perfectly painted lip. Big danger signal from Maggie – that's how obvious she got.

'Ladies and gentlemen,' Birse boomed, 'I give you Her Majesty, the Queen.' The entire company stood with filled glasses, turned to the bigger-than-life-size portrait of the Queen hanging on the far wall and drank,

'The Queen,' they chorused apart from Suzie with a zed, who giggled then hiccupped. Perfect, tiny white teeth nibbled at red lipstick.

The Loyal Toast over, almost everyone immediately pulled out cigarettes and cigars. All except Councillor Wiley, who was a man of the people, a self-proclaimed Bennite, the purveyor of simple tastes who, of course, smoked a pipe. It suited his public image even if it was a hand-crafted Chacom, number 288 of a limited edition of 1,245 as he never tired of telling people.

'Maggie, come n join us, doll.' Grimes' polite accent was slipping badly as the booze kicked in. Now that his favourite brandy was on the table he was in his element. Maggie could feel several pairs of eyes on her as she walked the length of the room. It was hardly surprising and she knew it. That's why she had chosen that dress – close fitting, thin straps and a thigh-length slash at one side. If the men around the room were thinking of her body the poor souls wouldn't be capable of carrying any other thoughts and that suited her fine. As it suited

Grimes. 'Ah was jist telling Baillie Wiley here what a dab hand you are at the accounts books. Definitely gifted ye know.'

'Oh, you learn as you go, Andy. Keeping accounts for a club or two is child's play compared to what you do, Councillor Wiley.' Maggie leaned forward as she spoke, watching Councillor Wiley's eyes follow her cleavage as her hand reached into her dainty handbag and switched on the even daintier tape recorder. 'Or you, Councillor Scully.'

'Oh, I don't know,' blustered Scully.

'Ah always say,' started Wiley, 'if ye can do the housekeeping ye can be an accountant – same skills. Women are . . . very underrated,' puff, puff, 'in my opinion.' Wiley never quite managed to step down off the hustings, with every sentence sounding like some pronouncement from his personal manifesto. Maggie considered him a shallow man full of his own bloated self-importance. But she did like the aroma of his tobacco – something between burning peat and cherry – a safe, strong reliable smell.

'I get that Bob Benson to do my economics,' offered Scully in a timid tone that overcame him after a few drinks. 'He's a braw lad that Bob. Rely on him for everything.' At the bottom of the table Bob Benson was nodding politely as Birse spoke but there was more enthusiasm in his eyes which were firmly focused on Suzie with a zed.

'Councillor Scully was just tellin me, Maggie, that we should speak tae Bob aboot that clearance notice,' Grimes said.

'He's a terrible man, Councillor Scully. Which development was he bothering you about over dinner?' Maggie asked, right on cue.

'Och, it comes wi the territory, Maggie. Ye get used to yer life no being yer own,' Scully replied as stoically as he knew how.

'I don't know how you cope with it,' Maggie said, her head turned to the side, eyes for him and him alone.

'Hmmmph, well anyways,' embarrassed now. 'It was they old properties at the east end of the city centre. Near the district court.'

'Oh those, yes they're in a terrible state. Hardly anyone lives there now.'

'Ah wis telling him that they old tenements are a disgrace,' said Wiley. 'The people deserve better than dampness, rats and junkies. Knock the damn lot doon's whit Ah say.'

'I'm sure the planning committee would look favourably on any application,' said Scully. 'But it's a matter of procedure and . . . and . . . and priorities. Bob's yer man for that. Keeps me right.'

'But we can discuss the proposal for demolition with Bob directly?' Maggie asked.

'Course you can, hen. An Ah've already told him Ah want it tae happen,' Scully said. 'He keeps me right about the procedures but Ah make the decisions.'

'Thank you, Councillor Scully, you're always so helpful.' Maggie reached out and squeezed Scully's arm, setting him blushing and sweating more than before.

'An don't you forget, Maggie, Ah'm oan the planning committee as well,' Wiley winked slowly as he spoke.

'We're very grateful to both of you for your support.' Maggie leaned further over the table than was necessary to reach Wiley's arm. All three men stared at the V of soft white flesh revealed by her drooping neckline.

'We're being honoured by Councillor Scully and Bob Benson as our overnight guests tonight, Maggie,' said Grimes, drawing his eyes away from her breasts and his mind back to the script. Ignoring Maggie's charms was easier for him after long years of knowing that she never put out to any man he had ever known of.

'Wonderful, perhaps we could arrange a breakfast meeting then?' said Maggie, sitting back up straight but crossing her legs to expose her stocking-clad thigh.

'Aye . . . aye, breakfast would be rerr,' stuttered Scully his eyes flitting around in their sockets, uncertain where to look.

'There's been too much business talk tonight already,' said Maggie. 'You men and your work,' she reprimanded, receiving in return preening, chest-swelling gestures from the two councillors and an open-handed who-me look from Grimes. 'What about you, Councillor Wiley? Will you not join us?'

'Oh, I'd love to, lass, but I've got tae go home. Wife's expecting us . . . she's no very well.'

'I'm so sorry to hear that,' replied Maggie. 'Nothing serious I hope.' Maggie already knew what was wrong with Mrs Wiley. An inoperable cancer of the stomach, the medical report said. Months to live at most.

'Naw, naw nothing too bad,' Wiley replied. 'Besides, I always go home. Like to put my head down in my own territory, my scheme so tae speak.'

'You'll let us call you a cab then,' offered Maggie.

'Naw, hen, thanks for the offer but Ah'm a bus man. It's the only season ticket Ah possess.' Wiley had often been photographed stepping on and off the city's green and orange buses. Along with his pipe the pictures had become an emblem of his status as honest man of the people.

'Sure? It's late you know?'

'Naw . . . naw thanks, hen. Plenty of time tae catch the last bus . . . Ah know the timetable better than the bloody drivers dae.' Wiley's oft-repeated comment set the company laughing and agreeing, talking of the old tram system and how they should never have done away with it. The turn in the conversation signalled that Maggie's work was done in this corner, but she had other unfinished business. Taking her leave, she headed back to the other end of the table, feeling eyes on her finely wrapped buttocks, and gently switched off the tape recorder in her handbag.

'Suzie, can I have a word please?' Maggie asked.

'Supercalifragilistikexpial . . .' Suzie's reply, delivered with a broad grin, set Bob Benson sniggering.

'In private,' Maggie smiled, taking hold of Suzie's shoulder, innocuous and friendly to the observer but leaving the young woman in no doubt. Maggie led the way out of the private room and through the main lounge of the Delta Club. The sudden rush of noise was deafening after the idle, booze-driven chatter of the night. Groups of men and women sat at white-clothed tables all around the room. Having had their dinner, now came the dance. A rumble of bodies jigged up and down in a small space in front of a raised plinth where a man in an ill-fitting tuxedo struggled with his false teeth, singing a compilation of Abba's greatest hits. As the two women edged through the crowd, the singer had moved on to 'Super Trouper' while his organist accompanist was still struggling with 'Dancing Queen'. The audience didn't seem to notice or care. Maggie couldn't help thinking of west of Scotland weddings and wondered when the standard issue punch-up was going to break out.

In the Ladies, Maggie checked all the cubicles before pulling Suzie roughly into the one farthest from the door.

'Listen you little cunt, and listen well,' Maggie started, watching her uncharacteristically crude language having the desired effect on Suzie. The girl was paying attention. 'All night you've been acting the fucking madam. As if you know the score. Think you're your own woman on your own time . . . well, that's shit.'

'Ah didnae mean anything by it . . . jist trying tae be good company,' Suzie pleaded her case, having to stretch her neck back in the confined space to look up at Maggie Small who towered over her.

'This is your work. We pay you, you little cow, and we tell you what to do.'

'Ah wis . . .'

'And what we tell you to do, you do.'

'. . . trying to make them . . .'

'Are you arguing with me, you dirty little bitch?'

'But . . .' Maggie slammed Suzie against the rattling cubicle partition pinning her there by both shoulders.

'You do not argue with me? Right?'

'Maggie, Ah wis jist trying tae say . . .'

'You do exactly as I tell you and no fucking buts.'

'But . . .'

'Kiss me,' Maggie ordered.

'WHIT?'

'You heard. Kiss me.' Maggie moved closer to Suzie. There was no smile, no frown, no hint of emotion on Maggie Small's face. Just that beautiful determination that she carried with her at all times. Suzie stood up on her toes and kissed Maggie on the cheek. 'Call that a kiss?' Maggie pursed her lips. Suzie's eyes filled with tears. She reached up and pecked Maggie on the lips. 'Again . . . properly this time.' Suzie's knees were shaking, her shoulders ached where Maggie's weight leaned against her, tears crystal in her eyes. She reached up and with quivering open lips kissed Maggie on the mouth. Maggie roughly grabbed the back of Suzie's neck with one hand and kissed her deeply, her tongue sliding in and out of the girl's mouth, feeling her teeth. The girl was gagging but Maggie didn't care or stop. With one hand she pulled up the girl's dress and deftly undid the studs at her crotch. Holding the girl against the cubicle wall, Maggie stood back and under the white glaring lights of the toilet forced Suzie to watch her looking at her sex, playing with her lips, parting her legs. Just looking and touching. 'See, you belong to me. Body mind and soul. I do with you what I choose. Right?'

Suzie was crying now. Wanted to curl up. Cover herself. Throw the bolt and flee from that place. Memories of her mother and the man she was forced to call father. Her following his instructions. Him laughing and getting cruder with every drink till he'd mount her and ride her with her mother naked nearby, too drunk to move, too stoned to care. 'Right?' Maggie's long fingernails jabbed into the girl's vagina while her eyes were staring at her face.

'Right,' mumbled Suzie.

'Pardon? Can't hear you?' Soft tissue ripping with another, deeper thrust.

'RIGHT,' Suzie said so loud that it echoed in the toilet's empty space.

'Good. That's better. So let's get you ready for work.' Abruptly, Maggie swung the door open leaving the girl there to fix her underwear and pull her dress down. When she emerged from the cubicle Maggie was standing in front of the mirror freshening her make-up. 'Better make yourself look decent, Suzie with a zed,' Maggie ordered. 'You have a long night ahead of you.' As Suzie dabbed at her eyes Maggie lit a long thin cigarette and watched. 'You're quite a good-looking girl you know. Work hard and you could do very well.' In the mirror, Suzie was surprised to see Maggie Small's reflection smiling, leaning casually against the edge of a sink, acting as if nothing had happened.

'Thanks, Maggie, I want to learn,' Suzie ventured.

'Good girl. Well, first piece of advice . . .'

'Huh?' Suzie turned to face her, keen schoolgirl looking up to teacher.

'Throw out all of your teddies.'

'Why? I mean, okay.'

'Men are fumbling idiots when it comes to studs.' Suzie nodded her head as if granted great words of wisdom. Maggie smiled and continued, 'Right, here's your instructions for tonight. Listen carefully . . .'

Back in the room, Maggie wandered around the table slipping keys to various men and whispering to the girls. All matches were now made, apart from Scully that was. He had special tastes: the largest bed you could find, a deep bath, well-stacked miniature bar, room service all night, absolute solitude and a thick envelope full of used tenners. He got the best suite the Central Hotel could provide. The guests slipped away one by one to be followed two minutes later by Maggie's selected girl.

Out on Union Street, Councillors Scully and Wiley said their goodnights to Grimes, Birse and Maggie Small. One lane of the street had been cordoned off by the police as the site of a murder scene.

'Uniforms only,' Birse thought contemptuously. 'Fucker must've been scum right enough.' The warm, steady drizzle would wash away any clues before long and the police on duty didn't look at all perturbed. There were more hazardous ways of working your shift in Glasgow on a Saturday night. High above them, Ba Bru kept on pouring his drinks.

'Are you sure we can't get you a taxi, Councillor Wiley?' said Maggie Small. 'You'll get soaked in this rain.'

'Naw, hen, no thanks. Good Glesca rain never killed a soul yet that I'm aware of. It jist makes you feel like you're deid.' The jibe went down well and Wiley took his leave, waving too vigorously as he headed towards George Square to catch a night-service bus. Scully departed to take up his berth in the nearby Central Hotel, dreaming of all-night orders of smoked salmon sandwiches, bottles of chilled Chardonnay and a thick envelope on his bedside table.

'Fucking hell, that was one long drag the night,' Grimes sighed once his guests were well out of earshot. 'You get that taped, Maggie?' Maggie Small eased her boss's anxiety by pulling the tape recorder out of her handbag, rewinding and playing an excerpt, 'An don't you forget, Maggie, Ah'm oan the planning committee as well,' Wiley's rasping voice sounded slightly hollow and metallic in the open air.

'Not much,' said Maggie quietly, 'but it will add to the collection.'

'Perfect. We'll hook that fucker in yet,' boomed Grimes. 'Ye're a star, Maggie. Right, Alex, you and I have tae talk about this Addison cunt.'

'Ach, it's a bit late the night, Andy, come oan, eh?' Birse complained.

'Too late fuck all. Ah'm no very satisfied wi whit you and yer toy sojers are playing at.'

'We've got a couple o leads,' Birse countered.

'Spare yer patter for the newspapers, eh! This is real life here, man. An Ah'm no very fucking happy.' Behind Grimes, a large Volvo sat tripled parked on the street, its engine running and the driver patiently smoking a cigarette. In spite of the Volvo's position impeding the flow of traffic, as well as encroaching on a crime scene, the police ignored it. They knew better – it was one of Grimes' cars from one of the taxi firms he owned.

'Aye, aw right but no here, eh? Bit public like,' Birse looked around him as if to illustrate the bodies still milling around the city centre well beyond the witching hour.

'C'moan back tae the Cat's then.' Grimes was impatient, angry and in no mood to delay.

'Right, you coming, Maggie?' Birse asked, trying to weigh up what he would be facing and hoping that Maggie would be going along to keep Grimes under some kind of control.

'No, past my bedtime, Alex,' Maggie replied with a smile.

'Drop ye off oan the way then?' Birse offered.

'Naw, she'll no accept. Never does eh, Maggie?' Grimes answered for her, knowing fine well that Maggie Small never let anyone know where she lived. Not even Grimes. She even refused to use any of his taxi services, preferring instead to pay her own way. He wrote it off to a need to keep her private life separate from her personal life. Of course he could have had her followed at any time. With anyone else he would have. But if Maggie had sussed out he'd been spying on her she would have quit promptly – a risk he was not willing to take. Besides, she was the one person he trusted and the only one he felt no need to go checking up on. If she wanted her domestic life kept far apart from work that was unusual but it was her choice. Something he understood, though didn't share. Business was Grimes' life. The Volvo's suspension visibly heaved under the weight of Grimes and Birse as they clambered into the back seat. As the car pulled out into the flow of traffic, Grimes was still berating the effectiveness of the police.

As Maggie Small walked to the taxi rank at the front of the Central Hotel, she looked up and scanned the windows, wondering which rooms her girls were in and hoping they were working well. In one of the best rooms in the place, Suzie with a zed sat on the edge of the bed watching Bob Benson unpack his overnight bag. After the humiliation from Maggie she was anxious to do well, to give herself to this man in whatever way he wanted. To wash away the feel of the woman's long fingernails probing in the folds of her fanny. He was taking his time, fastidiously hanging up his clean shirt and suit, making sure the trouser seams hung just so. Suzie's eyes moved from Benson to the TV screen and noticed it was just a boring report from the Berlin Wall. Just more crowds of people gathering there and shouting. She wished she could change the channel to a late-night chat show or maybe an old movie. But Benson had put the TV on at that programme and what

Bob Benson wanted, Bob Benson would have.

At last he turned from the wardrobe and walked towards her, a smile on his face and a prominent bulge in the front of his trousers.

'So, Suzie-Floozie, what do you want to do now?' he asked, walking up close to the young woman so his erection nudged against her arm.

'Whatever you want to do, Bob,' Suzie replied, smiling as sweetly as she could.

'I know what he wants you to do,' Benson said, pushing his hard-on against her.

Suzie started to undo his belt and asked, 'Wonder what that could be?' and giggled.

'And I know what I want to do to you,' Bob Benson continued.

'Mmmmmmm,' replied Suzie in a manner she thought soft and seductive while she worked at his zip. Benson leaned over and whispered his wishes in her ear as if they were too bad, too sinful to be uttered out loud. At that Suzie freed him of his trousers and underwear, letting them fall to his ankles, his hard penis staring her in the face. Or it should've been. Instead it hooked to the right, towards the TV as if it was keenly interested in the events in Berlin.

'FUCK SAKE, Bob, didnae know ye were THAT bent,' screamed Suzie. She didn't explain if she meant his whispered instructions or the angle of his knob. She didn't explain and didn't care. He would do to exorcise the touch of that woman.

Alone at last, Maggie Small sat in the back of the cab and smoked a cigarette. The hackney carriage stopped at the lights at St Vincent Street and Maggie idly watched the people moving around. Through the grey rain she spotted the erect form of a well-known figure tapping his pipe against the sole of a shoe, sending short-lived red embers scurrying along the pavement in the breeze. Satisfied the pipe was out, he pocketed it and continued on his way, walking past a group of young boys, none older than fourteen, hanging around in the light of a shop front. Other people would not have noticed his signal but Maggie Small was a grand master at observing people. She saw the nod and the chosen youth follow the man at a respectful few steps distance. Follow him into the iron-fenced entrance to St Vincent Street toilets and down the stairs to that cavern beneath the ground. St Vincent Street, the only twenty-four-hour public toilet facility in the city centre. Kept open by the good judgement and at the cost of the local council to prevent late-night drinkers from needing to foul the streets. St Vincent Street, the centre of the gay market for cottaging and specialising in chicken prostitutes.

'Well, well,' thought Maggie Small. 'Councillor Wiley, man of the people. You and I are going to be chatting again very soon.'

A DOG'S LIFE

'Come oaaaaaaaaan, ya rasper.' Fergie punched the air in a series of short, sharp jabs. 'Aw, pleeease. Come oan, Little Willie man,' now pleading, pathetic and hopeless.

'You off yer nut?' Joe was staring at him, open jawed and disbelieving. 'Whit?'

'You actually bet oan that lame hound?'

'Aye, well . . .'

'Are ye fuckin illiterate or sumthin?'

'Whit ye mean, Joe?' Fergie now sounding hurt, tearing his betting slip up slowly.

'D'ye see who the fucking owner is?' Joe wasn't going to let his pal off lightly.

'Aye, course Ah did – G. Small,' pronounced Fergie indignantly.

'An whit's that stand for then, smart arse?'

'You taking the piss?' Fergie turned to Joe, his face angry, full of challenge.

'You avoiding the question?' Joe stared back.

'Nuh, but yer treating me as if Ah'm a wean.'

'Who's the registered owner, Fergie?' insisted Joe. Fergie shook his head looking at his feet. He turned his head away from his friend and muttered. 'Cannae hear ye, man,' shouted Joe. Fergie shook his head again and jerked round to face his friend.

'Grimes Small,' he muttered through clenched teeth. 'Mr Andy Grimes and Miss Maggie Small tae be precise.' Joe's turn to look sad.

'An you bet oan the hound?'

'Aye,' said Fergie, staring at some place far in the distance.

'Why, man? Ye know fine well it's likely tae be stuffed full o rice pudding.'

'Ah know how they wangle it, Joe,' said Fergie, hurt and insulted. 'They handicap it till the fifth or sixth outing . . .'

'. . . tae raise the odds,' Fergie interrupted. 'Ah know aw that, Joe, jist Ah thought it WAS the fifth outing.' Joe shook his head staring straight at his friend.

'How often dae you come tae the dogs?' he asked.

'Three, maybe four times a year,' Fergie answered, knowing that his friend knew his preferred location for gambling was the bookies and on football or horses, seldom greyhounds.

'Precisely,' said Joe, as if that explained everything. Then he relented, 'Ye need tae gather more intelligence when yer a part-time punter. Know?'

'Aye but . . .'

'That was the beast's third outing.'

'You sure? Thought it was oan the card when Ah was here last year? Had tae have five races in,' persisted Fergie.

'Close – that was Little Whiskers,' smiled Joe. 'Asked Wee Archie,' explained Joe, referring to Shawfield Stadium's resident one-legged tipster. 'An so should've you.'

'Aye so Ah should've,' conceded Fergie. 'But Ah was running late for our meet, man, just had time tae post a bet and find yese.' Joe nodded sympathetically. Standing at the dog racing without a bet was joyless.

'Know your trouble, Fergie?' said Joe, making it obvious he was about to answer his own question. 'You like taking risks.'

'Aye,' replied Fergie with a grin, 'Ah'll gie yese that. But then Ah've no taken tae wearing long johns and drinking Ovaltine before ma bed like you, eh?'

'Cheeky bam,' smiled Joe, reaching out and pretend-slapping Fergie on the cheek.

Fergie turned away and looked round the stadium. Mainly men, muffled against the cold in spite of the warm weather. Why was it that sports grounds and cemeteries were always cold places? At the other side of the ground the bodies were masked in a silver-grey haze, like looking through half-shut eyelashes. It was something to do with the lights – too strong or too white. Something he didn't understand. The dogs for the next race were being paraded into the ground.

'How much did you go down for?' Joe couldn't remain angry with his pal for long. Fergie kept his head turned away and stayed silent. Joe put one hand gently on his shoulder, 'C'moan, Fergie. How much, eh?'

'Fifty,' was the reply, but still the man looked away.

'Whit? You bet fucking fi . . .' Joe caught himself in time. His pal was embarrassed, feeling like an idiot. Lesson learned, time to lay off him and build bridges. 'Yer last fifty by any chance?' Joe knew his friend was feeling angry with himself. Angrier than he would be just for failing to suss the fixed dog.

'Aye. Daft Fergie throws his last few quid away . . . so what's fucking new then, eh?'

'Here,' Joe tapped Fergie lightly on the shoulder.

'Naw, Joe, Ah owe ye a fortune already, man.'

'This is no a loan,' Joe pushed his hand forward, a roll of tenners in his fist. 'Ah owe ye.' Fergie turned towards Joe, a look of quizzical disbelief souring his face.

'Whit for?'

'It's occurred tae me lately that ye're aye by ma side.'

'Aye, so? Ah'm yer pal.'

'Aye, but now and then Ah need somebody tae be there.'

'Aye, so . . . like Ah said. Pals.'

'So ye'd dae it onyroads?'

'Aye, course,' Fergie sounded indignant.

'So Ah can gie a pal some callidosh then,' said Joe, smiling at Fergie, 'if Ah want tae.'

'Smart bastard,' Fergie smiling back.

'That's why you're ma mate,' Joe grinning.

'Hard work, but somebody needs tae dae it, eh?'

'Cheeky bastard, so you are.' Joe pushed the bankroll forward and Fergie took it with a curt nod. To say more would have breached their laws of mutual respect and they never did that.

Fergie and Joe watched the next race purely from an academic spectator's perspective with no bets running on any dog. Joe checked his watch and signalled for Fergie to follow. They walked through the crowds of men, the smell of stale beer rising with their breath into the chilly night air. Here and there men nodded in their direction – short, curt, unsmiling greetings. Betting was entertainment, and they took it seriously.

'Hello-rerr, Joe.' The small man waved effusively, barking his greeting in a voice that could grind steel.

'Don Chico,' was Joe's reply and a raising of his head. The man's double-breasted, broad pin-stripe suit carried lapels reaching his shoulders, each cuff having a strip of too many buttons. His trousers were wide, the turn-ups almost covering highly polished brogues. A wide multi-coloured tie was thick knotted at his neck and a glass-jewelled pin sparkled in the artificial light. Over the tie lay a thick gold chain and on each hand he wore full knuckleduster sets of gold sovereign rings. On his head sat a fedora, the blue smoke from his fat cigar curling slowly over its wide brim. Fergie kept his head down, watching his feet take step after step, smothering a chuckle bursting in his throat, till a few yards of safe distance lay between them and Don Chico.

'Fucking Godfather Two-and-a-Half,' Fergie spluttered at last.

'A wannabe, a wannabe,' laughed Joe. 'Have we given him an Oscar lately?'

'No for a few weeks at least,' replied Fergie.

'Cunt deserves another one Ah'd say,' said Joe. 'For perseverance at least.'

'For valour in the face of good dress sense, a special lifetime achievement award to . . . the stupid-looking cunt in the corner.' Joe and Fergie laughed loudly together. Their bristling niggle of a short time before all forgotten as they slagged off one of their favourite targets – anyone who acted the gangster.

Don Chico was their name for the man really called Chic McKenzie. Chic's street record was minor and well known, as everything was in the small village atmosphere of street life in the city of Glasgow. Some of the usual brushes with the law as a kid, couple of sentences for shoplifting, a two stretch for reset, then he settled down to do what he did best – running a chain of tanning studios and living off a reputation that was all his own invention. As his tales of organised crime were spun over the years he came to believe in them himself, somehow deluding himself they were true. Chic truly believed his self-constructed history was fact and thought everyone else did likewise. Some chance. Some played along with Chic's game. After all, he'd made a hefty fortune from Glaswegians' fascination with the sun – real or fake – and someone in Glasgow with cash was someone who could buy muscle. And Chic did so often to defend his fantasy reputation. Joe and Fergie simply took the piss.

'Marlon Brando must have styled himself on that wanker,' chortled Joe.

'Aye, and Edward G. Robinson. Mean Chic's run the mafia for yonks, man,' Fergie laughed and the two mates made their way happily to the exit.

Outside the stadium, groups of men stood about in the car park holding their own private meetings, talking quietly beyond the earshot of each other, hushing their voices as each person passed by. Joe and

Fergie kept going across Rutherglen Road, grimacing at the low-level stink of raw sewage in the air. The wind was blowing in the wrong direction, carrying the stench from Rutherglen up on their left down through Oatlands to their right and beyond into Gorbals, as if the good folk there needed additional grief. Their pre-planned destination was a square of wasteground across from Shawfield Stadium.

'Hamburgers, hot dogs and whatever ye fancy – get nourished here.' The stallholder was unusual in shouting his wares, but his day job was at the Barras, Glasgow's flea-market, and it was a habit he couldn't break. For his night-time job he pulled his converted caravan round a series of public events – Ibrox, Parkhead, Shawfield, car auctions, raves – and served quick greasy food at exorbitant prices. Around the stall an aura of blue light matched the reek of over-fried onions and hot lard. At least it almost blunted the stink of barely processed faeces floating down the street.

'Two cups o tea,' Joe ordered.

'Whit ye want tae eat? Gie ye that first so's yer drink disnae get freezing,' the stallholder insisted.

'Eh, nothing. Just tea,' Joe replied.

'Jist tea? Tea an nothing else? Listen, Bud, this is a hambuger stall. See, it says it oan the sign. H...A...M...B...U...R...G...E...R...S,' he spelled it out. 'No a fucking tea shop.'

'So, why you selling hot dogs, smart bastard?' Fergie intervened, always ready to enter a fight on the inconsequential.

'Whit you saying, wee man?' The fat man leaned perilously far out of his hatch and glowered down at Fergie.

'Ah fucking said . . .' Joe stopped his friend with a sharp elbow in the ribs. They had business to attend to and no need of a scrap over such a trivial matter.

'He said he'll have a hot dog,' offered Joe.

'Don't want a fuc . . .' Fergie halted by another sharp nudge.

'That's better,' breathed the stallholder. 'And whit aboot you?'

'Naw, nothing for me. Just the one hot dog and two cups o tea,' Joe replied.

'Ye cannae come here . . .' The irate hamburger salesman stopped mid-sentence. Joe had simply stepped into the circle of light beaming from the stall hatch and looked up at him. Recognition fluttered across the fat man's florid face. 'Right enough. One hot dog and two cups o tea coming up.'

'Ye've been clocked,' whispered Fergie.

'So whit?' replied Joe.

'Thought ye'd want tae keep a low profile the night?'

'Aye, well, Ah'm just enjoying a night at the dogs wi ma mate. Like ye do.'

'Aye and . . .'

'And that guy was getting right oan ma nipple,' Joe admitted.

'Best hot dogs in the city,' the stallholder butted in on cue. 'Fucking prime sausage aw the way frae New York city – the capital o the dog. Best fucking pork ye can buy. Sammy Davies Junior used tae eat these – even after he turned Jew boy.' The man was chattering away while he cooked, oblivious to any other conversation his customers might prefer, the heavy wheeze of accordion-driven reels blaring from a fancy ghetto blaster on a shelf. Joe really despised that heedrum-hodrum old Scottish stuff. Made him embarrassed to belong to the same nation as that prat in the manky, greasy white jacket.

'Any chance o a few bob fur a cuppa tea, mister?' The old tramp looked ancient and worn out but could've been any age. His face was ghostly grey-white in the half darkness and the fresh scab on his forehead shone scarlet. The old guy's stink was so rank Joe wondered if it had been the sewage works he'd smelled earlier or had he just met the source?

'Ye hungry, pop?' asked Joe.

'Starving, son, no eaten in a week.' An arthritic gnarled hand was shoved closer to Joe.

'Here's a few quid, get yersel stuck right in.' Joe handed across a fiver.

'Thanks, son, yer a saviour.' The old man turned and hobbled away.

'Jesus, Joe, yer a right easy tap wi the jakies. Must have a sign above yer heid saying SOFT TOUCH.' Fergie was always berating his friend's acts of spontaneous generosity, seeing himself as not too far removed from the old beggar.

'Ach ye never know the day.' Joe dismissed any remarks suggesting he was kind. That reputation wouldn't do at all. Besides it's just something he did but did not talk about.

'Best hot dogs oan the planet. Aw the trimmings,' the burger man carried over two bundles of steaming food. 'An extra one in case yer wee pal's hungry,' he nodded at Fergie, paused and added melodramatically, 'oan the hoose.'

'Eh, right, cheers.' This was a first for Joe. Free drinks, yes. Women offered for the night, occasionally. Cheap deals on cars, anytime. But buckshee hot dogs? With a grin he handed both bundles over to Fergie who stood there spilling onions and mustard over his boots.

'Cheeky fat cunt,' Fergie mumbled. 'Does he think Ah need feeding up?' Fergie found himself physically incapable of accepting the tea he did want, being simply one hand short. He looked around at a big oil canister, one end cut off transforming it into a makeshift bin and started heading that way.

'Nuh,' warned Joe. 'Dinnae want to insult the man now, do we?' Fergie spotted the old tramp hobbling slowly down Rutherglen Road away from the stall and took off after him.

'Woah, old timer, yer rushing away empty handed,' Fergie said when he had easily caught up.

'Aye, well, son, ye've got tae ration yersel ye know.' The old man's breath smelled of something rotting, decomposing. 'Yer pal's fiver'll last me a good while.' The old man turned to leave.

'Here,' Fergie held out his two handfuls of hot dogs.

'Whit's that?' the old man looked over his shoulder, stretching his face into a sneer.

'Some grub for yese.'

'No thanks, son. Widnae eat a thing frae that van. Manky bastard would poison ye.' And the old man limped away before pausing to look back. 'Besides they onions spoil the taste o the cider, ye know?' Off he went, abandoning Fergie with his two sodden bundles and nauseous bile bubbling in his stomach.

'You enjoy they hot dogs, pal?' the fat man asked on Fergie's return.

'Rare. Best dogs Ah've ever tasted,' he answered, taking a long swig from sweet, lukewarm tea while out of the side of his eye he watched an emaciated, mange-riddled dog taking a tentative sniff at the steaming parcels he'd dumped in the gutter.

'Is this our man?' said Joe, scanning the road down to the Gorbals.

'Aye, has tae be. No many look like that,' replied Fergie.

Even in the darkness on the pavement, sheltered by the overhanging branches spilling out of Richmond Park, Beano's profile was a giveaway. Tall and rangy, he walked with a swagger, a saddle-sore cowboy, except Beano's hands were always buried deep in the pockets of his ankle-length black leather coat. His hair grew down past his pectorals and was wild like sharp-snouted snakes dancing around his skull. A full, straggly beard lay on his chest. The tramp spotted Beano approaching and crossed to the opposite side of the road. Up close, Beano's face was strong boned and unremarkable apart from a nose broken in some long-forgotten street battle and eyes so dark they appeared black.

'How's it goin, guys?' he greeted Fergie and Joe. 'Long time no see.'

'Yer late, Beano,' said Joe. Usually a warm friend, this was business and discipline was necessary.

'Aye, sorry about that. Got held up oan a wee bit transaction,' Beano replied.

'More important than this?' Joe persisted.

'Naw, it's jist if Ah hadnae dealt wi it – well, might've got in the way like.' Joe nodded, beginning to accept the rationale. 'Needed tae clear ma feet,' Beano explained. Joe wandered away from the burger stall, his two colleagues following him as well as the shouts of the stallholder.

'We'll see ya again Ah hope. Welcome back at any time so ye are. Hot dogs on me.'

'Fuck sakes, no idea who that daft cunt thinks I am,' muttered Joe.

'Maybe he disnae think, but knows who ye are,' said Fergie.

'Aye, Ah'd thought o that . . . worst option. You recognise him, Beano?' asked Joe, nodding back at the lights of the stall.

'Ach, aye. Two-bit wheeler and dealer. Up tae every trick tae turn a buck.'

'How would he know me though?' Joe persisted.

'Maybe he disnae,' said Beano.

'Fuck sakes, let's no start at the beginning again, eh?' rattled Joe. 'How might he know me?'

'Well,' Beano scratched at his beard, a sure sign he was giving the question some serious thought, 'unless ye've turned pervo in yer auld age.'

'Whit?'

'Greasy Joe's hobby is the dirty mac brigade. Know – porno movies, strip joints, hand jobs frae working lassies.'

'Ah've telt ye, Joe, get a woman, man. An snappy,' Fergie grinned, receiving a glower from Joe in return.

'Fucking Cat's Whiskers,' spat Joe.

'Whit ye oan aboot?' asked Beano.

'Been in there a few times lately tae sort oot business wi that fucker Grimes.'

'That'll be it.' Beano slapped his thigh to emphasise the point.

'If he knows you at . . .' Fergie's contribution was halted by Joe's fierce look.

'Right, this will have tae be a quick meeting . . . don't like being spotted by that bastard,' concluded Joe.

'Ach he's no a problem,' said Beano.

'Maybe aye. Maybe no. Let's get the business done,' said Joe. 'First thing, Beano, this is big. Needs a solid team. A dedicated team.'

'Aye, as usual,' Beano replied.

'With no distractions. Like the night?' Joe gave Beano a chance to respond.

'Aw, that'll no happen again. Come oan, Joe, you know me, man.'

'Aye, that's why yer here. But Ah've heard a wee rumour yer into the drugs.'

'Me? Naw, no fucking chance,' said Beano offended. 'Ah'm clean, man, cannae stand that smack shite. Wee bit o blow, okay, but Ah fucking hate junk – no going tae poison masel, am Ah?'

'Heard ye were dealing,' said Joe quietly.

'Dealing? Me? No fucking way. Like Ah said . . . oh, wait. You mean the jellies?' Beano started laughing. 'Aye, ye do, eh . . . haaaa, it's only fucking jellies.'

'Do Ah?' Joe wanted an explanation and wasn't conceding any ground.

'Ye get Temazepam on prescription, for Christ's sake,' Beano reasoned in an effort to quell Joe's concerns. 'Look, a wee while ago ma old dear goes tae her quack. Couldnae sleep. Fuck me but she comes away wi a hundred jellies. Two ton at street value for the price o a prescription and she gets it free now she's a pensioner. Fucking great the NHS, eh?'

'Beano, get oan wi it, eh?' Joe knew that Beano could spin a tale out all night if you let him.

'Old dear has no truck wi tablets so I prescribe a wee quarter bottle nightcap. Disnae drink so I mix her a toddy – hot water and sugar and whisky – rare if ye've a cold.'

'Beano . . .'

'Aye, right, sorry, Joe. So, Ah'm going through a wee sticky patch and thinks, fuck it, Ah'll sell the jellies. Every cunt uses them, man. The coke fiends, smackheads. Every cunt.' Fergie knows the score about jellies. Besides, Beano can go on and on. Looking around him, Fergie notices the stray dog has finally risked a nibble at one of the discarded hot dogs. The thought pleases him that the hassle with the burger man has benefited some being. 'So, Ah gie the old dear a bung oot o the proceeds – it's only right. Fuck me, does she no come in the next night wi another hundred jellies. Easy money she reckons. Before the end o the week Ah've her pals working the same trick. Tell ye, the Gorbals Health Centre is full o insomniacs or stressed-out folks, man. Well, is now like. Ah gie the old buddies fifty knicker for each delivery – they're tickled fucking pink, so they are. Tell ye, Ah'm keeping starvation frae their door.' Beano finished, believing he'd hit the moral high ground and his explanation was good enough.

'So ye're a dealer then, Beano?' Joe was pushing. He had no truck with the drugs industry or any who worked it. In his experience even the most hard-headed trader ran a high risk of coming to appreciate their own products. That was a risk he couldn't take in the enterprise he was planning.

'Naw, for fuck's sake. Ye canny get addicted tae jellies, man. The fucking junkies take them tae help them deal wi withdrawals. Same wi the coke heads. And they loved up cunts an their Ecstasy use them tae level up the morning after the night before. Besides, Ah dinnae touch them.'

Joe had known Beano since their days in borstal as kids. Not only was he cool headed and disciplined under pressure, Joe had always thought of Beano as one of the most honest guys he'd ever known. But for that shared past, Joe would've walked away right there and then. He didn't know why the druggies took jellies and didn't much care. That was their problem. But if Beano said he was clean, Joe believed him. The big guy had never lied to him yet and had mixed in on Joe's side at times when he could've easily walked away.

'Okay, Beano, sorry about that, but ye understand my concerns,' said Joe.

'No offence taken, Joe.'

'Good man,' said Joe. 'So, here's the score. We'll need a three-man team. No amateurs. You take the lead, one other handy guy and a driver.'

'Want me tae choose them as usual?'

'Aye, well, it'll be your team – you need tae be sure you can rely oan them.'

'Shooters?'

'Aye, but strictly for show. No trigger-itchy fuckers in yer squad right?'

'Christ no. Mind that time wee Alex went ballistic. Fucking almost did me in, never mind the blue meanie.'

'Is he aye in jail?' Fergie interrupted.

'Aye, they're a bit unforgiving aboot shooting up the polis,' Beano replied.

'Right, so no wee Alex types, right?' repeated Joe. 'Basic details the night. It's a building, it's oan in the next coupla months and if Ah'm right ye'll no have tae sell yer sweeties tae the weans for a while.'

'Thank fuck. Ah'm getting a bit fed up o handling they grey hairs. They get greedy know? Like the night – old dame hits ma hoose saying she's off tae her son's in Corby for a coupla weeks. How's about she registers temporarily wi the quacks doon there an brings me up a bundle a jellies. Ah'm going, "Aye that sounds like a smart move, hen", then the old cunt taps me for her train fare. Wid ye credit it? Smart old biddy.'

'Right, how long's it going tae take ye tae get the team sorted?' Joe was unusually uncomfortable and unreceptive to Beano's patter.

'Och, a week tops,' Beano replied.

'An mind . . .'

'Ah know, Joe, you and Fergie never come up. You do not exist. As far as Ah'm concerned Ah huvnae seen yese since the Christmas before last.'

'Good man. Listen, Ah'm a wee bit edgy the night. Can we leave it at that an Ah'll contact ye the end o next week.'

'Sure, meet here again?'

'No way, that fat burger man has given me the willies. Ah'm standing here feeling paranoid, man.'

'No like ye, Joe,' offered Beano sympathetically.

'Nuh, but it's been an interesting week. Maybe Ah'm just a bit oan edge.'

'AW FOR FUCK'S SAKE,' blustered Fergie.

'Whit?' Joe wheeled round and Beano's hand automatically reached into the inside pocket of his coat where he kept his open razor.

'Poor wee dog's just spewed his load. It's a fucking wee shame so it is.' Sympathy written all over Fergie's face.

'A fucking dog! Jesus Christ, man, Ah thought it was serious,' fumed Joe.

'It is,' insisted Fergie, 'for the poor dog.'

'Let's split, okay?' said Joe. 'Greasy Joe's giving me heebie jeebies and Ah don't like it. Keep thinking he's eyeing me.'

The three men said their farewells, agreeing to meet up again – when and where to be dictated at a later date by Joe. Beano hung around to talk with a group of young guys loitering in a nearby close mouth while Fergie and Joe split up and made their separate ways to Joe's car. By the time Fergie opened the passenger door, Joe had already hit the play button of the car stereo. Chrissie Hynde's plaintive, sensual wail bounced off the interior washing away the taste of the tea and the jarring echo of accordions. Heading through the dark expanse of Glasgow Green towards the city centre and another meeting, The Pretenders hit the opening riffs of 'Message of Love' and Joe visibly relaxed, sinking into sweet chords that never failed him. For a while, Fergie allowed the familiar magic to work on his friend before breaking the silence,

'He's a good man, that Beano.'

'Aye, one o the best,' replied Joe. 'Loyal, you know. Always taking care of his friends whatever it costs him.'

'Aye,' replied Fergie, nodding in the dark, wondering if the stray pooch was okay.

Back outside Shawfield Stadium, Beano had finished his discussion with the young team. In the short transaction he had handed over some money and a couple of strips of jellies. By the time the lanky bearded one was striding his way back to his hunting ground in the Gorbals, the young mob had gathered at the burger stall.

'Hamburgers, hot dogs and whatever ye fancy – get nourished here,' the stallholder rhymed off his line to his new customers.

'Mister, somebody's done in the tyres o yer motor,' replied the youngest, most angel-faced youth.

'The fucking bastards,' screamed the stallholder and rushed to his car parked further back on the unlit waste ground. 'So they have, the cunts. No just one tyre but the fucking lot.' As he bewailed the damage to his car, two of the group had sneaked in his caravan. While one emptied the cash tray, the other unplugged the ghetto blaster, only pausing to eject the cassette and with a sneer tossed it carelessly into the bubbling deep fat. The rest of the young team had been waiting for the burger man in the shadows, quietly emerging and circling him.

'Ah've a message for ye, mister,' slurred the leader, the first of the jellies kicking in, and to illustrate pulled a long-bladed knife out of his waistband.

'M'oan, son, please . . .' pleaded the fat man.

'You're no welcome here no more.'

'Why . . . why, son, please . . .' The stallholder's knees buckled and he fell backwards against his car. The youth leaned over him, holding the steel blade against his cheek and whispered,

'You made ma dog sick, ya filthy cunt.'

'Whit? Whit dog?'

'If Ah catch ye back here Ah'll use this tae make hot dogs oot o yer blubber. Catch ma drift?' The sound of urine streaming from the hamburger man's trousers onto the ground signalled he had understood loudly and clearly.

When the gang had gone, their threatener passed on, the stallholder cried with fear and shame. His was a hard business, but never before had he come so close to a serious doing. He was going to give up the van in the city. Just cover the Dunoon Gathering, the Royal Highland Show through in Edinburgh, tourist shortbread lid stuff like that. Safe places with half-decent customers. Then he started to get angry. How dare they tackle him. He knew people. Powerful people.

'Fuckers,' he griped out loud to nothing but the darkness and the back of his abandoned stall. 'Dae youse know who Ah'm are? Ah'm the man that served Andy Grimes hot dogs the night. Aye, that's me. Andy fucking Grimes just left here.' The man's shout faded into the darkness. 'It was Andy Grimes, wasn't it?' he asked himself quietly. 'Sure it was Andy Grimes,' he muttered. 'Somebody fucking important onyroads.' The stallholder sobbed and bit his knuckle, his face creasing into a muffled howl. 'IMPORTANT, YE HEAR. FUCKING IMPORTANT – LIKE ME!' he shouted, but no one was there to listen.

Out on the road, the stray dog started to eat its own vomit.

3 SEPTEMBER 1989

Dead time, that's Sunday mornings in Glasgow. I like to get up early and look around. It's the best time to catch them unawares. So I go out and sniff around.

This morning it was a wander round to Cathy Brodie's place. Stupid really, too risky, but I had to be sure she was still there and in one piece. So I put on the tracksuit, pulled the hood up and went jogging. A lot of the middle-class types from up in Shawlands go running through the badlands - well, on Sunday mornings at least. Too dangerous at other times. Place was deserted apart from the occasional straggler coming home from some late-night party, their bag of Glasgow rolls and a *News of the Screws* hanging from one hand, an open bottle of Irn Bru in the other. Perfect sugar boost hangover cure for whatever substances they had been consuming.

Funny how the police have melted away from the street. This time two weeks ago the place was hoaching with them. What are they up to? Cathy at her window with her baby in her arms. Thought for the second I glanced up she started and recognised me. Just jitters. Besides, she wouldn't tell even if she had. Not Cathy Brodie.

Wanted to check out The Arse Bandit since his flat was nearby in Allison Street, Govanhill. At any one time I keep tabs on maybe twenty to thirty people, sometimes more, but The Arse Bandit has to be one of the most likely candidates for action. A right evil bastard I reckon. Just hasn't been caught out yet.

Running down Allison Street the smell from the kosher bakers made my mouth water. Was getting knackered, running with my head down, but still spotted Angie the Gopher coming out of the bakers hefting a full carrier bag. What did he want with bagels, cream cheese and smoked salmon? Angie looks like he doesn't eat. Looked tense, nervy but then

what's new? Maybe old Angie has some secret good
taste. Then again, more likely he'd maybe scored
lucky with some underage boy with taste.

The Arse Bandit's flat was showing no sign of
life. God knows what was going on behind those
closed curtains.

ACTION NOTES: Befriend some of the young smack
dealers that work for The Arse Bandit. Keep an eye
on Angie. In a couple of weeks get up even earlier
on a Sunday and deliver a thank-you wad through
Cathy's door. Get her out of that slum.

A

FURTIVE AL FRESCO

Angie the Gopher was convinced he could smell fried bacon. It was a puzzle since most of the houses were derelict and abandoned aside from this one, the one he was going to visit. And they wouldn't have bacon in there, would they? Not in a Jewish home. Angie wasn't stupid, he realised that Jews stopped practising as often as Protestants or Catholics or the Hindus he knew who loved minced holy cow and tatties. No, Angie wasn't as stupid as he looked but he was mean and the bill for the bag of goodies dangling from one paw lay heavily on his mind. If the ploy worked and got him over the threshold the investment would have been worthwhile. If it failed, Angie would be as furious as if the seventeen pounds and forty-five pence had been stolen from his wallet. There was nothing Angie hated more than thieves, well, thieves who stole from him.

The tarnished brass doorknob felt heavy and expensive. Inside the tenement flat the knock boomed and faded. They would have to be deaf not to hear it, but then they might be at their age. Angie waited, craning his long neck to cock his ear listening for any sign of life. Nothing.

'Patience, Farquhar,' he reminded himself, 'too much anxious rattling at the door will scare the buggers off.' Eventually he heard a faint, soft shuffle growing louder and louder till it stopped then . . . nothing. Angie thought he could hear breathing at the other side of the door but wasn't sure it wasn't his own open-mouthed wheezing in the silence of the close. He'd just given up and his hand reached out again for the knocker when the first bolt was grated and crunched. Several more followed and Angie stood up straight, smiling stiffly in a face he considered warm and welcoming. As the door creaked open slowly, Angie's style became stiffer and tense till his cheeks started twitching with the effort and his tongue dry and sticky.

'Mm?' the man was old, very old and as small as a child. He wore gun-metal rimmed, half-moon glasses with one missing leg which shook on the end of his nose every time he threw his head back in inquisition. 'Mm?' he repeated in a gruffer tone, a scowl twisting his jowl and hacking lines deeper into his broad forehead. Angie coughed, bringing spittle into his mouth and swilled it around his tongue.

'Mister . . .' Angie's voice was struggling so he coughed again. 'Sorry, bit of a cold, Mr Wise. Let me introduce myself . . .'

'MMMMM?' the diminutive figure looked furious as if every delay was an insult. Angie flipped open the ID card he had made up just the day before for this visit.

'I'm Jacob Goldberg from the social work department of Strathclyde Regional Council,' rattled off Angie, hoping his chosen pseudonym would ease the old guy's suspicions. 'I expect . . .'

'My name,' butted in the angry goblin without further explanation. 'I know your name Mr . . .'

'. . . is also Jakob.' The old man snatched the fake ID from Angie's fingers and holding his specs two inches from his nose, scrutinised the card with intense interest.

'I'm from the social work department, Mr Wise,' Angie blustered on, hoping that the man was as myopic as he appeared, scrunching his eyes tighter and moving the card closer to his face. 'The Jewish Welfare Association asked me to call.' Jakob Wise looked up, recognition softened his face for an instant then he returned to his examination of the ID. 'Just to be sure you and your wife are okay,' Angie continued. No response. 'I've brought some food.'

That did the trick with Jakob Wise. Food was useful while concern was not. Angie recognised the old man's body language, opened the carrier bag and went in for the kill.

'See, I've brought some fresh bagels, smoked salmon, cream cheese, chopped herring, butter and coffee.' Jakob Wise pulled the lip of the bag open and peered in, his watery eyes ticking off the checklist of his visitor's promises. Abruptly the old man stood back, held up the ID card next to Angie's head and nodded vigorously. Clearly he hadn't been able to read a word but faces he could compare. With that, Jakob Wise stood back from the doorway signalling for his visitor to enter. Angie stepped into the house and then quickly turned, remembering to touch the mezuzah screwed to the wall outside the door. Jakob Wise nodded his head and pushed his visitor gently into his home.

Picking his way through the hall, Angie was once again struck by the intensity of rubbish packed against both walls. The entrance hallway was where they stored newspapers. Stacks of them piled so high the tiny tenants must have used a chair or stepladder to make the final deposits. The place smelled of layers of dust and mildew from the newsprint leaning against the damp walls. The door at the end of the hallway was open about two feet, the full extent of its capacity reduced by black plastic bags cramming the place.

'Shalom, Mrs Wise.' Angie offered his prepared greeting to the back of the woman busying herself rummaging through a pile of carrier bags, empty and crumpled. Mrs Wise didn't respond and Angie silently prayed that when she turned round she would fail to recall his last visit to her house. Among the chaos the old woman looked neat and trim as if she was visiting not residing. Long silver-white hair was still thick and fixed in an ornate bob at the back of her head. Her outfit of a knee-length plaid skirt and cardigan was neat and implausibly clean in a place with no free storage space, no washing machine, no empty sink from what Angie could recall.

'Work, work, work,' the old woman mumbled. 'Never done in this factory. It is my labour and my duty. Work, work . . .'

Old Jakob Wise shook his head sadly and said, 'Come, Ruth. We have a visitor. Come sit with us.' She ignored him.

'Must finish before Papa comes in. Good mood and allow Ruth to go to dance. Wear her best dress on and have fun with sisters. Dance with Jakob, my Jakob . . .'

'RUTH. Oh, Ruth, I'm here precious. Here is your Jakob. Here.' The old man's cry was despairing, pleading, and had the exhausted air of an appeal often repeated.

'Mrs Wise,' Angie spoke out loud, 'I'm from the social work department. We've received reports of concern . . .'

'Who speak to you? Tell me who,' the angry, accusing tone had returned to the old man's voice and he squared his shoulders back getting ready for a row. 'You say the Jewish Welfare Association now . . .'

'That's who I meant, Mr Wise.'

'What is the reports? Show me reports.' The little man was clearly used to punching more than his weight and Angie hoped his fuse was slow burning to give him the time he needed.

'I meant a verbal report, Mr Wise, that's all. Just a phone call from the nice lady at the Jewish Welfare.'

'Work, work, work. Long day to work. Papa, can I dance? Papa, please?' Ruth Wise was still engrossed in flattening the empty carriers bags against her midriff, folding each one four times into rectangles and laying them one on top of each other on a battered old apple crate that was sprouting knitting needles at every angle. The old man sighed and turned to his wife.

'Ruth. Ruth, you're here with me. With Jakob. Your Jakob.' Angie looked at the old man sympathetically, hoping to catch his eye.

'Dance at The Institute. Bright lights and music . . .' the old woman continued.

'Ruth, we are here. Here in Glasgow now. Remember Glasgow? Our little shop. Lovely house. Just you and me.' Jakob Wise turned to face Angie and shook his head in exasperation. 'Half the time she thinks she is fifteen years old again in Berlin. The other half I don't know what she thinks.'

'It must be difficult for you,' Angie offered.

'Ach, yes,' the old man agreed.

'You should get some help. From the doctor or maybe a home help . . .'

'NO. No help. No visitors. No doctors. We manage fine.' The old man suddenly seemed frightened, an expression Angie recognised from many of his little bogus visits to other families.

'I can imagine how you feel, Mr Wise.' It was a situation Angie couldn't resist and he was automatically slipping into one of his favoured roles. 'But we can help you know.'

'They'll take my Ruth away. Stick her in the madhouse,' tears glazed the old man's face. 'No, no.'

'They'll help you here, with Ruth here. Or maybe get you a sheltered house. Together.' Angie knew his stuff.

'Shelter? Like in asylum?' the old man asked. Angie thought for a moment and concluded it was a very reasonable word when stripped of the slang madhouse connotations. A very reasonable word given the old man's perspective.

'Yes, asylum as in refuge from danger. A sheltered house together. Your own little place.' Angie was rather proud of his response and he'd remember it for future use. Jakob Wise nodded in short, sharp agreeable movements and Angie spotted him looking towards the bag of food still gripped in his hand.

'What am I thinking,' Angie said, slapping his forehead so vigorously his wig slipped a little. 'Here, this is for you and Mrs Wise.' The old man opened the bag and a smile crossed his lips.

'Real coffee,' he whispered in awe. 'You'll excuse me please, I'll prepare the food. You'll join us, of course?'

'Thank you, yes,' replied Angie politely and calmly while inside he could feel the adrenalin pump as he sensed the approach of opportunity.

'Come, Ruth, come with me,' Jakob Wise called gently, holding out his free hand.

'Work, work, work, work, work . . .' His wife responded and scuttled sideways a few steps, pulling another handful of crumpled carrier bags out of a cardboard box.

'Please, Ruth, just come with me to the kitchen,' the old man was pleading again.

'Work, work. So much work in this factory,' was the only response he received. Jakob Wise looked stuck, helpless and frustrated yet his still voice stayed low and sweet, no sign of losing his temper with his wife.

'Please, Ruth, for me. Please, Mama,' he almost wailed. Angie coughed nervously,

'It's okay, Mr Wise, I'll watch over her,' he offered. 'She'll be okay with me for a few minutes.' Jakob Wise looked uncertain. He never left his wife with anyone. On the days he found it impossible to persuade her to leave the house and join him in their small pawn shop, even then he hated to leave her alone, though the shop was just around the corner and he came back every half hour to check up on her wellbeing. He had to go to the pawn shop, though it had long since ceased to make any money, business floating away with the population and with the ready availability of easy credit. For years he had hoped the custom would return and he knew well enough that a business ignored was a business dead. So, he had to go to the shop, though these days he went for a touch of sanity rather than profit. But then he left his wife alone in her own home and never with a stranger.

Jakob Wise looked again at his visitor, seeing a dull-witted, soft man who did not appear too bright, always smiling and with a bad habit of wringing his hands. Jakob considered the man to be a simpleton do-gooder, a description those who knew Angie the Gopher would say was half right and half very, very wrong.

'Thank you,' replied Jakob, 'a few minutes only.' As he turned to leave he hesitated and added, 'I'm in the next room if . . .'

'I'll call you,' Angie reassured. 'Don't worry.' The old man shuffled out of the room, having to turn sideways to squeeze past piles of boxes and miscellaneous rubbish. Angie edged over to watch his progress. In the hall, Jakob Wise opened a door that Angie hadn't noticed before, it being half hidden by a column of newspapers. Angie stayed at his vantage point, keeping an eye open for the old man and occasionally turning to reassure himself that the old woman hadn't suffocated herself with a plastic bag. When he started to smell fresh coffee he decided to move, and quickly.

Angie pushed aside an old armchair piled high with what looked like woollen rags and opened the cupboard door. There were the gilded Kiddush goblets he had considered stealing on his last visit. On another shelf was an eight-stemmed menora he reckoned was made out of gold and certainly worth a few quid. But he was after more interesting loot. There it was on the shelf, the old biscuit tin with the Coronation pose of the Queen and Prince Philip on the top. Slowly, he prised the lid open carefully so it opened with a douce, reassuring FLOP. The top document carried the emblem 'Bearer Bonds' in old-fashioned, fancy script on heavy, expensive paper which was old and folded so often that fine threads showed here and there like down on a lady's lip. Angie couldn't read the German words but he could make out the value: $10,000, 'gold grains' and the year of issue – 1934. The tin was full of bonds and he started to count. He hadn't reached halfway down when he felt a chill and looked round. There in the doorway was old Ruth Wise, just standing and watching silently, her eyes on his face.

'Ruth, are you all right?' he whispered, looking at her over his shoulder while his hands blindly peeled off the top bond and crammed it into his inside pocket. 'Is your work finished, Ruth?' Straining to see past her into the room, to check if her husband had returned. 'Your Papa will be in soon, you know.' Lid firmly on the tin and it returned to the shelf placed exactly in the rectangular shape formed by the undisturbed dust. 'He'll let you go to the dance if you've done well.' The woman stared back at Angie, her eyes never blinking, lips not moving. 'Come, let's go find Jakob, will we?' Angie had closed the cupboard door and was gently leading Ruth Wise back to her heap of carrier bags when Jakob Wise entered the room.

'Ruth! Mr Goldberg, is she okay?' For a second Angie the Gopher forgot his alias and looked about him startled.

'Aye, Ah . . . I mean YES, yes she's fine,' Angie said, recovering in time. 'She was just telling me about the dances and her work.' Jakob Wise visibly relaxed and rolled his eyes in conspiratorial camaraderie with Angie.

'Poor, Ruth, you know. She worked such long hours all her life.' The old man felt some explanation was appropriate. 'No children, then the war. Her family all dead. Starting over again here in your city. Struggling on and on for many years. Such long hours for what? For this?' The small man opened his arms and swung them around the chaos of the junk-packed room. Angie could see what he meant but the time and the need for showing sympathy had long passed.

'She has you, Mr Wise. Her Jakob,' Angie offered, using the only relevant information he had.

'Weeeell,' the small man hung his head and almost blushed.

'Mr Wise, I'm afraid I have to leave. Another appointment I'm sorry to say,' Angie hoped his excitement at his haul wasn't written across his face.

'Ah, but the coffee is ready and the bagels . . .'

'Thank you, I wish I could stay but I can't let people down,' Angie explained, trying to find a clear route to the door.

'So busy. You are a very kind man.'

'Not at all,' replied Angie, finding his way into the hall, 'it's my job.'

'But still kind, and thank you for the gifts,' Jakob Wise said, trailing Angie all the way.

'Goodbye, Mr Wise,' Angie called cheerfully out in the street while rehearsing in his mind how pleased Grimes was going to be at his success.

'Goodbye, Mr Goldberg, and do come back,' cried Jakob Wise, waving from the close mouth.

'Oh, I will,' called Angie. Then to himself, 'Bet yer fucking bottom dollar Ah'll be back, ye wee wanker.'

A hundred yards down wind on a stretch of wasteland an old homeless jakie was finishing his breakfast and only meal for that day. Shoplifted bacon flung on the embers of his campfire was the trick. Better with some bread and tea but he wasn't complaining.

The jakie was thinking of moving areas. All the residents had emigrated to the new schemes on the outskirts of the city, taking with them his pickings. All gone bar that old Jewish couple. Nowadays, he just stood around on his lonesome on this waste-ground watching the old couple's movements and they didn't get up to much.

The old jakie watched the strange-looking man in the old-fashioned suit with the long skinny neck wave cheerio to the old bloke. When the old boy had disappeared up the close the funny-looking geezer had whipped off his hair and broken into a sprint.

'Fucking weirdo, man,' the jakie grumbled to himself, a habit he had developed recently through lack of company. 'Places like this are magnets for fucking loonies. Time Ah moved oan, flitted like. Maybe the morra. Aye, the morra. But first maybe Ah'll have a wee look in the old buddies' flat. Aye, might still have something worth robbing, eh? Aye, maybe the morra.'

POWER BREAKFAST

Breakfast at the Central Hotel was a tawdry affair. The thick linen was frayed and the silverware pockmarked, though still bearing the faint inscription of better times under ownership of the British railway system. Still the place had enough class to feel a little special and for those who grew up in Glasgow it held respect as the best hotel in town, even though it had long been supplanted by the new American-owned chains dotting the waterfront and filling the gap sites.

The party had partaken of the full Scottish doings: a feast of saturated fats in the centre of heart-attack city. Unhealthy yes, tasty certainly. Extra pots of coffee had been brought to their table and cigarettes lit, aside from Councillor Wiley who fired up his pipe. Maggie Small noted how the sweet aromatic aroma of his tobacco made her nauseous in the late morning after the night before. Was it just too much too early or had the little scene she had witnessed with Wiley and the boy somehow reached her? Maggie worried that she was beginning to develop some scruples at this late stage – now those would be a damn nuisance.

'Aye, the room service here is rare. Ye cannae wack it,' Councillor Scully blustered enthusiastically.

'I hope they took good care of you,' offered Grimes, returned to his polite form of dinner the night before.

'Oh aye, aye, just perfect,' replied Scully.

'You get a sufficiency of everything?' Grimes asked.

'Just dandy,' replied Scully with a wee crooked smile and the good grace to blush.

'Did you get home all right, Councillor Wiley?' Maggie Small asked. The old man puffed leisurely on his pipe and answered out of the side of his mouth, 'Aye, lass, just fine. Had tae wait a bit for a late-night bus but as Ah always say ye learn a lot waiting among yer ain folk.' Puff, puff – Wiley had that contented look a pipe stem in your gob bestows, enhanced by obvious satisfaction at his little clichéd slogan.

'And your wife, how is she?' Maggie added, her face beaming sympathy.

'No bad, lass, no bad. She's a brave one ye know. Always has been.'

Social chitchat made Grimes impatient, a necessary price he had to pay in working with officials and politicians. He noticed that Bob Benson had gone quiet and looked at his watch twice in the last minute. It was important to act now before the man made his excuses and slipped away.

'Do you mind if we discuss a little business now, gents?' Grimes asked.

'Not at all, son, that's why we're here, isn't it?' replied Wiley. 'Sundays are just another day for me. People's problems never take a holiday.' Puff, puff. Benson smiled but looked at his watch again.

Grimes and Maggie Small cleared a space on the table and from his briefcase he extracted a street plan which he spread out, flattening it carefully. The plan was no ordinary map but a blueprint slipped to him by Bob Benson following an earlier social outing. The council had intentions of clearing ground and developing at various points covered by the map and Grimes pointed these out to his guests.

'They,' he started, as if three of the people now slouched over the map had nothing to do with the local council, 'they are planning to demolish here, here and here. Build some of those little dolly style houses here and here and convert this site into a sort of park cum children's playground.' Three heads nodded as if hearing this information for the first time, though all had sat through innumerable committee meetings making just those decisions. 'Now,' continued Grimes, 'that means this area here is left as it is for . . .'

'Three years,' butted in Bob Benson.

'Thanks, Bob, and that's just the problem,' said Grimes. 'If you were to visit Dalmeny Street you would find properties lying in a more dilapidated state than some that are to be demolished.' Wiley shook his head sagely while Scully's cheeks reddened, his smooth forehead glistening. 'Not only that but with these properties left as they are . . .'

'Ye'll have junkies and glue sniffers and whores and winos crawling all over the place,' butted in Wiley. 'Fucking disgrace, excuse ma French, pet,' he apologised to Maggie Small, patting her on the shoulder as he would a small child or a lapdog.

'Aye, and your new tenants are going to be burgled at every turn as will the new shops planned for here,' Grimes drew his finger across a line in the map.

'Bob?' Scully turned to Bob Benson, forcing the official to reply on behalf of the politicians before Wiley said too much.

'The option was examined thoroughly, chair,' the fat man's lips seemed wet with the grease of the morning's repast. 'The clearance of this area here up to Rutherglen Road here was fully explored and assessed.' Grimes knew this since Benson had previously passed him the confidential reports. 'Officials recommended that the area be levelled and redeveloped. Committee was kind enough to concur and accorded this phase a top-rated priority along with the adjoining sites.'

'So, see, Andy, we are ahead of you, so tae speak,' Scully butted in.

'Ah'm Ah right in recalling that some o the proposals were knocked back due to lack of finances?' asked Wiley.

'As ever, Councillor Wiley, your memory is impeccable.' Bob Benson showed no shame with his ingratiating tone.

'Thought so . . . it's the bloody government's financial limits,' boomed Wiley. 'Ah'm Ah right, Bob?' Wiley was taking over the meeting as Maggie Small had predicted to herself. 'See, Andy, it's no just a question o the council deciding what should be done. It's a question of what they can do with the means allocated to them . . . unfortunately.'

'In fact, Councillor Wiley is being modest, Andy,' added Scully. 'The council was successful in negotiating additional allocations from central government – inspired by Councillor Wiley's constant interventions.' Wiley sat back and sucked on his pipe.

'So, while we would dearly love to action your proposals, Andy, it becomes, eh, more complex on the grounds that the council have recorded formal decisions on the self-same issue.'

'I understand, Councillor, but the council are well known for their ability to review decisions where there's a good reason.' Grimes was used to this type of shadow boxing with the politicians and officials. He much preferred dealing with street players or bent coppers where he could come to the point and the pay-off quickly and crudely.

'The original costings,' Grimes offered, 'were based on the average of invited tenders.'

'Yes,' Benson replied, 'including your own Oxford Street Properties, of course.'

'What if a lower price was possible?' Grimes played the card the councillors would need to reintroduce the issue to formal proceedings. Scully looked at Wiley, who kept his lips firmly around the stem of his pipe, his face half obscured by the hand holding the smooth briar bowl.

'It would be a factor worth considering, of course,' replied Scully.

'How much less?' Bob Benson was in hurry to leave and pushed the conversation to the nitty-gritty.

'A third off our original quote,' said Grimes.

'Very generous offer, Andy,' Benson offered too quickly.

'It certainly is, Andy, and worth considering,' added Scully.

'It could've brought the project into feasibility you know, chair,' said Benson, 'at the time.'

'Absolutely, and could save the council some embarrassment from the, eh, local difficulties that might arise,' said Scully. All the while Wiley continued to suck nosily on a pipe that had long since gone out, just sucked and said nothing.

'It's an offer made in good faith,' said Grimes, 'in recognition of the close partnership which has developed between the council and Oxford Street Properties. To put it another way, it's a price that wouldn't be offered to any other client for the same work.' What Grimes omitted to say was that Oxford Street Properties had no other clients bar the council and that if he couldn't get another sizeable contract on the books, the company faced bankruptcy in a few months. That in itself didn't bother Grimes but what he also stood to lose bothered him very much.

Oxford Street Properties was a cover for a range of illegitimate enterprises – substandard flats rented out at exorbitant rates, illegal money lending, car ringing scams, brothels, a protection racket covering most city-centre pubs, a busy trade in supplying firearms to gangs, not to mention a means of laundering money from heroin dealing and the growing demand for cocaine. In addition, Oxford Street Properties had bases in the Republic of Ireland, Spain and North Africa. The company had no contracts there, it just appeared to have. The lorries making regular trips back to the Glasgow base carried hidden supplies of drugs, cheap booze and the increasingly lucrative market in duty-free cigarettes. Oxford Street Properties was also useful in covering for other firms. Like the security company, SPS, run by ex-police who ran legitimate deals, but also a sideline of highly irregular earners which would not stand scrutiny. For a fee and a few favours, Grimes cleared those earnings through Oxford Street Properties. When the Inland Revenue and VAT men came to call, Maggie Small, the registered owner, could present them with accounts ledgers which stood up to all their tests.

Officially, Oxford Street Properties was a profit-making concern and business was prospering in the demolition trade. In reality, its one client, the council, turned a blind eye to its underpaid and unqualified non-union workers, poor safety conditions and its constant tendency to go over the deadline and way over budget. Almost a quarter of the names on the payroll never visited a site but spent their time in other illegal activities on behalf of Grimes. For this little thriving empire to exist, one major building contract was needed on its books at all times. Their one contract with the council would be ended within months, even if Grimes conned them into the usual extensions, so Grimes needed this proposed project badly.

'So how come,' blurted Councillor Wiley, 'if ye don't mind me enquiring like, how come ye can afford tae drop yer prices now and no before?' Wilcy's attention appeared to be devoted to fiddling with his pipe. He produced a little silver tamper from his pocket and carefully teased out the black tobacco tar from the inside of the bowl.

'Well, that's business, Councillor Wiley,' Grimes answered, 'the market's changing all the time, as you know.'

'Oh aye, the market, yon old chestnut,' mused Wiley, still playing with his pipe.

'Prices have gone down since we tendered,' Grimes continued. 'Other companies have gone under. Oxford Street Properties prides itself on being able to adapt, to weather the storms.'

'Right ye are,' answered Wiley with all the conviction of a constipated turnip.

'It's true but,' Grimes was almost shouting. There was a limit to his patience and this conceited old git was giving him a lump in his tonsils.

'If I could explain, Councillor Wiley,' offered Maggie Small, moving in on the act before Grimes started threatening the old boy – not too far off if she read him correctly.

'Wish ye would, pet,' replied Wiley, looking up for the first time to give Maggie a thin, I-know-it-all smile.

'As you know, the Tory government is cutting back on all public expenditure,' she continued.

'Ah, only too well, lass,' he replied.

'And this affects the building industry more than most. Why should the Tories bother to provide decent housing for working folk after all?' Maggie asked the question rhetorically but Wiley heard her literally.

'Cos they've no respect for good, decent working-class folk. No compassion for the less well off. Never have done never will . . .'

'You put it so well,' Maggie interrupted, 'and so passionately.' Wiley visibly preened himself at the compliment. 'Decent companies are having to compete harder for the available contracts. When they lose they have to pay off workers and we all know about the ravages of unemployment.'

'Aye, that we do, only too well.' Wiley was relighting his pipe which was crackling and bubbling like a pot of boiling water on an open fire.

'When the company pays off men we tend to lose them,' Maggie continued. 'They move on to other jobs if they are lucky but these days they're more likely just to give up.'

'Bloody disgrace so it is.' Wiley spoke so loudly he attracted a school-mam glower from the dining room's only other occupant and a yelp from the pink-white toy poodle lying at her feet. Wiley didn't appear to notice or care. If the nosy one was staying at the Central Hotel she was probably a Tory in his opinion.

'Demolition work is a lot more skilled than people imagine, you know,' Maggie said. 'Just because the men work in a dirty environment and need to be strong . . .'

'Aye, folk think they're no bloody damn good, hen,' Wiley finished off Maggie's sentence as she hoped he would.

'So, we already have a large team in the area, having won the council's other contracts,' Maggie said. 'A large proportion of the budget in any such work is bringing the men, the lorries and the machinery onto the site. If we can keep them there and trim our profits to the bone – we can afford to carry out this work at a much reduced rate.' She was finished and watched Wiley's face for any sign of her likely success at persuasion. Certainly his words had indicated that he approved of many of her sentiments and he was sitting there nodding his head and sucking on his pipe as if he was thinking over her argument carefully.

'Aye, Ah understand what you're saying and Ah'm no going to disagree with ye,' he eventually said. 'Bit Ah don't think it's possible, is it, Bob?' Bob Benson jumped at the mention of his name. Grimes had noticed that the fat man was getting more and more anxious, didn't want to be there. Under the table Grimes felt the wind of Scully's foot sharply digging into Benson's shin bone.

'It will require extraordinary procedure, councillor,' Benson replied. 'But it can be achieved if, say, two influential members raised the matter with the council leader.' Benson had decided that to spell out what he meant would be taking too many risks with Councillor Wiley. But Wiley had understood him perfectly.

'Oh, aye, ye mean like the chair of the planning committee and vice-chair of finance who also happens to be deputy leader of the council?' Wiley said more as a statement than a question. 'That'll be what you meant right enough.'

'I . . . I . . . I . . .' Benson couldn't find his next word, uncertain of how to respond to Wiley's barely muted sarcasm.

'Right, well, we'll look at that option, maybe,' said Wiley.

'Good, I'm glad, Councillor Wiley,' butted in Grimes. 'I'm sure you've made the right decision.'

'Oh have Ah, Andy? Have Ah made the right decision?' Wiley paused as if waiting for an answer. 'Damn clever that when Ah've made no decision at aw.' Grimes' face fell while Maggie retained her calm, polite exterior. Inside she was cursing Wiley. 'First things first,' Wiley continued. 'Ye'll have tae submit a full detailed proposal and Ah don't mean a copy of the council's own plans like ye've been showing us this morning. Second, we'll need a fully costed proposal and Ah want tae see where ye've made the cuts. Ah'll get one of our top accountants tae look over yer figures.' Wiley paused and tapped his pipe into an ashtray, 'Then and only then might I consider tae raise the matter.'

'Councillor Wiley, that'll take a long time,' argued Grimes.

'Well, ye shouldn't be sitting here and blethering then, Andy. Ye've got work tae see tae . . . an so have Ah.' Wiley stood up and delivered a curt farewell nod to the three men before turning, 'Maggie, it's been a pleasure. Ah think yer talent's wasted in the Tory private sector. Nae offence, Andy. Ye should come and work with us, Maggie, for the people.'

'Thank you for the compliment, Councillor Wiley,' replied Maggie.

'No problem, Ah mean it. Come and see me sometime and we'll chat.' With that and a wave, Wiley strode off in the direction of the foyer. Watching his back disappear through the doorway Maggie muttered,

'You'll be seeing me sooner than you think, Councillor Wiley.'

'Ah'm sorry, Andy, he's a very difficult, man,' blustered Scully.

'It's no problem, Councillor Scully, I understand his concerns,' answered Grimes politely, while his fingers clenched his papers so hard his knuckles were white, tense blobs on bright red fingers. 'What do you think, Maggie?'

'We'll find a way of . . .' Maggie's answer was interrupted by the sight of Suzie with a zed limping into the dining room still wearing the same outfit from the night before. When Bob Benson spotted her he blurted hurried goodbyes, picked up his bag and scurried to the exit, passing Suzie with his head down.

'Ah have tae be heading as well, Andy,' said Scully, oblivious to Suzie's approach. All young people looked the same to Scully these days and he didn't recognise Suzie from the night before. 'Phone me and we'll arrange a meeting after ye've thought about what you propose tae do next.' Scully had cleared the table by the time Suzie hobbled up.

'Whit the fuck dae you want, ye wee cunt?' growled Grimes.

'That fat bastard Benson's napper oan a plate,' replied Suzie, ready for a slanging match.

'You stay the entire night?' demanded Grimes.

'Aye an Ah wish Ah hadnae,' grumbled Suzie.

'That's against the rules, ye wee tart,' hissed Grimes, barely managing to keep his voice down. 'Maggie sort her oot, for Christ's sake, Ah've goat tae make a quick phone call.' Grimes was too preoccupied to notice that Maggie Small was smiling uncharacteristically, almost gleefully at the young woman.

When Grimes had gone to a call box and the women were alone, Maggie asked,

'Wee bit sore, Suzie with a zed?'

'Aye, agony. That fat fucker . . .' The penny slowly dropped. 'How dae you know?'

'Ask you to do something special did he, our Bent Bob?' Maggie Small was almost laughing.

'Ye bitch, ye could've warned me,' squealed Suzie so loudly that the toy poodle in the corner started yelping vigorously while her owner pretended not to hear and stayed absolutely still where she sat. 'You knew, didn't ye.' It was an accusation not a question.

'Yes,' replied Maggie still smirking and remaining seated. 'Just as I knew you'd stay the night and accept payment for extras. Just as I knew that you'd break the rules.'

'Ye could've warned me,' Suzie stood in front of Maggie, refusing any of the empty chairs scattered round the table.

'No need,' replied Maggie.

'Whit? He butchered me.' Suzie rubbed tentatively, gingerly, at her rump.

'No need, if you'd followed my instructions.'

'But Ah didnae know . . .'

'What? That he was bent?' Maggie's eyes mocked Suzie.

'Naw, that he . . .'

'Wanted to hurt you?'

'Aye,' grumbled Suzie in a low voice. 'He enjoyed hurting me.'

'Well, that's men for you, wee sore Suzie. But tell you a secret,' Suzie's pained expression, her posture leaning a little forward at the waist finally brought a chuckle out of Maggie Small, 'not half as much as I enjoyed him hurting you.'

'Right that's me done,' Grimes arrived back at the table his phone call made. 'Let's get back tae the Cat's and think o plan fucking B.'

'Can Ah get a lift wi ye, Andy, Ah'm awfy sore,' Suzie tried to muster her best little-girl look, holding her head to one side and smiling up at Grimes.

'Andy? Who the fuck said you could call me Andy? Eh?' he roared and the toy poodle whined and crawled under her mistress' legs.

'You did when ye . . .' Suzie stammered.

'Jesus, whit a mess ye are,' Grimes continued.

'Aye, Ah know,' whined Suzie, mistaking Grimes' statement for sympathy.

'Get the fucking bus back tae your place pronto and tidy up for fuck's sake,' he growled, and as he and Maggie walked towards the door he called over his shoulder, 'An don't be late for work the night – full house an yer oan the table remember.'

After Maggie Small and Grimes had left, Suzie stood frozen to the spot wondering if she would have stopped bleeding by night-time when she was scheduled to strip. There had to be easier ways of making money and she was going to find them.

In the car on the way back to The Cat's Whiskers, Grimes wondered out loud how they were going to be able to fix Wiley.

'I think I've found a way, Andy,' Maggie offered.

'How?' he demanded, half irritated, half pleased.

'Let me phone a few people before I tell you – want to make sure.'

'You are the business, Maggie,' he enthused, 'fuck knows what I'd do without you.'

'What about your phone call back at the hotel? I take it was to do with this business?' Maggie asked.

'Oh, aye, this business right enough. Let's just say I've, eh, engaged an independent contractor tae hurry the council up in their decision,' Grimes smiled, pleased with himself.

'Oh, Andy, you didn't, did you?'

'Whit?' said Grimes in that guilty tone trying hard to pass off as casual.

'You didn't phone HIM again did you? Not after the last time?' Grimes didn't answer, he just smiled out of the car window watching the straggle of Sunday pedestrians on the city pavements and thought to himself,

'Mugs, so ye are. Nothing but fucking mugs.'

GO TO WORK ON AN EGG

The young boy was cold. All down his back, his buttocks, his ankles and the soles of his feet. Even his scalp was freezing, not just at the back where the hairdresser had shorn it close with the electric clippers, but at the base of his skull and at the top of his head where the natural double parting threw his hair in uncontrollable directions.

He lay still and wondered what he'd been bothered about. So, the way his hair fell naturally meant that, even clarted with gel or greasy Brylcreem, it did what it chose rather than what he wished. So what? Small problems, small minds, his father used to say. His father, how long had it been? Two years, no, longer. Four years? He didn't know anymore. Just too long without saying goodbye. Small problems, small minds. He'd never be like that again if only he was allowed to leave this place.

The boy hated the smell of eggs boiling in the pan. It smelled of the night before giro day and a main meal of eggs and toasted bread borrowed from a neighbour. That's what was missing – the smell of the bread heating and browning. A soft, soothing smell. Hospital food. Recuperation. Invalid's digestive system. Easy and comforting. The toast dulled the acidic farting stink of the eggs and turned them into . . . well, food. Without the toast, the smell of eggs spelled poverty and despair reminding him of where he was and why.

Cold down his back and warm on his front where his skin rubbed against the wool of an old khaki blanket. Something wet slithered down his buttocks onto his thighs. Or was it a shiver? Too cold to know. Sniff the air. Maybe it was an accident. Just because he was grown up didn't mean accidents didn't happen. It had happened to his big mate Jake in Goa. All that grass and Es and fruit and curries and he shit himself. But nobody minded because there they all shit themselves sooner or later.

Fuck Ibiza. That was like a fortnight in the city centre except with sun. The hippy route. That's what he was following. All the way. Goa, he was meant to be going to Goa one day. Promised himself he'd raise a stash and get out quick to Goa. Take it cool and keep his options open. Fuck, it was the type of place you didn't mind taking your time over a wee decision like what to do with the rest of your life – if Jake was right. Jake was his mate, he wouldn't lie about something that was important, about escape, about Goa.

Christ almighty, he hated the smell of eggs boiling. It was like when he was a kid and his ma made him walk beside the pram full of their dirty clothes down to the steamie. He was only a nipper but he had to walk and the dirty kegs got to travel easy. Inside that steamie it was all women's loud voices, hot hissing air and that dank, dull smell of the week's dirt being sloshed out of the gear. Bloody smell smelled of nothing except the steamie. Bit like boiling eggs.

The guy at the steamie door, what was his name, he was a right cheeky bastard and took liberties. If his da knew the things that guy used to say to his ma, that guy would be dead for certain. It was another promise he made himself. As soon as he was in long trousers he was going down to the steamie one night at shutting time and dunt that cheeky bastard on the head with a brick. Why a brick? Why had he thought of a brick? Fuck knows, but a promise is a promise.

He'd been through several pairs of long trousers before that thought came back to him. A promise made and not kept is a promise broken. Then he got to think that maybe Ma should've taken the steamie man up on his offer. Maybe then she wouldn't be so lonely without Da and wouldn't cry so much. Maybe. He wanked off that night imagining his ma, his young ma, with the steamie man. Christ he'd felt guilty about that for weeks. His poor ma. What was she thinking now? Thinking the worst of him likely and no wonder, he'd asked for that.

Eggs. Boiling fucking eggs. He couldn't think of boiling eggs without thinking of his Ma scraping by and doing her best. Christ he'd hated her for those eggs. Instead he should've loved her.

'Soft or hard? Yer eggs Ah mean, ye dirty-minded wee sod. Ha, you no had enough? Jesus yer a slut right enough but Ah likes a slut so Ah dae.'

The man's voice made him start, buckling at the waist as far as the ropes would allow. Somewhere in the flat he could hear a radio, some faint radio. What was that song? Think he could make out Madonna's voice singing what's it? 'Like a Prayer'? Her stuff all sounded the same to him now. She was fucking number one and he couldn't understand why. Lassie couldn't sing, was a mediocre dancer and, as for looks, he'd had better knee-tremblers up a close. Still, his host had sung along to her in his deep voice, breaking at the high notes and incapable of holding a tune.

The news came on the radio and all he could make out was 'Berlin Wall'. Looked like something was going to happen there. Not that he cared. Cold, dreich fucking city full of grey uniforms. Bad fucking place where they killed you for wanting to move from one part of the divide to the other. Bad fucking place, mind you, but he'd like to be there nevertheless. Be anywhere rather than in this room.

'See eggs are very good for you. Full of calcium, protein and . . . other kinda stuff. Me, the way Ah look oan it is if ye scoff an egg it's like yer eating a chicken. A wee chicken right enough but the whole fucking works, man. Got tae be good for yese.'

The voice was in the same room, he thought. With his head like this and his lugs pointing down he couldn't be sure. It didn't make any difference anyway. The man was in the house and in control and that was enough.

'Ah'm gonnae make you an egg, see. Tae keep yer strength up. Ah know whit they say aboot me oan the street. Aw bad things, right? But Ah'm no really, Ah'm Ah? Or Ah widnae be making you an egg, eh? A hard-boiled egg for ma wee man.'

He'd never met the guy before. Oh, he'd seen him in the street and knew who he was right enough. Everybody knew who that guy was. He'd made a point of avoiding that guy just because he knew enough about him.

'Bad News' Jake called him. That was the worst thing Jake ever said about anyone. What an understatement. Mind, he'd also used it to describe that bloke who raped his sister. Now he was locked in here and Jake was out there somewhere. The guy kept asking questions about where Jake might be. What did he know about Jake? Hadn't seen him in a week. Could be back in Goa as far as he knew. Jake was like that, always disappearing. Now this guy was demanding to know where Jake was. Fucking Bad News right enough, Jake, wherever you are.

'Soon be ready. Ye'll be starving, eh, after no getting any kip last night. Yer a wee raver so ye are. Ah wish Ah'd noticed ye before. Still Ah've noticed ye the now right enough.'

Fuck, there he goes humming some Kylie number. What is it with that guy? And what about the eggs? He wasn't going to feed him after what he'd done? Mind, he knew the address and the bloke's name so maybe now it's make up time. So he wouldn't grass him up. Might feed him eggs, then let him clean up. Maybe give him a bit of money and some smack just so he would keep quiet. Aye, that will be it. Maybe some dosh and some smack.

'That's the eggs ready, ye wee thing. Shite, why is it the fucking phone rings every time ye don't want it tae? Why the fuck is that? Wee minute . . . Hello. Aye, Andy Grimes, how are yese? Long time no hear. Whit? Ah thought ye'd served me a dizzy oan the work front. Whit? Aye, well, that last job didnae go so smooth. No, Ah'll no make the same mistake again. Aye, Ah know, keep ma tadger oot o the business. Andy, Ah dinnae want tae lose yer work. Grimes is the biggest name oan the street – of course Ah dinnae want tae lose yer business. Ah'll behave, man. A wee torch job, no problemo. Dalmeny Street near Rutherglen Road? Of course Ah know it, Ah can almost see it frae ma flat. Top flat. Jist the top flat? Ah'll dae the whole fucking block if yese want. Naw, aw right then the top flat it is. Want it done the night? Naw. Ye'll phone and tell me when? No problemo, senor. Good working wi yese again, Andy.'

Andy Grimes. Christ he was letting everything slip. Maybe he meant all those things he had said last night. The nice things he said while he was doing him. Made the boy feel sick at the time. Humiliated and ashamed but maybe it was going to save him now. Maybe the pervo bastard of a guy was actually in love with the boy, or in lust, what did it matter? As long as the boy got out of there.

'Right, where was we? Aye, egg's nice and hard and ready just lying in the boiling water. First things first. Need tae make sure ye're comfy. How's the wrists and the ankles? They ropes no hurting yese too much? Naw, didnae think so. Let's just make sure they're nice and secure. Aye, good. Now a wee bit o the old magic ointment. Vaseline, man, whoever invented it deserves a medal. Stays greasy for days. Magic so it is.'

What was the guy greasing up the young boy's arse for? That phone call from Grimes seems to have put him in a good mood again. Maybe he was going to do him again before breakfast. Fuck, not again.

'Yer a bit sore looking doon there. But no problemo, this is yer last time, wee man. God, Ah get a hard-on just looking at yese.'

That's it. One last time. One last time and he was out of there. Maybe with some money and a bit of smack. He could put up with it one last time. He'd have to.

'A wee bit extra Vaseline. There that's it. Now the glove. Fucking scalding they boiled eggs so they are. Sure ye'll no tell me about yer pal Jake. Last chance? Naw, didnae think so. Right, ye ready? Good boy. Just prise yer wee bum open. Christ yer cute. And now the egg. Ah'm gonnae enjoy this egg much more than you, wee man. We'll just pop it up yer hole. Nae wonder they call me The Arse Bandit, eh?'

Bud Wilson (aka The Arse Bandit)
Late twenties, just over five foot, as broad as he's
tall. Mousy brown hair cut in a bowl shape, pudding
face to match. Has a flat in Allison Street. As a
kid, joined and was thrown out of more teams than
in the SFA. Too violent even for the street gangs.
Enjoys hurting people. Done time everywhere but
short sentences only. His big stuff never gets
reported for good reason.

Aggressive homosexual who is into rape.
Speciality is taking young boys hostage and shagging
them for days on end. When he can't get it up he
tortures them. No one wants to work with The Arse
Bandit but some – unscrupulous, cheap or desperate
– will hire him on one-off jobs only. Send him out
on a simple task and it's a toss-up between him
doing the job or just having his kind of good time
with the guys involved. Bad, bad bastard who seems
to enjoy it even when he gets hurt. Psycho case.

A
September 1989

ALARM CALL

Sitting in her car at the lights at the bottom of Byres Road, Jeannie Stirk suddenly felt on familiar territory. The old tenements and trendy shops selling everything from Sunday morning papers to aromatherapy oils, from giant-size Rizlas to Indian wood carvings somehow reminded her of her streets in Edinburgh in the Grassmarket or the top of Leith Walk. Even the traffic felt the same, nose to tail even at that ungodly hour on a Sunday. The west end of Glasgow is where Birse, barking down the phone and waking her from her slumbers, had instructed her to be.

'Where?' she'd asked, half awake, half in noddy land.

'The fucking west end. Ye know, the opposite o the east end,' he'd growled.

'No, where will I meet you?' she persisted, feeling unnerved by Amanda-Jane's restless sleep-filled movements lying in the bed next to her.

'Cul de Sac, wee restaurant in Ashton Lane. In a half an hour, right?' and with that Birse hung up the phone.

Jeannie Stirk was grateful he'd ended the conversation so abruptly, saving her from the temptation to ask where Ashton Lane was or try and negotiate more time, knowing Birse would see such manoeuvres as weaknesses. Amanda-Jane's arm snaked out and her hand stroked Jeannie's stomach where the soft flesh turned sensitive and taut over the bone of her iliac crest.

'Morning,' Amanda-Jane had croaked, her voice still sticky from her sleep. This was only their second night together and their new lovers' fascination with each other had only just begun. They made love till exhausted and again as soon as they woke up. Not that morning.

'You're going to have to go,' Jeannie had said abruptly, lifting her friend's arm off her and rolling from the bed. The call from Birse had made her feel as if he could see into her bedroom and she saw him there at the other end of the phone sneering and nodding at having found her out. 'Come on, Amanda, move it,' she'd screamed, hopping around the flat throwing open cases and boxes searching for clothes to wear, cursing herself for not yet making the time to unpack properly.

'Want coffee?' Amanda-Jane had asked, stretching as she padded naked in the direction of the kitchen.

'Are you fucking deaf?' Jeannie had screamed, 'I said get out. You have got to go NOW.' The rest had been a blur for Jeannie but she could sense the hurt in the young woman as she dressed sullenly and quickly. Jeannie wanted to say sorry and explain but was panicking too much, was too focused on Birse and what he wanted. When the door slammed she knew that Amanda-Jane had walked out of her life.

Now she was manoeuvring up Byres Road, steering one-handed, a street map of Glasgow clutched in the other. At the sight of the first car park she veered right into University Avenue against the traffic lights, receiving blared horns and two-fingered insults from other drivers. And she was an advanced driver approved by the police. She had to calm down quick or Birse would make mincemeat of her.

'Yer late,' Birse didn't look up from his plate, continuing to shovel forkfuls of savoury smelling crêpes into his already crammed mouth. 'Grab a pew,' he added but made no effort to free a chair by moving his coat or a pile of thick Sunday broadsheets. Jeannie was surprised that Birse read at all, let alone broadsheets. As for the crêpes, she'd taken him more for a full fry-up man. 'Fucking city, cannae get a decent fry-up oan a Sunday morning. But these fancy pancakes are no bad, gie them a go.' He nodded at the menu.

Jeannie didn't feel like eating, but since Birse seemed in no hurry to explain why she had been summoned she picked the menu up and did as she was told. The restaurant was dark and smelled of last night's smoke and stale lager. On the tables, burnt-out candle stubs gave the place a sad and forlorn feeling. Three small groups of diners were scattered around the place and they looked like students from the nearby university, too spaced out to bother with anyone else. Jeannie noticed that Birse had selected a corner seat, his back to the wall, where he could watch the only door and movements from the kitchen – the gunslinger's seat. Somewhere a member of staff turned on the sound system and gentle waves of Miles Davis' soothing sax wafted through the room.

'Fucking monkey music,' grumbled Birse.

'Boss, wha . . .' Jeannie started.

'How are ye with women?' Birse's question shook Jeannie, confirming her worst fears. Did he know? Was this what this was about

– a quiet word in her ear followed by her voluntary application for yet another transfer? 'Like, dae ye get oan okay with female con artists? Some folk don't. Cannae stand them masel.'

'Erm, yes, okay I suppose,' Jeannie said, relieved at the different direction of his queries.

'Mmm, okay. Look Ah'll come back tae that. You and me's no got off tae the best o starts,' Birse conceded, much to Jeannie's shock. 'Bad timing you arriving right slap bang in the middle o this, eh, complicated business.'

'I'm used to that but I . . .'

'Oh Ah know, hen, Ah know. Had a wee chat wi your ex-DCI this morning,' Birse said. Jeannie wondered if he'd phoned in the middle of the night to catch her former gaffer, an early Sunday morning golf fanatic. 'Sun shines oot o yer arse according tae him. Didnae know you were involved in that big heroin dealing case. That was a good catch.' Birse shovelled in more food and immediately washed it down with large gulps of coffee.

'Yeah, well, I have experience,' Jeannie offered almost apologetically and then continued with more confidence, 'it's just what's going on around here – well, much of it I don't understand. Like how the street teams relate to each other, who is in with who and against who. How the deals go down.'

'The bloody geography, eh?' Birse said in a barbed reference to her being late and an implicit confirmation that he had deliberately given her no directions to their meeting venue.

'Yeah, I suppose so . . . but I can learn.'

'So I believe, but how quickly?' Birse stopped eating and leaned across the table looking hard at Jeannie, waiting for an answer.

'I'm a quick learner, Boss.' She was embarrassed at deliberately calling him by that term but she reckoned that was the type of language Birse thought signified respect. What's in a name after all?

'You'd better be,' he still stared at her, his big jaw twisted into aggressive challenge mode. 'Got a job for you.' Birse abruptly lightened his tone, picking up his fork and going at his food once again. 'Two cons, Joe Murphy and Sean Ferguson. Heard o them?'

'Murphy, yes.' Jeannie was delighted to demonstrate some knowledge and hoped that her memory would back her up. 'He was part of the group we looked at in terms of those security van robberies a few years ago.'

'Oh, aye, joint operation. Serious Crime Squad boys all over the shop. Were you involved in that?' Birse was impressed.

'Just in support – I was a little girl blue at the time.' Jeannie risked a smile.

'Well, you hit it spot on, hen. Aye, bastard was never fingered though, eh? Story o Joe Murphy's life, that. Even the stragglers we caught refused tae grass him up in spite of the usual incentives.'

'Lucky Joe, eh?' offered Jeannie.

'Luck's got fuck all tae dae wi it. Joe Murphy's clever and careful. Uses the noggin,' Birse tapped his forehead, 'except in one respect. His wee pal Fergie's a bit o a loose cannon.'

'Never heard of him,' said Jeannie.

'No surprised, strictly small beer. A wee tadpole in a great big ocean full o sharks, but Murphy likes him, sticks by him. So here's the drill.' Birse signalled the waitress for more coffee as she brought some crêpes Jeannie had ordered. 'Murphy's been mouthing off and making threats aboot protecting this Addison bastard. Question is why? Addison's never needed protecting before.'

'Think there's a link?' Jeannie asked the obvious question having learned long ago that these were savoured by those who liked the sound of their own voices – by men like Birse.

'Aye, maybe the closest,' Birse raised his eyebrows and nodded. 'Now Ah reckon Murphy's time has come for his next trick. Ah can hear the fucker thinking frae here. We'll never trip him up but his wee chummy oan the other hand . . . easy meat, man.'

Jeannie was getting the picture. Birse suspected that Murphy knew Addison, or could even be Addison. To get to him they'd go via Sean Ferguson. Straightforward, but why her? Why not one of his long-standing team members?

'We need a face that's no known,' Birse continued as if reading her thoughts. 'That's where you come in. Yer ignorance fills the role just the ticket,' he grinned, showing dark green flecks of spinach splattering his large gravestone teeth. 'Fergie's no the full shilling, but he's jumpy and he knows every bloody polis in this city and a helluva lot elsewhere.'

'What do you want me to do?' Jeannie was short, simple and direct.

'You no eating that?' Birse signalled at the taupe envelopes lying on her plate ignored, cold and congealing. She shook her head and Birse pulled her plate over and forked half a crêpe into his mouth. 'Christ, whit's in this? Rancid wi fucking garlic.'

Jeannie couldn't even remember what she'd ordered so asked instead, 'Don't you like garlic?'

'Aye, like it fine but in a curry hoose late at night or even a Tally but no first thing in the morning.' Birse continued to eat throughout his protestations. 'First, get yer arse doon the road and read their files. Murphy's will take ye ten minutes but ye can cancel the rest o the day for wee Fergie's. Wee bastard needed a second file by the time he'd left school, that's if he'd gone to school in the first place. But ye need tae get tae know him better than yer boyfriend, right?'

'Of course,' Jeannie's collusion with his ignorant prejudice in assuming her sexuality didn't faze her at all. She was used to pretending she liked men.

'Then ye stand by. You and me'll meet from time tae time – tae keep ye briefed – but at some point, when it's right, Ah'm gonnae ask ye tae trail oan Fergie. He likes his bevvy and his women, if ye catch ma drift,' Birse winked. Jeannie caught his drift precisely. 'Have ye any tart-up gear? He likes them to show a bit o thigh annat.' Jeannie had more tart-up gear than Birse could imagine or would ever see. The question was what exactly did he expect her to do?

'I'll fix something up,' she replied.

'Talking o tarts, there's another wee matter.' he was scraping cold melted cheese off the plate and eating it straight off his knife. Jeannie thought of Amanda-Jane, so gentle and neat at a table you hardly noticed her eat. She waited for Birse to mention Cathy Brodie, expecting him to ask her to apply the softly-softly approach while he played Mr Angry. 'Ye're gonnae accompany me on some visits tae a certain club. Now officially we're there tae question a murder victim's relative – well, they're always suspect, right? This time the guy's no a suspect but you never mind that, Ah'll deal wi him privately.' Birse had lost Jeannie. 'Ah'll go into his office leaving you, the wee lassie like, in the club. Your job is tae get chatting wi a Maggie Small – friendly, eh – like women dae. Chat aboot her outfit or men or her hairdo, whatever ye fucking gab aboot. You are gonnae be her new wee pal.'

'Can I ask why?' Jeannie had never heard of Maggie Small and was struggling to understand this move.

'For the now, let's just say Ah don't trust her. Besides, she needs a pal, aw right? Christ, is that the time?' Birse looked at his watch. 'Better move ma arse, got a heavy date with a few pints at the Supporters' Club.' Birse was rising from the table and rifted loudly, hardly to Jeannie's surprise. 'God, ma guts are aching. See this job it's an ulcer oan a plate so it is.' As he flipped open his coat and struggled to find the arms, Jeannie smelled old cigar smoke. 'And the last thing – no a word tae nobody. Ah mean fucking nobody – public or polis or boyfriend. As far as the world's concerned you havnae heard o Joe Murphy, that Fergie shite or Maggie Small. You went tae church this morning. Get it?'

'Of course, but the files?' Birse looked at Jeannie as if she'd asked about a green Martian standing on the table rather than regular police files. 'How can I get the files without going into the office?'

'Fuck me, what am Ah thinking.' Birse slapped himself on the forehead. 'The papers are for you, thought ye'd no have the time tae buy them this morning.' He pointed at the hefty bundle of broadsheet newspapers sitting on the chair next to Jeannie. 'For you,' he insisted, pointing closer. Jeannie peeled back the wedge that was the *Sunday Times* and there were the fat files stuck inside a Haddows off-licence carrier bag. 'Slip them back tae me, and only me, when yer finished,' Birse ordered, and without further comment turned and marched to the door. Through the restaurant window, Jeannie watched Birse out in the lane, an oddball among the young people strolling by chilling out in the morning, in no hurry to go anywhere. Birse paused and lit a panatella, sheltering his lighter under his coat, and then was gone.

Jeannie ordered a large cafetiere of coffee and pulled a battered packet of Marlboro Lights from her handbag. She didn't smoke much but she needed a cigarette now to enhance her thinking time. She fought off the temptation to feel relieved, to believe that Birse had chosen her for a special role. Trusting her instincts, she didn't trust him. Jeannie hadn't fallen for his line that she was useful because she wasn't known on the street. Did Birse have a problem with his own men? Were some of them on the payroll of the gangsters? Or was she chosen because she was dispensable? Or expected to fail? What about Maggie Small, whoever she was? Why ask her to become involved with Small when the witness to the murder was meant to be Cathy Brodie? Was Joe Murphy more dangerous than Birse had let on? Whatever Birse was up to, Jeannie Stirk didn't like it at all.

12 SEPTEMBER 1989

I hate funerals. When I'm there to grieve for a friend somehow all the funerals of my life come back to haunt me. Doesn't matter if the deceased is a hundred and ten years old and their death is no surprise. It's the funerals themselves that remind you of everyone you've ever lost. For me that's my grandmother, my old grandad and my mam. My mam who I'd lost for so long and found again just in time to bury her.

I knew what had happened to her - the booze, the debt, the sad shell. That I was going to fix, take care of her. Then she died and my chance was gone. My fault, I waited too long. Everybody needs their mam, even me.

Come to think of it, it was at a funeral I started this malarkey. Old boy from the scheme popped his clogs and I went along to pay my respects. In the pub later one of his old pals recognised me, remembered my old grandfather. Took me aside and told me about my mam, what her landlord was putting her through. She fell into arrears with her rent, he lends her some money then comes back demanding big interest. Wee Mam was still drinking and hadn't a bean. So he took her benefits books and her body for years. No wonder she ended so sadly. When the old boy told me I sniffed around on my own. Landlord was up to all sorts of rackets, leaning on folk who couldn't fight back. Bad guy - so I killed him. That was the start and it started at a funeral.

Years later and that fat brother of Grimes is up to the same manoeuvres. When I heard about Cathy Brodie it was the last straw for him. Maybe not the smartest thing I've done, to take out Grimes' brother. Not smart but right. And it all started with a funeral.

Tomorrow's funeral will be different. That's work. But I still hate funerals.

A

COLD ENOUGH FOR COATS

'See's a turn o the bag, eh?' The young girl was leaning against a tree, her denims and knickers around her ankles.

'S'fucking great buzz, man,' replied the young boy, 'that Paki sells ace gear.'

'Industrial Strength Solvent . . . WARNING,' the girl read from the tin. 'Warning my fanny.' The girl held the crisp bag over her face and nose and inhaled deeply again and again. As she did so, the boy fingered her and rubbed his half-hard penis against her thigh.

'Man this glue's doing ma nut right in,' he grumbled.

'You're no goin tae fucking conk oot oan me again, are ye?' she asked, coming up for air.

'Naw, started seeing things but.'

'Have you been dropping acid, ye cunt, cos yer meant tae share wi me.' Buzzed up or not the girl understood her rights.

'Naw, naw, it's jist Ah'm imagining there's a fucking thingy doon there. Know one o they motors wi a coffin in the back,' he pleaded his case while still frigging the girl.

'Where?' she pushed him away and staggered from the tree to look in the direction his wavering arm was pointing in. 'Ye fucking daft bastard ye.'

'Whit?'

'It's just a fucking funeral.'

'Eh?' his muddled brain didn't understand the link.

'Where are we? Eh? Where the fuck are we?' she demanded, angry and convinced that he was too stoned for glue alone. He must have had something else and held out on her.

'Jesus, you that oot o it, man?' The boy thought that she didn't know where she was.

'Naw, it's a simple fucking question. Where are we?' She was going to drop him soon if he was going to carry on like this.

'Sighthill, course,' looking at her as if she was stupid.

'Sighthill whit?' He staggered back and immediately stepped

forward again, leaning against her and running his hands against her naked legs.

'Aw come oan, let's just have a good time, eh?' he pleaded.

'No until ye tell me. Sighthill whit?' In spite of her protestations she did nothing to stop his hand moving between her legs. She was cold and numb and buzzed up and felt very little anyway.

'Gie's a kiss,' he nuzzled her neck.

'Fuck off. Ye honk, man.' She half-heartedly pushed him back. He started pulling up her top.

'Gonnae let me, eh? C'moan lie doon.'

'Whit you like,' she giggled and flopped on to the wet grass. Looking up, her sky was revolving fast, clouds zigzagging, overtaking each other. Dodgems of the sky, just the way she liked it. 'By the way, it's a cemetery, like, Sighthill Cemetery.'

'Ah've always fancied you.' It was the limit of his standard seduction line muttered as he settled between her open legs not caring where they were.

'An Ah've always fancied giving you a doing.' The man's voice came from somewhere behind them. Gerry Kirkpatrick, known on the streets as Deadeye, was standing over the young couple and he didn't look pleased.

'Fuck dae you want?' grumbled the boy looking over his shoulder, peering up at Deadeye's black shape silhouetted against the meagre autumn sunlight.

'Want yer two's arses shifted oot o here pronto. This is a fucking cemetery and there's a funeral happening,' Deadeye ordered.

'Fuck off,' said the girl, 'we were here first, man.'

'An Ah'm here last, now shift, ye wee shites.' Deadeye was not in a mood for bargaining. He leaned over and gripped the boy by the scruff of his hair and yanked. The young couple held on to each other and their combined weight was too much for Deadeye. 'Wee cunts Ah warned yese.' Deadeye kicked the two young folk hard and repeatedly, raising nothing more than muted yelps. The lovers were too out of it to feel much pain. Maybe fear would work. Reaching into the back waistband of his trousers he pulled out his pistol, a small unobtrusive affair chosen for the solemn occasion. Squatting down, Deadeye shoved the barrel close to the young couple's faces. 'Now shift.'

'Wee problem here?' it was one of Birse's plain-clothes team, all black tied and suited for the burial but on official duty, scanning the mourners on the possibility that the murderer might attend, a macabre but common ritual – or so the police believed.

'Na, no problem,' replied Deadeye slipping his gun away, 'Romeo and Juliet here were just leaving.' The young couple were sitting on the ground frantically trying to pull up their trousers but the glue's impact on their coordination was making that simple task difficult.

'Cracking wee minge there, doll,' said the cop. 'See if Ah wasnae oan duty Ah'd maybe offer ye wee shot masel.' The girl was terrified, panicking, but she'd learned enough about survival at the sharp end. She turned and smiled at the leering cop.

'Nae respect these days, weans,' offered Deadeye.

'Yer right there,' replied the cop.

'Ah hate that shite,' said Deadeye, kicking the discarded tin of glue down the grassy slope.

'Aye, it's brain-rotting filth right enough,' agreed the cop. The two men stood side by side surveying the cemetery.

'Fancy sharing a wee one?' Deadeye drew a stubby three-skin joint from his inside pocket. The two kids had abandoned any ambitions for modesty in favour of escape. They were running as fast as they could to the far wall of the cemetery and the high flats where they lived, the top half of their lily white arses still showing, hands hiking at concertina-crumpled trousers.

'Aye, why no?' replied the cop. 'Last chance before the doings start, eh?'

Down below, a coffin was being ceremoniously removed from the back of a hearse. Andy Grimes stood close by between a freshly dug grave and row after row of floral wreaths. Hundreds of mourners stood round in a broad semicircle, all unmoving, silent and respectful. It was a gathering of who's who in crime on Glasgow's streets.

'Ma baws are freezing aff, man,' Fergie mumbled to Joe.

'Told ye tae wear a coat, ye daft bam, cemeteries are always cold places,' Joe half whispered with no sympathy.

'Dinnae have a coat. They're for old geezers,' Fergie answered. Joe turned to look at him, turning up the collar of his own black woollen coat. 'Aside from yersel, that is,' Fergie added with a grin.

'You saying Ah'm old fashioned?'

'Naw, naw. Mean no offence, Joe. Good piece o material and that it's jist . . .'

'Whit?' As much as Joe liked Fergie he found himself at times being so easily irritated by him.

'Jist look around, eh. Count the men in coats in this cemetery.' The two friends casually and silently looked round the group of mourners. 'See whit Ah mean?'

'Aye, aw right. Catch yer drift,' Joe conceded.

'Ye've yer team boys in their ankle-length leathers – think they fuckers could've changed oot o their working gear, eh? Birse, the polis brass in his cashmere job and his troops in the standard issue blue anoraks ower their suits. Who the fuck wears an anorak ower a suit? Fucking contradiction, man.'

'Aw right, Fergie, enough, eh?' Joe didn't need this. He had more important things on his mind.

'Aside from that lot,' Fergie ignored Joe's plea, 'ye've got Grimes, they two old fellas, Don Chico and you.' Joe's irritation faded as it always did where Fergie was concerned. Though he wasn't looking at his friend he knew there would be a sly grin on his face, pleased to get the opportunity to tease his more successful pal. In street terms it was like saying 'I love you' – a phrase that would never cross any of their lips.

'Place is mobbed with faces, eh?' said Joe.

'Aye, Ah know,' Fergie agreed. 'Check the amount o scars, man. It's like a gathering o the Failed Assassins Association.'

'Polis will have a field day here, and the press,' added Joe. 'Bet their cameras are up there,' nodding in the direction of the nearby Sighthill flats. 'Paid some poor sod for the view from their front room.'

'God, Ah didnae know Ah was gonnae be in the papers.' Fergie licked the palms of his hands and made a show of smoothing down his short, neat hair. 'Think they'll catch ma best side?' he postured with his neck jutted out, the broadest sleaziest grin he could manage spread across his face.

'You split me up, Fergie,' Joe sniggered, trying not to laugh. As much as he hated Grimes he was against showing the man any public disrespect unless it was absolutely necessary. 'Ah'm glad you're ma mate.'

'Aye?' Fergie turned towards him. 'Because of ma good looks, acute intelligence and vast vocabulary?'

'Naw,' replied Joe, 'cos ye make me laugh, even here. And Ah fucking hate funerals.'

Scotch Brian wasn't having a very good time. He had arrived that morning off the train from Manchester and taken a taxi straight to the cemetery. He knew where he was going because his contact down in Mosside had written it out for him, knowing that Scotch Brian's memory wasn't so good these days. Not that Scotch Brian didn't know the city. He had been raised in Glasgow and spent the first ten years of his adulthood working the streets with all the top teams. Then he'd got out, sensing a more lucrative scene in the north-west of England. But now he was back to do a one-off job for Grimes. Shooting some guy called Addison he had heard of but never met – easy work, well within Scotch Brian's speciality. Couple of days tops, his boss had said, give Brian a chance to catch up with some old comrades.

Scotch Brian knew all that but why here? Why a cemetery? He stood in the damp grass and looked around the graveside crowd searching for a face he recognised and failing. This place didn't feel right, didn't smell right. When he was younger and lived here he'd be asked to go south to do an occasional hit job for some of the London firms. Once he travelled to Spain to see off some guy who'd run off with the proceeds of a big heist. Every time he came back to Glasgow he could smell it, knowing he was there with his eyes shut. He used to think that no other place in the world smelled like Glasgow, now he thought that this place didn't smell like Glasgow. Scotch Brian wasn't happy at all.

'Who's that fat cunt waving at?' Scotch Brian said out loud as Grimes gave him a salute and a nod from his station by the grave. One or two other mourners heard him and turned, looking angry and muttering their disapproval. 'Does he think Ah'm stupid?' Scotch Brian continued. 'No way Ah'm going near that hole, man.' Increasingly of late, Scotch Brian talked to himself. None of his associates in Manchester were brave or foolish enough to tell him. Grimes had heard him and glowered back, his cheeks reddening with temper, an anger that would have to wait.

Scotch Brian looked at the grave and around him. Everyone seemed to be waiting and nothing happening. What were they waiting for? Why that grave? Was it for him? He looked round again feeling the hefty bulge of his Magnum in his shoulder holster and tried to work out if anyone else was tooled up. Then he remembered that in Glasgow they carried their pistols stuck into their belts, at the back under their jackets. Out of sight, sneaky like. Scotch Brian had given that habit up when he had adopted his first .357 Smith and Wesson. Now that was some armoury, blast through anything. Even if he was stoned out and managed to hit his target off centre, the guy was likely to die just from the impact, never mind the gaping hole ripped through his flesh. Great guns, and he'd stuck with them ever since, along with a substantial and varied stock of killing machines. Scotch Brian needed a selection of arms for different professional contracts but he also liked them, loved them for their own sake. But always he carried the Magnum in his shoulder holster.

'Bunch of sneaky fuckers,' Scotch Brian roared. 'Ah know what you're up to. Think Ah came up the Clyde on the back of a jobby boat?'

More muttering around Scotch Brian and some men started to slowly sidle away from him. That grave looked too convenient. All his adult life Scotch Brian knew he was going to end violently. He'd been a freelancer, taking contracts purely on the basis of the right price being paid. That suited his temperament but it also ensured that he had enemies in every quarter. After thirty years of killing he was hard pressed to think of a firm or a team or a family he hadn't hit.

The grave seemed to be getting larger and moving closer. Scotch Brian could feel the cold dribble of sweat running down his back. His forehead was drenched and he looked up, putting his hand out to check for rain that was not there. Some guy in a clerical collar began to speak. Scotch Brian couldn't hear his words for the sound of crashing sea waves in his head. So he watched the holy man's mouth get larger, showing teeth, sneering and repeating his name.

'Scotch Brian. Scotch Brian. Scotch Brian . . .'

'What are you saying, you wee cunt?' Brian shouted. Grimes looked at Scotch Brian, the fury shining in his eyes. 'Ah know what you're saying – well, you're out of luck, Fred. Ah'm off.'

Scotch Brian backed through the crowd turning from side to side, watching anyone for sudden dodgy movements. Those who knew who the crazy man was held their arms up, palms open and showing. Reaching the road running through the cemetery, Scotch Brian decided he was in desperate need of a smoke.

The first parked car he tried was open – who steals cars at a funeral? He slipped into the front seat and fished out his pipe – four to five inches long, made from brass. He sat and hurriedly smoked a cigarette with quick draws, tapping the ash into the bowl of the pipe. Below the bowl and stem ran a fixed brass pipe with a small screw at the end which Scotch Brian quickly opened, being very careful now. Gently he tilted the pipe till a small white crystal rolled out on to the palm of his hand.

'There you are, wee sweetheart,' he cooed, 'just in time for your daddy.' Carefully he placed the freebase cocaine into the bowl and replaced the foil mesh cover. Zippo lighters came with a guarantee and Scotch Brian's classic silver model didn't let him down. Lit first time and would burn as long as the petrol held out. Flaring up the crystal it turned into sizzling oil lying on its ash cushion. Scotch Brian was smoking some of the highest quality gear available. Back in Mosside he had a reputation for being fussy about the quality of coke he was willing to buy. Promise him excellent gear and deliver only good or mediocre – well, he'd been known to shoot people for less. Not surprisingly, he was always sold only the finest cocaine and Scotch Brian had become a top-notch rockhead, needing hits of increasing frequency just to stay level.

Three blasts later and the sweats had gone, the shaking stopped, angry waves disappeared from his skull and the world looked normal. Scotch Brian pushed open the car door and inhaled deeply through his nose. Glasgow smelled like Glasgow again. Scotch Brian suddenly realised he was on familiar territory. 'Sighthill,' he murmured, 'got a few old pals buried here. Where the fuck did they skyscrapers come from? Fuck sakes, nothing stays the same.'

Brian remembered he had a job to do for Andy Grimes, a guy he used to run with when they were young men but whom he hadn't seen in years. He'd not believed that Grimes had risen to be one of the top street players. Apart from a vicious streak, Grimes was more of a bully and a backstabber than a brain or a leader. Still, Grimes was willing to pay his fee. 'Ah'll work for any tosser me,' Scotch Brian mumbled.

'How ye doing, Brian?' Deadeye stood by the open car door. 'Boss sent me tae take you tae the pub – few drinks and sandwiches annat.'

'Who's your boss? Besides Ah'm no hungry.' Scotch Brian didn't like the look of Deadeye.

'Start again, will Ah?' Deadeye offered. 'Andy Grimes said tae drive ye tae the pub. Says he and you can talk there. An something about some o yer old pals going along.'

'Grimes? Right, suppose so then,' Scotch Brian conceded reluctantly. Deadeye Kirkpatrick jumped into the driving seat and was surprised to find Scotch Brian climbing out of the passenger seat and getting into the back.

'Hey, Brian, yer among friends here,' exclaimed Deadeye, who was very familiar with the strategic significance of the back seat when taking a driver hostage. 'You're no gonnae pull oan me, are ye, Brian?'

'That's for me to know and you to find out,' grumbled Scotch Brian. 'Just fucking drive, right.'

'Riiiight,' muttered Deadeye who, for two pins, would have taken the middle-aged hitman out but for the hassle he'd get from Grimes.

Down near the graveside, Joe and Fergie watched the mourners queue up to pay their respects to Grimes.

'Bunch o arse lickers, eh?' said Fergie.

'Aye, Ah suppose,' muttered Joe.

'Yer no going doon there are yese?' Fergie nodded at the huddle around Grimes.

'Fuck off, you,' Joe turned and glowered at Fergie

'It's just Ah know you and yer fucking ethics. Aye up tae the right thing just because you think it's right.' Fergie was in flow again, released from the constrained silence of the burial ceremony.

'That's right, and so?' Joe turned to look at Fergie.

'Well, fuck, it's Grimes – look, that bastard Birse has gone up tae shake his hand. A fucking copper shaking his hand in broad daylight.'

'That explains ma stance in this matter,' Joe nodded in the direction of Grimes and Birse in deep conversation.

'How?' Fergie couldn't keep up with Joe's thinking some of the time.

'Well, Birse is a bent polis, right?' Joe sounding reasonable.

'Every cunt knows that,' Fergie exasperated.

'Well the right thing to do . . .'

'Aye?' Fergie impatient.

'. . . the moral thing to do . . .'

'Christ, get the point would yese.'

'. . . is to take ma mate to the pub and buy him loads o drink,' Joe smiled.

'Now yer talking, but Ah still don't understand, man,' Fergie's brow was knitted, perplexed and he was still not following his pal.

'The last thing Ah'd do is shake Grimes' hand, especially in condolence for the death o that sleaze bag, dirty scum o a brother o his,' Joe spat, wanting to shout the words at Grimes, holding back his temper. 'So much so . . .'

'Aye?' Fergie worried that Joe was going to do something stupid.

'. . . Ah'd even rather buy you loads of drink,' Joe smiled.

'C'moan then, let's get oot o here.' Fergie turned towards the cemetery gates and the two men walked slowly through the stragglers trying to avoid standing on the graves, though neither understood why. 'We're no going back to the pub Grimes has booked, are we?' asked Fergie, the worrying thought just occurring to him.

'Christ almighty, Fergie, do you no listen?' Joe stopped and turned his friend by the shoulder till they were standing face to face. 'Watch ma lips . . . Ah'd rather set masel on fire than spend another minute in that Grimes fucker's company.'

'Just asking, Joe,' Fergie muttered, half hurt, half apologetic.

'Aye, Ah know, an Ah'm just telling yese.' The two walked over to their car and headed for a pub, any pub, as long as it was on the opposite side of town from the funeral party.

In the rear of the long black Mercedes that didn't come as part of the deal with the undertaker, Grimes sat beside Maggie Small, talking to Birse through the open window.

'Ah want that cunt Addison fingered in the next twenty-four hours,' ordered Grimes.

'We're close, Andy, real close, but Ah'm no sure we'll get him that quick,' Birse replied, looking sheepish and waiting for the retort.

'Quick! Fucking quick! Ye've had weeks, man.' Grimes was in less of a reasonable mood than usual, which was saying something. Scotch Brian's outbursts and insults were nagging on his mind.

'Ah'll pull the stops oot the night,' Birse backtracked, 'see what we can do.'

'Ye'd better finger him and tell me pronto . . . hear me?' Grimes demanded.

'Aye, we'll . . .'

'No arrests, Alex, no reports, no fucking records,' Grimes interrupted. 'Just you tell me where he is then get your mob tae vamoose.'

'Ah can sort him for yese, Andy, be easy,' Birse said.

'Naw, no need. Ah've brought somebody in tae see tae that. Top man, top dollar. Nice and squeaky clean.' Grimes was talking about Scotch Brian as if the hitman's behaviour at the graveside did not worry him. Maybe Brian had deliberately behaved like that to make the public and the police believe that there was bad blood between him and Grimes. Now that thought reassured Grimes very much.

'Outsider? Yer walking close tae the line, Andy. If this gets back tae me it could be fucking difficult,' Birse spoke in an angry, anxious whisper.

'No worries,' Grimes leaned over and patted Birse on the arm, 'told ye, Ah've brought in a top man.'

Deadeye Kirkpatrick was getting very worried. Ever since he had arrived at the pub, Scotch Brian seemed to be getting more and more agitated. Pacing the room, jumping at noises, the sweat rolling off his forehead. Deadeye didn't like the look of this one bit.

'There's gonnae be fucking trouble the day yet,' he told himself.

A WEE DRIVE IN THE COUNTRY

'Brian, how yese doing? Long time no see, ma man.' The man had just returned from the jukebox where he had selected what he thought appropriate funeral music. Johnny Cash's 'A Thing Called Love' rolled out of the speakers. Now he stood at the bar, a drink in his hand, smiling at Scotch Brian.

Scotch Brian said nothing, just eyed him up and down. He didn't like country and western and he didn't like the look of the guy. Long straggly grey hair in need of a wash, three days' growth on his chin, a mug full of scars. Scotch Brian thought that he was the type of guy he should have recognised but didn't have a clue who he was. He did recognise the coat – a black, ankle-length leather job – and automatically checked for the tell-tale signs of one long, prominent, unforgiving fold. But no, the guy wasn't carrying a shotgun.

'Kamikaze, mind?' the man offered his open hand. 'We ran together in the south side. Mind, wi the Govan mob, when they ruled this fucking dump? Naw?' Scotch Brian continued to stare at the man and said nothing. 'You gave me ma nickname, mind? That night at the Wee Black Man when the Toi attacked n Ah was the only cunt standing there. Chatting up a wee bird so Ah was and they fair spoiled ma patter, man. Lumbered her the next week right enough.'

Deadeye watched the two men from the far corner of the bar. He wished people would leave Grimes alone for a minute so he could warn him before Scotch Brian blew up. 'Got this scar that night,' Kamikaze ran one nicotine brown finger down the length of his most conspicuous scar. 'You did in the guy that sliced me – brought me back his blade and his thumb. Fucking cracker, man, Ah kept them oan ma mantelpiece till the missus complained aboot the stink.' Scotch Brian turned and walked away, leaving Kamikaze still talking to him, in midflow of yet another tale of their early years.

The room was filling up. Scotch Brian stood with his back against a wall and watched these strangers with increasing nervousness. The sweat was rolling down his forehead and onto his face, nipping his eyes, blurring his sight. He checked his watch.

'Half an hour,' he spoke aloud to himself. 'Only half a fucking hour. My hits are getting closer and closer.' An old guy standing close by thought he was being addressed and leaned over with a genial smile, holding one hand behind one ear. Scotch Brian barged through him, spilling his drink, on his way to the toilets. Deadeye turned and watched the door swing closed behind Scotch Brian. He felt for his piece in his waistband and contemplated going in after the man.

A wall of cracked white ceramic to urinate against with the drain blocked and the tiled floor beginning to flood – the place had the acid piss and stale beer stink of the standard facilities in any Glasgow pub, football stadium and the lanes in the city centre on weekend nights. Off-white panels of the one private cubicle in the corner of the small room bore a range of graffiti in bold markers of different colour.

> BURN A HUN TODAY
> *GOD BLESS THE POPE*
> *NEIL SIMPSON FOR KING*

Ran some of the football orientated slogans.

> *WEE BILLY SUCKS COCK*
> PHONE MADGE FOR A RIDE
> *JULIE THE BARMAID TAKES IT UP THE ARSE*

Ran the sexual messages – the majority – resplendent with crude, caveman drawings and contact telephone numbers. None of that interested Scotch Brian, he just wanted to smoke his pipe in privacy. Pushing at the cubicle door, it creaked and protested but didn't budge. Over the engaged sign someone had tacked a rag of lined paper, torn roughly from a jotter, on which was scrawled, 'BOG BROKE'.

Scotch Brian swore but he didn't much mind. Who was going to mess with him just because he was doing some drugs? Fishing out his pipe he started his familiar routine, smoking a cigarette and flicking the ash into the bowl. He had unscrewed the brass pipe and was carefully rolling out a white crystal when the toilet door swung open and in walked the little old man who he had just barged past in the bar. The screech of the door's hinges startled Scotch Brian's fraught nerves and three white crystals plopped on to the piss-soaked floor. He looked at the freebase cocaine dissolving rapidly at his feet.

'Aye, aye,' said the old man, unbuttoning his fly and taking his stance at the urinal. Brian recognised that guy from somewhere but he couldn't recall where. Maybe he was being followed? That feeling had come back where everything seemed too real, too threatening. The old man twisted his head round while he peed and said, 'Grimes has put oan a good show for his brother, eh?'

Brian wondered what he knew about Grimes and what was he looking at and why was he following him? The Magnum was out of the shoulder holster in Scotch Brian's hands, gripped in both fists pointing at the back of the old guy's head.

'Put your paws up,' muttered Scotch Brian.

'Eh?' the old man twisted round again and looked into the barrel only inches away from his face. 'Oh for fuck's sakes, mister.' The old guy's hands shot into the air, his neck still twisted round, piss dribbling down his trousers and over his shoes. 'Ah've no got much, son, but take it. Just dinnae hurt us . . . PLEASE, eh?'

'Face the fucking wall,' growled Scotch Brian. The old guy complied. 'Hands flat against the wall . . . NOW.' As the old guy leaned forward, Scotch Brian kicked at his feet, opening his legs wide.

'Son, ma wallet's in ma inside pocket – there's just a few quid but . . .'

'Just shut the fuck up you . . . head against the wall,' barked Brian, whisking off his captive's cloth cap and ramming the guy forward. With the Magnum held in one hand and always pointing at the old guy, Scotch Brian gave him a rub down, pulling the contents out of his pockets. When he was finished, the old man's wealth lay scattered in the piss on the floor. A cheap fake leather wallet, twelve pounds in singles, a thousand peseta banknote, a faded black-and-white photograph of a smiling young woman, a bus pass, a dental appointment card, a betting slip, a worn cough sweet tin now filled with tobacco and cigarette papers, the horse racing section of the *Daily Express* and a dirty handkerchief, crispy hard and snotter stained.

'Take it, son, Ah'll no say nothing,' pleaded the old guy, still staring at the wall.

'Just shut the fuck up, you,' shouted Scotch Brian. 'Now turn round slowly. Very fucking slowly,' and to help the man on he thrust the pistol barrel into his ribs. The old man's head was grazed where it had been shoved against the wall, his lip was bleeding where dislodged false teeth had cut, his penis was shrivelled with fear, a small one-eyed, wrinkled stub above his piss-drenched trousers. 'What you sniffing around for, ye bastard?' Scotch Brian was wiping the sweat from his eyes, having difficulty in seeing anything.

'Ah wisnae, son, Ah just came in a for a slash. Honest.' The old man was looking down the barrel of the massive pistol.

'Right, strip,' ordered Scotch Brian.

'Whit?'

'Fucking clothes off, NOW.'

Deadeye opened the toilet door to an unexpected sight. Sitting in the middle of the floor was an old man, stark naked, weeping, his hands under his buttocks, his clothes and bits and bobs scattered all around him. Scotch Brian hadn't heard the door for the waves crashing again in his skull, echoing and roaring, louder and louder. Oblivious to Deadeye's presence, Scotch Brian went on ripping up the old man's jacket, searching in the lining for the hidden gun he was convinced had to be there. Deadeye spotted the Magnum brandished in one of Scotch Brian's big fists and backed quietly out of the door.

'We've got a fucking serious problem,' Deadeye whispered into Maggie Small's fragrant ear, having chosen to go via her rather than risking Grimes' wrath by interrupting his chat with well-known faces. A short summary is all it took for Maggie to grasp the seriousness of the situation. A quiet word from her to Andy Grimes and the three of them were standing out in the car park having a crisis summit.

'Whit ye mean he's got a bazooka in there?' demanded Grimes, his incredulity mixed with anxiety.

'A Magnum. He's got a Dirty Harry special trained oan the old boy. If Brian starts shooting the fucking bullet will go straight through the old yin's body, right through the bog wall and kill some cunt or two sitting in the bar.' Deadeye's language was not technical but he knew his guns.

'Shiiiit.' Grimes was thinking fast and was finding no answer. It was the one area of business he couldn't seek Maggie Small's advice, though she stood there with them, an honorary member of every war cabinet.

'Ah was gonnae jump him, man, but if the fucking gun went off . . .' Deadeye didn't need to finish his sentence.

'Gonnae have tae try and get him oot o there,' concluded Grimes, stating the obvious.

'But how?' Deadeye asked, wary that Grimes would order him back into the toilet.

'Fuck knows,' spat Grimes, 'but we need tae get him oot o the bogs, oot o the pub and oot o ma hair.' Deadeye silently let the message sink in and Grimes continued, 'Sharpish. Fucking sharpish. Whit did that old cunt dae tae annoy Brian anyroads? Maybe we can just have a quiet word wi Brian and say it's a bit messy in the pub and offer tae take him tae a safer place tae kill the old fucker. Whit ye think?'

'Think that'll work?' Deadeye still suspected that he was going to be ordered to be the messenger and wanted to sustain the conference for as long as possible.

'Well, here's your chance to find out.' It was the first comment from Maggie Small since they convened in the car park.

'Whit?' asked Grimes, and in reply Maggie nodded towards the door of the pub. He saw the old guy first – grey faced, walking slowly, stiff legged. His arms were held away from his sides and he was barefoot, wearing only his trousers and shirt, the tails flapping in the breeze. Inches behind him walked Scotch Brian, his gun out of sight but his hand resting inside the left lapel of his double-breasted suit.

'Brian, how ye doing? Andy Grimes,' Grimes held out his hand.

'You're no Andy Grimes. Ah know Andy Grimes,' muttered Scotch Brian.

'We all change, Brian.' Grimes patted his substantial girth. 'Ah didnae recognise you either,' he lied.

'Ah'm really pleased you've agreed tae dae this wee job for us.' Grimes was keeping up a cheerful front but his legs were shaking, his fingers constantly clenching and unclenching. Scotch Brian looked perplexed, wiped some sweat from his face and the penny dropped.

'Yeah, the job. Aw, no problem. Happy to oblige.' As the two men spoke the old man stood between them ignored, visibly shaking, knees buckling, tears running from one eye.

'Should be arranged for tomorrow – is that okay?' asked Grimes.

'Tomorrow will be dandy,' replied Scotch Brian, ' but Ah've got a wee problem right now.' Scotch Brian prodded the old man in the back with his free left hand.

'So Ah see, ma man, has he been bothering you?' The old man then thought of saying something, what had he to lose? But terror had dried his throat, turning his mouth tacky and the words would not come. He was lucky.

'Bastard's been following me all day,' replied Scotch Brian.

'Bad business,' sympathised Grimes.

'But Ah know who's likely put him up to it.' Scotch Brian nodded sagely, sending a shower of sweat tumbling from his brow. 'And Ah'm going to fix this bastard good,' Scotch Brian patted the right breast of his jacket, 'as a wee message.'

'Catch yer drift,' replied Grimes, 'but tell ye, it's a wee bit public here.'

'Yeah,' agreed Scotch Brian, looking around at the cars and nearby main road.

'What say ye Ah get the boys tae take you and chummy here tae a more secluded spot?' Grimes' expression was friendly, collusive. 'A wee drive in the country?'

Scotch Brian silently considered the offer. 'Is it far?' he finally asked.

'Two or three miles,' replied Grimes. 'Why?'

'Ah've a little errand to run,' replied Scotch Brian, as if talking about going to the supermarket. 'Find myself a little short of my friend Charlie,' he explained. 'This little bastard caused me to spill some goodies in that shit house in there.'

'Ye wee fucker,' spat Grimes and slapped the old guy hard across the face. 'But listen, Brian, we can fix ye up wi Charlie, ma man. As much as ye need.'

'Is it good stuff?' Scotch Brian asked, a sceptical sour look on his face. In his detailed knowledge of the cocaine market he knew that much low-grade, adulterated powder was sold into Scotland. He knew because he shipped it north.

'The best Colombian,' replied Grimes cheerfully.

'Better be,' replied Scotch Brian.

'Oh, it is . . .'

'Or Ah'll do you, you fat bastard,' spat Scotch Brian. Grimes' face flushed. He wanted to scream to Deadeye to kill the insulting madman right there and then but he knew that he would be caught in the firing line and the first to go.

'Deadeye will see to it won't you, Deadeye?' Grimes turned away from Scotch Brian and stared at Deadeye, no smile on his face just plain anger and hate.

'Sure, boss, Ah'll take care o whatever Brian needs,' replied Deadeye nodding curtly at Grimes.

'Good man, take a couple of the boys with you. Just the ones that are HANDY, eh?' Deadeye nodded curtly again, message received loud and clear.

The old man's blubbering was the only sound above the purr of the Mercedes engine as the car cruised through the concrete wasteland of Easterhouse and onto a single-track country road.

'Is that the burn where that kid drowned the wee nipper?' asked the driver as the car crossed a small bridge.

'Ah'm no sure,' replied the man in the front passenger seat, 'was that no Drummie? Or was it Castlemilk?'

'Shut it,' ordered Deadeye and silence was immediately restored.

The old guy was in the back, wedged between Scotch Brian and Deadeye. When Grimes had seen the state of the old boy's urine-soaked trousers he had ordered him to take them off and cover himself with a black bin bag bearing the legend of the local council. It was the type distributed for the disposal of rubbish. Business was business, but Grimes wasn't going to risk his nice leather seats being stained or left with that acidic stink. The car slowed down and turned onto a rough road hewn through a field by a builder's crew, turned off again and came to a gentle stop beside a copse of trees.

Scotch Brian pulled the Magnum from its holster and edged backwards out of the car.

'Right, you, get the fuck out of there,' he ordered the old man, waving the gun at him. The old man edged slowly, reluctantly, over the car seat, his flesh producing wet squeaky, sticky noises against the leather on account that he'd wet himself again.

'Take him a good bit into the trees,' shouted Deadeye. 'Ye get they mental ramblers and farming types coming doon this road.'

Scotch Brian prodded the old guy in the back, pushing him forward, walking behind him, his gun trained on the old man's skull. The old guy's bare feet caught on stones and thorns and his progress was slow. He knew he was going to die and he tried to think of a prayer, a love poem to his dead wife, wishes for his grandchildren, something significant. But all he could hear was the nearby roar of traffic from some hidden road and all he could think of was that he was going to die.

'Right, you, this'll do,' ordered Scotch Brian. They hadn't walked far into the small wood but the sweats were on Brian again and that loud swishing noise was back in his head. He just wanted to kill the old man and go off and get a fix. Scotch Brian looked down and saw that he had stood deep in a cow pat, slimy green shit covering one shoe.

'Fuck!' he shouted and lifted the gun against the back of the man's head. When the first shot rang out the old guy collapsed, a blanket of blackness creeping over him. He never heard the other three shots.

When the old guy came to he first saw the base of the tree trunks and then he saw them – digging his grave. They were going to bury him alive. He had somehow survived and they were going to dump him in some hole in the middle of nowhere. There was no pain but he'd read somewhere that the more powerful the gun, the less the victim felt. He had thought that was rubbish but it must be true because he felt nothing and his right leg and arm wouldn't move. That was it then, shot down the right side. He closed his eyes tight, in case they noticed, and wondered what to do.

'Oy, you. Old yin, Ah'm speaking tae yese.' Someone was shaking him roughly but still he kept his eyes shut, playing dead. 'Come oan, man, it's time tae split. If ye dinnae waken up we'll leave ye here. Ye'll catch yer death o cold lying there.' Was this a trick? But then why bother, they could just shoot him again. Somebody started slapping his face.

'Aw right, for Christ's sake, leave us alane,' the old boy grumbled, stirring into a half-sitting position.

'Think that mad bastard's dead?' Deadeye was asking one of the men digging into the wet, peaty ground.

'Ye fucking shot him four times,' the digger answered. Scotch Brian was lying in a crumpled heap with half his body on top of the old man's right leg and forearm. In the fast fading light the old man could make out that Scotch Brian's eyes were closed but his mouth gaped wide open. The old guy lost it.

'Ye big fucking arsehole,' he screamed, punching and kicking out at Scotch Brian, 'come oan then. No so fucking big now, are yese, ye piece o shite.'

'Ho, cut it oot, wee man,' shouted the man who'd been driving, 'show some respect for the deid, eh?' And the group laughed, even Deadeye, who took the shovel from the digger's hand, lifted it above his head and smashed it down on Scotch Brian's face – twice.

'That'll be him deid now then,' said Deadeye handing the shovel back. 'Chuck him in, eh, that's deep enough.'

'Ye sure?' said the grave digger.

'Aye, and throw some leaves and branches on top,' replied Deadeye. 'Nae cunt comes oot here. Besides it's getting dark, man.'

Driving back through the schemes, the old man's nerves finally broke and his relieved weeping could hardly be heard above the jovial, relieved post-job banter of the three murderers.

'Nae wonder you're greeting, old yin,' offered the driver. 'You've got tae explain tae Andy Grimes about pishing in his car.'

13 SEPTEMBER 1989

I was right, I still hate funerals. The Grimes' one was more interesting than most though. Every street face in the city in attendance, even some of Grimes' sworn enemies. Why is it they do that, then the next day are plotting to kill each other again?

As soon as he started bawling out I knew it was Scotch Brian. It's my business to know important faces and he is one. A top hitman for decades. A mean player on the streets of Manchester where even brave men wilt. He and Grimes used to run together when they were young, so folk will think he just came up to pay his respects.

Scotch Brian didn't look too healthy. Appears to have lost a screw or got a serious drug problem. He always was dangerous, he'll be lethal and unpredictable now. But less for me to bother about I think. Ten years ago it would have been a worry to be chased by Scotch Brian but now, well, let's hope I'm right.

A

SINGING THE WRONG SONG

'Taken care of?' Grimes was sitting behind his desk in The Cat's Whiskers late, sometime before midnight on the day of his brother's funeral.

'Aye, no problem, boss,' Deadeye replied.

'The stiff hidden safe?'

'Middle of nowhere,' replied Deadeye, knowing better than to relate the exact whereabouts of Scotch Brian's body. This was one of the perks Grimes insisted on for paying the wages – lack of incriminating knowledge on many of the crimes he ordered. His hand had never touched a bag of coke or heroin. He often passed a sociable hour at a club his men were holding to ransom for a weekly pay-off. He never paid any of the under-age hookers he used and abused regularly. He left those business transactions, procurement and payment, to Maggie Small, just like he was now leaving the entire responsibility of Scotch Brian's murder with Deadeye Kirkpatrick.

'Good, good, and the old guy?' asked Grimes, setting Deadeye wondering if his boss had developed some compassion in his old age.

'Aye, a bit shook up but fine.'

'Is he still walking and talking? You fucking daft? Whit if he opens his gob?' Grimes' mood had changed instantly as it was wont to do.

'Aw, ah dinnae think he'll dae that . . . too shook up,' Deadeye had read this one entirely wrong. Then again, Grimes hadn't sent him any hidden verbal messages on the old guy, like describing the men he should take with him as being 'handy' meant that they should be carrying arms.

'See tae it.'

'Boss, Ah . . .'

'Fucking see tae it. NOW,' Grimes roared.

Deadeye knew the score. Follow orders or leave the team. And if you left the team don't start reading any long books – you'd not have the time left alive to finish them. He felt the weight of his booty, the Magnum, pulling hard against the waistband of his trousers. Poor old sod was going to get it after all. And to think that when they'd dropped him off at his house, a corrugated-iron windowed council flat in the Priesthill scheme, the old guy had recovered his nerve and was thanking them all profusely. Shaking their hands, offering them money, trying to make arrangements to give them a night out on him. Last thing he promised was to pay the valet cost of the pish-stained back seat of the Merc before he turned and tottered up the wrecked close wearing nothing but his shirt and a black bin-bag kilt.

'Move yer arse, you. Every second is a risk,' shouted Grimes. Deadeye turned and dragged his feet out of the office. This was one job he wasn't going to enjoy.

As Deadeye walked through the club, the festivities were reaching an end for the night, the licensing arrangements recently being restricted by the council due to complaints of street fights and drunkenness. They were restrictions that Grimes was working on and would soon see lifted, though the fighters and boozed-up punters continued to hit the street unabated. At the door of the club Deadeye met Birse and Jeannie Stirk coming in.

'Cheers, Gerry,' Birse greeted him but Deadeye didn't answer, just kept walking on by into the street. 'Fucking don't speak then,' Birse muttered. Then to Jeannie, 'Strange one that. Never know how you're gonnae find him.'

Jeannie wondered exactly how friendly her boss was with the patrons of the club and made a note to ascertain the identity of the sullen-faced young man. Inside the club, in spite of being on duty, Birse ordered a large whisky for himself and orange juice for Jeannie, the driver for the night. The drinks were brought over by the most striking, beautiful woman Jeannie Stirk had seen in a long time outside of Hollywood movies and glam mag shots of models.

'Maggie Small – Detective Constable Jeannie Stirk,' Birse said by way of introductions. The two women shook hands. Jeannie felt smooth silk purses, smelled vanilla and musk and looked up into large, green eyes smiling down at her. 'Jeannie's just moved through from Edinburgh, Maggie, Ah'm showing her the ropes, that sort of thing.'

'Hope he's treating you well, Jeannie,' smiled Maggie, 'if not, just you let me know.' Maggie Small leaned over and stroked the back of Jeannie's hand conspiratorially, 'I'll tell the boys where he lives.' Maggie Small delivered a stage wink in Jeannie's direction as Birse laughed. It was the first time Jeannie Stirk had heard her new gaffer laugh and his deep-toned boom sounded forced, out of place with the rest of what she did know of the man.

'Ah'm looking for a favour, Maggie,' Birse said.

'Nothing new there then,' replied Maggie. Jeannie liked her – a woman who oozed confidence and stood up for herself with relaxed ease.

'Have tae have a wee word wi Andy. Just some old business like,' Birse continued.

'A talk about the football and a couple of brandies more like,' Maggie Small said with a sly grin.

'Well, if he's offering. But Ah wondered if Ah could leave Jeannie in your capable hands for a wee while.'

'Sure, delighted, we're closing up anyway,' replied Maggie.

'You're a star. Is he free the now?' asked Birse.

'Yeah, think he's waiting to see you,' replied Maggie, remembering Grimes' angry outburst earlier in the evening about Birse having to come up with the goods and pronto.

'Ah'll go right in then, eh?' replied Birse. 'Half an hour tops.'

'Take your time,' said Maggie as Grimes came out of his office and waved angrily for Birse to follow him. 'I'm sure we'll be just fine.' Jeannie Stirk wasn't so confident.

Inside his office, Grimes was fuming. What a day he'd had. Burying his brother whose killer still walked free. Having to have his hired hitman hit. Now this old geezer had to be seen to and Deadeye clearly a reluctant party for once. Next he was expecting Birse to come barging in with information on who and where Addison was. If he did, what could Grimes do now? No hitman, Deadeye away in the huff and no other team member he could trust with putting this Addison guy down. No matter how angry Grimes was with Addison, he understood well enough that the man couldn't have survived anonymously this long without being good, very good. No, he'd need to get a top man to take care of him. Birse knocked on the open office door and went straight in slamming it behind him.

'Andy, Ah'm sorry,' Birse started off even before he reached the desk.

'Sorry for whit?' Grimes asked, genuinely perplexed.

'Ah've let you down, man, and Ah'm sorry,' Birse eased himself into the big chair across from Grimes.

'You mean . . . ?'

'Not a sign of him. That lassie Cathy Brodie will no tell us a fucking thing even if Ah pulled her teeth oot one by one,' said Birse, starting to explain himself.

'Naw, Ah know,' nodded Grimes, 'but ye could have some fun trying though, eh?' He grinned across his desk at Birse.

'Aw, Ah've no forgotten aboot her. Ah'm gonnae go back when the time is, eh, right.'

'So, you've done sweet FA, as usual.' Grimes was getting into role.

'Naw, naw. Ah've followed up a better lead – your suggestion aboot that Joe Murphy.'

'Now yer talking.' Grimes leaned over the table pouring brandy into two goblets knowing Birse wanted the drink without having to ask.

'Reckon the way to Murphy is through his wee nyaff of a sidekick,' said Birse, grimacing as he took his first swallow of the brandy.

'Feckless fucking Fergie, aye,' Grimes nodded.

'So, Ah'm thinking o setting a wee honey trap up for him,' said Birse, raising his eyes. 'New lassie, dead keen tae impress. She'd better impress or her arse is back in a beat uniform, right.'

'Like it, so when?' Grimes asked.

'That's just the thing. She's just new, it's gonnae take a couple of weeks.' Birse waited for the onslaught.

'TWO FUCKING WEEKS?' roared Grimes so loudly he could be heard over the sound system in the bar playing 'Moon Over Bourbon Street' just because one of the barmen liked Sting's music and all the paying customers had gone. Then in a lowered voice, 'Ah've paid for a top man tae be in the city like now and you're telling me Ah'll have tae wait two fucking weeks and maybe, only maybe then, if it fucking works and Murphy is our man and he's daft enough tae tell that wee cunt Fergie.'

Grimes' face was scarlet, a blue vein pulsed at his temple. But inside his head he was trying to think of who else he could hire who could be in Glasgow in a fortnight now that Scotch Brian was clearly out of the game. Sure as hell he wasn't going to admit to Birse that he'd contracted the drug-crazed madman, never mind arranging for the same man to be killed. That would be embarrassing. In Grimes' world a lot of power came from reputation and he wasn't about to lose face with Birse. No sir. He, Andy Grimes, was the chief honcho. A fortnight – plenty of time to arrange a new hitman. Grimes' thoughts were interrupted by Birse's radio going off.

'Fuck, thought Ah'd switched that off,' Birse cursed then answered it, relieved to have some diversion from Grimes' fury. 'Where?' Birse said into the radio. 'You're joking. Fucking hell. A whit? Fuck sake. The Royal, right. Be there shortly. Aye, something else to see to first, half an hour.' Birse switched the radio off and turned to Grimes and smiled.

'Whit?' Grimes demanded, his brow still marked with his feigned anger.

'You know anything about a man, early fifties, kinda English accent, carrying a shoulder holster, wearing a bullet-proof fucking vest, a wee .22 strapped to his ankle, his body caked in mud and both feet clarted in cow dung?' Birse smiled as he ended the question.

'Whit is this, a fucking riddle?' Grimes glowered back at him.

'Naw, a road traffic accident report,' Birse smiled.

'Stop acting the wise cunt,' Grimes growled.

'A polis car has just run over Scotch Brian staggering across the M8.' Birse was grinning now.

'Scotch who?' Grimes persisted with his act of ignorance.

'The fucker Ah first arrested as a beat cop when he was a teenage razor merchant. The Mosside hitman. The fucker that was at the funeral the day. The man you hired tae kill Addison.' Birse's look told Grimes that he wasn't born yesterday, that he'd recognised Scotch Brian at first glance, that Grimes should come clean.

'Aw, him,' Grimes answered quietly.

'Aye, HIM,' Birse said with a flourish.

'Cunt's meant tae be wasted,' Grimes swallowed the remnants of his brandy.

'Well, he's alive and kicking and in the Royal Infirmary,' Birse informed him.

'Fuck's sake.' Grimes held his head in his hands. 'Whit next?'

'Ah know, Andy, Ah know,' Birse sympathised while struggling to stop himself from laughing, 'ye just cannae get the staff these days.' Jeannie found herself uncharacteristically tongue-tied, feeling embarrassed and gauche. Not just because Maggie Small was the perfect host with a comprehensive repertoire of chit-chat she succeeded in conveying as interesting and pleasant but also because Jeannie couldn't remember a single word of the conversation. Yet that's why she was there – to collect information.

'You're useless,' Jeannie Stirk chided herself, 'you're meant to be the one befriending her not the other way around. Acting like a teenager with a crush.' Maggie held the conversation going, showing no obvious sign of boredom. Jeannie Stirk knew well enough that, if you were skilled, what you showed did not necessarily reflect what you felt. She brushed at non-existent fluff on the shoulder of her trouser suit – one of several she had as standard work clothes – utilitarian enough but plain, sexless and dowdy. Jeannie Stirk felt under-dressed sitting next to Maggie Small in her strapless black evening gown with the thigh-high split.

'I'm sorry, Jeannie, but I have something to see to with the girls before they go,' said Maggie.

'Oh, of course, don't let me get in your way, please,' Jeannie replied.

'You can come with me if you want,' Maggie offered. 'It won't take long.'

Two minutes later, Jeannie Stirk was standing behind Maggie Small on the raised stage of the club. The club's working girls filed on looking tired and sullen, though each displayed a beauty of a very different form – blondes, brunettes and redheads; voluptuous, pert and statuesque – and all appeared next to naked.

Jeannie worked out that they had each been developing new routines and had been given new costumes. This was the final touch and Maggie had the final say before the acts started the following day. Maggie approached the first girl in the line and, without warning, reached out and yanked at her low, fake fur neckline. The woman's costume was left dangling from Maggie's hand and the blonde stood there smiling in nothing more than a glittery, string thong.

'Perfect,' Maggie smiled, 'well done.' With that approval the woman took her outfit from Maggie and half skipped, half ran off the stage, going home at last.

When Maggie turned to the full-figured brunette with the chalk-white skin, bored face and Oriental eyes, there was a problem. Her mandarin outfit didn't quite fit her on the bust, or so Maggie thought. The velcro strips at the back were undone and the girl stood with her breasts exposed as Maggie tried to get the top half of the costume to fit better. As she manoeuvred the silky, transparent material, her hands smoothed over the woman's breasts several times causing her nipples to rise and become taut. Neither Maggie nor the dancer seemed at all nonplussed by the intimacy. Jeannie could feel the heat of a blush and told herself it was just their work, nothing beyond the boundaries of normal behaviour. That whatever anyone thought about strip acts or lap dancing, to the performers it was just show business. Jeannie was losing the argument with herself to her overwhelming curiosity of what it would feel like if it was her with Maggie's hands on her breasts instead of the brunette.

'Stirk, we've got tae go . . . NOW,' Birse shouted as he marched into the club.

'Maggie . . . thanks . . . I . . . I've . . .' Jeannie stuttered. A tinkle of laughter came from Maggie Small and a full-lipped smile. She took Jeannie by the arm and led her away from the earwigging group of women.

At the edge of the stage, Maggie whispered into Jeannie's ear, 'It was a pleasure. Come again when you're not working.'

Flustered, Jeannie Stirk stepped back and took Maggie firmly by the hand, shaking it vigorously while saying in a loud voice, 'Thank you for your hospitality. Hope I wasn't too much trouble,' before stepping smartly off behind Birse and straight out of the door. Maggie stood, the picture of sophisticated charm and ladylike beauty, and smiled to herself till the two cops had left the club.

Turning sharply she marched straight up to Suzie with a zed. 'What the fuck do you call that?' she demanded and didn't wait for an answer. 'You're meant to start erotic and end up obscene – not the other way around.' She pulled Suzie's schoolgirl gymslip outfit off her. 'Might as well shove your fanny in their faces.' She hooked her fingers into the girl's G-string and ripped it off. 'There, what do you think, girls?' The other women giggled. 'Think we should make Suzie dance like this?' Suzie with a zed said nothing and didn't move. She listened to the other women laughing at her and kept her eyes on Maggie Small's perfectly made-up face. Suddenly, Suzie ran to the silver pole rising from the centre of the stage. She leapt high, grabbed the bar with both hands, swinging round. As she turned to face the women, she twisted her mouth and eyes grotesquely and opened her legs wide – getting lower and lower and lower till she was sitting on the stage, legs splayed, face contorted.

'Obscene enough for yese, Maggie?' Suzie pouted. The women were laughing with her, making crude remarks. Maggie Small walked across to where the girl was sitting on the floor and said, 'Nice pussy, pussy,' and stroked Suzie's hair. In an urgent tone, 'Right, move your butt over here. Now that the filth has left let's discuss the important business.'

The women, including the naked Suzie, gathered round Maggie

listening to her every word. 'Who's free tomorrow night, we need two?' asked Maggie. Half the women raised a hand. 'It's a group, private party, girl-on-girl show then the full works.' The women's hands stayed raised. 'A twenty-first party. Still too old for you, Suzie.' The women laughed. 'It pays forty each and half of whatever else you might raise on the night.' All hands stayed up. 'Okay, you two,' Maggie pointed to the bored-looking brunette and Suzie.

'Yeeeeess,' hissed Suzie and the others giggled.

'Just one thing, Suzie,' said Maggie, her face back to its habitual stern expression, 'cheat me and you'll not work again and maybe not walk either.' Suzie frowned and said nothing. 'Right,' Maggie continued, addressing the entire company, 'that's all the specials for tonight.' Some of the women grumbled in complaint at the lack of business. It was the kind of motivation that Maggie liked in her girls. Hungry for cash they made good, reliable workers as long as she kept them busy. 'Don't worry,' she interrupted, 'there's still something for everyone.' The women went quiet and listened to Maggie. 'We've had a special order on credit cards.' Mumbles of approval. 'A regular customer has upped his order,' continued Maggie. The regular customer was Joe Murphy, but the women would never know his identity as far as Maggie was concerned. Just because Joe and Grimes had had words recently and may end up at war, that was no reason to stop the trade.

Joe had a scam going whereby he employed a team of people to use stolen credit cards to obtain goods and cash. It was a good, low-risk earner and he was extending the operation. Maggie ran girls who worked as prostitutes as well as strippers. Who better to supply the cards? It was an arrangement of convenience, a business agreement from which both benefitted. Grimes knew all about the deal, of course, the payments contributing a small but steady flow into his income.

'The usual terms,' Maggie went on, 'twenty quid a standard card and we'll look at anything special like platinum.' The women were chattering, all happy at the prospect of some extra earnings. All except Suzie, who was quietly questioning the price to be paid. Surely the cards were worth hundreds, maybe more. If she had shared her thoughts aloud the other women would have told her not to be so stupid. Punters rarely admitted that their wallets had been stolen by a prostitute and cashing in on the cards was the big risk – a risk they did not have to take. It was easy, safe money.

'REMEMBER,' Maggie shouted above the rising din, 'take other items as well – driving licences, library tickets, bus passes, passports – anything with ID. You'll get paid by the customer.'

The women were nodding, eager to be seen by their boss to be receiving her instructions loud and clear. A few of the women went to stroll away from the group believing that the briefing session was over. 'AND,' shouted Maggie, 'only work the patches I've allocated. Anybody found freelancing will be in big trouble.' As she made this final warning, Maggie stared at Suzie and Suzie frowned back, resentful of the more powerful woman who seemed to be able to read her mind.

At that the office door banged and Maggie turned to see Grimes fully coated up and standing in the middle of the club.

'Got a wee bit business, Maggie,' he shouted. 'Might no be back. You okay tae lock up?'

Maggie nodded and asked, 'Anything I can help with?'

'No, no, just going to see an old friend. Besides, Ah fancy an early night.' Grimes waved and headed for the door. Maggie got the message and wondered who was in trouble now.

Birse directed Jeannie Stirk as she drove the dark streets of Glasgow's city centre. Either the place changed its character at night or Birse was taking her down all the back roads, she decided, not recognising anywhere. Between instructions, Birse briefed her on what they were travelling to.

'Some stupid wanker's got himself run doon oan the motorway.' Jeannie was thinking of Maggie Small. 'Apparently he just came staggering oot onto the road.' She had never lost it at work before, never let sexual attraction get between her and work. 'Only chooses a fucking polis motor tae run intae.' Then again she'd never met Maggie Small before. 'Thing is there's a few irregularities aboot the guy's, eh, appearance. Probably just some spaced-oot copper's imagination.' Long fingers, with red nails on white breasts. 'An somebody thinks he looks familiar but cannae place him.' Soft silk purses of palms. 'These fucking guys aw want tae be Colombo annat. Closest they'll get is tae lose an eye – if they're lucky.' Vanilla and musk. 'So how did ye get oan wi Maggie then?' Green, green eyes and red, red lips. 'Jeannie, Ah said how did ye get oan wi Maggie?'

'Eh, sorry, what?' she said, feeling herself blush at Birse's intervention in her daydreams.

'Fuck sakes, you aw right?'

'Yeah, fine . . . just a little . . . you know . . . it's been . . . well . . .' She wanted to say delicious but needed to find something sober, serious and it wasn't going to be 'a long day'. No way, that's what they all wanted to hear about women cops. Too weak to take the pace and besides she was wide awake, too awake.

'Well, how did ye get oan wi Maggie then?' Irritation had entered Birse's voice and she found it strangely reassuring.

'Fine, fine. Just made small talk, you know,' she replied, lying through her teeth.

'Nothing interesting then?' Birse asked and she resented it. He hadn't told her yet what was supposed to be interesting to the police about Maggie Small.

'No, just took it gently,' she replied, now back in the real world. 'Like you said, befriend her. Girls' talk that's all.' She told the truth and acknowledged to herself that she wanted more than just talk. Jeannie Stirk knew she was in big trouble.

'Smart girl. Well done, they stupid university graduate fast-trackers would be jumping in, grilling the target like something oot o the fucking Inquisition. Smart girl. Patience, Ah like that.'

They were driving through what was obviously an old part of the city. The dark shapes of off-centre, old-world buildings could be seen through the drizzle and something bigger, looming. Jeannie reckoned correctly they were in the east end of the city centre near the cathedral.

'Pull in here,' Birse suddenly shouted. 'Never mind the signs, we're polis.' Jeannie steered the car into an accident and emergency ambulances-only bay. What she had taken as the cathedral turned out to be the Royal Infirmary and she was glad, hoping that the cathedral had more beauty, more majesty. Even through the dark, the Royal appeared threatening, evil and spooky as well as ancient. 'Listen,' said Birse, 'there's no need for you tae hang around. Just knock off for the night. Ye must be knackered.'

'No, really, I'm fine. I'll come in with you,' Jeannie insisted.

'Tell ye the truth,' Birse said solicitously lowering his tone, 'Ah think this is gonnae be a big waste o time and, eh, Ah'm knocking off as well shortly.' He coughed and winked. 'Have a wee, eh, personal rendezvous arranged, if ye catch ma drift.'

Jeannie Stirk was so taken aback by Birse apparently confiding in her that he had a personal life outside the police that she was still sitting in the car when he was already marching through the hospital reception area. She steered the car out into the traffic and turned right, a smile across her face, happy at the prospect of some uninterrupted thinking time. Dreaming time. Maggie Small time. She'd deal with the complications tomorrow.

One uniformed policeman stood guard in the corridor.

'You oan yersel?' barked Birse, all hustle and bustle, bringing the outside cold in on his coat.

'Aye, sir,' the young cop stood erect, at attention, face forward.

'Got a fucking green one here,' mused Birse.

'There's another officer being sent oan, sir, it's just that they're down troops at the station and it's been a bit hectic – trouble in the city centre,' the young copper rushed his words out in one breath. Only a few months in uniform, he recognised Birse from the TV, now here he was in person turning up on his shift.

'Right, son, let the dog see the rabbit.' Birse walked straight past the cop and opened the ward door. Two doctors in white coats were working on the patient and a nurse was busy messing around with mysterious-looking machines attached to the bed by a crazed set of tubes and wires. But for the quiet voices of the trio the room was silent, yet at the same time full of action. Birse found the scene discordant, somehow unreal, unnerving. One of the doctors turned to Birse.

'You're not supposed to be in here,' he said politely but firmly. He was a young black man, the ebony skin of his face shining with health though his eyes were weary, worn out.

'DCI Birse,' Birse replied as if that would be enough.

'Prove it.' The black doctor had turned again to his patient, adjusting a tube in his mouth.

'DCI Birse,' Birse repeated but this time having fished his ID out of his pocket, holding it open towards the bed.

The young doctor glanced quickly over his shoulder before turning back to his patient and saying, 'Good, but you're still not meant to be in here. This patient is critical.' Birse ignored him and edged closer to the bottom of the bed. The man in the bed looked grey faced, lifeless, the skin hanging loosely from broad cheeks and his mouth held open by some gadget. The rigmarole would have made his own mother difficult to identify but clocking people was Birse's job. It was Scotch Brian all right.

'Look, I said . . .' the young black doctor started, only to be stopped by his colleague with little more than a sympathetic look.

'You finish here, okay?' she said quietly. 'I'll talk to the DCI, brief him on the details the police need to know.' The young man sighed and smiled at her, nodding, accepting. In the bright lights of the green-painted corridor, Birse saw that she too was young. Long, sandy fair hair tied loosely off her face. Pale skin, peach complexion. Blue eyes that a man could fall for. Yet her face was drawn and pinched. Exhausted. 'Please forgive Ola, DCI Birse,' she started. 'It's been a while since he's had a break.'

'How long?' Birse asked.

'Yesterday morning,' she replied in a matter-of-fact tone. 'The long hours, well, you never quite get used to them.'

'God save me from falling ill in Glasgow,' Birse thought. 'Ye get treated by sleep-starved kids.'

'The patient?' Birse asked, walking alongside the doctor who seemed to be taking him somewhere.

'Identity not established. He was speaking when the ambulance picked him up but just gibberish from what they could gather.' She pushed open a door marked FIRE EXIT and Birse followed her out on to a metal platform from which stairs zigzagged down to the back of the hospital.

'Did the ambulance guys tell ye what the gibberish was – could be meaningful tae us,' he asked.

'Phew,' she sighed, drawing in a deep breath of the damp night air, 'not much, except he kept asking for someone called Charlie. The paramedics kept asking him who Charlie was but he didn't answer. Probably couldn't hear them let alone understand.' The young female doctor flipped back one side of her white coat and from a pocket at the side of her skirt brought a crumpled packet of cigarettes and a lighter.

'Probably just a relative or nothing at all,' Birse lied while lighting the woman's cigarette. 'So what sort of state is he in now?'

'Not good.' She inhaled the smoke deep into her lungs. 'A broken leg, a few ribs, two bones in his left hand and severe bruising all over, especially on his chest. Strangely, he's got all the standard multiple bruising he would get from being run over except on his chest and back where he was protected by the bullet-proof vest. It's the first time I've seen one of those – maybe I should get one for my shifts on the casualty ward on a Saturday night.' The doctor smiled at Birse.

'Ah'm sure nobody would want tae hurt a good-looking lassie like you, doc,' he smiled back and she took the comment as a harmless compliment, just grateful to be having a break away from the endless round of patients.

'But on his back, it's strange,' she continued, 'there are three very deep, distinctive bruises and a similar one on his chest. Like someone had hit him with the sharp end of a heavy pick.' The doctor looked at the starless night sky and dragged on her cigarette, allowing the information to sink in.

'Aye, weird one right enough,' said Birse who had worked out exactly what those bruises were.

'But the worst is the damage to his skull. He must have rolled in a strange way when the police car hit him,' she said.

'How's that?' asked Birse.

'He's got serious damage to the front of his skull as well as here at the top.' The doctor demonstrated with her hand and her own head where Scotch Brian's injuries were. 'It's like two separate accidents,' she sighed. 'He's got some unspecific brain damage and that's the bottom line.'

'Brain damage?' Birse was relieved that she had reached the important details without his impatience interfering and egging him on to push her – an approach he was sure would do nothing but make her back off. 'You mean he's going to die?'

'Who knows?' she replied. 'He's in a coma. Look, you know the way it always is on the crappy television programmes and in the films? Major character slips into coma, still looks good but he or she's in a coma? Nobody knows if or when they're going to come out of it?'

'Aye,' Birse added, 'and there's always a good-looking saint-like doctor who never gives up on them.'

'That's the one,' she giggled. 'I'm always criticising that plot line. It's unrealistic, uncommon and the portrayal of the doctors . . . well.'

'Seems true enough tae me,' Birse smiled and she smiled back.

'Just in this case, that's exactly the state the patient is in . . . except he'll never look like a Hollywood star again.'

'No loss there then,' thought Birse, 'Scotch Brian was always an ugly bastard.'

'How long you think he's gonnae be out of it?' Birse was holding open the door as they re-entered the disinfectant stink of the green corridors. In response she pulled him a face which asked if he had been listening at all. 'Sorry, doc, Ah have tae ask ye what yer best guess is.'

'Well, there's something else wrong,' she conceded. 'He's not responding to the medication. Has the typical responses of a problematic heroin addict but has no other signs: track marks, poor body weight . . . I don't think his chances are good.' They were approaching the naive new cop still standing at attention as the black doctor and the nurse wheeled a clattering trolley out of the ward. 'We all done, Ola?' she asked.

'Yeah,' Ola answered with a weary smile, 'done as much as we can.'

'Thanks, doc.' Birse shook the young woman's hand.

'What for?' she asked.

'Using plain English to this ignorant polis,' he smiled. When the medical staff had moved on to their next emergency, Birse turned to the uniformed policeman, 'Couple o things, son,' he started in an officious tone. 'First, Ah'm off tae make a phone call and, second, for Christ sakes relax – it's gonnae be a long boring shift.'

Returning from his sortie to the public phone box, Birse was reduced to ordering the young cop to go to the canteen for a break.

'For fuck's sake, son, dae ye think Ah'm no capable o guarding a guy in a fucking coma?' he glowered at the cop.

'No, sir. Of course not, sir. It's just, sir, I'll wait for my relief due any minute now,' the young policeman insisted.

'Relief!' Birse laughed out loud. 'You think they're gonnae send someone else so's the two o yese can guard an unconscious bloke that hasnae even committed a crime – that we know of? You fucking daft, son?' Off the cop went with strict instructions not to return sooner than half an hour. Andy Grimes was waiting by the door of the canteen when the uniform cop turned up. Watching the blue serge suit disappear, Grimes headed towards Birse and Scotch Brian.

'You sure he's in a coma?' demanded Grimes of Birse as they stood staring down at Scotch Brian's prostrate form.

'Naw, Ah think he's playing deid,' Birse drawled back. 'Whit's it fucking look like tae you?'

'Like he's fucking sleeping,' said Grimes, staring at Scotch Brian as if trying to suss him out.

'Aye, you sleep wi tubes up yer arse and wired tae the mains dae ye?'

'It's just . . .'

'Look, Andy, the doctors have said, man, no me. Ah just jail the shite – they fix them up.'

'Still, maybe Ah should make sure.' Grimes looked at the machinery surrounding Scotch Brian's bed, searching for the plug that was keeping him alive. The switch they switch off when the patient was beyond all hope. Grimes searched and couldn't see one. Birse read his thoughts.

'No fucking way, Andy,' he hissed. 'Ah'm oan duty here and the fucking Lone Ranger doon in the canteen is incapable o lying – catch ma drift?' Birse leaned out and gripped Grimes by the arm to emphasise his point.

'Aye,' mumbled Grimes. 'Right. But ye sure he's zonked an no just playing at it?'

'Andy, what else can Ah say?' replied Birse, exasperation echoing in his voice. 'Doc reckons he'll be oot for a good long while and maybe no live.' Grimes was half listening while searching along the edge of his coat lapel for something. 'Doc reckons he'll no be a well man IF he survives,' continued Birse, fully aware that he was exaggerating what the doctor had said. But it could be right. Whatever happened, no way did he want Grimes to start panicking now – not over some guy in a coma.

Grimes had pulled a long hatpin from his lapel and was looking at Scotch Brian trying to make a decision. 'Like maybe he'll no be able to walk, or feed himself, wipe his arse or even speak,' Birse explained. 'What the fuck?' Birse spotted the hatpin in Grimes' hand.

'Proof,' Grimes explained pulling back the bedclothes. 'Just need some proof.'

Grimes peeled back the material covering Scotch Brian's groin, lifted the prone man's penis up and shoved the hatpin into the nearest testicle. Birse grimaced and felt his anus tighten. Scotch Brian didn't budge.

'That's oot o fucking order, man,' exclaimed Birse.

'How?' asked Grimes, genuinely perplexed. 'Nae cunt'll notice a hatpin mark doon there.'

'Right enough,' conceded Birse.

'Ye say he might kick it?' Grimes sought confirmation.

'So the doc reckoned.'

'Let's hope,' Grimes nodded, 'but if he comes to. Wakens up . . .'

'Ye'll be the first to know,' Birse said in a sing-song voice.

Jeannie Stirk was lost and didn't care. Her knowledge of Glasgow streets was bad enough anyway, but at night, in an unfamiliar area and with

Maggie Small on her mind – disastrous. She'd turned right, heading up through Royston, past Blackhill, wound her way round Ruchazie and on to the motorway leading out of town. Soon she realised her error – the signposts for Edinburgh and Carlisle being a big giveaway. But she didn't care and decided to go for a straight, fast drive to a soundtrack of blaring music, the way she enjoyed driving. The car stereo seemed incapable of picking up anything other than Radio Clyde on which the late-night DJ was playing songs for lovers or broken hearts, there not being much difference between the two. Not her taste usually but tonight she didn't mind. By the time she had found a cut-off and turned back towards the city, Jeannie was singing along with the country-and-western love dirges, the soppy ballads and howling the blues.

At last she found herself back where she started. Now she stood a chance of finding her way home. Stopped at some lights near the Royal Infirmary, her mood was still melancholy enough to join in with Perry Como, asking his lover to lay her head upon his pillow.

Jeannie was holding the last note longer and stronger than Perry when she spotted Birse in a minicab crossing the junction to her far right. Who could miss that big ruddy face and shock of white hair even at that distance at night? Birse was sitting in the passenger seat having an animated discussion with someone in the back. Jeannie giggled, wondering if the person was his secret rendezvous and peered through the dark to try and catch a glimpse.

Andy Grimes' angry profile sailed past her and away. What the hell was Birse up to? If he and Grimes were in cahoots where did that put her and Maggie Small?

Jeannie was still contemplating the questions when startled by the blast of a car horn behind her. The lights had turned green. Maggie Small had been given her rightful place again. From now on Maggie Small was strictly work.

29 SEPTEMBER 1989

It's not like me to act on a whim but I've been following an American guy round town.

Americans in Glasgow come with cameras slung round their necks, plaid trousers and wallets stuffed with travellers cheques. This bloke has none of the trappings and is certainly travelling economy. Or rather staying economy because he isn't moving. Cooped up in McLean's Hotel, more the kind of place you find homeless people. Slinks out at night usually and ends up in locations you expect to find low-level street players, working girls, ten quid bag smack dealers. No harm in that, but this guy looks like a player and he's been trying to see Grimes. Why? Anything to do with him has got to be illegal. No harm in that. But why should this outsider seek him out? How does he know about him in the first place? He's got to be a player with some deal. What has he got to set up? And why Grimes?

Whatever the Yank is about he doesn't want the law to know – why else would he be living in a flea-pit, walking the streets and chancing his neck in Glasgow's drinking dens? Normally Grimes' day-to-day business wouldn't interest me but a Yank in Glasgow is unusual. Besides, for as long as Grimes is chasing me I'm interested in everything he gets up to and in everyone interested in him.

Got a name for the Yank from his hotel register but Hiram Holliday might as well have called himself Mickey Mouse. Maybe I'm wasting my time?

Angie the Gopher seems to have changed his style. Keeps visiting an old couple in Dalmeny Street. Maybe they have grandchildren and I haven't seen them. Not sure what to do about Angie. If I knew he abused the kids I would know what to do for sure. But Angie just likes to talk with them, pretending he's a social worker. What does he get out of that?

Deadeye Kirkpatrick is now a regular visitor to Priesthill. I don't trust that man. Is he planning something behind Grimes' back with the team from that scheme? If he gathered a crew in from Priesthill, Nitshill, Pollok — they'd be a force all right. But Deadeye doesn't usually work with others — strictly a lone wolf. Has he changed? Maybe I should just stand back and let him get on with it?

Trouble with this game I'm playing is that I can't ever come out and put my hand up. Never own up to what I've done or offer to help in any way. I'm on my own in the shadows. From there I'll keep watching Deadeye — it's all I can do.

Everything has gone quiet around Cathy Brodie and I don't like it. I expected Birse and his troops to move in one night. But no sign. Mind you watching over Cathy has made me fit with all that running. Still I'm worried for her — bastards like Birse never let people go.

I've heard from a source that Scotch Brian is out of harm's way for the minute. Question is, what will Grimes do now? It's not in his nature to do nothing.

Big weakness of Grimes is impatience. Sometimes the best strategy is to watch and wait. Like I'm patiently waiting his next move. Let's hope I'm right and he's not closer to me than I think.

A

CHICKEN TEETH

Angie the Gopher was an anxious man. Bad enough that he kept wanting to urinate but found that he couldn't. His mother would have said he'd caught a chill but it couldn't be that. He'd be constantly dribbling and now he wasn't dribbling at all. Not for days.

He'd read somewhere that men of a certain age sometimes developed the problem. Some kind of gland got swollen and, well, they couldn't pee. Angie was sure there would be more to it than that but he hadn't read the whole article, no need. Still, it couldn't be that. It only happened to men of older years and he was still in good shape, he thought. He looked at himself in the stainless-steel tiles of The Cat's Whiskers' Gents and smiled. A fine-looking man, if he said so himself. Just a small adjustment to his wig, a full smile with his new dentures – a fine-looking man – but still he couldn't pee. Bad enough all that, but now there was a meeting going on that could spell big trouble for Angie the Gopher.

A long time ago he'd learned that there was one thing worse than failing to carry out Grimes' orders and that was promising him something then letting him down. It wasn't that Angie had promised Grimes anything at all. All he had said was the Bearer Bonds in the old Jewish couple's house could be worth money but Grimes interpreted that as an absolute promise of great gains, a promise from Angie of wealth to be had. Now Grimes was in his office meeting with some official types and they were going to get an accountant to look at the bond Angie had blagged out of the old biscuit tin. It would be thumbs up or thumbs down for Angie. Christ, he wished he'd pretended he hadn't seen that old box but it was too late now. Angie wanted to pee again but wasn't hopeful.

'Good of you to visit my little club, Councillor Wiley,' said Grimes as Maggie Small served afternoon tea. Tea at least for Councillor Wiley, though Councillor Scully, Bob Benson, Grimes and herself preferred the freshly ground coffee she poured from a cafetiere.

'Aye, no problem, Andy,' replied Wiley. 'Ah wanted tae see this bit o town anyroads. Ah reckon the city-centre Clydeside is a prime site for blue-chip development in the near future.' Scully was nodding his head in agreement while Bob Benson just sweated, slurping his coffee and munching his biscuits.

'Ah'm glad you think so, it was a reason I based this club here you know,' smiled Grimes.

'Aye, well, an what sort o club is it . . . exactly?' asked Wiley, staring at Grimes over his teacup poised inches from his lips.

'Ah, entertainment, just entertainment,' blustered Grimes. 'You know, drinks, a cabaret, meals.'

'Herrumph, Ah heard it was a strip club,' Wiley sipped his tea, 'an worse.'

'Naw, scurrilous rumours . . . rivals . . . just entertainment.' Grimes, flustered, was failing to string a sentence together. This wasn't how the meeting was meant to be going at all. Wiley hadn't come as a friend but to challenge him. He had to get the meeting back on track and quick.

'Never mind all that the now.' Wiley dismissed the subject assertively as if Grimes had raised the diversion. 'Whit about this clearance proposal? How far have ye got wi it?' Maggie Small recognised the old fox in Wiley and had to admire his strategy, albeit grudgingly.

'Well, Ah thought we could discuss some aspects further,' piped up Scully, 'Bob?'

'Yes, aye, thank you, Chair. After our last discussion at the Delta, I saw fit to revisit my department's appraisal of Area Two's future projections, paying particular attention to socio-economic implications to the wider area and, of course, to reappraise the social risk assessment of the neighbourhood not currently included and brought to our attention by Mr Grimes.' Bob Benson rolled his blueprints out on the table and handed out reports to all in attendance. 'Now, as you will recall, the area under question is here,' pointing to the plan, 'covering Dalmeny Street up to the junction with Rutherglen Street here. Having examined the current billing progress for work under current sites here and here, and having reached a possible compromise arrangement with Mr Grimes, we find there is some, eh, leeway in the budget. Add to this our fresh cost-analysis assessment of leaving the Dalmeny Street area in its current state, well, we find . . .'

'WE? Who is WE, Mr Benson?' Councillor Wiley roared. 'Would that be you and Mr Grimes? Don't tell me – the bottom line is that the council could sanction this new work at no extra cost at all. Ah'm Ah right? Well, am Ah?'

'Uumm, well,' havered Benson, 'with a minimum extra cost which Mr Grimes has . . .'

'. . . agreed to spread over several years on the basis that the contract is signed in a hurry except some months down the road he'll find some extraordinary reason to charge extra, AGAIN, and you will convince the planning committee, AGAIN.' Wiley stopped to take a breath, and in a quieter voice, 'Ah'm Ah right?' No one tried to answer, not even Maggie Small, who had expected this turn of events even if it had occurred sooner than she had anticipated. 'Ah'll be having a word wi the council leader about your behaviour in all of this, Councillor,' Wiley spat out the word full of sarcasm, 'Scully. Whit is it? A backhander frae Grimes here? Man, he's nothing but a bloody pimp.' Wiley was collecting his things together. 'Bunch of thieving capitalist bastards so ye are.' Wiley was striding to the door and didn't notice Maggie Small a few steps behind him. As his hand gripped the door handle she caught up with him and touched his shoulder.

'I wouldn't go out there if I were you, Councillor Wiley,' she whispered.

'WHY NO?' he roared, 'Ah've got nothing tae hide,' he said, turning to glower at the three men sitting at the far end of the office, 'unlike some folk.'

'It's just a couple of your friends have popped in to see you,' said Maggie, edging the door open a few inches. Peering through the narrow gap, Wiley saw the two boys.

To anyone else they looked like two underfed, scruffy, bored young schoolboys drinking some Coke. To Wiley the boys represented carbolic air, locked cubicles echoing drunken shouts, long skinny limbs, instant erections and soft mouths round his cock at ten pounds a turn. The two boys reflected just some of his shame.

'Scully and Benson know nothing of this . . . yet,' whispered Maggie. 'They don't need to, do they?' Wiley slowly closed the door, his chest slumped forward breathing heavily.

'How much?' he croaked.

'How much what?' Maggie replied.

'How much will it take?'

'Not much,' she smiled at the back of his head, 'just your cooperation.'

With Wiley and Maggie Small back at the table, Bob Benson, sweating more than usual, was asked to continue. Benson kept staring at Wiley's face. He had never seen the old fellow traveller look so shaky and wan. But continue he did, in a staccato, stilted delivery, line by line.

'So,' he concluded, 'if councillors Wiley and Scully were to raise an emergency motion at the next meeting of the full council the matter could be addressed.'

'Naw.' It was the first word Wiley had said since his tête á tête with Maggie Small at the door. The group turned to him and gaped. 'No that way,' he continued. 'The leader will rule it out of order as a matter of principle. He's like that, Scully, you should know that.' Councillor Scully continued to smile his benevolent smile but was lost to Wiley's meaning. 'He makes a point of treating his own folk hardest of all. Suits him, he's popular.' Wiley rubbed at his head wearily. 'We'll need, whitya call em . . . precipitating factors. A sort of REAL reason, then a proposal at pre-agenda meeting. Then, if, and I say IF, he agrees we're oan. If no, we're doon the plug.'

Maggie was trying to catch Grimes' eye, terrified he wasn't following Wiley's explanation. When Grimes looked over she gave him a wide stare and slightly nodded her head. He frowned, looking angry and frustrated, and eventually said,

'Think Maggie's got something to say.'

'Thank you,' she lied, 'and thank you, Councillor Wiley, for your insight. I believe the circumstances you describe are very likely to present themselves in the near future.' Maggie kept her eyes on Grimes who was still lost, still angry. She continued, 'The young people of the area are, let's say, fractious.'

'Oh aye,' bellowed Grimes, 'aye, right enough. Real fucking fractious and real impatient.' He was smiling, nodding his head. 'The question is, are youse two up for it?' addressing councillors Wiley and Scully. 'Well? Are yese? Or dae Ah call the shots?'

Before he received an answer the door sprung open and in sashayed a young teenager, one of the boys who had caused Wiley so much upset.

'Look, youse people Ah've been waiting oot there for hours and hours and hours, man.' He stood over the group, one hand on his hip, all exaggerated feminine posturing but hard-faced cheek in his voice. He was scared of no one. He sucked the cocks of the city's manhood. Why should he fear anything? The streets had made him that way. 'If

Ah drink anither Coke Ah'll piss maself. Now,' pointing at the group, 'Ah'm Ah getting trade the night or what?' The group were staring at the young boy, all, that is, apart from Wiley, who had buried his head in his hands. 'Hello,' said the boy lightly, his tone suddenly changing to soft, tender. 'Ah thought Ah recognised youse. How yese doing?' He edged his hip onto the arm of Wiley's chair. 'Youse aw right? What's up? Are they bastards no treating youse right? Aw come oan,' rubbing Wiley's shoulder gently. 'Whatever it is it's no worth it, pal, sure it's no.' Patting Wiley's head he turned to the group, 'You bastards should be ashamed o yersels so youse should.'

Grimes was on his feet approaching the boy. 'Listen, son. He'll be aw right. Nothing tae dae wi us, right? He's just upset like, tired an aw that.'

'Keep yer fucking paws aff me ye fat arsehole,' screamed the boy, holding on to Wiley's shoulder. 'Ah'm no leaving tae Ah'm sure he's aw right, and yese can stuff that up yer cunts, so yese can.'

'C'mere you.' With one fist Grimes grabbed the boy by the throat and started to lift him off the seat. The boy coughed and spluttered and thrashed his arms and feet, drowning in mid-air. 'Ye little poof, coming in here an acting like ye own the fucking joint,' Grimes cursed. 'Ah'm the fucking boss in here an Ah'm about tae show why, ye wee arse wipe.' The boy was flapping and jerking when Wiley's arm snaked out and reached round him. The old socialist looked up at Grimes, his face filled with tears, eyes bloodshot red. He looked up and begged ease, comfort, not for him but the boy-man with the bruised throat. The look on the old man's face disgusted Grimes. It wasn't fear or a plea for mercy – those he was used to and ignored at will. All Grimes knew was that it was something soft yet strong. Something that didn't suit his notion of the old councillor who had him by the balls only minutes before. It didn't fit, it wasn't right and on Wiley's face it scared the hell out of Grimes like no prospect of brutality ever could. If Andy Grimes had bothered to learn a half-decent vocabulary he would have chosen the word compassion. Grimes dropped the boy and grumbled, 'Get the fuck oot o ma sight.'

'Whit aboot ma money,' the boy croaked at the door. 'Ye promised me payment.'

'We'll see you fixed,' said Maggie, 'the barman has an envelope for you and your friend. Just ask him, OK?'

'Right,' said the boy then finally warned, 'youse better leave off him, right?' Silently, Benson and Scully gathered their things and left the room with Maggie and Grimes, leaving Wiley in peace with his tears of guilt.

'If that cunt Wiley gives us any more bother Ah'll fucking crucify him.' Grimes was back to himself, standing in his club, a large brandy in one hand pouring it down his throat as fast it could.

'Andy,' said Maggie Small with a long sigh, 'that's not likely.'

'Naw? Could've fucking fooled me.' Grimes downed the rest of his brandy and watched Benson and Scully leave the main door of the club.

'Boss, is there a decision?' Angie the Gopher suddenly appeared beside Grimes.

'A whit?' roared Grimes. 'Oh, aye, Ah've decided yer a fucking waste of space.'

'Naw, boss, Ah know that, Ah meant the meeting.'

'Whit the fuck ye oan aboot?'

'The meeting with the finance guy and,' Angie reduced his voice to a whisper and moved his lips close to Grimes' ear, 'the Bearer Bonds.'

'Shit,' hissed Grimes.

'Whit, boss? Whit's up?' Angie the Gopher cowered back as he asked the question.

'FUCKING STUPID BASTARD,' screamed Grimes and slammed his fist into the bar.

'Naw, boss, whit is it, eh?' Angie was backing off farther.

'Shit, Maggie,' groaned Grimes.

'I know,' she replied.

'Ah forgot tae ask him tae get an accountant set up.'

'Hmm, me too,' Maggie conceded with a smile.

'Fucking here in ma pocket tae.' Grimes extracted the bond.

'Yeah,' said Maggie not looking at Grimes.

'One of us is going to have to ask Wiley,' Grimes spoke quietly, horror mixed with disgust in his voice, 'in there. In the office.'

Maggie Small straightened her dress, snatched the Bearer Bond from Grimes' fingers and walked towards the office door. For a second or two Grimes watched her walk. He loved seeing the way her hips swayed and her buttocks moved the fabric of her dress, although he knew he would only ever get to look and nothing more. As she knocked and disappeared through the door, he turned and said,

'It's sorted, Angie, don't worry. Got the guy under oor wee finger.' Grimes took some quiet satisfaction at Maggie's proposal that they get

Wiley to connect them with an accountant from the council to advise on Bearer Bonds rather than use the three different firms he employed for some of his legitimate enterprises. Accountants were like lawyers, coming close to an understanding of what lay behind his public façade. They all knew what Grimes was, just never spoke of it or admitted it publicly. As soon as they saw a Bearer Bond in his mitts they would know it was bent. Next stage would be for them to expect a certain generosity and that was against Grimes' nature. Some underpaid git from the council on the other hand, what would he know? She was a bright one that Maggie Small, right enough.

Grimes sighed with quiet satisfaction and looked round into empty space. 'Angie?' he called but received no response. He gestured to a barman restocking the gantry, 'Where the fuck's Angie the Gopher disappeared tae?' The barman looked around him then shrugged,'No idea, boss, he was standing there just a minute ago.'

'Fucking arsehole, so he is,' grumbled Grimes.

The barman started wiping at an already dry glass then said, 'Fuck sakes, forgot tae say, boss, but that Yank was in again asking for yese.' Grimes turned and scowled at the barman. 'Right big, mean-looking fucker an aw.'

'Whit is it wi this Yank? Whit the fuck's he want?'

'Didnae spell it right oot, boss, but he was right, eh, insistent annat. Said he'd goat yer name through connections an he wanted help in tracking some folk doon. Widnae gie me a name, jist said it was a couple o relatives. Ah said tae him tae go tae the police an he looked at me as if Ah'd shit oan the bar – obviously they're no his favourite company.'

'Hunt the body tricks. Pah!' spat Grimes. 'Hate them. Small change, man, Ah cannae be bothered wi them. Did ye no ask him for his name?'

'Aye, said it was Hiram Holliday or sumthin,' said the barman with a serious, straight face.

'He was taking the piss,' laughed Grimes.

'Aye?'

'Aye, Hiram Holliday – funniest TV show when Ah was growing up.'

'Aye?' The barman's face betrayed his ignorance.

'Aye, wee speccy, baldy guy in a suit wi n'umberella annat.' Grimes was laughing at the memory of more innocent kicks beyond the ken of the younger and poker-faced barman.

'He was right insistent annat, boss,' the barman offered, feeling uneasy with a smiling Grimes. 'Wouldnae take a telling, know?' In danger of falling into a good humour, Grimes caught himself and returned to type,

'Aye, Ah know. How did ye shift him then?'

'Ah well,' the barmen smiled broadly 'asked they two wee poofs tae hassle him, know?'

'They two wee hookers?' asked Grimes.

'Aye, right in there they went. Fucking Yank looked like he could kill em wi a scowl, know? Two minutes, man, Big Yank's oot o here muttering hostilities as he runs tae the door.'

'Fucking cracker! Maybe Ah should gie the shirt-tail lifters a job as bouncers?' Grimes laughed.

'Cost me two double voddies in their Cokes,' said the barman.

'Ho, that's fucking illegal, man, they're under age. An awfy expensive. Think Ah'll stick tae the usual bears, eh?' The barman walked away, chuckling and shaking his head. The humour between the two men served as close as Grimes would ever get to congratulations and gratitude. The barman understood he was in his boss's good books, for the moment.

Grimes turned to the large TV screen playing in the corner. It was another report from the Berlin Wall.

'Fucking life,' he grumbled, 'even the TV's full o the same old boring stuff.'

Outside the Gents toilet lay a little bundle of jet black hair. Angie the Gopher had been in a hurry to go. But when he got there he still couldn't go, in spite of all the taps running and his tuneless whistling. Angie had a feeling that life was changing and would never be the same again.

TWENTIETH-CENTURY CHATS

YOUNG AND OLD
GLENLORA DRIVE, PRIESTHILL, GLASGOW (OCTOBER 1989)

'Ah've no always lived in this scheme, son,' said old Joe, opening the first of the six-pack of super lager Deadeye had brought him. 'Naw, Ah'm a Brigton boy me. Used tae run wi the Billy Boys – well, whit was left o them by my time, which wisnae fucking much. But a few of us youngsters kept up the tradition for a while.' Joe slurped at his beer and started to roll a cigarette. Deadeye was always fascinated by old Joe's arthritic claws of hands still being able to roll perfectly formed, tight little cigarettes.

Deadeye was carefully rolling a joint. The Rizlas already gummed together, he teased the tobacco out before turning to fire up his lump of dope. The sweet smell of cannabis floated into the room.

'Yer a dab hand at setting up the wacky baccy, eh? Aw ma life Ah've been smoking they wee skittery things. There wisnae a lot o dough around when Ah wis a boy. Depression and then the fucking war – one thing after another. Ah signed up right away. Cheeky cunts said Ah wis too wee. Ah says tae them, "How big dae Ah need tae be tae kill Germans?"

'Ah thought Ah wis gonnae get a knockback because Ah'd done time in the jail an Ah wis ready for them. Ah wis gonnae tell them that every bastard in ma street's been in borstal and the BarL for fighting, just like me. "We are ideal candidates for a fucking war," Ah wis gonnae say tae them. But naw, yer too wee, so beat it. You cauld, son? Naw? Ah'm a bit parky masel, must be ma age, eh? Fucking quack says ma blood's too thin or something. Wanker so he is. So there Ah was for two year working the trams annat and some cunts are telling me Ah was a coward. Fucking gave them a right doing. Mind, it was a good time for the nooky. Aw they men oot the road there's just a few young guys an loads o hairies. Fucking desperate for it so they were. Great for the nooky. Great. Ah ended up getting caught. Well, ye did back then. We aw did. So there's me hitched wi a new wean an sharing a single end in Crownpoint Road wi her folks an her auld granny. No exactly fucking ideal, right? But the bastarding army could've chosen a fucking better time tae change their minds, eh? Suddenly Ah'm big enough for them. Aye, big enough tae get killed.' Old Joe opened another can of super lager. 'For three year Ah hardly saw them. Comes rolling back wi ruined lungs, a demob suit that didnae fit, nae money and nae job. Bad fucking years, son. Aw Ah brought in was a cairry-oot an a bad temper. Three fucking weans that lived, three that didnae. Ripped her insides oot so they did. She's cleaning fucking offices tae raise a wee bit buckshee an aw the time she's no well. Never said. Never complained once. Then it was too late. Two days aifter Ah buried her the welfare came for the weans. Last Ah seen o them. Have Ah shown ye her photie?'

Old Joe asked the same question on all of Deadeye's visits. Deadeye decided not to remind Joe that he had seen the picture before, lying in the piss on that toilet floor as he crouched naked and Scotch Brian ripped up his clothes. Best not to raise that day for any reason. Best that old Joe kept it as far away from his mind – and his mouth – as possible. 'Aw, son, see that wee holdall ye've left wi me? It's just that Ah've got the Gas Board coming in tae change ma meter. Think ye should maybe move it oot o the cupboard, eh? Ah didnae want tae touch it masel cos ye said no tae. Ye could put it in that press in the bedroom – Ah'm never in there onyroads.'

Deadeye went to the cupboard and hefted the sports bag through to the other room. Once away from Joe's company he unzipped the bag and checked the contents. They were all there, tied together exactly as he had left them – the revolver, sawn-off shotgun, bullets and cartridges. A good safe haven for when he needed them next. Better than killing old Joe as Grimes had ordered, Deadeye used him. Now that was smart. 'Ye away already, son? Ach ye never stay that long but it's good tae see yese. Naw, naw, there's no need for that.' Deadeye placed a few tenners on the mantelpiece. 'Ah just like yer company, son. Besides, Ah owe you – ye know, for saving ma neck yon day. Owe you big time, so Ah dae.'

'Just keep thinking like that,' thought Deadeye, 'an you and me will get oan jist dandy.'

A PROMISE
DALMENY STREET, GLASGOW (OCTOBER 1989)

'Ach, it's such a long day, Ruthie, when business is quiet.' Jakob Wise settled down on one of the two junk-free seats in the flat. 'Not one single customer the whole day . . . again. Maybe we should move, whatya think? Hmm, Ruthie, move to a better area? One with people?'

Ruth Wise sat across from her husband nodding to herself, sewing an imaginary piece of cloth with imaginary needle and thread.

'Up near Allison Street, now that's full of people. Long, long street, Ruthie, and all tenements and all full of people. There are black people moving in there I hear. Whatya think? Maybe not such a good idea, hmm?' Jakob leaned down and undid his laces, eased his shoes off his feet and sat massaging his toes.

'Move again? Paah, what am I saying? All that moving for all those years. First in Berlin, you remember Berlin, Ruthie?' Jakob didn't wait for his wife to respond. 'Yes you do, though maybe not today,' he muttered, embarrassed to be referring to his wife's confusion in front of her, as if it made any difference. 'So many people, eh? Such good people. All gone now. Gone.' Jakob Wise looked at the far wall but saw further and more.

'Do you remember the dancing? Course you do, my Ruthie. You were so beautiful and full of life. Dance, dance all night – you never wanted it to finish.' Jakob fished a half-smoked cigar butt out of his cardigan pocket, fired it up and followed the billow of blue smoke with his eyes.

'Then they took over and it all changed. We were so lucky, hmmm, Ruthie? So lucky. My father, he said it was stuff and nonsense. That Hitler wouldn't last. Stay and work, he told us, our people have moved too much. Stay and work, he insisted, and the German people will see that no harm comes to us. Stay and work, he pleaded, this is the twentieth century.'

Jakob rose from his chair and crossed to his wife. He pulled her shawl up over her shoulders, tucking it in around her neck. Ruth Wise was still sewing the imaginary cloth, a thin pleasant smile on her face, humming a tune under her breath so low he couldn't make it out. Dance music, he reckoned and stroked her cheek gently with the back of his hand. His wife looked up and smiled at him through half-blind navy-blue eyes.

'You remember the train rides, Ruthie? So many trains. Chopping and changing at every tiny station so they wouldn't catch us. Ha, even when we were supposed to be safe we didn't trust them, did we? We knew all about collaborators – it's just the word we didn't know. Marseilles, paah, what a place. Full of black skins and Brown Shirts. Sea captains cramming their boats at double fare heading to the Americas, slipping back after a week, their passengers gone. We knew what they were up to, didn't we, Ruthie? Paris!' Jakob Wise turned his head and made a disgusted spitting noise. 'More Nazis in Paris than in Berlin. Heh? Then that lorry rattling through Belgium, crammed in the back breathing in the smoke from the engine. How much did we pay the driver? No matter. Amsterdam, where you were so frightened you'd pull your shawl over your head. That crammed warehouse for months. All those stinking, unwashed bodies and the squabbles. On and on, all day and night. Fighting for enough room to lie down and sleep. Haggling at the queue for water. Stealing bread from each other. Ha, and they called themselves Jews. Then England. Remember how we held each other and wept so when we saw the shore? Such tears. I prayed out loud and you sang a dance tune. We didn't stop smiling till we arrived at the internment camp. From one jail to another. I argued with them. I told them we were Jews, seeking asylum, a safe refuge, not prison. They said we were Jews second and Germans first. We could be spies! "Tell that to Hitler," I said to them. But you, Ruthie, you held my hand and told me that it didn't matter. Nothing mattered now that we were safe and together, and you were right.' Jakob sat nodding silently, remembering the lost years.

'What am I thinking,' he started. 'Sad thoughts. We have no need of sad thoughts. We are alive. Me and my Ruthie, we showed them. Showed them all and here we are. But no more moving huh, Ruthie? Whatya think? I promised you when we came here that we would stay and never have to move again. A promise broken is a stab to the heart. We'll stay here. We've much to be pleased of, heh? Nice house, a little business and our precious little collection. Our little box of paper gold. Eeeh! We should be happy, heh?'

Jakob opened the cupboard and lifted the biscuit tin. The weight of it felt good in his hands. The rectangle of dust-free space it left on the shelf warmed and reassured him. Pop, he loved the sound of the tin opening, and there they were, just as he had left them. Bonds from heaven. It had been so tempting along the way to sell them on to help through barren times. But that would have been at a great loss and he and Ruthie shared an abhorrence of such waste. Besides, what they had

had to do to get the bonds in the first place – Jakob and Ruthie never spoke of those deeds. So they had gone without, almost starving at times, all in order to hold on to their little box of paper gold. One day soon the paper would truly become gold and the worth of their lives would be matched by their wealth. Jakob was sure of that. He felt it in his bones. Any day now.

The biscuit tin returned carefully to its position, back in the living-room Ruth Wise hummed her tune louder. Jakob recognised it as one of their favourite waltzes back in their courting days.

'You want music, Ruthie, will I get you some music?' Jakob moved a pile of carrier bags Ruth had folded that very morning. He moved them carefully lest she think her work undone and start folding them all over again. There he located a large, old-fashioned transistor radio with one large dial on the front and three buttons to change the waveband. The dial produced nothing but high-pitched white noise till it broke into orchestral music. The old man's wavering hand took several attempts to settle on the station. Jakob sat down to a broad smile from Ruth, moving to the music, humming along, sewing her imaginary piece of cloth. Suddenly the music stopped,

'This is BBC World News at 5 p.m. Growing unrest in Berlin today has been heralded as a further step towards the reunification of Germany . . .'

Jakob quickly got off his chair and turned the radio off. 'Berlin! May Berlin rot in hell.' He stroked his wife's cheek and knelt painfully at her feet. 'I'm so sorry, Ruthie. I didn't mean to shout, to startle you.' Tears were streaming down her cheeks. 'No, no, my darling, don't worry so. We'll not go back. We'll not go anywhere. You and I, heh, we'll stay here forever. Whatya think? We'll never leave here. Promise you, Ruth. Promise you.'

CREDIT DUE
MELVILLE STREET, POLLOKSHIELDS, GLASGOW (OCTOBER 1989)

'Miss Brodie?' the man was tall, heavy and leaning against the frame of Cathy Brodie's front door.

'Ms,' she replied.

'Whit?'

'Ms Brodie tae you, tae everybody in fact.'

'Aye, well, whatever ye say.' He was looking down at her, a sleazy grin all over his face. 'Ah'm frae SPS Ah'll only take a minute o yer time.' He went to enter the house but Cathy barred his way.

'Don't need no insurance, no hoover, no new kitchen, no credit card or anything else ye're selling.'

'Aw, Ah'm no selling, Cathy,' he grinned, 'Ah'm from SPS – Strathclyde Professional Services – a private detective agency, security advisers and, oh aye, debt collectors. Ah'm here tae save the roof ower yer heid.'

'Whit? Whit dae ye mean?'

'Ah'm here aboot yer rent arrears, as well as a few other outstanding debts.' His smile was getting wider and wider. 'Think we better chat aboot this inside, eh?' Cathy stood back from the door and the man strode in, followed by another man of similar build and dress.

'Hey, who's this?' Cathy barred the second man's entrance. This was beginning to feel familiar, they spoke and even dressed like beat coppers, trying to adjust to plain clothes and failing badly.

'That's my associate, that's all,' said the first man. 'Ye've nothing tae fear from us, Cathy.'

'So how come it bloody well takes two of ye?'

'It's just procedure,' he smiled.

'Show us yer ID,' Cathy demanded.

'Och there's no need for that . . .'

'Show us or Ah'll phone the police.' The two men started laughing.

'Where from,' he said, 'the phone box doon the road? Ah can tell ye for sure it's oot o order. Some bastard's panned the money box and shit in it for good measure.' In spite of his response the two men flashed official-looking IDs showing their pictures, a blur of small print and SPS in large bold print. She noticed that the cards were the same colour as Strathclyde Police IDs. 'Pretty nifty, eh? Now shift and let ma mate in.'

Cathy moved away from the door and the two men entered the

room. The second one held his arms stiffly a few inches from his sides and his feet pointed outwards as he walked on legs which seemed incapable of closing. Cathy reckoned he worked out, pumping iron and downing steroids. She read somewhere that the steroids made men look grotesquely macho but shrank their balls and shrilled their voices. She hoped they did but wasn't to find out since he never spoke, leaving the brainwork to the first man.

'I didn't catch your name,' said Cathy to the first bloke.

'Never mind that, Cathy, let's talk about your responsibilities,' he replied. At that the baby stirred in his cot, giving a little moan and whimper and then silence. 'Aw, wee Timmy.' He moved over to the cot. 'Cute wee guy, eh?'

'How dae you know his name?' demanded Cathy, biting her lip for being so blatant in showing her alarm, her fear.

'Aw, Ah know everything there is to know aboot you, hen, from ma time in the polis,' he sneered. 'Right doon tae yer favourite position in the sack.' He stuck his tongue out drawing it slowly over his lips. Cathy was flustered, noticing her clean washing ready for ironing with her underwear on top. She whisked the laundry basket up and lodged it behind the bed out of his view.

'Your new landlord is after his rent. According to this,' he pulled a notebook from his hip pocket, 'there's over two hundred quid owing. That's a lot a dough, Cathy.'

'Ah didnae know Ah had a new landlord,' she said, 'who is it? Ah've a right tae know – in fact Ah should've been notified. In writing.'

'Great one for yer rights, eh?' he smiled. 'So happens Ah have a wee letter for you here.' He pulled a piece of typed paper out of the same hip pocket and handed it to her. She unfolded and read. It was headed Oxford Street Properties and signed M. Small. Cathy Brodie knew exactly who Oxford Street Properties were.

'Andy Grimes. Shit,' she sighed and slouched in resignation like the wind had been knocked out of her chest.

'Aye, well,' he smirked, 'who dae ye think his bro would leave his business tae? An while we're at it there's another wee matter. Yer outstanding loans.'

A shiver ran through Cathy. It's what she had dreaded, nothing changing and everything staying exactly it had been before the fat man was killed.

'What loans?' she tried to brass it out, knowing it would be hopeless.

'Whit loans? Ha, good yin that, Cathy. Did ye think it would die wi that poor man oot oan the pavement, eh? Naw, he kept a book and that book's been handed oan tae Andy Grimes an he's a bit anxious tae collect. But this time he wants money, no nooky.'

Cathy's world collapsed on her. She'd been so naive thinking that the debts would disappear. People like this never got out of your life. When one died or was jailed another just stepped right up to fill his place. In this case, a bigger animal than the first one.

'How much?' she groaned.

'About a monkey, five hundred, give or take a few coppers,' he scoffed. 'But Ah've tae advise ye of new terms.'

'What?'

'Interest rates, they're now twenty-five per cent a week and very reasonable too, if you ask me,' he mocked.

'Ah . . . that's . . . couldn't pay . . .' Cathy felt tears of frustration well up in her eyes and fought them. Early in life she'd learned how to deal with threats and rule one was show no emotion, especially when you were terrified.

'First payment due today,' he smiled and put his hand out palm upwards. 'Ah'll accept fifty oan the rent and two hundred oan the loan.' The smile was replaced by a serious, menacing stare.

'Ah've no got it,' Cathy said in a tiny, weak voice.

'Ye'll have tae get it then,' his poker face glaring down at her, 'or there'll be penalties.'

'What ye're doing is illegal,' she sobbed, 'and you ex-polis.'

'Aye, EX-polis. But we'll start legal wi yese. For example, Ah know yer oan a list for non-payment of poll tax. We'll arrange tae have yer case nudged up the queue, get an eviction order oan yese and the next ye know the sheriff officers'll be oot flogging off yer gear. An, by the way, SPS are also registered sheriff officers – just so's ye deal wi a familiar face like.'

'Fuck the poll tax.' Cathy had found her voice again, 'Ah'm no paying the poll tax on principle.'

'Aye, an ye'll be homeless oan principle then.'

'Ah'll get the anti-poll tax protestors to help me – you'll no evict me.' Cathy was up for it again.

'That bunch o left-wing pansies, paah. They'll no bother us.

Besides, we keep anti-social hours – lot o night-time working – if ye catch ma drift.' He was smiling again. 'There is a way tae get oot o yer little difficulties though.'

'Whit?' Cathy's answer was abrupt, aggressive, expecting the big slob to want the old deal, to want sex. No way was she going to fall into that again.

'Naw, naw,' he jibed, reading her expression of horror. Rubbing his crotch slowly he continued, 'Ah'd love a blow job but unfortunately cannae take ye up oan yer kind offer. Naw, a wee bit information is aw it would take. Just a name. A description. Take yese two minutes and yer oot o hock.' He walked to her sink and stared out of the window, 'Good view o the shooting frae here, eh? So who was it? Whit did he look like? That's aw we want, just that.' He waited, looking quietly out of the window, then turned to face her, 'So whit's it to be?'

Cathy had expected the police to return, not this crew of licensed thugs bringing with them the old debts. She was ready for the police, had been well trained by her father all her life. But this, this she had to resolve herself. She stared at the wardrobe with the rickety door. From where she was standing she could see the edge of the white envelope, the one full of ten pound notes and with the words '**In Appreciation**' typed in bold on the front.

Till half an hour before she had thought that was her dilemma. The envelope was pushed through her letterbox one night. As soon as she realised what it was and who it was from she had put it away without even counting the money. Cathy had been raised to do what was right according to street rules. The one thing you didn't do was accept payment for keeping to those rules. She didn't tell the police anything about the young gunman because she thought that was the right thing to do. And now he had paid her. She had thought her only problem was how to return the money. Besides she had only caught a glimpse of the man. She thought she knew who it might be but couldn't be sure. Even if she had been certain she would mention it to no one. That wasn't the problem. The money – that was her problem, till now.

'Come oan, you, make yer fucking mind up,' he growled, 'we're wasting our time here. Money or info – fucking decide quick will yese.'

'Have you a receipt book with you?' she asked.

'Aye, but what the fuck dae you need wi a fucking receipt book? Jist tell us aboot the guy and we're oot o here. C'moan, be smart, eh?' From the top of the wardrobe Cathy pulled the envelope down, kept her back to the two men, and ripped it open. She counted out seven hundred pounds, stuck the envelope into the pocket of her jeans and handed over the money.

'Paid in full, I think,' she said, and this time it was her turn to smile. His face fell.

'Thought ye'd no money?' he said in a spoiled child tone. She had ruined his fun.

'Just write a receipt and fuck off out of my home, eh?'

The two men slammed the front door on their way out. Cathy stood at the window and watched the tops of their heads appear in the street, praying for the appearance of a small young guy with a gun.

When the men got into a big black car and drove off, she pulled the envelope from her pocket and flicked the remaining banknotes with her thumb. There were hundreds left in there. Now she was in debt again. But she reckoned she'd rather be in debt to James Addison than to Grimes and his team any day. But it was still a debt and she would repay it. The question was how and where and when. That was a question that would have to wait till another day, the baby was crying.

OLD FLAME
STEWART STREET POLICE STATION, GLASGOW (OCTOBER 1989)

'Aggie Lipstick, long time no see.' The voice sounded friendly, welcoming, while the expression turned sour, full of dread. The tired old Desk Sergeant at Stewart Street police station didn't need this, not tonight.

'Hellooo, Sergeant Dick,' she announced from the main swing doors, 'Ah've been expecting a call frae youse.' Aggie Lipstick was on her best behaviour, trying to speak proper, the way her Mammy had always told her to.

'Aw, Ah've been awfy busy, Aggie L,' he whined through sinuses blocked and irritated by his forty-a-day habit and untreated due to his terror of doctors. As a new cop thirty years before, watching a drunk police quack deal with some injured prisoner had been enough to terrify him for life. No way would he trust any of them, ever. 'Sss a murder enquiry annat oan oor patch.'

'Aye,' she lisped, prancing and wiggling her way towards the desk, her tight short skirt constricting her strides. 'An Ah'm het.' She arrived at the desk, craning her neck up at the Sergeant and smiled.

'Whit?' he gasped in mock horror, 'ye killed the man, Aggie L, an Ah thought ye were an angel tae.'

'Naaaaw,' she giggled, covering her mouth with her hand, 'though he wisnae nice, know?' Her tone dropped to serious. Dangerous to talk ill of the dead. 'Ah'm the woman that phoned him in.' The Sergeant kept his head down, lost in thought, writing slowly and carefully. 'SAAAAID,' she insisted, blowing the fumes of raw gin up over his face competing with the citric bight of her cheap perfume. 'SAAAAID, Ah phoned in the shooting.'

The Sergeant continued writing, pausing now and then to knit his brow and suck on the end of his pen. Aggie Lipstick waited. She was used to waiting. It was one of her roles in life. Waiting patiently, politely, was the mark of a true lady, an artisan, and she was all that and more. 'FUCK THIS PALAVER, YOU!' she screamed after less than a minute. 'LISTEN UP NOW OR AH'LL THROW UP OAN YER DESK.' Even she had her limits. The Sergeant sighed and looked over his desk. There she was, just as she had always been. Diminutive, well short of five foot. Short, quilted embroidered jacket, low-cut V-necked top covering a chest flatter than a schoolboy's, skirt to halfway down her thighs displaying legs so skinny her knees protruded, PVC leather look-alike boots reaching just below her knees.

Was it his age or had Aggie Lipstick been wearing the same rigout for the last twenty-five years and more? If she had changed her clothes she certainly hadn't altered her make-up, that he was sure of. From her brow to her chin was covered in flour-white paste so thick that cracks appeared at the side of her mouth when she spoke. Both cheeks carried concentric rose-red circles that reminded him of dolls, old fashioned even when he was in nappies. Her eyebrows were plucked bare and replaced by thin arches of black mascara. Her eyelashes were long and curved and black and false – he could tell because one was peeling off. Lips. Now those he knew nothing about because he had never seen them. Where her lips should be she had painted in bright red lipstick her notion of the perfect pout, which grew larger every year.

Aggie Lipstick. She had been given that name before he had started on the beat – one divorce, three grandkids and a hernia ago. He never understood that nickname. Surely it should have been Aggie Geisha? Especially with that hair, the long pageboy style dyed so black it hung stiff, unmoving.

'So happens, Aggie, Ah was jist making the report oot as ye waltzed through the door.' He smiled down at her.

'Aye?' She craned up, standing on tiptoes, still failing to get close to the desk surface.

'Aye,' he boomed, trying to sound officious, 'very important information.' Aggie Lipstick nodded, her perfect mouth open, face poker straight. 'Could ye jist run ower it again for me?' Aggie nodded and thought. She rammed three knuckles of her right hand into her mouth and bit, smearing one side of her perfect lips all down her cheek. The Sergeant wrote some more as he waited.

'Weeeelll,' she started and then paused. 'Weeeelll,' she took a deep noisy breath, 'it was a wee young guy and he was coming tae ride me but he bumped intae that bad bastard who widnae get aff the pavement so he had tae shoot him and the bad guy said sumthin real bad so he had tae shoot him again though he didnae really want tae and the bad guy had made a mess o the road so the wee young guy had tae vamoose oot o there case the road sweeper came aboot an he goat the blame an he was that sorry cos he couldnae come up ma stairs and have a right good shag but he'll be back an at's for sure cos Ah'm the best nooky he's never had.'

Aggie finished and gasped, drawing her breath noisily through her mouth. Rummaging through her pockets she fished out a half-smoked cig, bent in the middle. Straightening it carefully she looked up at the Sergeant and asked, 'You got a spunk, by the way?' Without looking at her, the Sergeant fished a lighter out of his tunic pocket and leaned one arm over the desk. As Aggie sucked in smoke he continued to write.

'Very interesting, Aggie,' he said not looking up from his work. 'You've added a few details that were missing from the original report.' Aggie nodded sharply and looked up, frightened, alert. 'But tell me, how dae ye know he'll be back?'

Aggie shoved three knuckles back into her mouth and worried. The Sergeant looked over his desk and grinned to himself. Aggie Lipstick! He could've written her turning up in a sealed envelope last week, predicting she'd be in. How many times had she claimed to have witnessed murders in the city? He had lost count. Three or four times she had even claimed to have actually committed murders, though she knew sod-all about them. Too much gin and too much time lying on her back with her legs open for a few quid. She was a lonely old soul. How old? Well into her sixties. Her trips to the police station were probably just an excuse for company. Okay, this time she lived on the right street but all that meant was that it was more likely she came in to report some cock and bullshit story. No way was he going to be wasting any time on Aggie Lipstick.

'He looked up,' she blurted.

'Whit?'

'He looked up at ma windae an kinda smiled like this.' Aggie grinned stiffly displaying isolated, higgledy-piggledy teeth all covered in deep red lipstick. Maybe that's where the name came from? 'An then Ah knew he'd be back.'

'Yer right, Aggie.' The Sergeant looked down at her and smiled. 'Ah'm sure he will.' Aggie smiled back and nodded. 'Fact ye better get yersel doon the road – case he comes a calling.' Serious worried frown from Aggie. 'Ah'll jist fill in yer report here – take me a while yet – an Ah'll see that the detectives come interview you the morrow.' Tomorrow, the first of two days off for the Sergeant. 'Aw right?'

'Aye, right. Ah'd better go, eh?'

'Ye'd better hurry, Aggie, ye dinnae want tae keep the young guy waiting.'

'Right, right. A'm . . . eh . . . cheeeri . . .'

As Aggie disappeared through the swing doors the Sergeant kept his head down still writing. He was struggling with one part. Having to concentrate, suck his pen. He stood up straight and turned, calling through to an adjoining office where three drowsy constables slouched at their desk.

'She as in Hazel in Brazil,' he called.

'WHIT?' came the reply.

'She as in Hazel in Brazil.' No response. 'Seven letters across.' Silence. 'Third letter T.' Still nothing. The Sergeant beat a drumroll on his desk top with the fingers of his left hand.

'NUTTERS,' came the shout.

'Whit?' he asked.

'NUTTERS.'

'Fuck aye, nutters. How did Ah no see that?' The Sergeant filled in the little squares. Three more clues to go and he would have finished the evening paper crossword. Five more hours before he was finished his shift. It was going to be a long night.

PAPER CHASE

'Security guards are leaving the bank. One's stopped and speaking tae an old woman. Looks like the wanker's giving her directions. Aw nice, the wee boy scout, eh?' The man in the driver's seat nudged black-framed glasses up his thick nose and mumbled as he pretended to read a newspaper. Strictly a *Daily Record* and *News of the World* tabloid man, he'd bought a broadsheet for better camouflage.

'Aw missus, gonnae hurry up, please. Think the old dear's a wee bit corn beef. Wee fucking shame so it is. You guys okay under there?'

The two men crouching in the foot-well of the back seats, concealed by a tartan travelling rug, said nothing. Their pulses were racing, hearts thumping. No matter how often they did this, the tension was always Red Road flats high. Exhaust fumes from the idling car engine were beginning to crawl through the panels of the floor, making them nauseous, light-headed.

'Here we go. Last man's on board. Door's shut. Counting now: one thousand, two thousand, three thousand . . . and we're goin' in.'

The driver's voice betrayed an edge of excitement but his actions oozed the bored calm of everyday routine. He slipped the car smoothly into first gear, indicated and pulled out into the road. Indicated again, waiting patiently for a gap in the traffic and pulled in to the spot vacated by the security van. To onlookers he was an anonyomous shopper looking for a better parking space in the chaos of the city's traffic congestion. 'Pulling in now . . . parked . . . GO!'

The travelling rug was thrown back and the two men stepped out of the car. Without looking right or left they marched straight into the bank. From a distance they were just two workmen in navy-blue boiler suits. Even since the slow demise of the shipyards there would be thousands of the same brands in Glasgow. No one would look at their feet, but there they wore plain black training shoes of brands popular with young folk. Just workmen in comfortable light shoes, good running shoes. But they were cold workmen, hands covered by leather gloves and ski masks pulled down over their faces, only their eyes and bridges of their noses exposed to the elements and view. As they barged through the glass doors the leading man plucked the revolver from his pocket and the tail pulled the sawn-off shotgun out of his boiler suit.

'DOWN,' roared the shotgun man, 'HIT THE FUCKING DECK, NOW!' He walked quickly among the few customers, holding the shotgun in front him, showing it to the cowering women and startled old-age pensioners.

His partner stepped quickly to the counter and in two leaps was up and over the bandit screen rising halfway to the ceiling. It was a difficult leap but that was why he had been chosen. At school, on the few days he attended, they said he could be a gymnast or a goalkeeper.

'Touch any buttons and yer deid,' the revolver man said quietly to the tellers. 'On the ground NOW,' he screamed. 'FACE DOWN, ARMS OAN THE BACK O YER HEID, LEGS WIDE FUCKING OPEN.' One young woman whimpered and curled into a foetal position, 'FLAT OOT, HEN,' he yelled, pushing her over on her face, 'AND LEGS OPEN LIKE YER SHOWING YER MAN A GOOD TIME.' He kicked her legs apart and turned to find his target.

'TWO MINUTES,' yelled the shotgun carrier, moving quickly about the bank growling at everyone. His role was to control through terror without firing his gun. Sometimes on the same type of job he had carried the shotgun unloaded. But not this time. Something this time had made him nervous and he'd loaded the breech, throwing a handful of cartridges in his pocket for good measure.

'ONE MINUTE THIRTY,' he roared, leaning over a young man edging along the floor belly down. 'Now, son, Ah widnae budge an inch,' he said quietly. 'Yer lassie widnae fancy yese wi the kinda parting Ah'd gie yese,' and he placed the cold metal of the barrel against the young man's neck.

Behind the counter, his colleague was throwing yellow and red canvas bags onto the floor, rejecting them. They were full of money but of low currency only.

'HURRY THE FUCK UP, WID YESE,' screamed the shotgun carrier. He knew he was right to have doubts about that guy. Shouldn't have broken his rule never to work with anyone he didn't know as a friend. Bloke gave him the shivers. Something wrong with him, sinister, he'd always thought that.

But Joe Murphy had brought the job forward having found out there was a big delivery. They had to get a team together in a hurry and Beano's usual associates had all been otherwise detained: one with a broken leg from playing football, another had been dragged off to the Costa del Sol by his missus and two courtesy of Strathclyde's constabulary. Normally they would have just cancelled the job and bided their time till the next opportunity was spotted. But the normally cool-headed Joe Murphy had been keen to go ahead, as if he needed the money badly. Not like Joe. All right for him, he was the spotter, the setter-up and wasn't stuck on the job.

So happens this guy had been pestering Beano for some freelance work just the week before. Beano had been surprised when Joe gave the guy the nod. He thought there was bad blood between the two of them. Good timing or bad timing? They'd find out very soon.

'ONE MINUTE,' howled Beano, the shotgun man. Behind the screen his colleague was busy, having found what he wanted. He was stuffing green bags into the heavy-duty canvas kitbag he'd brought. Green was the colour of real money, high-value currency of tenners and twenties. They weighed less and were worth more and there was a stack of them just waiting to be harvested.

'THIRTY SECONDS – NOW – WE GO NOW.' Beano's fears were being confirmed. The guy was still collecting booty, throwing thick green packages into his kitbag. 'LEAVE IT – TIME'S UP.' He was ignored.

Beano rushed to the teller's window. 'COME OAN – SHIFT. YE'LL NO BE ABLE TAE LIFT THE LOAD OWER THE SCREEN.' The man couldn't resist one more green bag, pulled the drawstrings of the kitbag tight, slipped his hip on the counter and in one movement was up and on his feet, throwing the kitbag over before vaulting into the bank hall. Beano lifted the load one-handed and screamed, 'NOBODY FUCKING BUDGES, RIGHT? YE'LL BE FINE.'

The two men ran out of the door, straight into the back of the car, pulling the plaid over their bodies, crammed in with the added bulk of their spoils. This time the car shifted with speed but not so much as to turn the heads of casual pedestrians.

'Looks like it's a done deal, guys,' the driver prattled nervously. 'No sign o the meanies.' Beano wasn't so sure and he knew the driver was experienced enough to know that the next few minutes were crucial. Certainly someone in the bank would have pressed an alarm. Somewhere there were police cars speeding towards them. The average time taken for the police to arrive at the scene was four minutes. That's why they allowed three and even then it was a calculated risk. The madman with the revolver had wasted valuable escape time for the sake of a few quid. All they could do now was stick to the plan and pray.

The police sirens howled and wailed, ebbing and flowing as they caught up then sped past. The driver of the innocuous little family saloon was courteous like all the other drivers, slowing down to a crawl, pulling over to let the police cars pass. They were just three young men going about their business, dressed in casual tracksuits, singing along to Meat Loaf's 'Bat out of Hell' blaring from the radio.

'Helluva noisy they polis.'

'Aye, they like tae show off.'

'Aye fancied a go at being a polis driver,' said the driver.

'You?'

'Aye, rerr. Ye get tae speed n nae cunt pulls ye up.'

'You, in the polis? That's a good yin.'

In the boot of the car was some unusual luggage. One large kitbag loaded with money, navy boiler suits, black training shoes, ski masks and the driver's disguise of black, heavy-rimmed spectacles, a false moustache and soft cap. In a black bin bag was a sawn-off shotgun and revolver.

It had been Joe's idea to drive in this direction and it was making the three of them nervous. When they'd exchanged one stolen car for another, they drove back in the direction of the bank, following the same route as many of the police cars.

'Whit dae robbers usually dae?' Joe had asked.

'Get the fuck oot o it.'

'Precisely, they run away. Helicopter's oot looking for a motor speeding frae the scene. You are gonnae drive slowly, casually, right past the bank like ye've nothing tae hide.'

He was a smart one that Joe and had never been wrong before. But this time his strategy was making the crew anxious. It went against their grain to be alongside the police, even if they were duping them.

The rest of the plan was straightforward. Change cars again – this time to legally registered ones. They'd all split up. The driver would take the money to Joe while Beano took the disguises away and burned them in the incinerator of a local school where his uncle was janitor. Three days later the three of them would meet up again and Beano would dish out their cuts, minus Joe's substantial share for spotting, setting up and funding the job.

Then came the golden rule — no extravagant spending. No new outfits for girlfriends, big nights on the town, surprise holidays and especially no new flash cars. Even if they had debts, they had to pay off just enough to keep the heavies from the door. Any team member caught infringing this rule was in for a serious talking to and much worse.

Funnily enough, on this account Beano wasn't worried about the revolver man. Deadeye was well known for his simple tastes — a lot of dope and work. He had obviously been keen on this job for reasons other than raising his standard of living. Whatever those reasons were, Beano didn't give a shit. Now the driver, he was another kettle of fish. Totally reliable in everything else, he was well known to be easily parted from his cash and he had well-developed tastes in good-looking, fast-living women. He too had been fitted in at the last minute.

'Hey, Ah was thinking,' the driver turned and smiled at Beano, 'dae ye think Ah suited that moustache?'

'Made ye look like Saddam Hussein, ye daft cunt,' chuckled Beano.

'Mind, he's a handsome man — for a tyrant bastard.' The driver was serious.

'Either old Saddam or that guy oot o Village People,' mocked Beano.

'Aye,' the driver was joining in, laughing at himself, singing 'In the Navy', blowing Beano kisses.

'Aye. Naw,' said Beano, 'ye just look fine the way yese are.'

The driver peered at his face in the rear-view mirror, smoothing his upper lip with one leather-gloved finger, imagining his new facial hair. Beano was going to have to speak to Joe about this. They hadn't even dumped the money and the driver was making plans which no doubt involved women and high living. No, Beano didn't trust him at all in this and he'd have to warn Joe. Joe would have to do something about Fergie and fast.

30 OCTOBER 1989

Today is his anniversary. 30 October 1963. RIP. I'm told I look like him but that could be just one of the things people say to make you feel better. There's a list of questions I have for him, I wish I could've asked. Mostly they don't bother me unless I'm tired or it's his anniversary.

The old guy I met said he was some character. His own man. Ran with The Powery when they were a top team. But back then they were an Orange mob, Protestants to a man. Not now, not for a long time. Yet he was a Catholic. How does that work? Do we think of the sectarian streets in clichés? Were they ever anything other than a gang? Sometimes I think we make life easier by attaching labels. Doesn't matter if they are accurate as long as we understand them. Then again some folk cover themselves in them so they mean something to the world. But not him apparently. He was just him – take him or leave him, love him or hate him.

What did it mean when he upped sticks and went off to Spain to fight against Franco? He was a wide guy, smart with his fists, into smuggling and bank robberies – he wasn't meant to have principles apart from greed. But he must have, mustn't he? From being top dog in his patch in Glasgow to tackling the Spanish Army with only a rusty .303 rifle and a bunch of amateurs for comrades. Now that was mental unless it was important to him. Maybe he was on the run, needed to get out of the city. But surely there were easier places? Maybe he was political – a socialist or a communist. Then again maybe he just didn't appreciate big teams leaning on wee guys. Maybe. I wish I could have asked him.

Back in Scotland they wouldn't let him join the British Army for World War Two because of his criminal record. What was that all about? So he took to smuggling big time. Made a few quid through the war running boats to Ireland and bringing in a load of gear. Would sell anything to anyone. Took orders from petrol to Guinness. But the old guy told me he'd delivered bacon, sugar, tea, flour and stuff to every house on his patch - no charge. Just doled it out and never said why. I'd have like to ask him. But then maybe the old boy just told me that to make me feel better about never having met my father.

He must've been a fair age when he met my wee mam. A few years together and then they got him. Choked on his own vomit, they said officially. But he wasn't known to drink much and was strong as an ox. Corpse covered in bruises the police claimed were already on him when he was lifted.

I was once arrested in Govan and held in the cells at the Orkney Street Police Station. Cold stone efforts out back in the quadrangle of the station. Wind and rain blew in through the bars. Dull light in the corner and a stench of drains. I spent all night wondering if it was the same cell. His cell. Knowing that he had died there or close by in another dungeon. It was as if I could feel his ghost stalking the police, inviting them to one last square go.

I think that was the night I really changed. I used to feel bad that he died not knowing my wee mam was carrying me and they never had the chance to get married. But now I've borrowed his name. Turned it into a joke then into something useful, something serious.

Maybe it will be the death of me as well.

A

FREE LUNCH BLUES

'So whit ye telling me?' Grimes had given up all pretence at manners with the councillors and their bent officials. The little group of Wiley, Scully and Benson all knew enough about each other to make such a show redundant. They now had too much to lose and would keep each other in line. Maggie Small sat at the table and watched the men sweat with more than a little amusement.

'It's going to take a bit longer than we hoped,' mumbled Bob Benson through a mouthful of food. The group occupied a corner table in The Buttery, a dark and discrete restaurant, full of antiques and serving some of the best grub in the city. At lunch-time, the scattering of diners made it an ideal public venue for a confidential chat.

'Ah'm paying for the masters, no the lapdog,' growled Grimes, scowling at Wiley and Scully.

'Eh, Bob's right, Andy,' blustered Scully, his genial round face glowing damp scarlet. 'Council has, eh, a bit o a crisis oan its hands.'

'Fucking politicians. Ye're aye going frae one crisis tae another,' snarled Grimes. 'Fucking smokescreen if ye ask me. Covering up yer no doing any work.' Wiley sat holding his pipe, staring at its unlit bowl, cradling it in both hands. On the table in front of him lay his main course barely touched. Since the little scene at The Cat's Whiskers he had been subdued, wearing the depressed air of a beaten man. 'Well, this is no the fucking municipal board, gents, this is real life. So waken up and put up.'

'Naw, he's right,' so low a mumble that Grimes had to check twice it was coming from Wiley.

'Aw, he's alive,' said Grimes in a sarcastic tone.

'Big overspend,' continued Wiley, no energy or fight left in him to tackle Grimes' insult. 'Ah mean like millions. Leader's going spare and quite right too. Emergency meetings and service cutbacks.'

Grimes looked at him with raised eyes.

'So? Whit's it got tae dae wi us if the bins are no gonnae get emptied or home helps get sacked . . . again?'

'Your proposal,' Wiley coughed, looking up for the first time, 'will cost some money. Money that we don't have.'

'Maggie's shown ye the figures, man, it'll look as if it's buckshee, free, a fucking early Christmas present.' Grimes was getting exasperated. Oxford Street Properties' deadline was coming perilously close.

'The leader'll no look at it and we need his agreement,' Wiley explained quietly. 'Unless there was a bigger problem that needed fixing.'

'FUCKING BIGGER PROBLEM?' Grimes roared, only to be quelled by Maggie Small placing a hand lightly on his arm. He could shout if he wanted but not here, not in the hushed and dignified atmosphere of The Buttery.

'What I think Councillor Wiley is suggesting,' Maggie said quietly, 'is that if there were local problems at Dalmeny Street the council leader would look at it.' She'd simply said the same thing, just reversing the information to a positive statement rather than the troublesome negative that was leading them all to an unproductive bawling match. She sought confirmation, 'Councillor Wiley?'

'Aye, aye, Ah suppose that's whit Ah mean,' the old socialist murmured.

'Naw,' snapped Grimes in a stage whisper. 'Aw naw. No fucking supposed aboot it. If there's local trouble will you two comedians guarantee that our proposal will get through? Well?'

'Aye. Oh aye,' enthused Scully, taking a nervous swallow of his wine. 'For sure, Andy. Aye, aye, definitely.'

'Well?' Grimes demanded from Wiley. Slowly the white-haired head nodded without looking up. 'Good. In that case, consider it done. So, you guys better get yer act sorted, right? Work out yer spiel.' Grimes fired up a thick cigar, smiling and happy. Trouble he knew how to create, so if that was all it took he foresaw no more problems. 'When's yer accountant coming tae see us then, Wiley?'

'Eh, should be here shortly,' Councillor Wiley replied, looking at his watch.

'Good, Ah have a wee phone call tae make.' Grimes pulled his new mobile phone out of his pocket. It was the first he had owned, having decided to buy one when they were being produced small enough to be held in one of his big paws. That rigmarole with field phones simply hadn't worked. These mobile phones were the future, Grimes could feel it. 'Ah'll have tae go intae the car park. These gadgets have an aversion tae stone walls . . . bit like masel. Heh heh heh.' Grimes nodded and winked at Maggie Small. 'Ye'll forgive us for no inviting ye tae stay, boys, but it's wee private consultation wi the finance man. Maggie'll take care of yese though.'

Outside the restaurant, Grimes watched the three men leave as he spoke into the phone. 'Top flat mind and no mistakes,' he said, reciting the address that Angie the Gopher had provided. 'Want the roof off – so target the attic if there is one. No much petrol, lighter fuel'll do yese – it's just a big fucking hole in the roof Ah want. Give the fire five minutes or so and dial 999. Mind an get the fucking fire brigade oot you. This is a property job – nae casualties, right?' On the other end of the line Bud Wilson, aka The Arse Bandit, was smiling,

'You sure yese only want the one hoose done? Ah'll throw in a couple at the same price.'

'One building and make sure it's the exact one Ah gave ye. Dae aw right the night an there'll be other hooses other nights.' Grimes watched a middle-aged man in an ill-fitting, grey, off-the-peg Burtons suit. The guy looked like an accountant and the battered brown leather briefcase in his hand was the final giveaway. He was trying to work out which was the main entrance to The Buttery, obviously being unable to afford the cuisine on his local government salary. 'Got tae split. Meeting tae attend tae,' growled Grimes. 'That precise hoose, right?'

'Aye, right.' The Arse Bandit smiled and replaced the handset. He needed some company on this fire job and had a couple of young junkies in mind. Total smackheads but cute-looking young boys.

'Aye, they'll do the trick nicely,' he smiled to himself and pulled his jacket on, heading for the front door.

The accountant refused an alcoholic drink, settling instead for a cup of tea. As previously arranged, Grimes and Maggie made sure the new man was sitting beside her, close enough to smell her perfume, glimpse down her cleavage and occasionally feel her thigh rub against his. As intended, he was as jittery as a chicken on hot coals.

'Hmm, a Bearer Bond,' he started, holding the docket pinched by Angie the Gopher close to his face. 'Looks like the real thing, except in this light . . .' Grimes waved to a waiter and two minutes later they had an ornate standard lamp by their table. 'That's better,' continued the accountant.

In the brighter light, Maggie and Grimes could see that his serious, dull face was blushing.

'So whit is it?' asked Grimes.

'Very interesting,' mumbled the accountant, peering at the print as closely as he could.

'What we need to know is how it works, who owns it and if it's worth anything,' explained Maggie with a smile.

'Right, sorry, of course,' flustered the accountant. 'These were issued in Germany around the 1930s during the economic depression. The government was desperate to attract funds and to stop money going abroad. So, they created these bonds, which are a bit like government stocks. For a certain amount – see this one cost $10,000 – the investor was guaranteed a high rate of interest, cumulative interest.'

'Whit's that when it's at home?' piped up Grimes.

'Well, let me show you.' The accountant pulled a crumpled typist's spiral notebook from his briefcase. 'If you start at, say, this rate . . .'

'It's okay,' Maggie laid her fingers on his wrists, 'I understand it perfectly.' She knew that, in his head and at great speed, Grimes could work out complicated betting odds, the profit percentage to be made on cutting heroin with talcum powder and a whole range of other complex mathematical problems. But his strengths were focused on the practical while the theoretical, particularly explained in jargon, left him cold.

'Right, right,' the accountant blushed more, 'so you'll be aware that if left invested over a number of years, the interest can swell to a handsome dividend?'

'Oh yes,' Maggie said in a husky voice, 'I'm very aware of that fact.'

'Ya beauty,' smiled Grimes. 'So let me get this right. If these havnae been cashed in . . .'

'Oh they haven't,' the accountant interrupted. 'If they had been redeemed they'd be in the hands of the bank. They'd check the unique serial number here,' the accountant drew his finger under the small print, 'pay out and hold on to the bonds. You see they're called Bearer Bonds . . .'

'Aye, was gonnae ask you aboot that,' said Grimes.

'Put simply, whoever bears or possesses the bonds owns them.' Grimes' jaw dropped in amazement. He fully intended to gain from these bonds but this was beginning to sound like a gift. 'They're like banknotes except they accumulate interest. So, people could sell these on at a profit. Whoever bought them bought the guaranteed interest. This prevented people from being tempted to withdraw their money – very important during the time of a recession.' Grimes wasn't listening anymore,

'So, can Ah get this straight. If Ah take this bond tae . . .' he butted in.

' . . . the German government or the Deutsche Bank – any broker will do the work for you,' the accountant answered, anticipating the full question.

' . . . they'll gie me the ten grand plus the backdated interest for fifty odd year?'

'Yes, that about sums it up,' smiled the accountant.

'How much would you estimate this bond to be worth?' Maggie asked calmly and politely as across from her Grimes was grinning and nodding his head.

'Difficult to say,' answered the accountant. 'Depends on the original level of interest agreed and the various factors since. But taking a conservative stab at interest rates,' quick fingers on his pocket calculator, 'oh, I'd say in the region of $500,000.'

Grimes' eyes were popping. A vein in the side of his head had swollen up dark blue and pulsed visibly.

'About £300,000 each?' Grimes croaked.

'Now don't quote me precisely but there or there about,' smiled the accountant. Grimes was on his feet shaking the accountant's hand. Maggie Small slowly uncrossed her legs, lingering as she lifted one leg over the other, offering a flash of stocking top to the accountant. The poor man didn't know which way to turn as Maggie Small pushed an envelope into his hand.

'A small appreciation of your professional services and in thanks for your discretion in this, mmm, sensitive matter,' she smiled, lifting her leg higher as she finally completed the uncrossing of her long limbs.

'Abb . . . so . . . yes . . . yes, of course. Naturally – it's only, hmmm, professional.'

When the accountant had left, Maggie Small and Grimes ordered large liqueurs and sat smoking and plotting. If the Bearer Bonds were worth so much, a couple would take care of Grimes' business problems. But Angie the Gopher had claimed there was a whole tin of bonds. Angie could exaggerate, in fact he was an inveterate liar. Only one thing stopped him and that was fear. Fear and terror, that was what

Grimes held over Angie, so he'd scare the weirdo into going back to the house and lifting the whole tin of bonds. Maggie and Grimes concluded they'd chanced across a goldmine. They were going to be rich.

As the accountant walked away from The Buttery, through the rundown council scheme of Anderston, he could still smell Maggie Small's perfume on his suit jacket. Vanilla and musk, it was the most beautiful smell he had ever smelled. He was a bit embarrassed by how he had behaved. He knew his strengths were pedantry and detail. Some might call his style boring but he knew they were essential values, especially in his profession. But he'd tried to impress Maggie Small with his knowledge. Did his best to come across as suave and sophisticated – and failed miserably. He hoped he hadn't gone overboard. He hadn't wanted to admit that his entire knowledge of Bearer Bonds had been gleaned from one lecture he'd attended as an undergraduate almost thirty years before.

'I'm sure I remembered everything important about Bearer Bonds,' he thought to himself. Just then the rain came on and he searched in his briefcase for his umbrella – unsuccessfully. 'No, I'm sure I didn't forget anything.'

DEAR HARSH PLACE

'Richard Burton and Liz Taylor used tae come in here, know? Just for the oysters,' Grimes slurred. 'Man, there was some heat between they two, eh? Ah think they used tae shag for real in their films.' Grimes and Maggie Small were sitting in the Rogano where he had diverted the taxi on the way back to The Cat's Whiskers. Sitting with a plate of oysters and a bottle of the best champagne, Grimes pointed out the football players, TV presenters and any other name in the place. He was in the mood for celebrating his new-found gain of £300,000 in the Bearer Bond. Maggie, as ever, was more concerned about business. In particular, getting their hands on the rest of the bonds and what was worrying her was the phone call Grimes had made from The Buttery's car park. She decided to break into her boss's good humour before it became truly drowned in the booze.

'What about Dalmeny Street, Andy?' she asked quietly.

'No problem,' he whispered, 'wee torch job the night.'

'The old couple's house?'

'Aye, well, burning an empty hoose'll no move the council.'

'True, but . . .'

'A threat tae a couple o grey hairs oan the other hand . . .' he let the statement hang knowing Maggie would catch his meaning.

'Who have you got to do the job, Andy?' Grimes looked awkward. 'Andy?'

'Arse Bandit,' he muttered, almost embarrassed.

'Shit.' When Maggie swore the words sliced home.

'It's only the roof – he's under precise instructions.'

'Wasn't he under precise instructions the last time?' Maggie knew that Grimes knew the answer.

'Aye, but . . .'

'And three people died.'

'Aye, but . . .'

'This time you've got a box of bonds to think of.' Maggie wondered at how obtuse Grimes could be at times. 'Maybe you can't have it both ways this time.' She watched as Grimes bit his lip and rubbed his face, a clear sign that he didn't like what he was being told. 'Andy, it is The Arse Bandit we're talking about.'

'Shite. Of course yer right,' conceded Grimes, slapping his great mit of a palm on the table. He pushed his way out of the booth, barged through the crowd of Chardonnay sippers and headed outside, mobile phone clutched in his hand. On the pavement he dialled the number, made a mistake and was forced to redial, cursing loudly as he did so. At last the ringing tones buzzed in his ear and buzzed and buzzed and buzzed.

'Oh FUCK,' he screamed and threw the phone on to the ground, little pieces of black plastic, wires and batteries skittering over the pavement. On the way back into the Rogano he noticed a public phone to his left, an engaged public phone. The young woman didn't know what hit her when she was suddenly gripped by the collar and yanked away from the phone. Grimes didn't care what she thought, he just dialled and prayed – to no avail. Hanging up the receiver, he didn't notice the young woman standing in the foyer digging her way down into hysterics.

'No luck?' asked Maggie when Grimes had returned.

'Naw, fucking Arse Bandit'll be roasting they fucking bonds as we speak. We better get the fuck oot o here and NOW.' On the way out of the Rogano, they passed a waiter and waitress trying to calm down the hysterical young woman. In the background the manager was discretely phoning the police. Obviously the young woman was off her head. They were getting a lot more of that sort of thing lately and he blamed the drugs.

On the south side of the city, The Arse Bandit stood on Dalmeny Street with two young boys and three gallon canisters of petrol.
'It's easy,' he told them for the umpteenth time. 'Just kick the door in, right? Pour the petrol oot, stand by the door, drop a lighted match and yer oot o there.'

The Arse Bandit had decided the requirements of setting fire to the attic were asking too much. He had felt obliged to bribe the two boys with a couple of hits of his finest smack and some dope. They were having problems staying awake, never mind clambering up through a loft. He would have done the job himself, of course, but for one minor problem, his big secret. The Arse Bandit was terrified of fire. He was also frightened of dark small spaces and he wasn't too fond of birds, or rather their feathers. But he wasn't for telling anyone that, was he? Not The Arse Bandit – he was the terror of the streets and that was the way it was going to stay. 'Hurry up, eh? Sooner we get this done, sooner we can go back to my place and get another hit cooking.'

That was the time of the night he was looking forward to. All that smack and dope wasn't going to go to waste on just this piffling little torch job. When it was over he fancied having the two boys at the same time. Maybe pass them some speed or Es as well to give them a bit of up and at it.

Of course the two boys knew nothing of The Arse Bandit's plans and neither did their girlfriends or their mothers.

'Just pour it, light it and get the fuck oot o there?' one of the boys asked.

'Aye, nae problem, eh?' The Arse Bandit reassured.

'C'moan, man, Ah'm needing another hit soon,' said his pal. The two boys staggered towards the close mouth, their drug-heavy limbs weighed down by the real weight of the three gallons of petrol.

'Top flat, mind.' The Arse Bandit shouted behind them, hoping that they'd heard.

The two boys might be junkies but they were far from stupid. They remembered it was the top flat. The door lay ajar, having already been smashed down and the flat lay empty aside from an array of empty beer cans, the charred doings of heroin works, a few used condoms and an old black-and-white TV set with no plug. Hefting a canister of petrol each they set off from opposite corners of the flat backing their way through till meeting again in what used to be the living-room. The acrid smell of fuel would have turned most people's stomachs but the drug-deadened senses of the boys protected them.

'Fucking easy money this, eh?' said one.

'Aye, nothing tae it man.' With that they both struck matches, threw them on the petrol-soaked floor, turned and ran through the nearest door – into the kitchenette. The fire caught quickly and spread. The youngsters hovered at the door, terrified to move, petrified to stay still. Then they saw it. The forgotten third canister of petrol, still full, sitting in the middle of the living-room, flames licking all around. They looked at each other, pulled their denim bomber jackets over their heads and ran through the fire towards the front door.

Grimes had hailed a taxi and given the driver orders,

'Oatlands, ye know where Ah mean? Just past the Gorbals near Shawfield? Right then, drive an Ah'll tell yese where tae pull in.' Maggie and Grimes travelled in silence, only too aware of many Glasgow taxi cab drivers' dual role as runners for the teams as well as informants for the police.

'Fuck sake, that's some blaze.' The taxi driver was the first to break the silence and when he did Grimes knew they were close to the site.

'Just pull over, driver, and wait for us, please,' said Maggie cool as ever.

'You aw right, love?' asked the driver, looking at Maggie via the rear-view mirror. 'Nothing wrong is there?' he asked, nodding imperceptibly in the direction of Grimes his eyes still staring at Maggie.

'What? Oh yes, fine,' she said with a reassuring smile. In spite of the mess and possible massive financial loss she found the driver's concern amusing. Maggie and Grimes got out of the cab, crossed Rutherglen Road and walked down a way till they had a good view of the fire engines, ambulances and attending police car. The whole scene was lit up by fire brigade spotlights but still the roof blazed fiercer, brighter.

'Fuck youse doing here?' The Arse Bandit asked, almost bumping into Grimes on the pavement. 'You checking up oan me?'

'Naw, just trying tae stop yese, ye arse wipe,' answered Grimes, buzzing with the day, up and ready for any aggro The Arse Bandit wanted to dish out, slipping his hand inside his jacket where he kept the pistol.

'Think yer too late annat,' smiled The Arse Bandit, gesturing with his thumb over his shoulder.

'Whit's burning?' demanded Grimes.

'You lost it, Grimes? It's a fucking tenement, man,' The Arse Bandit chuckled, 'THE fucking tenement.' Grimes tucked his chin down and glowered at The Arse Bandit. 'The top fucking flat like yese said, aw right.'

'You sure?' persisted Grimes.

'Whit's it look like?' and they all turned and looked back at the building, its roof ablaze but dulling fast under the steady bombardment of water curving up and down from four different directions.

'You sure the rest is aw right?'

'Aye, hunky, even the auld couple oan the bottom are fine,' said The Arse Bandit. 'Ye didnae tell me it was a couple of grey heads.'

'Would that have made a difference?'

'Naw.'

'So, no casualties and the bottom flat is safe?' asked Grimes.

'Bottom flat's safe but there was one wee mishap,' said The Arse Bandit. 'His wee pal,' nodding over his shoulder to the young boy standing behind him, 'he got a bit, eh, burned up like.'

'A bit? How fucking burned up?' demanded Grimes.

'Fucking roasted, man, ye should've seen him,' said The Arse Bandit, his eyes gleaming with excitement and relish. 'Come oot o the close with fucking flames rising from him, man. Well cooked so he is.'

'I'm sorry,' said Maggie Small, talking to the young boy who just shrugged and held his head down.

'How old was he?' asked Grimes of The Arse Bandit.

'Fucking whit? Maybe fourteen or fifteen. Whit age was he?' turning to the young boy.

'Ma age, fourteen,' he mumbled. 'Fifteen next March,' he added as if it were important.

'Can we get you anything,' Maggie asked the young boy. 'Take you anywhere?'

'Naw,' he half whispered. 'Just need a hit, man.'

'Your wish is my command,' The Arse Bandit smiled. 'We better be shifting.'

'Aye, aw right,' said Grimes and grudgingly, 'Eh, well done oan the job the night but sorry tae hear aboot yer loss. Ye know, yer team annat.' Relief was such a healer for Grimes that he was temporarily capable of sympathy even towards The Arse Bandit.

'Aye, thanks,' said The Arse Bandit quietly, standing in the dark, his teeth shining white on the backcloth of his smoke-smeared face. 'Still,' he continued putting an arm around the young boy's shoulder, 'cannae complain for small mercies, eh?' With a slow, lewd wink The Arse Bandit moved on along the pavement, his arm held round the young boy's back.

As the taxi wound its way towards The Cat's Whiskers, Maggie and Grimes sat silently in the back. Grimes was pleased with himself that the day had turned out not too badly at all. First he finds out that he is sitting on a paper fortune that may be worth millions then The Arse Bandit comes through, saving the bonds and probably Oxford Street

Properties. Two hours before, Grimes would have settled for the bonds and sacrificed his business. Now he could have both. Nothing wrong in taking it all when you could get it. Nothing wrong with that at all.

'Thought you said you weren't going to work with him again,' said Maggie Small quietly after the taxi driver had turned on his radio to break the monotonous silence. Some retro night-time DJ was playing The Rolling Stones ballad 'Nineteenth Nervous Breakdown' and the taxi driver was singing along in a strained falsetto voice.

'Whit? Naw, Ah'll no. Ah'm finished.' Grimes smiled out of the side window at the dark ghost of the People's Palace and the hookers stamping their feet on the ground to fight off the cold, shading from the rain under the trees on Glasgow Green. 'Ah love this fucking city,' he thought. And he did, right there and then, love Glasgow. He had more in common with that dear harsh place than with any person he had ever known. 'Naw, Ah'll no need tae use him again after the night. That's a guarantee.'

DEAD OF NIGHT

'Ah'll need tae phone The Arse Bandit, Maggie.'

Grimes sat at his desk in The Cat's Whiskers, hands out, palms up and a look of sad resignation on his face. 'No choice left.'

'But you said . . . oh, Andy, he's trouble. Serious trouble, and you bloody well promised,' she replied.

'Ah know but whit Ah'm Ah supposed tae dae?' Grimes' voice begged for forgiveness in a discordant tone that made Maggie's scalp crawl with suspicion. He never begged, rarely asked and forgiveness was a gift he had no use for. What was going on here? What else didn't she know?

'Look, Ah have tae tell ye,' Grimes conceded. His relationship with Maggie was part business partners, part George Washington and his parent. On drunken, lonely nights he had chosen her and only her as mother confessor, to lay the weight of all of his darkest deeds on her shoulders. 'Scotch Brian's woke up and they promised me he was going tae peg it. Or be fucking totally disabled. Bastarding quacks never get fuck all right when ye want them tae.'

'I thought he got run over?' Maggie had only been told half the story. 'Oh,' realisation rung her bell, 'what did you do, Andy?'

'He was going totally fucking mental, Maggie, Ah had tae have him seen tae.'

'Seen to by Deadeye?' she asked.

'Aye, Deadeye,' his head was down, small child waiting for a deserved chiding.

'So why not use Deadeye again?' Mother was in a forgiving, helpful mood, as ever.

'Whit, Deadeye versus Scotch Brian? Look, Brian might have been in a coma for weeks, have a few broken bones, wakened wi one side of his face paralysed and no be able tae speak but he'd eat fucking Deadeye alive in a straight head oan.' Maggie sent him a sceptical look.

'Last time,' Grimes explained, 'Deadeye jumped him. Besides, Scotch Brian was oot o his nut oan rock or crack whatever. Now the cunt knows we're oot tae get him. Naw it'll have tae be someone else and The Arse Bandit's ma only choice. But if yese like Ah'll send Deadeye with him?' he offered.

Maggie conceded gracefully. It was accepted between them that such affairs were Grimes' speciality while matters of commerce and negotiation belonged to Maggie. She just prayed that The Arse Bandit wouldn't bring them all down. 'Right,' Grimes said, returning to form, 'Ah'll just phone Birse. Get him tae call his man off the door.'

Scotch Brian sat in his bed and fretted. He had been in a coma for weeks, getting stuffed full of the finest drugs to keep him regular, pain free and alive. He was of the old school, rising to prominence on the street on the basis of a ferocious physical strength and a constitution that could survive nuclear fallout. It would take more than a mashed skull to finish him. Now that he'd wakened they had reduced his dosages and he found that the monkey was right on his back, sharp claws digging into his brain.

Twenty years on the finest cocaine, ten years on the purest freebase coke and Scotch Brian was in a love affair that would last his entire life. With the sweet highs of the hits came the rages of withdrawals and it would remain that way till he finally pegged out. What he needed was a smoke of his pipe or maybe just a line or two of Charlie to get him straight. Some blues would do, or even a handful of jellies. Something, anything. So Scotch Brian assessed his predicament and plotted. He'd a broken leg in plaster, one of his hands ached, his chest felt like a tight metal band was wrapped around it, his face was twisted so he drooled all the time. He couldn't speak a word, he was in a hospital-issue gown with no clothes and there was a young polis guarding the only door out of the room.

'Ach, been worse,' he thought, 'but not much.' A young female doctor came in carrying a tray.

'Wide awake? Are you a sight for sore eyes,' she smiled. He nodded, sending a stream of saliva tumbling over his chin. 'We thought we'd lost you. Welcome back,' she clutched at his hand which didn't ache and squeezed it.

If he had met her when his consciousness first crawled out of the dark he would have taken her for an angel. Scotch Brian didn't have much time for women, though it was women he preferred. But this one had the eyes of someone you could fall for and she smelled . . . clean. That was it, clean. God, how he missed clean. 'Now I'm going to give you some medication.' That's more like it. 'A little something for the pain.' Bingo. 'Before I do.' Shit. 'Can I ask if you can write? With your good hand?' What did she want? Noughts and fucking crosses? Just give us the dope. 'It's just it would be good to have your name. If you feel up to it?' He gripped the pen she offered and on her pad, slowly and painfully, scribbled, *Gerry Kirkpatrick*.

Where the fuck did that come from? He knew who he was and he wasn't going to tell the doc that, angel face or no angel face. But whose name had he written. Gerry? Gerry? Didn't mean much. Then Deadeye's dour face came alive in his head. Ah, that Gerry Kirkpatrick. That back-shooting, cowardly, doomed Gerry Kirkpatrick. That dead Deadeye Gerry Kirkpatrick.

Over the doctor's shoulder he noticed the young cop speaking to someone in plain clothes with an ugly face he'd never forget. It was Birse. Might be decades older and a few stones heavier but that was the same Birse who lifted him that very first time when he was a kid. Birse had caught him square and round for shop breaking but, not satisfied with that, he'd given the young Brian a right kicking and added three more offences to his charge sheet. Offences he had not committed but still went down for. Birse was an old score waiting to be settled.

Angel doctor was busy saying something but Scotch Brian wasn't listening, he was watching the young cop collect his things. Birse waited for the uniform to disappear, then turned to look through the window in the door. Catching Scotch Brian's eye, Birse smiled, waved, mouthed 'CHEERIO, CHEERIO, CHEERIOOOOO', football-chant style and walked away. Angel eyes was shooting some muck into his arm that he prayed was diamorphine, heroin, smack, junk. That would be the ticket and had arrived just in time. Scotch Brian had business to attend to and first off he had to get out of that hospital bed before the hit squad arrived.

With the doctor gone, Brian carried out a survey of his room. Yanking his plaster-stiff leg over the edge of the bed he lowered himself to the ground. The room was spinning, slowly but effectively. It was just a white-out and would pass, he hoped. By the time he'd staggered to the wardrobe, discovering it empty apart from a tatty hospital dressing gown, and come back to his locker, his balance was as stable as could be expected for someone who had just emerged from a coma. In the locker he was surprised to find a packet of cigarettes and a lighter. They couldn't be his – all his clothes and belongings would be in the forensic lab – they must have been left by an earlier patient. The fags were a cheap brand and one he didn't care for, but a smoke is a smoke. Thinking time smoke – he had to get out of that hospital room.

Throwing on the faded and frayed tartan dressing gown, Scotch Brian padded cautiously out of the door and down the green corridor, holding on to the wall for balance and listening for noises. He was grateful for the shortages in the NHS – no staff around to confront him and halt his progress. Eventually he found a door marked EMERGENCY EXIT and on the other side a metal platform at the top of metal fire escape stairs, turning sharply, repeatedly all the way to the ground. The stagger down the corridor had exhausted Scotch Brian, his bad leg ached and he was covered in sweat. Half-fit, he wouldn't have hesitated to shimmy down the fire escape, even dressed as he was. That night he needed a breather and time to think. Pulling the cheap fags from his dressing gown pocket he fired one up and with the first draw the dizziness returned with a vengeance.

The rear of the Glasgow Royal looked like an enclosed quadrangle to Scotch Brian, like some of the ancient prisons he knew only too well in Victorian buildings designed to terrify the inhabitants. Except worse. The Royal looked like a madhouse or a film set for a horror movie. The place was giving him the raving heebee-jeebees. Men's voices, nearby, down below. Scotch Brian pulled himself back into the shadows and listened.

'Ah'm in charge here so Ah go up first.'

'Yer too fat. Ah'm no taking the risk ye slip.'

'Fat! Cheeky cunt, this is pure muscle.'

'So yer telling me.'

'Fucking show yese as soon as this job's done. Now shift.'

The allegedly fat man started to climb the fire escape ladder next to the one Scotch Brian was having his smoke break on. In the still of the night, the man's strained, sharp breathing reached Brian's ears. When, eventually, he had reached three-quarters of the way up he came into Brian's view. An ugly man, short and squat with a bowl haircut and a pudding face. As he climbed, his tongue hung out of the side of his mouth. Nasty looking, yes, but a stranger to Scotch Brian. Not like the second man, Gerry Kirkpatrick, the doomed Deadeye. Scotch Brian knew they were the hit team.

'You aw right, Arse Bandito?' said Deadeye. 'No want a wee seat after that bit exercise?'

'Whit you calling me, ye wee runt? Nobody calls me that,' said The Arse Bandit.

'Aye, tae yer face.' Deadeye was looking up at the rear end of The Arse Bandit and was looking for trouble. Scotch Brian hoped the bad feeling between them ran high enough to distract them.

'Go on,' he thought, 'shoot each other. Go on, fucking dare you.'

'You an me's gonnae sort this oot between us after we've killed this old cunt,' declared The Arse Bandit.

'Fine by me,' replied Deadeye. With that they sprung the door open and crept into the hospital corridor.

There was no dilemma now. Scotch Brian went for the stairs. With every step his plastered leg made a metallic clunk that echoed in the night air, each shock jarring into his groin. He ignored the pain, knowing he had maybe two minutes maximum to reach the ground before they searched in this quarter. As Scotch Brian trundled down the stairs he was being watched by another patient sneaking a smoke on a platform across the way.

'Go oan yersel, big man,' the sole audience shouted, 'run for it. Ah'm coming wi yese.' Scotch Brian tried to shout threats at the man but all that emerged from his mouth was more drool.

Reaching the ground, Scotch Brian took off, peg-legging it across the quadrangle heading for the rear of the hospital, praying he could hide in the dark before the death squad emerged. As he reached the far side, the observing patient called out,

'Run for it, Jimmy, they've spotted yese.' Up on the metal fire escape The Arse Bandit and Deadeye, their sight not yet readjusted to the dark, were drawn by the man's shout. When the shot rang out, Scotch Brian ducked and headed down the side of the hospital, hobbling towards what looked like black oblivion. He'd recognised the shot as coming from a Magnum, his Magnum, and now knew for sure that Deadeye was going to be a dead man.

Scotch Brian tottered down what looked like a country lane till the mass of the back of Glasgow Cathedral loomed into view. It was so close it was frightening, like standing at the bottom of a skyscraper and looking upwards. On he panted, across an old single-track bridge and onto a winding, steep path. The sweat was dripping off his head and the pain in his leg and chest were agony but to stop would mean paying a greater price.

Nearing the top of a high knoll, bushes appeared and Scotch Brian dived for cover. Flopping on thick wet grass he listened to the sound of his own heaving chest, trying to breathe more slowly to cut down his noise so he could hear if his pursuers were still on his trail. Nothing. No sound of footsteps. He'd given them the slip.

'Yer claimed, mister.' Scotch Brian swivelled round to see a group of three or four young boys and a couple of even younger girls standing feet away. In the half-moonlight they looked pale faced, thin, ephemeral, ghostly. 'Yer claimed,' the young spokesperson repeated, having received no response from Scotch Brian. 'This is oor territory and yer oan it.' Scotch Brian clambered painfully to his feet. 'This is oor patch and yer trespassing.' The young boy flicked open his razor. Scotch Brian gained his feet and stood before them holding his arms out to keep his balance. The kids got their first good look. Tall and wide, wearing a gown like a shroud, bare legs glowing white in the dark. Sweat-soaked hair sticking up on end and a face twisted to one side, drooling down his chin. And a smile, just a little smile. Real people they could handle, but this was too much, especially in that place. The kids vanished. Disappeared. Vamoosed into thin air. And the shakes were beginning to hit Scotch Brian again.

He leaned backwards against a tree, needing a rest and to make sense of it all. The trunk felt hard and cold, stone like. When he turned the tree had metamorphosed into a high gravestone. Startled, Scotch Brian staggered away. It wasn't just a gravestone but a big fancy affair, as tall as a house, with angry, fierce goblin faces staring out at him. He took flight.

The sweats were back along with the shakes and all he could hear in his head was the crashing of waves. Whatever that doctor had given him it wasn't smack and it wasn't enough to keep the horrors at bay. More gravestones, each one bigger and uglier than the last. They were chasing him, hunting him and Scotch Brian was fleeing. He sensed he had come to Glasgow to die but there was no need for this. He'd done bad deeds, plenty, but surely he had done some good? Surely they could see that? If only they let him live, he'd change. He was tired anyway. Worn out. He promised. Anything. With each turn he faced a new grave each with his name inscribed. One gravestone bent over reaching out its tentacles, feeling out for him and he leapt through a hedge right into trouble.

Suddenly the dark broke and there in a valley in front of him was a massive spacecraft. All bright lights, shining aluminium and exhaust fumes. They had come for him and it was all too much. Scotch Brian backed off over a sheer ledge and fell a hundred feet.

'Think he's deid?' asked The Arse Bandit coming across Scotch Brian's body an hour later lying crumpled in the lower reaches of Glasgow's oldest cemetery.

'Ah'm no taking any chances this time,' replied Deadeye, putting the Magnum against the back of Scotch Brian's overtly smashed skull. The blast ricocheted around the Necropolis, off the gravestones and back. High above them a small boy crawled out of the bushes and peered down, carefully. When he and his friends had confronted the ghost they took Scotch Brian for, the others had scooted off home. That option wasn't open to him unless he was in the mood for another beating from his father while his mother lay dead drunk. Rather the company of spooks than that.

'Think he was thirsty?' asked The Arse Bandit, nodding over his shoulder at the Tennant's Lager Brewery, all bright lights and aluminium pipes.

'Aye, that's a good yin,' conceded Deadeye. 'He was dying for a pint, eh? Eh!' The Arse Bandit laughed. The kill had worked for both men in lifting their spirits, the bad-tempered gibing from earlier in the night all but forgotten.

'Whit we gonnae do wi him?' asked The Arse Bandit.

'Aw, just leave him,' said Deadeye. 'Grimes was quite happy for us tae do him in his fucking hospital bed, wasn't he?'

'Aye, but he's no there, is he? And you've just put a traceable bullet in the fucker as well as back at the hospital.'

'Aye, Ah suppose Grimes would be even happier if we tidied up the job,' conceded Deadeye.

'Aye, an maybe more generous.'

'Got an idea,' said Deadeye. 'Where dae ye hide a pin?'

'Whit ye oan aboot, man?'

'Best place tae hide a pin is in a box o pins, right?'

'If ye say so.' The Arse Bandit still wasn't following.

'Look, you humph the stiff up tae the top there and I'll go fetch something – show yese.' The Arse Bandit wasn't sure that Deadeye wasn't taking a rise but the good mood of the hit won over his suspicions and off he set.

Deadeye later found The Arse Bandit, sitting on a large, thick granite slab laid over a grave in front of the headstone, with Scotch Brian's corpse, his forehead a black hole, leaning against it as if sunbathing.

'Perfect,' said Deadeye.

'Whit?' puffed The Arse Bandit.

'Taaararaaa!' Deadeye produced a pick and spade from behind his back. 'We are gonnae bury the cunt under there.' The Arse Bandit looked at the slab he was sitting on, got the point and smiled.

Sometime later they had managed to raise the slab about a foot off the grave.

'See they slabs?' The Arse Bandit asked, as if Deadeye hadn't noticed the chunk of granite they'd been struggling with. 'They were put there by relatives, know, tae stop the grave robbers.'

'Aye? Whit's there tae rob?'

'The bodies annat – for doctors at the Uni,' explained The Arse Bandit.

'Aye? Must be the first time somebody's made an extra deposit then.'

Two hours later, the weak sun was threatening to rise into a sky turning reluctantly from black to dark grey. Scotch Brian had been successfully interred and the slab returned to its precise position. The two gravediggers were checking the area for any obvious signs of disruption when Deadeye whispered,

'Don't look up but we're being watched.' The young boy was peeking at them from a vantage point behind a nearby bush.

'Ach, it's just a wean,' whispered The Arse Bandit.

'Aye, a kid that saw too much,' grumbled Deadeye.

'Right enough,' said The Arse Bandit, 'ma turn for a suggestion. You take the pick and spade tae be dumped so they think it was just a wee bit o petty thievery, eh, and Ah'll take care o the wee fella.' Deadeye knew all about The Arse Bandit's taste in young boys and he didn't approve. But tonight, as usual, business came before morals for Deadeye.

'He's no tae be in a position tae grass us up,' added Deadeye, concerned that his associate was simply chasing his own pleasure principle.

'Ha,' laughed The Arse Bandit quietly, 'that's guaranteed cast iron, ma man.'

'Deal then.' Deadeye stood up and lofted the spade and pick.

'Ho, son, nice night for it, eh?' The Arse Bandit's voice was all friendly uncle. 'Fancy a wee smoke? Ah've got a bottle o ginger here tae.'

Deadeye walked away, the tools weighing on one shoulder, as the boy emerged from his hiding place and took a long swallow of lemonade and a cigarette off The Arse Bandit. The night had been a profitable one. Not only had they successfully dispatched Scotch Brian and pleased Grimes but Deadeye had learned something.

'Maybe The Arse Bandit isnae as bad as he's made oot,' he thought. 'Maybe him an me can work the gether oan a few joint projects.'

Up on the knoll of the Necropolis, The Arse Bandit put his arm around the young boy's shoulder leading him away to his lair. He'd learned something too that night and as he smiled reassuringly at the boy, he thought, 'This is a rerr place for hiding the evidence so it is.'

DEADLY DIVISIONS

LEFT-WING PANSIES

'YOU ARE CAUSING AN ILLEGAL OBSTRUCTION. CLEAR THE WAY OR I'LL BE FORCED TO MAKE ARRESTS.'

The uniformed policeman had glittering Christmas decorations for epaulettes and fancy braid on his helmet. 'I REPEAT – MOVE ASIDE OR I'LL ORDER MY MEN TO MAKE ARRESTS.'

The crowd consisted of all ages, all genders, all social classes. The one thing they had in common was their refusal to budge. More people with placards were streaming in off Rutherglen Road to join their comrades. Someone started singing a half-chant, half-song and everyone joined in. No one was going to be evicted from Dalmeny Street today.

'Look, Bob,' the big man in the suit addressed the police top brass with justified familiarity. They had worked side by side for twenty years in Strathclyde Police. 'Why don't your men just shift the cunts. Get the batons oot and get in amongst it?'

'Aye, you would like that, eh?' the policeman replied. 'Liked it a lot in your day I recall.'

'They are breaking the law, man,' the suit protested. 'SPS have a legally binding eviction order on the basis of health and safety issues, man. The fucking building is roofless.'

'Aye, and the old couple don't want tae budge and, let me remind you, I'm the law here, no you.'

'Okay, why don't you let ma boys an me charge in?' the suit persisted. 'An if we can't manage it your team can pick the lefties off.'

'You're no dealing with a bunch of kids here, ye know,' the brass replied. 'These people are experienced, organised and some would have your overweight thugs for breakfast.'

'Aye, right ye are.' The suit dismissed his comments with sarcasm. 'How the fuck did they find aboot this onyroads?'

'Look, man, these are anti-poll tax campaigners,' the brass sighed, trying to explain what he thought was obvious. 'Somebody at the housing department's phoned and alerted them. Told them that the old couple werenae for budging regardless the state o the hoose. This crowd are just up to stop evictions, any evictions an they know they can win. Anti-poll tax, man, no weans. They are deadly serious and experienced. Christ's sake, look at them properly and see who you recognise.'

The suit trailed his eyes down the crowd, taking in one face at a time rather than the mass. There was the well-known young socialist who was involved in every demonstration and strike that happened. Two down there was an ex-gang member from Pollok, shopped him himself for a couple of affrays. What? Had he converted or something? Three more faces he had known through his police work. A young Church of Scotland minister. In front of the group paraded a bunch of scruffy-looking kids. In the lead, the oldest boy held a large phone piece to his ear and behind him trailed his brothers and sisters holding a khaki-coloured case, wires and switches and something that looked like an aerial. The McElhone kids – back in his beat days he had lifted their mother for prostitution more times than he cared to remember. Some of his colleagues still visited her house to give her a go for old times sake. Somehow the children added to his view that this was one solid gathering, one worth the watching. Christ, he'd love to mix it with them.

The suit's eyes lifted up from the crowd to the house in question. At one window Jakob and Ruth Wise watched the events, their old faces strained with a lack of understanding and an overdose of terror. They had seen such events before and feared that Berlin had finally caught up with them.

The suit knew nothing of how the old couple felt and cared less. He was just frustrated that he couldn't get through to get his hands on such easy targets. Could carry them out himself, one under each arm, if it wasn't for this bloody crowd of anti-poll tax campaigners. But who was that standing behind the oldies? If the suit wasn't mistaken it was Angie the Gopher. What the hell was he doing in there? The suit made a mental note to tell Birse and Grimes as soon as this charade was over. Oxford Street Properties were paying most of his wages after all.

Back to the crowd. A whole bunch of women, housewife types. Their menfolk should keep them in order, was the suit's view. A bunch of kids that should be at school. And a grinning, familiar face, staring at him, just him. What was she doing here? Cathy Brodie slowly stuck her tongue out at the suit.

'The left-wing pansies are here,' she called over to him, 'What ye waiting for?' Both her arms in the air beckoning him forward with her hands, 'Come ahead if yer able.'

The suit turned back to the brass, 'That's fucking it. Ah'm taking ma boys in and youse can dae whit ye like.'

'I'll arrest you if you move one step towards that house,' the brass replied quietly without looking at him.

'Whit the fuck?' growled the suit. 'Whose bastarding side you oan, man?'

'Law and order, of course,' replied the brass. 'Oh, and good publicity.' He nodded his head to the end of the road where the TV crews had already set up, their cameras rolling. Alongside them, photographers from all the main papers were standing on top of cars, wide-angled lenses covering the whole scene. 'Now, shift your arse,' barked the brass. 'This operation is formally abandoned.'

'Alex Birse is no gonnae like this,' warned the suit.

'Shift, before I lift you for breach of the peace, ye dim arsehole,' threatened the brass.

A short distance away, the whole proceedings were being watched by a tall, distinguished-looking man with white hair. Councillor Wiley had come to watch more of his shame, to feel the weight of his failure. He had decided to put an end to all of this.

HIPPIES AND HELMETS

'Look at them, man, mental.'

'Pure head cases, the lot o them.'

'Think they Commie guards are gonnae turn nasty?'

'Naw, watch this man, watching, right.'

'Fuck's sakes, a wee while back they were shooting any cunt that looked at em.'

'Mental.'

'Widnae be me but.'

'Whit ye mean?'

'Ah'd let some other mugs go up first.'

'Whit?'

'Make fucking sure the shooting wisnae still oan the cards, know? They Commies are serious fuckers.'

'Where yese been the last few weeks? Fucking hibernating as usual?'

'Cheeky cunt, whit ye getting at?'

'It's been oan the TV for weeks, man. Saying this was gonnae happen.'

'Aye?'

'Aye.'

'Aw, Ah dinnae pay much attention tae the idiot box, man, too busy.'

'See, look there. See that?'

'Whit?'

'Fucking guard's got his helmet aff, an look there's another one wi a fucking wee pansy or thingy in the barrel o his shooter.'

'Fucking soft right enough. The fucking Commies – who would've thought.'

'Mental.'

'Whit are you fuckers up tae?' Grimes shouted as he steamed into the office making all his team jump. The entire contingent was sitting around watching reruns of the news of the fall of the Berlin Wall. They thought it was historical, important, more important than work, but their views weren't unanimous.

'Ye watching this shite for?' They turned and stared at Shuggie

Reid, aka The Mouse, who was back in gambling debts to them all again and knew he was being handed the short straw. The Mouse felt round the edge of his surgical collar, pulling it away from his throat to help him breathe, cool down. Somehow the metal clips in his skull felt tight again, though he hadn't noticed them for days.

'Boss,' The Mouse started, 'we just thought it was like, eh, important annat.' Cringing as he finished his short sentence.

'Aw, like whit's going oan ower there in a foreign fucking country wi a bunch o hairy hippies oan a dope rampage is like more important than whit Ah pay ye tae dae?' Grimes was just warming to his act.

'Aye, boys, the boss might be right, eh?' The Mouse was going to attempt appeasement. 'They Fritzes look fucking stoned right enough, eh?' Grimes gripped his fists into knuckles and headed in The Mouse's direction as the small man sprung to his feet and scampered as far away as the room would allow.

'Boss, Ah didnae mean anything, just meant that ye were right,' the small man shrilled.

'Ye better believe it, Mouse,' and Grimes kept heading for him.

'It's jist that the young folk, boss, they think it's good reason for a party, ye know, the stupid wee wankers.' The Mouse tried a laugh but fear strangled it in his gullet and it came out sounding more like a cough. Just then Maggie Small walked in the room.

'Is that right?' Grimes asked of the company. 'Young folk like here, in Glesca, might be celebrating?'

'Aye, boss,' shrieked The Mouse.

'Think he's right, boss,' said Angie the Gopher.

'Aye, any fucking excuse for sex and drugs and music these days, man,' agreed another. Grimes had come to an abrupt halt some yards away from the cowering Mouse, the effort of a change of mind knitting his brow. Maggie Small approached Grimes.

'Need a quiet word, Andy,' she said. They moved to the far end of the room and she continued, 'I've just had a call from Birse. One of his newspaper pals has passed him the word that Councillor Wiley was killed tonight.'

'Whit?' he struggled to take in the information.

'Apparently he just walked out in front of the traffic in the city centre. Just walked straight out, drivers didn't have a chance,' she continued. 'Given the state he was in recently it might look suspicious to us but is likely to be written off as an accident.'

'Aye.'

'Unless he's left a note or a letter or anything.' Maggie was trying to cover the angles they would have to think of but Grimes was in a thought-ridden, speechless trance. It was upsetting news, but Maggie didn't expect to see Grimes so moved.

'We'll have tae apply Plan B, then, eh?' Grimes finally strung together a sentence, revealing that, as usual, it was his business he was thinking about, he didn't give a toss about Wiley's death.

'Plan B?' she asked.

'Aye, tell yese aboot it later,' he chirped up and turned away to face his men again. 'Right youse lot, collect empty ginger bottles an start filling them up wi water.'

'Whit?' exclaimed a couple of the team at the same time.

'We're celebrating the fall of the Berlin Wall,' explained Grimes, 'A great historical event. Come oan, boys, this is history annat. Celebrate . . . we're setting up a rave for they youngsters.'

The men looked at each other, shrugging, then did as they were ordered. 'There's lot o dough tae be made oot o history, man,' Grimes explained. 'By the way,' he yelled, 'anybody seen Deadeye?'

'Naw, boss, he's no been in aw night,' Angie the Gopher answered.

'That Deadeye is never around these days,' Grimes thought, 'What the fuck is he up tae?'

10 NOVEMBER 1989

Well it's finally happened. I grew up with that Wall as a way of life and yesterday it came to an end.

As a child you learn that people are so lethal sometimes we need to build fences to keep them out. That Wall made it feel as if that kind of self-interest was the way to be: natural, necessary.

And hate. We all hated the Communists as we grew up, or at least they tried to get you to think that way. My generation of kids didn't play Cowboys and Indians, we played Cops and Robbers or War. It was the Germans, the Japs and the Commies that wore the black hats not us. As if Communism was a state of mind, a state of wickedness. As if we had been at war with them for years. Later I realised they are just ordinary people like you and like me.

It's been a strange year. The Soviet Army got kicked out of Afghanistan with a terrible loss of life. If it had been the Yanks or the Brits or the Aussies or almost anyone else in the world it would have been a cause of international mourning. To listen to our media you'd believe it was a cause for celebration that young guys got killed — over what? Does anyone really know?

Then Tiananmen Square. I'll never slag off students again. Apart from their dress sense. The image of that young guy playing tig with that tank. Now that's balls and for what? — just to demand a say? Wish more folk here demanded a say. Then one night the tanks roll in and crush them in their sleep. A short while later Thatcher's lackeys are over there doing business with the government. What kind of signal is that? Fuck with us and we might roll over you too?

That mad Ayatollah Khomeini kicked the bucket. His funeral was like a battle. A million so-called mourners, all men, beating their chests till they bled and so desperate to touch the little man that the coffin ended up on its side and his corpse half naked. Grief? So where were the womenfolk? Do they not grieve? What was that all about?

It was getting to the stage that it was all bad, crazy news. If you thought about it too long it felt as if the world was crumbling into despair and madness. Then down came the Wall. I stayed up last night watching the film over and over again. The folks pulling lumps of stone away with their bare hands, just seemed like normal folks. The youngsters looked like those students in China. Felt like them. The good news, the bad news from one continent or another – the people all looked the same. Has it always been like this?

Yesterday was a strange day. I went to check up on Angie the Gopher. He's been spending a lot of time with that old Jewish couple. I've noticed the man hardly ever leaves the house now but Angie still visits. Not like him. Then the mob arrived. I hung back, too many police. Got chatting to an old jakie. Cost me a few quid and a packet of fags but was worth it.

We watched the battle in silence from his small campfire on a piece of wasteground – I suppose he calls it home. The anti-poll tax campaigners looked just like the people that tore down the Wall later that night. The police looked like police anywhere. Noticed that SPS mob right in the middle of the action. The KGB of the private market.

It's like a retirement home for bent coppers that firm. The main suit used to be inspector rank in the Scottish Serious Crime Squad. A high flyer till he got hauled off the streets, investigated for his involvement in a scam smuggling diamonds in from Amsterdam on small planes landing at Glasgow Airport. Trouble is it was an internal investigation – most of the team knew him and were in Grimes' employ. The suit got off and resigned early only to step right into a job in private security with SPS.

Officially Grimes has nothing to do with SPS but it is registered as one of his Oxford Street Properties. No doubt there then who set up the eviction charade.

Finally worked out what Grimes wants from Dalmeny Street. Tracked down a working girl who regularly sees to Bob Benson. Gave her double her rate and just asked to talk - she appreciated that. Before long and without me trying she was talking about the wee fat man, with the long knob bent at 45 degrees. Seems Benson likes to talk too - brag more like - in between his S&M games. If Grimes doesn't get a new contract to demolish the Dalmeny Street area Oxford Street Properties goes bust. If that happens, he has no cover for his illegit income or various scams. He fears the Inland Revenue more than the police - the tax folk are not that open to sweeteners. One of his plans is to extend his counterfeit money lark into Europe - acting as a clearing house for various firms in several countries. So he isn't just risking what he's got but what he intends to get. Dalmeny Street looks like a group of dilapidated slums, but for Grimes it's a big deal.

Advised the working girl to move patches. Told her I knew that there was a police operation going to hit the women who work around Blythswood Square - think she reckoned I was a copper, not unusual in her game. I dread to think what Grimes would do to her if he found out what she knew.

I've got no problem with Grimes' rackets but I do have a problem with the attention he's paying the old couple. Realised that the old guy used to run a couple of pawnshops. Went there a few times years ago to sell on stolen goods. He wasn't the most generous payer but then no fence is. At least he was reliable - nothing ever fired back at me. So why is Grimes giving them so much grief? There are plenty of other houses to torch.

Heard from one of the local dealers that one of his smackheads was flush the other night as well as honking of petrol. When the guy teased him about sucking petrol out of cars' tanks being one down on blagging car radios the junkie got all indignant and started boasting about doing a job with The Arse Bandit. Now who employs that unreliable beast to do what? How come the young junkie was free and not getting shagged? My guess is Grimes was the paymaster and something nasty like torching the old folk's tenement was the target. Aye, and there was more than one young guy with The Arse Bandit that night.

I'm going to have to move in on Grimes and The Arse Bandit pronto. I'm not having them hurting the old couple - no way.

A

LOVE ON THE CLYDE

'Whit are we doing here, man?' Fergie sat in the passenger seat as Joe drove down the back roads beside the Clyde, the streets dark and ill lit, bumpy with potholes and slippery with wet, worn cobblestones.

'Just want tae see whit Grimes is up tae,' Joe explained for the umpteenth time, concentrating hard on steering the car on the perilous road surface.

'We'd be better off going some place else, Joe, this sleuth game yer fond of is a real bore,' grumbled Fergie.

'Look, we'll take a shifty and if it looks like nothing's going oan or ye dinnae like it we're oot o there.'

'Promise?'

'Aye, cross ma heart an hope ma balls drop off,' laughed Joe.

'So yer no that bothered if ye break yer word then,' mumbled Fergie, 'mean yer no really losing much, are yese?'

'Cheeky fucking bam.' Fergie squealed like a young boy pretending to struggle with Joe as he slapped out with one hand and steered with the other.

'Shit,' shouted Fergie, 'think we might have arrived, man.'

For some time they had been driving alongside massive but long-redundant granary warehouses. Close up they were just solid walls of endless red brick without a break or relief. Here and there a disused loading chute broke the monotony but there was no sign of life till now, where it was buzzing. Coaches and cars lined the street for a hundred yards. On the side of the building someone had hung a series of joined white sheets and spray painted 'THE WALL CAME DOWN' in six-foot-high letters. Young people were patiently queuing at the open double doors of a loading bay and light beams flooded out into the dark street. Above the noise of the engine, the thud-thud-thudding bass of loud music reverberated through the car.

'Fuck sakes, Joe,' exclaimed Fergie, 'dinnae think that's Chrissie Hynde they're playing, man.'

Fergie and Joe parked and jumped the queue. On the door were some bouncers from The Cat's Whiskers who waved them through, as did the two women from the club, sitting at a table collecting the money. The sloe-eyed brunette smiled broadly at Joe as she always did.

'Fucking fancies you, man,' Fergie teased his mate in an old vein, 'either that or yer wallet.'

'Aye, right, she's just being friendly like,' Joe dismissed his comments.

'Never had a Chinkie bird, have you, Joe?' Fergie persisted.

'Naw.'

'Well?'

'Well, we've business tae attend tae,' Joe replied brusquely.

'See your trouble, Joe,' Fergie started, 'yer just too fucking serious for yer own good.' As Joe pushed open the main doors the wave of sound hit them like a full-scale gale on top of the Sighthill flats. It wasn't just loud, it was painful. Joe's discomfort could be discerned by a slight grimace. Fergie was less subtle, clutching at both ears and bending over, trying to cower under the music and failing, of course. The granary was packed out with young adults, most wearing skimpy outfits, gyrating, hugging, blowing whistles, dancing and even managing to talk with one another. Joe wanted to find Grimes. Fergie just wanted to leave.

At the back of the hall they found Angie the Gopher and The Mouse, both looking as if they had experienced a life-threatening shock. Fergie couldn't be sure but he was convinced Angie's wig was bouncing to the music. The Mouse appeared to be attempting to pull his head down into his surgical collar and looked like a slightly animated version of the old graffiti declaring 'KILROY WOS HERE'.

The Happy Mondays kept raving on through the sound system but as far as Joe and Fergie were concerned it could have been anybody. In Glasgow you were either club or street and, so far, the two friends were decidedly street. As far as Angie and The Mouse were concerned, it wasn't music but torture.

When Joe's efforts at communicating with the two distressed older men failed, Angie signalled everyone to follow him. He had discovered an office adjacent to the main hall but separated from it by an almost effective panel of double glazing.

'Boss ordered us no tae hang oot in here,' explained Angie, though his words sounded hollow and ill formed as the after-effects of the music still battered around his brain. 'Said we couldnae watch whit's going oan properly. Tae make sure things went smooth like and tae get the money oot o the place if the polis raided us.'

'Polis?' asked Fergie, trying to clear his ear of wax. 'Why would the polis be interested?'

'S'no quite legit,' mumbled The Mouse through his surgical collar. 'Fact, no legit at aw.'

'Naw, fucking owners dinnae know we're using this dump,' added Angie, 'an we dinnae have a licence.' Fergie's ears perked up.

'Licence? Any chance o a beer then, boys?' Both The Mouse and Angie the Gopher shook their heads.

'No bar,' said The Mouse sadly, 'jist selling fucking water and these things, whatever the fuck they are.' The Mouse held up a Safeway carrier bag half full of Ecstasy.

'WATER?' Fergie was confused. 'Who the fuck wants tae drink the stuff?'

'They kids,' replied The Mouse, 'cannae get enough o it. Got tae dae wi they F drugs annat.'

'F?' it was Joe's turn. 'Eh, you mean Es, Mouse?'

'Aye, whit ye say. Fucking Es then,' said The Mouse who couldn't have cared less. 'They pay a quid a go. For fucking tap water!' Joe's curiosity was now answered. There was no issue here for Grimes except that old hardy annual of profit. Twenty quid a head at the door, a pound for a bottle of water and Angie and the Mouse on duty to collect the empty bottles, refilling them from the only tap in the place held under a temporary padlock and key. Add to that the proceeds of The Mouse's other task of selling Es – Joe reckoned The Mouse had to be the most unlikely drug dealer in the country – and the profits on the night were huge. Minimal overheads, maximum costs equalled profit. Just the way Grimes liked it.

'Take it Grimes is no going tae be around the night then, eh?' asked Joe.

'Naw,' replied Angie, looking more and more like a half-scalped, startled rodent, 'says he cannae stand the racket.'

On their way through the crowd heading towards the door the DJ executed a seamless change from Happy Mondays to Jean Michel Jarre's 'Oxygene Part IV' and Fergie was off jigging with passers-by, grabbing a woman, getting down and going for it. Joe walked on and noticed a man looking as out of place as he felt. Tall and broad, in his late forties, blonde hair turned ash white, he was wearing an ill-fitting, baggy suit and casing the crowd. He looked like an undercover drugs cop too sloppy with his disguise. Joe made a mental note of the time, date and location and turned to wrench Fergie away from the dancing. Joe had other things to see to that night.

Fergie nodded briefly at Maggie Small when he entered the bar. He was there for a good time and wanted nothing to do with business, especially anything connected with Grimes, and Maggie Small was never off duty.

Bad enough that Joe had hit him with a thousand questions before he let him out of the car. That Beano must have put the mix in for him. The robbery had paid out better than expected and he was flush. Of course he would spend it as he saw fit and he intended to have a real good time. No new motors or fancy holidays or the kind of stuff that would attract the attention of the police. Just a real good night out and maybe pull a bit of female company if he got lucky. Not that he told Joe that before he drove off to some other meeting with person or persons unnamed. Fergie hated how Joe kept secrets but, on the other hand, expected him to tell all. So, to his friend he swore that he would be careful, of course he would. And he would. Fergie was just going to have a good night out. He'd earned it after all.

Maggie Small was on a recruitment trawl that night and had gone to one of her most successful locations, the Tuxedo Princess, a boat harboured on the river Clyde in the city centre and turned into a permanent disco, drinking den and nooky parlour, especially rich in underage girls. Maggie was perched at her usual stool by one of the bars, observing. Diagonally across from her a young man made his first approach to a girl worse the wear for drink, as were most in the joint. Within two minutes, Maggie timed them, they had started kissing and the boy's hand was stroking the girl's thigh. Within another two minutes the girl was in the throes of blatant advanced arousal.

'Lucky girl,' thought Maggie, 'gifted, but far too enthusiastic, an amateur.' She looked for the harder-headed girls with a gold-digger's edge, willing to do almost anything for a price. Like at another table, over in the darkest corner. One cute and very young-looking girl had been allowing her much older female companion to buy her drinks all night. It could be just a case of one being broke and the other happily standing the costs for her company on a good night out. Maggie's instincts told her otherwise. It was then she saw Jeannie Stirk.

Dressed up for the night with full make-up and a short dress which proved to Maggie she had been right about how good Jeannie's legs would look. Drink in one hand, Jeannie seemed to be circling the bar searching out a seat or for someone, maybe Maggie?

'I knew you'd find your way to me,' Maggie smiled as Jeannie drew near.

'Hello, Maggie,' Jeannie murmured, drawing a breath of that scent, the same as that night, just more of it. The hidden disc jockey let rip with some incomprehensible patter, laughing raucously at his own jokes as he changed the records clumsily. Within the opening riffs, Maggie piped up, 'Playing our song, I think.'

Pop music wasn't Jeannie's thing. She preferred jazz, blues, old Stones tracks, but a couple of lines in she recognised the group as the Bangles, an all-woman line-up, and the record 'Eternal Flame'. The jibe hit home.

'This is DC Fraser,' said Jeannie, turning to one side to reveal a man standing behind her. The male cop signalled his presence by wearing decidedly un-clubland casual gear from one of the chain stores, a square haircut he'd probably had since schooldays and a scribble of a moustache, the kind teenage boys grow for a few weeks just because they can.

'Ah,' said Maggie, ignoring the man, 'work it is. Shame.' Maggie believed in her ability to suss people instantly. The male cop she wrote off as an already married, faithful father of two, with neither the aptitude or the imagination to have an affair. Besides, she had also noticed the blush on Jeannie's cheeks.

'Yeah,' mumbled Jeanie, 'something like that.'

'Listen, Stirk,' butted in DC Fraser, 'you stay here awhile an Ah'll dae the single routine. See if any lassie offers me service.' Fraser decided that he held greater seniority than Jeannie and could decide the routine, though their length of duty and achievements told another story. A man among women he could impose his will on both Jeannie and Maggie. Another time another place, both women would have shot him down with a look, tonight they were more inclined to let him disappear, leave them alone.

As Fraser staggered off, overdoing his impression of the drunk man's gait, Maggie smiled to herself. Only the truly naive would fail to notice he was a cop.

'You're a strange one,' Jeannie started, her assertive tone catching Maggie by surprise.

'Why?' Maggie smiled and offered her companion one of her long thin cigarettes.

'You're polite. Obviously well educated. Extremely beautiful,' Jeannie's voice trembled a little but she was determined to put this woman in her place. Maggie Small was work, work, work.

'Why thank you,' smiled Maggie, reaching out her small gold lighter.

'It wasn't meant as a compliment,' answered Jeannie, her manner still serious. She lit her cigarette, puffed a generous plume of blue smoke above their heads and continued, 'Yet you work with Grimes, you hang around in this dive for God knows what purpose. Some of the women who work for you are hookers – maybe them all.'

'Good little girl's been doing her homework,' teased Maggie, enjoying the energy of Jeannie's newfound aggression.

'So you're obviously slumming it, Maggie.' Jeannie had moved closer, speaking quietly but forming her words carefully. 'Give you a kick, does it?' At last, Jeannie's turn to smile. Maggie turned and deftly flicked her cigarette into an ashtray. She sipped her drink and looked at Jeannie. Her face was calm, smiling, unworried as she looked down on Jeannie Stirk.

'Is that your way of asking me to tell you about myself?' asked Maggie.

'Yes and no,' replied Jeannie. 'What I'm really asking though is why you're wasting yourself here.' Maggie continued to look at Jeannie silently. 'Why stoop so low, Maggie?'

Maggie Small prided herself on being cool. Too often to count she had been furious, terrified, howling with grief and never did the outside world know. It was a self-control developed deliberately and had been hard won on the back of red-raw experience, all underwritten by loneliness. But now she found herself slipping.

'So, this is me down in the world is it, little middle-class cop's daughter?' Maggie started.

'How did you know . . .'

'A short history on yours truly – Maggie Small. Born and bred in Coatbridge. The pimple on the shit-smeared arsehole that's Airdrie. Council house, crap scheme. Eight brothers and sisters – three dead before they were school age. Mother invalided and died young through Catholic morality and too many kids. Father a bookie's runner. Simple honest man – too honest to dip the takings. Too simple to avoid being set up by his boss and some of your corrupt mates. When I was thirteen he was jailed for something he didn't do . . . Am I boring you yet?'

'No, no . . . I eh . . .'

'. . . three years in jail for something he didn't do. Me and the youngest two in a children's home. Care officer used to touch us up at night. When my father came out of prison he was a broken man – too shattered to care for himself, let alone us. I was shipped off to middle-class foster parents in the country. Foster father used to screw me at nights with his wife lying asleep next door. Me – I decided to take from them what I wanted. Went to their fancy school, four Highers later started at university – the pederast was so bloody guilty he paid for the lot. Soon as I had my degree, I took him for five grand . . . you falling sleep yet? Buying a flat I said. It was a lie. Five grand was my escape money. I fled to where I was from. Back to where I belonged. Back to where I was safe,' Maggie took a long drink from her glass and moved her face close to Jeannie's. 'Back to where no one was going to hurt me again . . . ever again.'

Maggie's last words hung in the air, a chant echoing in the empty church of Jeannie's mind in spite of the babble of background noise. Jeannie was stunned, their roles swiftly reversed. Throughout her speech, Maggie's words had sounded urgent, angry but her demeanour remained calm, sweet. Jeannie was torn between the urge to reach out and comfort her or shy away from the sting of her speech. The combined effect was a rush of passion Jeannie Stirk had thought she had exorcised. No chance, it was back in trumps.

'I've done it now,' Maggie chided herself, 'told her too much. Tight-lipped all these years only to break the secrecy tonight and with her – a copper.' Even as she reprimanded herself, Maggie Small kept smiling and knew, just knew, she wanted to get to know Jeannie Stirk better, much better.

'Place is hoaching wi underage drinkers – but that's it. No exactly a major crime wave, is it?' DC Fraser had returned with a sour face and just butted in as he had been taught from boyhood he had the right to do so as far as women were concerned. Maggie was hardly surprised that Fraser had failed to spot the obvious infringements of the drug and morality laws raging on every deck of the boat. Even the most spaced-out dealer would spot the policeman in him. Maggie winked slyly at Jeannie.

'What is it tonight?' asked Maggie. 'The usual dope, pills, under-age drinking or has the Tuxedo Princess suddenly gone up a league?'

'Anything we spot, really,' said Jeanie, hating herself for the return of that mixture of awkwardness and excitement she promised herself she'd never feel again in Maggie Small's company.

'So, what do you make of that then?' Jeannie turned round, looking in the direction of Maggie's nod. Under their table, the older woman had worked the young girl's panties halfway down her thighs. 'Now I'd say that was underage sex? What do you think, DC Stirk?' The heat rose to Jeannie's cheeks. She'd allowed Maggie to make her feel that way again and it was rubbing salt into her emotional rawness.

'Ah think it's fucking obscene,' butted in DC Fraser, 'thanks, Maggie.' Off he traipsed and gripped the older woman by the arm, Jeannie Stirk trailing behind him, still fuming, still wired up.

Maggie Small smiled as she tried to lip-read the conversation between the police and the women. Maggie admired the way the young girl had turned off the instant the coppers had arrived. Her body was covered and her face stony as she pointed to the older woman, all quiet blame and accusation. Maggie made a bet that the older woman would get huckled but the kid would be back in the bar within the hour. She had definite recruitment potential that young one. In the meantime, there were other events to interest Maggie Small. Fergie was holding up the bar, already very drunk, buying rounds for anyone and everyone. Looked like he was there for the night and had the money to last the pace. Now, for Fergie that was most unusual.

The Yank didn't know or care about a dive like the Tuxedo Princess. After failing to locate Grimes at the rave he had left and gone to Off the Record in the shadows of the *Daily Record* newspaper offices. All he was looking for was a drink. But he was depressed and lonesome. His work in Glasgow was not going well at all and he had made little progress. Soon he might have to reappraise and write it off as a lost cause. The Yank did not like failure. Twenty years in the NYPD had taught him that to accept failure was to invite in defeat as a regular habit. But he was in an unusual position having parachuted into this unfamiliar city on his own. All he wanted was to track down some relatives. People he had never met and only recently learned the significance of them to his own parents, his father. He still hadn't decided what he was going to do when he met them, a state of indecision that was unusual for him, made him nervous, careful. The

Yank didn't want anyone to know he had been in the city – well, anyone the authorities would believe. A phone call to an academic friend, a criminologist studying organised crime worldwide, and he had soon been given the name of Andy Grimes in Glasgow. It was standard practice for guys like Grimes to use their networks, their taxi firms, the bars they ran to track down names. Cost them little effort and the Yank reckoned he would have to shell out a few hundred bucks. But no questions would be asked and that's how he wanted it. Trouble was the Grimes guy didn't seem to want to be tracked down. Back in New York, the Yank would have had the street contacts to convince Grimes to cooperate but here, in Glasgow, he was all on his own and he was beginning to feel it. Back home, in the police he was always part of a team and more often a close partnership. Even when working on an assignment on his own he had his friends and the occasional lover still there in his life. Here he was a non-person, a shadow man and he didn't like it. He knew his police pension would never be enough and he'd have to work. But maybe he should have chosen a different kind of work, something a bit more regular than this project. But then this wasn't just about money, it was about honour.

Women in the bar, obviously working girls taking a break from the cold and the Johns, made him feel his aloneness more keenly. But if the girls used this pub for their recreation it meant they worked nearby. The Yank finished off his drink and went walkabout.

He had gone two blocks when she asked him for a light for her cigarette. Was it his sadness or were Glasgow's call girls particularly young and fresh? She was all that and beautiful.

Leading him down to a walkway by the river Clyde, hidden from the main road by a grass embankment, he listened to her chat. She never stopped. The river was black and trundling slowly, like the lazy warm rain he had become used to in that city. She wasn't in a hurry, not like the New York working girls he had used sporadically throughout his adult years. Hometown hookers came close to being friendly while you negotiated the price – close but not quite. After that it was tight-lipped resentment and speed, making him feel like some sort of turnover statistic in an efficiently run business. But this girl took her time, acting like she wanted to be wooed, won over. She might be acting but it made him feel good. She reached up and kissed him on the mouth, breaking the golden rule. Maybe she wasn't a hooker? Or maybe the rules were different here? At that time he didn't care to search for answers he just sunk into the kiss. The embankment reached up for him, pulling him down on to its spongy bed. Then he felt the searing pain in his head.

'He's no got a lot,' she was sitting astride his chest rifling through his pockets.

'Take whatever there is and let's split,' the man's voice was high above him.

'Fuck, jist forty quid and some credit cards,' her weight was heavy, painful on his ribs.

'Grab it for fuck sake and let's go,' there was an edge of rising fear in the man's voice.

'Wait, there's something else here,' she reached inside his other jacket pocket and pulled the envelope out. 'Fuck, just a passport, some letters and a plane ticket. Hey? Fancy a trip tae Noo York, Noo York? One way?'

'Jist fucking grab it,' the man's voice was angry, threatening, 'and let's split before we're spotted.'

'So ye'll no be wanting the shooter then?' she pulled the small pistol out of its side holster.

He shouldn't have reached up. Long lessons on city streets told him to play dead. But his eyes opened and his arms reached up for her. It was the last thing he knew.

'Next time Ah go through their pockets,' said the man, heading for the streetlights.

'Aye and you can winch them as well,' replied the girl. 'Let them touch up your tits if yese like.'

'Ye should've just grabbed his gear and split,' he repeated.

'Ye shouldnae have hit so hard the second time,' said Suzie with a zed.

'Aye, well, what's done is done,' replied Deadeye.

'Hope he can swim,' giggled Suzie nervously.

'Aye,' replied Deadeye, 'fucking long way back tae the States, eh?'

13 NOVEMBER 1989

The worst thing about this life is the necessary discipline. While others can relax, I'm always on duty, by my own choosing of course. Sometimes I watch others with their families, friends and lovers. Carefree. I can never be free of care.

Not that I would have it any other way. I can no longer remember or decide if I chose the life or it chose me. Not that it matters. It just is. I am the life. The life is me.

I started young with this other me, too young. But timing is never under our control in life - or is that just my bad karma? Two different people, two roles to play. I act the other so smoothly I wonder sometimes if that is still the real me. Then I return to my secret flat, the one those who know me would never expect me to have, and sit at this desk making these records. Then, now, I am Addison and I know this is really me. But who can I share me with? Till now it has been small black letters rattled out on the white page by this old IBM electric typewriter. Till now.

I started to write this chronicle as a record of my work. Notes, descriptions, dates and places. Facts and figures. It was meant to be insurance for the day they find me out and catch me unawares. But I've had to review that plan. Glasgow is a small village of a city. As safe as I consider this secret flat, I have to be ready for the day someone spots me coming here, perhaps someone following me on other business to do with the other me. It could be something simple like burst pipes in the flat when I'm away and the factor using his key. They don't know I've changed the locks but still they'd just batter the door down. A pipe worn thin and stressed under the floorboards. Mere domestic chance and my number could be up. Isn't life just like that?

So I thought of depositing these records elsewhere. A lawyer I thought. But it would have to

be the right lawyer. One I could trust. Not just
with my admissions of crimes, since everything James
Addison has done is against the law of the courts,
though well within the law of the streets. But it
would also have to be one who shared my agenda. If
I'm jailed or killed — one who would use whatever
power they have to take down the abusers of women,
children, old-age pensioners. One who felt the
difference between combatants and civilians. One who
shared the old-fashioned street code. Made the same
judgements as me. And that's the trouble. My agenda
is personal and deadly serious. Where could I find
a lawyer who would share my values?

But I came across another person by accident.
First I didn't trust them and tried to learn about
them. It was then I realised I was wrong. They were
as trustworthy as I am and, most importantly, have
similar reasons to hate the same people.

The night I showed my hand was the biggest risk
I have taken. 'I know Addison,' I said, and let the
comment hang in the air. 'I know Addison,' I
repeated, 'I don't just know of him like the rest
of the city.' And that could've been it. Hitmen
knocking on my door in the early hours. Curtains for
me. It didn't happen. Instead my new ally gave me
something back in return. Something they didn't need
to give. Something that showed good faith. I knew
its worth — I couldn't have got that type of
information on my own. It built from there.

Even now as I sit here at this desk I'm not
entirely convinced. But sometimes you have to make a
leap of faith over a blind wall. Either I'll land in
good company or a pit of my own making. Either way
it's too late to turn back.

So now I have destroyed much of my detailed
surveillance notes. I've realised that the street
trained me to retain details in my head and left me
bereft of the skills to record on paper. I felt like
a phoney anyway, a pretend cop, a wee boy playing

at spies. Besides, it's not my task to empower anyone else. Where are these chronicles likely to end up? In the hands of the police – Birse and his ilk. It's against my agenda to give him and his kind anything but grief. Give those fuckers nothing but pain. So I'll leave them nothing except the knowledge that someone else knows what they know and more.

I hope these chronicles will save anyone else for being blamed for being James Addison. I have acted, I am responsible. And maybe they will explain a little of what type of person I am – if anyone cares.

So I'll share my intelligence with my new-found ally. And give them access to these chronicles. I know it's a risk but I'm lonely – lonelier than ever before. So this is for them and me and us alone. But I wonder what they'll make of the increasing number of personal reflections? Maybe they'll see themselves staring back? I hope so. I'm betting on it.

Who are the real criminals? Am I wrong? Am I evil? Or do I see people the way they really are? Make up your own mind, I've already made up mine.

A

RIGHT IN IT

'POLICE . . . OPEN UP!' Two men were couched by the side of the door, bullet-proof vests over their blue tunics, pistols primed and ready to fire held in both hands, pointing to the ground at their feet. At the end of the garden path a marksman leaned on a fencepost, hairline sights marking X on the front door. In flats behind him, two of his colleagues with identical rifles perched at bedroom windows scanning the terraced house, covering the windows, the doors and even the roof. 'WE HAVE A WARRANT – OPEN UP OR WE WILL BE FORCED TO COME IN.'

'You no meant tae tell him yer armed?' Birse asked the officer in charge of the unit.

'Aye, ye know we are,' was the terse reply. Birse chuckled and his colleague continued, 'Look, Alex, tell bad bastards like this we're tooled up is just asking them tae play fucking Ned Kelly. You want tae interview him – Ah'll catch him alive.'

'Aw right, just asking like.' Behind the uniformed Chief Inspector's back Birse grinned. He liked nothing better than to take the piss out of the serious mob. But he did want their target alive. He had a few questions he needed answered.

'Right, guys, get ready,' said the Chief Inspector before raising the loudspeaker to his mouth, 'STAND BACK FROM THE DOOR – POLICE ENTERING NOW.' Next to him, his sergeant talked quickly and clearly into a walkie-talkie, notifying all the police at the scene to standby for entering. The Chief Inspector nodded.

'GO, GO, GO!' ordered the sergeant into the microphone.

Fergie was lying across the top of his bed not dressed and not undressed. Staggering home in the early hours of the morning, he'd managed to prise one shoe off and ease his trousers halfway down his legs before he passed out. The woman who'd come home with him had lifted his legs onto the bed, helped herself to her taxi fare out of his wallet, plus a little extra for her trouble, then left. That's where they found him, still snorting in his sleep, his dreams jumping between falling, falling, falling and his mother's face, her voice telling him not to do something she never made clear.

'Fucking sleeping beauty!' Birse strode into the bedroom after two armed policemen had kicked open the door and were standing at either side, their pistols trained on the prostrate body of Fergie. 'Place is bowfing, Fergie, do you no believe in fresh air?' Birse went to open a window and found the metal latch stuck, welded solidly together by several layers of gloss paint. 'High time you were moving oot o Balornock, man, the maintenance isnae whit it should be.'

Fergie stirred on the bed, his hand reaching up to clutch at his forehead in a vain effort to quell the porcupine rolling enthusiastically against the inside of his brain.

'Whit the fuck's going oan?' Fergie croaked.

'Just thought we'd pay ye a wee visit, social call like,' said Birse mildly. Then angrily, 'Yer done, son, fetch yer coat.'

'Whit?' Fergie slumped into a seating position on the bed, his head in his hands.

'UP. UP. ON YOUR FEET, NOW!' screamed one of the armed policemen.

'Whit?' Fergie squinted through the fingers of one hand. 'Whit the fuck's he oan aboot?'

'UP NOW,' the armed policeman repeated, holding his gun steadily on the bed as his armed colleague rushed in from Fergie's blind side, yanking him to his feet and ramming him against a wall.

'HANDS BEHIND YOUR HEAD. LEGS OPEN . . . NOW,' thundered one armed cop, roughly searching the length of Fergie's body as the other threw the bedclothes to the ground, shaking every sheet, ripping open the pillows and bending to search under the bed.

'Ah brought a squad tae search this dump, Fergie,' said Birse, 'but, fuck me, ye've got next tae nothing in here, eh? You believe in that Japanese minimalist shite the poofs are aye writing about in the papers? Never took ye for an arty-farty fucker.'

A cooker and an old sofa serving as his seat as well as his bed – that was all he had. The house had been next to empty since Fergie's wife had left him, taking most of the furniture. He kept meaning to buy a few things whenever he was flush but somehow always seemed to have greater priorities, like having a good time.

Still in the search position, Fergie was sliding down the wall leaning on his head till jerked up again by the armed policeman standing behind him.

'Whit's the score, Birse?' Fergie eventually managed to mutter. Birse ignored him and strode out into the hall.

'This place about all clear?' he shouted through the house. If Fergie had been aware that the squad were ripping up floorboards, pulling apart fitted kitchen units and tapping the plaster walls for secret cavities his hangover might have vanished instantly. As far as he was concerned this was just another shakedown with Birse going over the top as usual.

Fergie had been used to hassle from the police, putting up with it as a professional hazard since his teens. But the ante seemed to have been raised since he and Joe Murphy had teamed up. On other occasions even Fergie had noticed this and thought about it with no ready conclusions or, at least, any he considered palatable. This morning all he could think about was paracetemol, Irn Bru and sleep.

'Nothing,' spat Birse, coming back into the room. 'Nada. Nish. Not a fucking thing worth aw this fucking effort onyroads.'

'Whit ye expect tae find, gold fucking bullion?' groaned Fergie against the wall. In a second, Birse was behind him and with both clenched fists thumped him hard between the shoulder blades. In his fragile state, Fergie's body concertinaed and he crumpled on the floor. Birse flipped him over on his back, dropping down onto his chest with both knees.

'Get one thing straight, ye wee cunt,' growled Birse, 'you are getting done the day.' Birse wrapped a gloved hand round Fergie's throat and squeezed. 'Ah'm gonnae do you so fucking bad ye'll no recognise yersel in the mirror.' Long seconds ticked past as Birse continued to squeeze on his throat. Fergie was gagging wordlessly, his face turning from scarlet to blue, his tongue stretching out of his mouth, thick and dry. 'Get him intae the wagon,' Birse barked, getting to his feet, straightening his coat.

'You no supposed tae read me ma rights or something?' Fergie wheezed.

'Rights? Rights? Your fucking rights crawled oot the door as Ah walked in.'

Fergie was whisked past the desk sergeant at Pitt Street police station – no booking in for him – and dumped in an interview room with a taciturn, shorn-headed uniform cop for company. An hour later it was still the case.

'Need the toilet,' Fergie asked. No response. 'Ah've been telling yese for an hour, man, Ah really need a slash.' Nothing. 'If Ah don't go soon, Ah'll pish masel.' Nothing. 'Whit aboot ma lawyer? Youse get him yet?' The cop didn't even look Fergie's way let alone answer him. 'Get Birse in here, eh? Ah've got rights.' The broad crew-cut skull turned and glowered at Fergie. 'Need a drink as well. Ah'm parched.' Fergie's drinking session had dehydrated him good style. While he lusted for a bottle of cold Irn Bru, now he'd settle for lukewarm pond scum. 'Ah'm getting dizzy, man,' Fergie moaned and wasn't exaggerating. 'If Ah'm . . .'

The cop looked at his watch and suddenly sprung into action. He opened the door and a colleague entered. Together they secured handcuffs on Fergie's wrists and led him to the Gents. Some other prisoner had been sick and his vomit lay splattered across the floor. The small white room smelled as if the spew had been there a long time, cooking in the central heating for the appreciation of other prisoners. The two cops stood at either side of Fergie, so close he could feel the breeze of their breathing on his face. They watched his still cuffed hands struggle with his zip, staring at his penis while he pissed. Saying nothing, just watching.

'Need a drink,' Fergie announced again and headed for the tap at the sink.

'No chance, sunshine,' snapped the second cop, 'ye're oot o here.' The cops grabbed Fergie by each arm and hustled him quickly back to the interview room, planting him firmly on the seat behind the metal table screwed to the floor. 'You go get a cuppa tea,' the cop said to his suede-headed associate before taking up his post by the door and adopting his instructed demeanour – silence.

Three hours later, after Fergie had given up asking for anything, the door burst open and in swaggered Birse accompanied by two of his usual plain-clothes team.

'How ye doing there, son?' Birse asked in mock friendliness. 'Have the boys looked after yese aw right?'

'Where's ma lawyer, Birse?' Fergie rasped, his tongue sticking to the roof of his mouth.

'Aw, did ye want a lawyer? Dearie me, we'll have tae try and contact him,' Birse smiled. 'Aye, so we will, immediately after Ah've asked you a few questions.'

'Asked for a lawyer hours ago, ye bastard ye,' spat Fergie.

'Whit's that?' Birse cupped a hand behind his ear and craned his neck in Fergie's direction. 'Naw, cannae hear ye.' The men behind Birse sniggered, sneering at Fergie. 'BUT, now's your big opportunity.' Birse swung a package and dropped it on the metal table with a clatter, sending Fergie's already tense nerves tingling. 'Recognise that?' he asked quietly.

'Whit is it?' Fergie replied, seeing that it was a sawn-off shotgun.

'Don't come the wise cunt wi me, Ferguson, we found it in your hoose,' rattled Birse.

'Naw ye didnae.'

'And whit's more,' Birse continued, ignoring Fergie's denial, 'it's covered in your paw prints.'

'Lying toad.'

'And whit aboot this?' Birse signalled to one of the plain-clothes men who threw a clear plastic bag full of white powder on the table. 'Think there's enough Charlie there to ruin a few noses.' He turned to a plain-clothes cop, 'Where did we find that again? Oh aye, under yer bed. There are grains in every corner o yer hoose – well, leastwise, there will be by the night.'

Birse stood away from the table and the two detectives deposited the remainder of their goods on the table, this time placing them down quietly and shoving them in front of Fergie. The rock pipe, .22 pistol and ankle holster had never made it to forensics after Scotch Brian was admitted to hospital. They had been diverted to a cardboard box in a cupboard in Birse's room. He knew that Scotch Brian was going to have no future need of them and reckoned they would serve him some useful purpose. Even Birse hadn't reckoned on that opportunity presenting itself so soon. Grimes had arranged for the last item, an old army revolver, to be passed to Birse. It was the type of weapon no self-respecting street player would carry, unless they were robbing a bank and wanted to scare the staff rather than shoot them. The revolver was a dead ringer for the piece used by Deadeye in the bank job.

Fergie clocked each and every item. He looked up at Birse and shrugged.

'Know nothing aboot this lot, Birse,' he said.

'Shame yer prints are oan everything then, isn't it?' replied Birse with a grin. Fergie knew that would be Birse's answer, just as he knew he was in serious trouble.

'Know fuck all aboot them,' Fergie persisted.

'An whit aboot this lot then?' asked Birse pulling a plastic evidence bag out of his pocket and throwing them on the table. 'Ye've got a lot o credit, Fergie, an a lot o fucking names.' Fergie recognised them instantly. Credit cards and ID cards he'd picked up from Maggie Small the night before to hand over to Joe Murphy. It was a scam Joe ran using a squad of pickers to go round the shops and buy to order till the cards ran out or were cancelled. The identity cards he had adapted by a wee guy in Shawlands to suit any purpose and any customer. The cards were the only items really in his home, his jacket pocket. They wouldn't have been there if Maggie Small hadn't asked him at the Tuxedo Princess to pass the load on to Joe. The cards were no big deal. They were trouble but compared to the other 'evidence' they didn't even register on the scale.

'Son,' said Birse, turning to the uniform cop, 'could you gather up this evidence and take them up tae ma room? Good man.' As soon as the uniform had left, one detective stood with his back against the door while the other circled behind Fergie, still cuffed and seated. 'Now, Ferguson,' Birse continued, 'in case you hadnae worked it oot, you do not exist in this station. The polis have never seen you the night, right?' Birse grinned humourlessly, showing Fergie all of his front teeth. More of a snarl than a smile. 'An ye're heading for a serious stretch. The coke alone will get you twelve years and as for the weapons – well, armed robbery's no the favourite behaviour of the judiciary at this time.' Birse lit a cigar, taking the time to let Fergie wait. 'And that revolver, well we suspect it was used in a murder a couple of months ago.' Birse knew it had been, that being his one request to Grimes when he asked him for a revolver of that style. 'Young boy, decent family, he just got mixed up in a wee bit o debt tae some dealer. Fucking shame, isn't it? Scourge of our weans they fucking drugs. But it looks like you killed him.'

Birse circled the room a few times, smoking but not speaking. Fergie felt his thirst rage and his metal-encased wrists shake and flicker. The interview room had grown hotter, much hotter. What he needed was a drink and a sleep then he could begin to make sense of his position, work it out. Instead he was hoisted up from the back, one cop holding him still with his arms wrapped round his chest, as Birse dropped his cigar and punched Fergie in the breadbasket.

'Twenty years recommended,' puffed Birse and punched Fergie in the kidneys. 'Years in solitary,' kneed him in the testicles. 'The jails full o Grimes' men,' another fist in his solar plexus. Suddenly Birse backed off and wandered over to the cop at the door who handed him something. 'And Ah forgot the best part,' he shoved the package in front of Fergie's face, his eyes blind with tears, the pain in his abdomen firing his guts, making him heave and gag. 'Look at it, ye little pervo cunt.' Birse yanked Fergie's head back by his hair and held the package a foot from his face. It was a large colour picture of a young girl of about six years, naked, weeping, wrists tied to a bed's headboard, a man's arm crossing the frame from the left, two of his fingers jammed into her vagina. 'Hundreds o them in yer hoose, ye sick fuck,' spat Birse. 'They'll love ye up at Peterheid so they will,' kneeing Fergie in the groin again.

Then they left Fergie alone to ponder on his death sentence.

HOLLOW WALLS

DCI BIRSE'S OFFICE

Sit doon, guys. That was well done, by the way. The wee cunt'll be in that interview room all on his tod shitting himself. Christ, whit Ah'd gie tae hear what's going oan in his noggin. Fuck, can ye just imagine, eh?

INTERVIEW ROOM THREE

Come oan, Fergie, pull yer wits the gether, man. This is serious. The most fucking serious. Ah need tae think. Get ma act the gether. That big bastard's gonnae walk through the door any minute an charge me.

DCI BIRSE'S OFFICE

That was spot oan, eh? Did ye see the wee prat when we walked in? Aw mooth and patter. Like ye cannae scare me, Ah'm mental. Well, he WILL be mental noo, eh? Fucking wee shite. Who does he think he is?

INTERVIEW ROOM THREE

Work it oot. Come oan, imagine ye were Birse. Try an get intae his napper. Think like him. Need a drink. Christ Ah'm thirsty. If Ah just had a moothful o something I could think. FORGET IT. Ye're no thirsty. No thirsty, right. It's just a feeling. It'll pass. Think, he could be back any second and turn that tape oan. Tape oan, tape oan . . . Work it oot, ye slow cunt. Frae the beginning. Whit the fuck was there an armed squad for? Cos he'd planned it frae the start, right? Right. Ah'm being fitted up so how can Ah prove Ah'm being fitted up? Right, here we go . . .

DCI BIRSE'S OFFICE

It was just the right time tae hit him when he was that hungover. Whit's the name o that cop that gave us the nod? Fraser, was it? Tell him Ah'm pleased, eh? Christ we could've got him tae sign anything for a bottle o ginger and an asprin. Ha, serve the wee shite right. Thank Maggie for setting him wi that wee lassie. She did a rare job, eh?

DEADLY DIVISIONS

Mickey Finn? No need wi that bampot, Fergie, just flash yer tits and keep watching him drink. He'll put himself oot o the game.

INTERVIEW ROOM THREE

Rights, what are my rights? Work it oot, Fergie, come oan, man. Tae start wi, Ah wisnae booked intae the station. You do not exist, ma man. Then they didnae turn the fucking tape oan. Left ye in here tae make ye hurt and used the time tae set up their package o surprises. Fuck, that wee lassie in the photie, poor wee bitch. An Ah think Ah've got it bad? Stop feeling sorry for yersel, Fergie. Fuck, whatever, they had free run oan ma place. No problem wi nabbing a few prints then. Maybe there's no much in the flat but ma prints — everywhere, man. Empty beer cans, unwashed cups, ma fucking toothbrush. So much for yer training, Fergie. Aw this 'dinnae touch anything at the polis station' an aw that shite. They have a hoose full o ma prints, man. Ah'm well fucked.

DCI BIRSE'S OFFICE

How long do ye think we should leave him? If he was a bright cunt Ah'd gie him no time at all. Ah'd just do ma dinger. Beat shit oot o the wee bastard and charge him while Ah'm at it. See they bright cunts, they're easy and quick. A bit o a doing, shout a bit and they're a mess, man. Try that wi the wee neds an yer up shit creek. They cunts are well used tae the knuckle. But send them a wee message an let them stew a while — easy meat, man. Putty in ma mitts. Now, Fergie, he'd be a leave-tae-stew type. Nae brains at aw, that cunt.

INTERVIEW ROOM THREE

They've got me oan the bank job, that's for sure. Mean, whit's ma alibi that the weapons are no mine? Ma witnesses that Ah was driving and no carrying were fucking carrying themselves. Like they're gonnae volunteer the info? Aye, that'll be fucking right. The coke and the rock pipe and the child porn filth, that's aw lies. Jesus, they might as well kill me as sentence me for twenty years among the nonces and ponces. That's worse than death, man. As for the young boy that got shot, that's worse, that's set up by the cunt that did it. That bastard Birse'll know fine who killed the young boy. So that's it doon tae the bank job, eh? Aye, and the credit cards, but they're fuck all tae worry aboot. Maggie Small? Could it have been her that grassed me up? Why would she? She earns a good sideline oot o her girls blagging the credit cards frae their punters. Whit has she got tae gain? Nothing. No as much as Joe, that's for sure. Or even Beano. So whit dae they want? Is it names o the bank robbers? Or maybe the guy behind the job? Is that whit they want? A cannae gie them that, man, Joe's ma pal.

DCI BIRSE'S OFFICE

Whit ye think he's thinking? Ah'll tell ye whit he's fucking thinking. He's thinking fuck aw worthwhile. Tell yese, he's doon there thinking 'Mammy Daddy, Mammy Daddy' an shitting himself. Fuck it, let's leave him tae stew for a good while, eh? Anybody fancy a pint? Aye you, ye bastard, you're buying.

INTERVIEW ROOM THREE

Whose name's no on the line for that bank job? Naaa. Who stands tae gain? Naaa. Who said it was tae be organised in a hurry? Naaa. Who knew Ah was oan the fucking bevvy last night? Naaa. Who wasnae very fucking pleased wi me that last time we spoke? Naaa. Who thought Ah was gonnae grass them up? Aye, he did think Ah was gonnae grass him up. Prick, so he is. Ah dinnae grass. Cut ma cock aff first. Just like they cons are gonnae dae tae me if Ah go doon for fucking weans. Mean Ah left half ma stash wi him. Said, 'think Ah'm gonnae blow it, Joe, will you jist hang oan tae that load there'. Must've left the fucker wi forty thousand pounds. That's a lot o dough even for Joe. Seems tae have a big need of the cash right now, does Joe. Fuck, an Ah thought it was Beano. Big straight cunt he is. If he had a problem wi me he'd have said tae ma face. Well, Ah thought he would but he's that close tae Joe the cunt's probably in cahoots wi him. Aye, that's more like it. The pair of them the gether. He's a smart cunt that Joe. But maybe no smart enough, eh? Tell ye whit though. Whatever they fuckers say, Ah'm no gonnae gie that Birse fuck all. We've got history me and Birse. Birse is the enemy, isn't he? Isn't he? Naw, Ah'll find another way o dealing wi this. Ah'm telling Birse nothing. Come oan, ye big prick, dae yer worst.

DCI BIRSE'S OFFICE

Man, Ah shouldnae have had that Guinness. Gie's me wind so it does. Whit does an ulcer feel like? Fuck, this is the pits. Anyway, back tae wee Fergie. Think he's sweated long enough? Ah dae. That wanker'd get confused in ten fucking minutes. Tell ye whit he'll no forget though. Bastard hates me. Heh, heh. A mark o ma success as ye might say. If Ah go back in there he'll do an Alamo oan us. Tell us tae come ahead, an the more Ah hurt him, the more he'll ask for. Loves a bit o fanny though does oor Fergie. Eh, a mug for a whiff o fish, eh? Heh, heh. Go doon an tell that Jeannie tae get her mini kilt oan an get her arse in here for inspection. Well, ye have tae have some perks, eh, lads? Eh? Eh?

MEA CULPA

The handle of the door rattled then opened slowly, quietly. Fergie sat bolt upright, tensed his arms, flexed his thigh muscles and waited for the next onslaught.

'You can go.'

'Eh, Ah'm no meant tae.'

'My case now and I'm ordering you to leave.'

'Does Birse know aboot this?'

'Who gives a fuck?' replied Jeannie Stirk quietly to the uniformed cop on guard. 'Now beat it.'

Fergie's exhausted, dried-out brain watched Jeannie Stirk, balancing a tray with teapot and cups, crossing the floor in slow motion. His murdered nerves told him to be wary of the trick. He knew there would be one but just didn't expect it to involve a woman. A good-looking woman at that. He focused his bleary eyes on the door, expecting Birse to come rushing through any minute, backed up by his team of muppets, baton-handed. That was the treatment he had been used to over the years and he was ready. But his eyes wouldn't stay on the door, drifting back to that smiling face floating towards him. He remembered as a child wanting to stay awake to greet the New Year and being told that he could if he managed to stay awake. Sleep hit him too early and he fought it by trying to stare at his grandfather's face. But it slipped down, down towards sleep, the pull of a magnet, of gravity, of truth. As now, his eyes falling back on the wetness of her smile.

Jeannie poured Fergie tea, pulled the chair six feet back from the table and sat down. Upstairs, in front of the CCTV monitor in Birse's room, a detective muttered, 'Fucking women. Cowards.'

'Nuh,' replied Birse. 'Just following tactics. Watch her legs.'

In the interview room Jeannie Stirk crossed her legs, her skirt riding high up her thighs. Fergie's head dropped, his eyes zooming in on the soft Y of flesh. Too tired to be interested, too weak to be willing, his head and his vision followed stronger instincts.

'Sean,' Jeannie started softly, 'you are in serious trouble.' Upstairs, Birse hollered a whoop of congratulations. Jeannie Stirk was good, better than he'd hoped. 'I'm Jeannie Stirk. DC Jeannie Stirk. I think you and I can bring this trouble to an end right here and now.' Jeannie smiled again, Fergie frowned, a bemused look spreading over his face. His bludgeoned brain couldn't quite grasp that this was real. What was it, his alternative to the condemned man's last meal? Soft soap before the troops rushed in? Because if it was, he was ready. Ready to enjoy this woman's company and still meet the squad head to head. Now was now. Then was yet to come. Now he was sitting with a soft-spoken honey and now was all that existed.

'What do they want?' Fergie's voice sounded harsh, rasping, unfamiliar to his own ears.

'They haven't told you?' Jeannie Stirk all concern and disapproval.

'Told me they've set me up annat.'

'The evidence is quite . . .'

'Ah know,' Fergie was abrupt.

'I know you know.' Jeannie Stirk felt as if she was overacting, coming across as falsely sympathetic. Upstairs, Birse watched the monitor and thought she was playing a blinder. Most important, Fergie thought she was genuine. 'That's why I argued for a chance to settle this reasonably. Just between us, before things get out of hand.'

Fergie loved her voice. Low, almost husky, sure and certain. It was a voice that revealed who she really was behind the job, away from the stinking interview room. Or so Fergie believed. Jeannie Stirk didn't show it but she was disappointed and angry. She had prepared thoroughly for an undercover operation, reading so much she reckoned she knew Fergie better than he did himself. She had even prepared a couple of outfits, sassier than anything she'd wear at work, leaving them hanging in her locker prepared for short notice. At nights she'd driven round the city centre and the east end, checking up on the pubs and the clubs where she might be expected to bump into her target. Into Fergie. Instead what had she landed? One interview, with Birse watching her every move from upstairs. One lousy interview and she would be expected to get a result. It was make or break time for Jeannie Stirk in Glasgow and she knew it.

'Could you do something for me?' Fergie asked.

'If I can,' replied Jeannie.

'Give me a cigarette then tell me what you want from me?' Jeannie put two cigarettes in her mouth, firing them up, then passed one to

Fergie. 'As good as a kiss,' he said, bringing a smile to her face. 'Then again probably not.'

'Drink your tea,' she said, placing her cigarettes and lighter on the table within his reach. 'You need to drink. If you want more just say and I'll have them bring some.' Fergie nodded. 'You drink and I'll talk.'

'Okay,' agreed Fergie, pouring milk into his tea. 'But tell me, where have they been hiding you?'

'Exiled in Edinburgh,' she smirked.

'Aw,' he replied, 'ye've escaped then. Well done.'

'They know you were involved in the bank job, Sean. They know for sure. They even know the role you played and that it's not the one you are going down for.'

'Not good.' Fergie shook his head. She thought he meant the trouble but what he meant was that it was further proof leaning towards Joe's involvement. Joe going corrupt, who would have thought? Upstairs, Birse was cursing, accusing Jeannie of going back rather than forward. He had told her he would allow her twenty minutes only, not long enough to go back over what Fergie already knew. Did she not know what the good cop routine meant?

'No, not good, Sean, and they can make all the other stuff stick.' Her eyes down, soft, resigned.

'Aye,' he sighed, 'Ah know.'

'They've gone to a lot of trouble,' said Jeannie, as if the police had nothing to do with her. 'More than usual, you agree?' Fergie nodded his head.

'Aye, but why? Ah'm no big player. What dae they want?' Jeannie allowed a few seconds for Fergie's question to hang in the air. She pushed a lock of hair off the side of her face, edged her chair right up against the table and leaned close to her prisoner.

'They want James Addison,' she said quietly.

'Aaaaw,' Fergie sighed, 'him.'

'You do know him, Sean, don't you?' Jeannie was talking so quietly the CCTV wasn't picking up her voice.

'Oh aye, Ah know aboot James Addison aw right. Doesn't everybody?' he replied, lowering his voice to match her volume. Lovers whispering in the dark, best schoolfriends sharing a secret.

'But you do know who he is, don't you, Sean?'

'What if Ah did?' He moved closer over the table their elbows almost touching. 'Whit if Ah told you? Whit dae Ah get?'

DEADLY DIVISIONS

'You walk away,' she replied, 'no charges, no record, you haven't even been here.'

'And who protects me?' he asked.

'You don't need protection, do you?' she smiled, telling him what a brave, tough cookie he was.

'Not from most things,' he smiled, 'but from Addie . . . aye. Aye, Ah dae.' Smile gone from Fergie's face.

'What would you need?' she pursued the point. 'Safe house, change of name, pension, move out of the country?'

'HA, HA, HA,' Fergie's laughter came as a shock to her, pushing her back from the table. Had he been mocking her, stringing her along? 'Ye can put me oan a poky wee uncharted Mexican island, Addie'll still find me.'

'He'll be in jail,' she reasoned, 'for a long time. You'll be all right.'

'No, he'll no. No, Ah'll no.'

'We can hold the most difficult prisoners when we know they're difficult. It's the ones who we aren't warned about who escape.'

'Addie's no going to prison.' Fergie's voice was quiet again and as he spoke he rapped the cigarette lighter against the metal table. All that Birse could hear upstairs was a sharp rattle and white noise. 'They'll no let him live that long.' Jeannie looked away from Fergie's eyes and thought. She knew that he might be right and didn't want him to see her eyes when she was lying to him. Respect and trust are the first essential qualities of the confessional. 'Look, Jeannie, Ah cannae be seen tae be a grass oan Addie.' Her heart sank. She was losing him. 'But Ah can plead a defence oan the robbery since ye have me all tied up tae it. Now, if Ah named the other guys involved in that ye'd have tae make sure Ah was charged as well, but for driving, no shooting.' Jeannie had already put Fergie down as a driver rather than a gun merchant and believed he was now telling her the truth. There was a problem though, 'Sean, they'll not trade the charges for names of bank robbers . . .'

'But,' he interrupted, 'what if Ah tell you that the names Ah could give ye was Addie?' Rattling faster on the table with the metal lighter now. Upstairs, Birse was cursing and threatening to end the interview.

'What do you mean?'

'Has anybody ever wondered why Strathclyde's finest have never been able tae catch James Addison?' Jeannie shrugged. 'As in the guy that is James Addison?'

'Often, I'd imagine. Why?'

'It's cos they're looking for THE guy,' Fergie's voice raised loud and clear for the hidden microphone, the lighter held firmly in his hand. Birse was hearing every word. 'When they should have been looking for the TWO GUYS. How else dae ye think Addie has avoided the law aw they years?' Upstairs, Birse had gone deadly silent. He was sitting staring at the screen, slack jawed, wondering how he had managed not to consider that possibility for all these years. Not one James Addison but two James Addisons.

'They would be very interested,' Jeannie kept the momentum going to the target, 'to learn of the names.'

'Tell ye the truth, Jeannie,' Fergie spoke conspiratorially, 'Ah'm feart.'

'It's understandable,' Jeannie reached out and clasped the back of Fergie's hand, a doctor comforting a worried patient.

'Ah couldnae grass Addie,' he said. 'Ah'd no be here long.' Jeannie was searching for an encouraging line and had just decided to reiterate her offer to Fergie of a new identity abroad when he continued. 'But, if Ah write doon the names. Say, oan the back o this fag packet . . .' Jeannie smiled. 'Ye'll drop all the made-up charges against me.'

'Yes,' she butted in too quickly, too enthusiastically.

'And that so-called evidence Birse has . . .'

'What?'

'Ah'll be allowed tae take it wi me.' Jeannie was thinking, thinking hard and fast, coming up with too many options and not enough answers. Her deliberations were interrupted by a rap on the door. She stood talking to someone in the corridor. Someone who didn't want to be seen by Fergie but who couldn't disguise his hushed whisper of a voice. The boss was intervening. This was Birse's call, as it had been from the beginning. Jeannie closed the door and wandered back to the table.

'Agreed,' she said. 'All items previously shown to you can be removed by you from police property tonight.' Fergie smiled thinly, sickly, and nodded his head.

'One more thing,' he said, staring clear eyed at Jeannie Stirk, his confusion and uncertainty disappeared for the moment, 'ye have tae charge me wi the bank job. For driving at the bank job.' It was Jeannie Stirk's turn to be confused. Fergie had just negotiated a walk away and a few extra goodies besides. Why did he now want to put himself in jail?

'Sean, that's . . . why, for God's sake?' Jeannie flustered.

'So the street know Ah'm no a grass. If Ah walk and the others go doon they'll suspect me, won't they?'

'And it's so important that it's worth years in jail?' she asked. Fergie nodded his head and said,

'Oh, aye, it's that important.'

'Okay,' Jeannie nodded at the cigarette packet.

'Fuck,' sighed Fergie. 'Hope Ah'm doing the right thing.'

Sucking his breath in through closed teeth, Fergie reached over, plucked a pen from Jeannie's grip and began to write.

17 NOVEMBER 1989

Events have taken an interesting turn. Fergie was hauled in by Birse and his crew. That Birse isn't stupid and he has a nose for the weakest in any group. Fergie has told them something in order to be released after the police went to such trouble. Everyone on the street will know about Fergie – what will they do about it? What about Birse – what's his next move?

Trailing Birse is too dangerous to carry off effectively. He checks every street corner at every turn. The man has turned paranoia into an art form. He keeps his team in the dark till the last minute and sometimes even beyond then. Sends them out to carry out a specific task and doesn't tell them the significance of what they're doing or how it ties in with other plans. His squad of heavies are well used to his ways and don't question their boss. Except perhaps the new one, DC Jeannie Stirk. Maybe she hasn't learned the rules yet.

Stirk is a woman stuck among a bunch of the cream of sexism. She's new and will take time to work out the rules. But she's a DC so she has experience, coming to Birse's team with formed views.

I've managed to find out that she was foisted on Birse. Stirk was a high flyer in Lothian and Borders Police. Apparently, she had a relationship with a superior officer, a married woman. Her lover became possessive, wanted to leave her husband and move in with Stirk; tell the world. Jeannie Stirk knew they would also have to resign from the police and wasn't willing to sacrifice her job. So she ended the relationship but her lover persisted. Lost the place, started stalking her, threatened to resign anyway and go to the press.

Just as well for Jeannie Stirk she had a supportive boss. The old DCI pulled a few strings, spoke to both women, suggested a breathing space and called in a favour to have Jeannie Stirk transferred to Strathclyde Police. The business between the two women seems to have been effectively covered up. Birse thought he was being landed with some top brass's niece or young bit on the side. One of Birse's weaknesses is that he doesn't look beyond his own patch, Glasgow. Maybe we can use that against him?

A

LIGHT BULBS IN DARK CORNERS

'Angie, yer the biggest waste o space.' Grimes swivelled away his chair in disgust with the Gopher.

'But, boss, Ah'm telling ye, it's just no possible without grief, serious grief,' Angie sat in one of the chairs in front of Grimes' desk, the special chair with no padding and short legs. As Grimes swung back round to face him, Angie visibly cowered and kneaded his hands tighter together.

'It's a simple thing Ah'm asking. They're just oldies, surely tae Christ ye can nip intae the cupboard and nick the tin behind their backs?' Grimes found it embarrassing that he was even having this kind of conversation with one of his men. What would happen to his reputation on the street if this leaked out?

'The old dear, aye. She's oan a different planet each day an none o them planet Glesca,' Angie was explaining for the umpteenth time. 'But the old boy, he's as bright as a twinkle and he never leaves the hoose these days. No for weeks.'

'He must go for a shite sometime?' Grimes was exasperated. Angie shook his head. 'Tae buy grub?' Angie still shook his head furiously and felt the heat rise to his face, scared that Grimes would discover that he had been taking food to the old couple on a daily basis. 'Aw, Jesus H. Christ, we're just gonnae have tae knock them aboot a bit.'

Angie caught himself shaking his head and stopped abruptly. Rule two about Grimes – never contradict any of his proposals. But Angie couldn't help it. He had grown fond of Ruth and Jakob Wise. So fond he was now visiting them and no longer doing his bogus visits on families with young children. At least Angie was attributing his contact with the Wise couple for the change. If he'd thought carefully he would have noticed a few other changes in his life. Like his constant need to urinate then his difficulty in going. Like he hadn't been interested in the twink trade in a long while and his pile of gay porn magazines lying covered by a layer of dust by his bedside. He'd also started to lose a little weight, something he could ill afford. The changes Angie did notice he wrote off on the pressure Grimes was putting him under, that and his pleasure in the company of Jakob and Ruth Wise.

'He's right, Andy,' said DCI Birse sitting in the comfortable, leather armchair in front of Grimes' desk. 'If ye knock a couple o oldies aboot yer in serious bad press time. The *Evening Times* front page will be full of headlines screaming for the polis tae get the evil scum that did it.' Birse paused and sipped his drink, 'And I'm sorry tae say that's exactly what the polis'll be forced tae dae.'

'Aye, Ah know,' replied Grimes, 'but we can put somebody else in the frame. Throw yer uniform mates a couple o junkies annat.' Angie didn't like the sound of this at all.

'Fine, but even the junkies'll no want this one oan their nuts,' said Birse. 'The fucking doing they'd get in the jail. Na, even smackheads are no that suicidal.'

'Christ, all right, yer right,' said Grimes, turning to glower at Angie the Gopher who'd just let slip a loud sigh of relief.

'Whit's the big deal anyway?' asked Birse. 'Ye seem helluva keen tae rob this old couple's slum.'

'Told yese,' replied Grimes, casting a cold look at Angie to remind him not to think of contradicting his lie, 'they've a couple o antiques Ah've got a ready-made, cash-paying buyer for.' It was a readily believable lie.

Birse had done his homework, without Grimes' knowledge, confirming that the Wise couple used to run a thriving pawnbrokers. Where better to pick up the occasional rare piece. And he already knew that Angie the Gopher had some knowledge of antiques, being a bit of a specialist at blagging them or pointing out the gold from the crap in the proceeds of tie-up jobs.

'Well, ye'll have tae find a soft way,' said Birse. 'Better still, why don't you do it legally?' Grimes' face crumpled into a sour look of disgust, much as it would if Birse had just defecated on the desk and proceeded to eat the steaming turds. 'Make them an offer,' Birse continued. 'Buy the bloody things from them but well below the price.'

'Aye, thought o that,' said Grimes, 'but Angie reckons the old guy is still sharp enough tae be beyond being conned.'

'Fucking Jew boys,' muttered Birse, 'whit are they like, eh?'

'Eh, boss,' said Angie the Gopher, his voice timid, unsure. 'Ah think Ah know a way. A legal way.' Shock was written all over Grimes' face.

For as long as he had known Angie the man hadn't come up with one idea to his certain memory. Well, not one that didn't involve young boys.

'This'll be a fucking joke,' muttered Grimes with no sign of humour on his face. 'Come oan then, gie's a laugh, Angie.'

'There's a law,' started Angie.

'Aye, too many,' muttered Grimes.

'The National Assistance Act,' continued Angie. 'There's a section that allows a court tae order folk intae hospital. If they are found incapable o looking aifter their selves.'

'Angie, you've been pretending tae be a social worker too long,' bellowed Grimes, 'yer beginning tae sound like them an I for one cannae understand a fucking word yer saying.'

'Means ye can have them locked up,' Angie continued, 'like in a hospital, then maybe a wee old folk's home. Folk tae take care o them annat.'

'Aaaaaw, nice tae be nice, eh?' rolled Grimes, oozing sympathy that changed abruptly. 'WHAT THE FUCK DAE WE NEED IN ORDER TAE GET THEM LOCKED UP, YE FUCKING USELESS ARSE WIPE?'

'A doctor,' Angie blushed and muttered. 'Ye jist need a GP. A bent GP and the hoose is oors.' Grimes and Birse were silent. Angie cringed nervously waiting for them to bawl at him or, worse, laugh.

'Fuck me gently,' mumbled Birse stunned.

'Dae you believe that?' Grimes asked of Birse, though he didn't expect an answer. Angie shrunk further into his seat, his chin reaching perilously close to his sharp, bony knees. 'A bent GP?' Grimes asked quietly. Angie looked up and nodded before tucking his chin down again, holding his breath. 'Well, that's NO problem then Angie.' The Gopher shuddered. 'You are fucking amazing. Remind me tae gie ye a pay rise.'

'We could use that guy we caught over-prescribing,' offered Birse, thinking of the south side GP who had been seduced by the local smackheads into giving them prescriptions for massive doses of methadone. The same well-meaning man who had been given a choice between prosecution and the loss of his career, self-respect, friends and family or writing scripts for Grimes' dealers.

'Aye, aye,' agreed Grimes, obviously working through a list in his head, 'or what aboot that female GP we've got phcities o wi her tits tied up and her fanny oan display.' He was thinking of the gynaecologist who had been a regular customer at an S&M dungeon run by two of Maggie's girls.

'Naw, she's a hospital doctor, eh?' offered Birse. 'Ye said a GP didn't ye, Angie?'

'Eh, aye,' offered Angie, still not convinced that his idea had been accepted, expecting any minute that the two large men would turn on him and beat him up for wasting their time. 'Have tae say that they've known Jakob and Ruth . . . eh, Ah mean the Wise couple . . . for a while. As their doctor.'

'Angie,' said Grimes quietly.

'Aye, boss?' Angie ducked, expecting the onslaught now.

'Mind aw they times Ah gave you a doing for yer wee bogus habits?'

'Aye, boss,' Angie's head and torso flinched.

'Well, Ah meant it.' Angie knew they had been winding him up. 'But ye've paid me back a wee bit the night. Well done.' Angie's body was shivering as Grimes walked him to the door of the office. It was a door he had been thrown against by Grimes too many times to count but, being shown through it politely, this was a first.

'You just take it easy, Angie,' said Grimes, his hand on the older man's shoulder. 'Away and have a drink or two. Tell them yer drinking oan the house the night. Tell em Ah said, right. You just away an have a good time. Leave the GP business wi me, okay?'

'Okay, boss,' replied Angie. As soon as the office door was shut Angie took off running. Angie the Gopher needed to urinate again, badly.

'Who'd have thought it, Angie the Gopher, eh?' said Birse once Grimes had returned to the desk, the door shut and the two men alone.

'Aye, maybe Ah should start calling him by his Sunday name, eh?' laughed Grimes. 'Mr Farquhar A. Farquhar . . . aye, that'll be fucking right.'

'Hope he's right aboot that law,' said Birse soberly.

'Oh, he'll be right. For a conman, Angie knows his social work,' said Grimes, drawing a smirk from Birse. 'But listen, Alex, we have a wee bit o business that's more pressing.'

'Aye, ye said,' replied Birse, who had been called to an urgent meeting by Grimes.

'Couple o wee presents for ye,' said Grimes. Birse reckoned it would be an envelope fat with money. His arrangement with Grimes was ill defined, not contractual but always involved good payments coming his way in amounts that differed every time but were never less than generous. Grimes opened a desk drawer and pulled out a bulging A4 manila envelope, a larger payment than usual, unless the used notes were of low value. Then Grimes placed a smaller envelope on the desk. Finally he brought out a large, matt-black pistol and a box of shells. The gun was of a type Birse was unfamiliar with and that was unusual. Grimes had ordered it especially through his contacts in Liverpool. He'd asked for a weapon that was efficient and trustworthy but unusual on the British scene. His dealer had obliged by delivering a Czechoslovakian number, well tested in the bloody cauldrons of Afghanistan and the Middle East. The small envelope and pistol he pushed to his right, the manila envelope to his left.

'Whit's aw this, Andy?' asked Birse, now bemused and more than concerned.

'It's a deal, Alex. Just a deal,' smiled Grimes. 'Ah'll put it simply. If you take this,' he lifted the gun, 'and see to this,' he lifted the small envelope, 'you'll get this,' he lifted the fat manila package.

'How many?' Birse cut to the thrust, having been here with Grimes on several occasions before. Grimes tried to avoid ever giving straight instructions when the tariff was high and he could be implicated. So he played games.

'Just two,' replied Grimes.

'Travel or local?' asked Birse.

'Oan yer fucking doorstep.'

'Players or citizens?'

'Players, very active players.'

'Whit's that full of?' Birse pointed at the manila envelope.

'Twenties.' Birse looked at the wedge of notes covered by the shit-coloured paper. It was a big payout and Grimes wasn't known for his spontaneous generosity.

'They at war wi you?' he asked, which covered many questions, such as were they aware Grimes wanted them dead, would they be waiting for Birse?

'Not at all,' Grimes smiled. 'Let's say we co-exist quite happily . . . for now.' Birse pondered the information. Anything else he needed to know was in that small thin envelope. Birse reached across, picked up the pistol and stuck it into the pocket he had tailored into the lining of all his coats. That was the contract, the shake of hands. If Birse backed down now, Grimes would pay someone else to shoot him as well as the names in the envelope. Grimes leaned back in his chair, lit a squat stogie and said, 'Mind, not until ye get outside.' Birse nodded, stood up and left.

Andy Grimes was very pleased with how things were going. On the same day he found a way of getting his hands on the bonds with no one knowing a thing, he'd just hired a hitman to kill James Addison. The two men who were James Addison. Birse had never failed him before. It was a very good day for Grimes.

In his car parked in the street, DCI Birse tore open the small envelope. Turning on the car's interior courtesy light, he held the small card up to the weak beam and read the typed print. It was, as he expected, the two names Jeannie Stirk had connived out of Fergie. The two names of the men who Fergie claimed acted as Addie. Ever since he had read Fergie's scribble on Jeannie Stirk's fag packet, Birse had been amazed by the information.

'Fucking hell,' he had wheezed. 'Him Ah understand but no the other one. Something bad must have gone down between the two o them, man. Something real bad.' It was too late for such conjecture now.

A LUMBER

'This is a little number . . . sisters . . . us tonight. Good to see . . . than usual . . . power to the sisters.'

'Wish to fuck he'd stop jigging about while he's introducing the records,' thought Jeannie, 'or at least learn to carry the mike with him.'

'West End . . . Pet . . . Shop . . . Boys . . .' the DJ was long gone, lost in showing off in the admiring gaze of his one groupie, a henna-haired man well into his forties who thought he could pass for twenty because he was skinny and because of the clothes he wore and that hair.

'West End Girls! The fucking dickhead has never listened tae the lyrics,' growled Jeannie's drinking partner, a woman of indeterminate age wearing her grandfather's hand-me-down black suit. 'And ye cannae dance tae the fucking record.'

'She's right there,' thought Jeannie, 'what are you meant to do? Bounce up and down? Pogo? Cruise?'

Jeannie was meant to be celebrating. Her first night out in a couple of weeks. She'd won Birse over a bit, convinced him that she had the brains and know-how. Now she was out on the town trying to convince herself she had the staying power to let things run their course. That she was dispassionate enough not to try and take care of everybody's problems, particularly when they didn't deserve her attention. She knew what was likely going to happen to the two men named by Fergie and she didn't like the prospect one bit. It wasn't Jeannie's notion of justice, though it happened much more often than the public realised or the authorities would ever admit. Next act was to prove she didn't care. What difference would it make anyway if she sat at home and worried? Or worse, spoke to Birse? They were dead men whatever she did. So she had accepted the fact – sadly, reluctantly resigned herself to the inevitability – and decided to gain where otherwise she might lose.

'Fancy a beer the night wi the boys?' Birse had asked.

Without thinking she'd replied, 'Oh, I'd really like that but . . . ha ha . . . I'm on a promise,' and she'd smiled, not too much, just enough to tell Birse that she was doing the shagging. Like his bears always pretended.

'Aye, well aye,' he stammered, awkwardness screaming in his whole demeanour. 'Just remember tae leave some meat oan his bones, eh? Boy's probably got a mammy some place that worries aboot him.' And he slapped her on the shoulder, chummy like.

She had no plans to go out, not till she spoke to Birse. But now she had to, just to lessen the detail of the lies the next day. So it was back to Bennett's and maybe a meeting with Amanda-Jane. Jeannie couldn't bring herself to phone the young woman but a chance meeting at a disco? Now that she could handle. Trouble was, no sign of Amanda-Jane.

Then the dyke in the zoot suit turned up. Not Jeannie's taste at all. But she could dance all right. She'd obviously been a Northern Soul traveller. Whenever Marvin Gaye was played she'd go crazy, with legs to dance all night. Called herself Sid and smoked Marlboro Red with the tips nipped off. She smelled of Hi Karate aftershave and Jeannie wondered if she'd inherited that from her grandfather as well. Not Jeannie's type, but she could dance.

'Now girls,' the DJ held the mike up close to his mouth for once, speaking as low as he could muster, looking like he believed he was sex on wheels. 'Now girls,' the queens in the corner shrilled, blowing the DJ kisses, turning their backs to him, stroking their asses as their boyfriends smiled. 'Time for a change of pace,' the DJ kissed his boyfriend. 'Mister Gene,' the DJ took the mike away from his mouth, stuck his tongue out, rolling it over his chin and across his upper lip, 'Pitney.' The opening line of 'Something's Gotten Hold of My Heart' came on loud and strong.

'Cannae dance tae that shite, man,' shouted Sid. 'That's lassies' music.' Hands deep in her pockets, shoulders hunched, Sid strode off the dance floor. Jeannie was relieved. It was going to end in embarrassment. Sid would've wanted to take her home, bed her and it wasn't going to happen. Jeannie was relieved but also sad. She loved that song. Wanted to dance and wondered if she would feel okay dancing by herself. She might feel awkward, embarrassed. But why should she? Jeannie Stirk was a top cop in the country's hardest city and was respected by the notorious Birse. She could do whatever she wanted and would.

'They're playing another one of our songs.' The voice came from behind her but Jeannie could smell who it was with her eyes closed.

Without turning round she replied, 'That's because I willed it.'

'And do you get everything you will?'

'I will.'

'And now? Now what?'

Jeannie Stirk and Maggie Small danced slowly across the middle of the floor. Neither knew it but they were being watched, observed by those who would do them ill. Jealousy is bad, eats into you like a cancer. Sexual jealousy is the worst. But it was the fate of others that night. Not Jeannie Stirk and Maggie Small as the green-eyed monster dyke in her grandfather's suit stood and stared.

'I didn't know you smoked hash,' said Maggie Small, accepting a neat single-skinned joint from Jeannie Stirk. 'Isn't it against the rules, Ms Detective?'

'Well, I've learned a few things as well tonight,' replied Jeannie, giggling low, 'for sure.'

'It's just the start, wee Jeannie,' replied Maggie, stroking Jeannie's neck where her hair curled damp and soft.

'Tell me something,' said Jeannie.

'Anything,' lied Maggie. 'Whatever you want.' Jeannie stretched her naked legs out wrapping them around Maggie's thigh, soft and smooth. The alarm clock by Jeannie's bedside said it was two in the morning. She'd have to be up for work in four hours. She didn't care.

'Why tonight?' Jeannie asked. 'Why tonight of all nights?'

'It would have happened sooner or later,' replied Maggie, the sound of her inhaling on her cigarette whispering through the stillness of the room.

'Sooner would have been wonderful, later would have been good but why tonight?' Jeannie persisted, leaning up on an elbow in the bed, reaching out and kissing Maggie's cheek.

'You're too smart for your own good, wee Jeannie,' smiled Maggie and returned the kiss but on Jeannie's lips.

'Cannae kid a kidder, kid,' Jeannie laughed in her Harry Lauder mimicking of a Glaswegian accent.

'Ha, I'll remember that then, kidder,' replied Maggie rubbing Jeannie's naked shoulder.

'So, why . . .'

Maggie silenced Jeannie with a gentle finger on her lips. Kissed her lightly on the tip of her nose then said, 'There's somebody I think you might be able to help . . .'

ONE LINE'LL DO

'So where were you, Joe?'

'Whit? Fergie, come oan.'

'Naw, Ah'll no dae fuck all. Where were you?'

'Ah was seeing somebody.'

'No good enough, man. Tell me who or we're through.'

'Fergie,' Joe whispered, 'keep yer voice doon, man, folk are listening.' Around the bar the usual crowd of drinkers were trying to look nonchalant, pretending whispers to their company and all the while listening to the row between Fergie and Joe.

'Ah don't give a fuck aboot them,' Fergie roared, standing up, sending Viccies and one arm up to the lot of them with a, 'GET IT UP YESE.' The drinkers looked away and listened more intently. 'Ah can buy any cunt in this place.'

'Fergie,' muttered Joe through clenched teeth. 'Shut the fuck up, man.'

'Any o youse cunts want a drink?' Fergie was on his feet pulling a thick wad of ten pound notes out of his pocket. 'Hey, barman, get every fucker in the place a bevvy and doubles for you and yer mates.' Fergie pushed his way through the crowd and slapped a handful of banknotes on the bar. 'When that's done gie's a shout. Plenty o dough the night. Ah'm loaded, man.' Fergie went to turn from the bar and hesitated, 'Hey, Mouse, how ye doing, son?' Shuggie Reid was standing at the bar some ten feet away. Though his back was turned to Fergie, The Mouse was immediately distinguishable by his surgical collar, once off-white, now turning a shade of battleship grey. 'Barman,' ordered Fergie, 'get that wee man whitever he wants and keep pouring.' Fergie headed back across the bar, staggering as he went, bumping into drinkers, spilling pints, apologising, making it worse.

'You need tae calm doon, Fergie,' muttered Joe. 'And stop flashing the cash. Where the fuck did ye get it anyway?' Joe was talking quietly, privately.

'WHY CAN AH NO HAVE MONEY?' roared Fergie on his feet again. 'JUST JOE FUCKING MURPHY CAN HAVE MONEY, EH?

WELL, AH DID A WEE JOB, SEE? A BIT OF INFORMATION HERE AND A WEE WORD THERE. FUCKING EASY MONEY, MAN.'

'Fergie,' started Joe. 'Sean, come oan, Ah've got yer stash. Where the fuck did ye get that?'

In their time together Joe Murphy had watched Fergie earn a great deal of money. While Joe had used his to set up a few legitimate businesses, buy a house in a quiet middle-class enclave on the outskirts of the city, fund other jobs, run a couple of top-of-the-range cars, go abroad a few times a year and still have more than enough left over to have a good time – his friend was always broke. A long time before Joe had given up wondering how Fergie could spend so much on partying and good-time women. But he managed it consistently. Now he was carrying a wallet load while he had still forty thousand pounds lying with Joe from the bank job. Something wasn't right and the natives would notice. They knew Fergie's usual pecuniary state and would be curious.

'AH'LL FUCKING TELL YOU WHERE AH GOT MA DOUGH IF YE FUCKING TELL ME WHERE YESE WERE THE NIGHT AH NEEDED YESE. MAN, JOE, AH WAS HOT FRAE A JOB . . .'

'Fergie, shut up,' Joe said, pulling Fergie down by his arm.

'. . . THREE O US. POLIS ON EVERY FUCKING CORNER. THE OTHER TWO – FUCKING WANKERS, JOE – AH JUST NEEDED A PLACE TAE HIDE OOT, MAN. BUT YE WERENAE THERE.'

'Come oan, Fergie, come oan.' Joe spoke qietly. 'Let's just go back to my place and talk, eh?'

'YOUR PLACE, YE CUNT? IT WAS YOUR PLACE AH WANTED. BUT NAW, JOE'S OOT OAN BUSINESS OR SOME FUCKING THING. YOU'RE NO IN AND AH END UP GETTING NABBED, YE BASTARD.'

'Fergie, please, come oan . . .'

'IT'S YOUR FAULT AH TELT THEM, JOE BIG FUCKING SHOT CUNTING MURPHY. YOUR FAULT.'

Fergie got up, pushing and staggering his way through the crowd. At the door, a Salvation Army soldier came in carrying a collecting can and an armful of *War Cry* newspapers. Fergie looked him up and down, being watched by everyone in the bar.

'Put that in yer can, ye cunt,' Fergie screamed and butted his head into the Sally Army man's mouth, splitting his lip and dumping the guy on his arse on the ground. Fergie turned round and pointed across the bar, 'YE'RE A DEID MAN, MURPHY. AH'VE SORTED YOU, YE BASTARD. DEID MAN YOU, YE CUNT.'

'Fergie,' pleaded Joe, 'Ah don't know whit yer talking aboot.' Too late, Joe's comments were to Fergie's back as he slumped through the swing doors.

Once Fergie had left, the bar broke out in a chorus of animated mutterings. One or two regulars went over to Joe commiserating on his troubles and reassuring him things would be okay again once Fergie sobered up. Joe thanked them and sat on his own, his head held low, deep in thought about the repercussions of his friend's outburst. There was no doubt Fergie had just put himself in serious trouble. Fergie a grass? Joe couldn't believe it and wondered what he'd told the police about the bank job. Fergie might have been a close friend, his closest friend but now that had to change. Fergie had declared himself an enemy in the most public of ways. Joe would have to act on that, show he was above working with a police informant. The beer tasted sour in Joe's mouth.

Joe smelled her before he heard her. That rancid stink of years of unwashed shit was unmistakable. Madge stood in the middle of the pub floor, hiked her skirts up one tartan-skinned thigh and gave her loudest, squawking rendition of her second favourite song, the Platters' 'The Great Pretender'. As she sang the one and only line she ever got right,

'Yes I'm the great pretender
'Pretending . . .'

Joe's head slumped into his hands and he muttered,

'Why tonight, Madge? Why that song tonight?'

Shuggie Reid, having seen and heard everything, was slipping into the snug bar and out onto the street by the side door. He had information he had to share with the boss.

25 NOVEMBER 1989

I have broken one of my guiding principles and I've been wrong. Now it's time to act.

Always, I've judged individuals. Tried to look at them only, slicing out their unacceptable actions. Ignoring the other matters. To tackle the wider scene is like tackling life or changing human nature – commendable but impossible.

It's like German soldiers during the Nazi regime who worked in the concentration camps. Some claimed they followed orders and as soldiers that was their duty. My view is that all individuals take responsibility for themselves. They may live in a fascist state, work for an evil boss, be obliged to take orders from a corrupt superior. They may even work for good reason: to lift them and theirs from poverty, to give their children opportunities they never had. All valid, all understandable, but when they cross that line they cross it on their own and will be judged.

Don't ask me why I don't judge crime, the question is too big and becomes academic, unreal, impossible – that's the world of others who never want to be held truly accountable.

Ask me why I kill someone and I can tell you – he murders innocents, tortures the weak, takes pleasure in the pain of others. When the knife blade slips in it is in the hand of an individual. That I can judge as right or wrong. The rest I leave to politicians and their bedfellows, fat-arsed writers and grey-faced civil servants.

I have made a mistake, waiting for Grimes and Birse to show their game plan. Waiting for them I could wait forever. Action is the way forward as long as I'm sure every small step I take is right. Through action maybe I'll chance upon the answers, maybe not. As long as everything I do is for the right reasons then nothing is lost.

It is time to act. For some time I have known
who needs my attention and now their time has
arrived.

A

THE DEBT COLLECTORS

Deadeye didn't know he was being followed. He took his usual route to old Joe's house in the Priesthill scheme, as ever changing buses unnecessarily, getting off early, just short of the Pollok Centre, and walking past Glenlora Drive before stopping at an off-sales to buy Joe's beer, then cutting back through a school playground. Normally his routes were more complicated but it was only a social call after all. But his tail had followed him before and just cruised behind the first bus before guessing Deadeye's destination. By the time Deadeye arrived at old Joe's he was being watched from the muddy wasteland at the gable end of a nearby house.

'Ye shouldnae have bothered, son,' said old Joe opening his first can of super lager. 'Really, yer too kind.' Joe gulped quickly, killing the gnawing shakes that had plagued him since morning. His pension hadn't lasted the week and the bottle of weak cider, all he could afford, had failed to take the edge off his need for booze. Joe had prayed Deadeye was going to visit that night. If he hadn't, old Joe was in for a very rough time. 'Ye'll be wanting that old phone directory, eh, tae lean oan for yer wacky baccy? There it's there, son. Know Ah've never tried that stuff, never had the notion. Whit's it like? Like a good bevvy, eh? Or better? Once got tablets aff the doctor. Cannae mind whit they were but, Christ, did they make me feel rerr. Found oot later that the kids take them 'cept they cry them jelly beans or something. Would've paid me two quid a throw for them. Fuck sakes, son, if Ah'd known that Ah would've traded them. Sixty quid or something. Ah could've got steamboats for three days oan that.'

Across the way, Deadeye's tail watched the two men's heads through the curtainless window. Old Joe couldn't afford curtains and, besides, his living-room window was the only one not blacked out by sheets of corrugated iron. If he had enough money or his wife was still alive maybe there would've been a set of nice floral drapes. Joe's misfortune was unwittingly protecting his new young friend. With the lights blazing and the windows uncovered, Joe and Deadeye were talking in the equivalent of an illuminated goldfish bowl. But the time would come when Deadeye stepped out of the house. That would be the time.

'Ye sure, son? Dinnae want tae waste yer good smokes annat. Can Ah take this hashish wi the electric soup here? Cos if it's a toss up, ye know, Ah'll stick tae the devil's brew. Nae offence meant, son. Christ, this stuff tastes no half bad. Kinda nice smell, eh? Got used tae that smell since ye've been coming roon, son. Kinda makes me think o yese, ye know? Mean they weans just smoke it aw the time doon the scheme. Nice weans tae. Nae offence, son. Whit Ah'm trying tae say is that Ah used tae think folks that did drugs, well, they were aw junkies, ye know? Like mug yese as soon as look at yese. But this wacky, man, every bugger seems tae be smoking it, eh? Nice kids smoke it. Just like yersel, eh?'

Old Joe went quiet, embarrassed by the softness of his comments to the young man. Men simply didn't say things like that and Joe worried he was getting soft in the head as well as in the heart. But Joe had to admit it, he was a lonely old man and the company of his young friend was the only company he had.

'Who the fuck's that at this time o night?' Old Joe asked as somebody rapped three times on his door. 'Shite,' he swore, struggling to his feet, 'Ah'll bet it's the Provvie man. Ducked the bastard the other day but he's local, no the first time he's caught me oot late at night.' Deadeye understood that Joe would owe money to the Provident, most folk in the schemes did. Deadeye also understood that Joe would be broke. 'Whit's that? Och, no, son, ye've no need. Ah'll just tell him tae sing for it. Whit they gonnae dae? Throw me in the jail?' Deadeye insisted and stuck the envelope of money in Joe's top pocket. He was going to give him the cash anyway, just at the end of his visit to cut the embarrassing chitchat down to a minimum.

Joe teetered out into the hall, slowly, painfully. Deadeye had noticed how the old guy's legs stiffened when he had been sitting for any length of time. It was a sign of old age that Deadeye didn't like, telling him that Joe wasn't as fit as he claimed. Voice at the door. Old Joe angry, his voice raised.

'Naw, ye cannae come in. Dinnae gie a fuck that ye've a warrant,' he protested. 'Tell ye, yese must have the wrong address. Ah'm just an old man oan my own.' Heavy footsteps rushing down the hall into the living-room. Deadeye on his feet, gun drawn, aiming at the door.

'Gerry, come on, you don't want to make this worse.' Jeannie Stirk stood facing Deadeye, behind her were two uniformed cops. 'I'm here to arrest you in connection with a bank robbery. That gun makes it serious, very serious.' Deadeye said nothing, weighing up his options. There were only three of them and they weren't armed. Easy targets. Old Joe's house was in a perfect location. Deadeye could take care of the cops and hightail it down the back of Glenlora to the park, cross the main road and be in the middle-class neighbourhod of Crookston before the police knew there was anyone to chase. Deadeye had been in worse predicaments before. This was going to be easy.

'Whit's happening, son?' said Old Joe coming in the living-room door, grabbed by a policeman and pulled back.

'Leave him be, ye fucker,' spat Deadeye.

'Whit's happening, son?' Joe's voice from the door. 'Aw, son, dinnae dae this. They'll send ye doon forever.' Joe's voice, plaintive and pleading. Deadeye could take them but Joe was in the way.

'Move back, Joe, move away,' shouted Deadeye. 'Get oot the hoose an keep moving.'

'Naw, son, Ah cannae move fast. An Ah'm no moving till Ah'm sure yer OK,' said Joe, standing by the door.

'Gerry, just put the gun down, please,' said Jeannie Stirk, standing stock-still five feet away from the barrel of Deadeye's gun. 'No tricks, Gerry,' she said, lifting both sides of her coat away from her body to show that she wasn't armed. 'No agendas. Straightforward arrest.'

'Aye, till Ah get in the motor,' retorted Deadeye holding his gun steady, aimed at her abdomen.

'You are my prisoner, Gerry . . .' Jeannie persisted.

'Aye, an yer boss is Birse.'

'DCI Birse is on annual leave. I'm in charge and you have my guarantee,' said Jeannie. 'You are my prisoner and I will ensure your safety while in custody.' Deadeye didn't believe her. It was a straight call and he had the upper hand. Old Joe was going to get in the firing line but so what, he was meant to have been killed a long time ago. Deadeye looked at his old friend's frightened, pale face and tear-filled eyes. An arthritic claw reached down, rubbing slowly at an aching thigh.

'Your decision, Gerry,' said Jeannie Stirk, continuing to look calmly into Deadeye's face.

Handcuffed in the back of the police car, Deadeye swore that was the last. No more friends, no more soft touch. It made him weak and now more than ever he had to be strong, ruthless. As the car pulled away from the kerb, Deadeye looked back, watching old Joe wave timidly from his front gate. That would be the last time he'd see the old guy, the last friend in Deadeye's life.

In the shadows of a nearby gable end, the hunter turned, slinking off into the dark, cursing. He'd missed the easy target, the obvious one. But he still had business that night.

PALS' ACT

He could feel he was being watched through the peephole in the steel-enforced door. Being watched for a long time, though it was only seconds. He was giving up hope, about to turn away. Then, the door opened slowly. The young boy stood in the close, shaking with fear. The last time he'd been here he'd been subjected to such horrors. Such personal atrocities so disgusting, so demeaning he couldn't tell anyone, not even his best friend. He should have told his best friend. He really should have told him.

'Jake?' the man answering the door spoke quietly, meekly. 'Have ye come back tae me then?' He spoke through a gap of a few inches, the door being held securely by a number of chains.

'Aye, listen, Ah'm sorry aboot the smack,' replied Jake holding his head down, his knees jerking with fear. 'It's just, well, Ah had tae get away, know?'

'Forget it. It was just twenty tenner bags.'

'Aye, but Ah flogged them like ye said.'

'Aye, well, it's no exactly hard tae shift smack, eh?'

'And Ah owe yese the money.'

'Forget it, let's write it off tae a wee mistake.'

'Thanks,' Jake's head still turned down, ' Ah was wondering . . . Ah was just wondering like if Ah could deal for yese again. Naw, sorry, that was stupid.'

'Would it cost me twenty tenner bags every time?'

'Naw, Ah just need some work,' said Jake. 'Need tae raise some money. Skint like.'

'Aye, well, ye'll have tae come in and we'll talk aboot it, eh?' This was the part Jake was dreading. He knew what the invite to go in meant. The visions of that last visit flitted through his mind in vivid Technicolor as they had every day since.

'Aye, okay,' Jake mumbled. The chains were undone one by one and the door was pulled open wide. Jake was yanked out of the way,

'POLICE. ARMED POLICE. DO NOT MOVE ,YOU ARE UNDER ARREST.'

The two armed coppers stood in the door, their pistols pointing straight at The Arse Bandit's head and guts. It was too much, even for him. Bud Wilson, aka The Arse Bandit, surrendered for the first time in his life. He turned against the wall, his hands behind his head, showing the revolver stuck into the waistband of his trousers. One armed policeman whipped the gun out, emptying the shells, while the other covered him. Then they swapped roles, the second cop swiftly but thoroughly shaking The Arse Bandit down while his colleague held his gun steady at his back,

'Does Birse know aboot this? Whit aboot Grimes?' The Arse Bandit asked, keeping his head facing the wall.

'No, I'm the arresting officer,' replied Jeannie Stirk walking into the hall of the flat.

'Ha, a lassie,' sniggered The Arse Bandit. 'Well, ye'd better get oan the blower tae yer boss then wait for yer arsehole tae be kicked.'

'And why would that be, ye piece o filth?' DCI Birse walked into the flat and punched The Arse Bandit in the kidneys. 'Sorry, Jeannie, sorry,' muttered Birse, 'your arrest, Ah'll back off.'

'This is unexpected, sir,' said Jeannie, trying to keep her cool, 'I thought you were away for a few days' leave?'

'Aye, aye Ah was but Ah came back early. Heard ye had a shout oan and, ye know, couldnae resist catching this wide cunt.' Jeannie smiled.

'Good to see you, boss,' she said and this time she meant it, but not in the sense he assumed.

'Whit we got the bastard oan?' Birse asked, nodding at The Arse Bandit's back.

'Suspect in an armed bank robbery,' Jeannie replied. 'But what is definitely sticking to him right now is the small matter of dealing in Class A – namely heroin, assault, assault to permanent disfigurement, assault with a serious weapon and whatever else we can work out from torturing and raping an underage boy for three days.'

'Yer a lying cow,' squealed The Arse Bandit.

'You should choose your victims more carefully, Bud,' said Jeannie, 'and make sure their friends don't care for them more than they're frightened of you.'

'That wee cunt Jake,' screamed The Arse Bandit, turning and moving fast, only to be grabbed by two cops and thrown back against the wall head first. Jake edged into the doorway, still terrified, his stomach flipping nervously, feeling sick.

'You ruined ma pal,' Jake started quietly. 'You almost killed him, ye big fucking prick ye. An he's just a kid. An ye burnt his arse oot. Damaged him inside bad, man. Fucking ruined him.' Tears streaming down Jake's face, he was edging closer and closer to The Arse Bandit his arm lifted, fist clenched, his teeth gritted. Jeannie stepped in front of him.

'Come on, Jake,' she said, 'we've got him now. Let us take care of him, eh?' speaking softly, stroking Jake's shoulder. 'We'll put him away, good style.' Jake slowly nodded his head.

'Ah'll testify against him tae,' Jake said.

'He's a lying wee wanker,' howled The Arse Bandit.

'He did the same to me. He raped me for three days and nights. Jist he went further,' Jake weeping now, his head in Jeannie Stirk's shoulder, 'wi ma pal.'

'Liar, Ah dinnae need tae rape,' screamed The Arse Bandit.

'AH'M GRASSING YOU, YE CUNT, AN AH DON'T CARE WHO KNOWS ABOOT IT,' screamed the young man. Jake had appeared at his local police station, volunteering the information of his own assault in the den of The Arse Bandit. He didn't mention the small guy who had approached him in the pub one night. The pub in Edinburgh close to the flat of his new girlfriend. The place he had run away to after his torture by The Arse Bandit. Healing himself on weeks of sweet feminine company, good hash, nights on the town without looking over his shoulder. He never asked the guy how he had tracked him down. The guy didn't know about him and The Arse Bandit, just wanted to tell him about his friend. Jake hadn't hesitated. Straight on the train and a taxi to Glasgow's Victoria Infirmary. Ten minutes after he walked out of that ward he knew what he had to do. Straight to the local nick.

'JEANNIE! Better come look at this,' shouted a uniformed cop from another room. In the living-room, forensics were examining brown powder from one large bag and in a score of smaller, clear, plastic packages. The bedroom stank of sweat, spunk and shit. A young boy was tied face down on the bed. Naked, legs spread-eagled, his buttocks smeared with faeces and Vaseline. Down his back ran a series of fresh cigarette burns. The police photographer took several quick pictures from different angles and distances then the boy's hands were released.

'I'm Jeannie Stirk. What's your name?' No answer. 'How old are you, son?' asked Jeannie, helping him up to a sitting position, wrapping a blanket round his shoulders.

'Want tae go home,' he whimpered, 'ma ma disnae know where Ah'm are.' The young boy from the Necropolis graveyard had decided there were more dangerous places than sharing a house with a drunken, violent father.

Out in the fresh air of the street, Jeannie Stirk watched the dawn creak the day to life over Glasgow. It had been a long night and the day would be longer. She lit a cigarette and exhaled, leaning with her back against the tenement wall, looking up at the stars still winking in the half daylight.

'That's a good collar,' said Birse moving alongside her, looking up to see what she could see. Jeannie nodded, said nothing and pulled on her cigarette again. 'Been after him for years so Ah have.' Jeannie said nothing. Birse turned, moving close, leaning down, his mouth next to her ear, whispering, 'You an me, Jeannie, we have tae work the gether, right? Work wi me an you'll be fine. Do well. Catch ma drift?' Something hard, weighty and bulky in Birse's coat leaned heavily against Jeannie Stirk's arm. She turned to face Birse up close, her head raised, their lips almost touching.

'I noticed, Alex, your shoes are all covered in mud.' Birse frowned down at her trying to make sense of her comments. 'Muddy scheme that Priesthill.' Jeannie threw her cigarette on the ground, brushed past Birse, stopped and turned, putting a hand up and squeezing the shape of the pistol in his coat. 'And you need to lose some weight.'

Jeannie Stirk walked back into the tenement close leaving Birse alone with her words and his thoughts. He was going to have to be more careful, or maybe more vicious, maybe with her. What he did know, however, was that as of that moment he and Jeannie Stirk had trouble between them for as long as they worked together or lived in the same city.

12 DECEMBER 1989

Even though I try and reduce life to its most simple components, still competing forces duel against each other. That is one reason why I look only at simple acts, yet still they rise and bite you in different ways.

Till now, I was going to protect them. I had even reasoned that a simple, ill-guided, weak man should suffer if he became a party to their harm. Now that seemed straightforward and there will be those who judge me badly simply because of who these people are and what they've had to endure. I'm with them on that but even the persecuted can be guilty no matter how evil their persecution has been.

I wonder if what I'm doing is akin to the jailing of men and women for crimes they did not commit on the presumption that they have done other ills. I don't believe so. At least I am not lazy, not prejudiced. I base my judgements on the acts themselves and don't pretend the punishment is for one thing when it is really for some figment of my imagination or the wish fulfilment of my prejudices.

Is it so difficult to support someone for how they have been treated, to be willing to fight to prevent it ever happening again and, at the same time, to punish them for acts which are beyond acceptance? People, we can be saints and sinners and never miss a beat. Me, I just judge them for the sins against decency. As for the rest, I am on their side.

Tomorrow is a day that may not work well for me. As I type this, I'm aware I may not have another chance to explain. So, you need to know I have taken precautions. I have already typed out and copied the reasons for my actions. If you read this and I'm dead or in jail, don't judge me till you read on. If I survive, wait for me, I'll explain all.

Like history, these chronicles are not written in objective, logical order. Like history, they are written for a purpose. My purpose. Make of them what you will.

A

INTO SAFE-KEEPING

'This is not right! Not fair!' Jakob Wise howled and wept.

'It is for your own good, man, now shut up.' The doctor was stressed. Bloody ambulance was late as usual, leaving him standing outside the old couple's house and it had been an hour since his last hit of methadone.

'Jakob, come, let's find some things for you and Ruthie to take with you.' Angie the Gopher was in his element. Not only had the bent GP introduced him as Ruth and Jakob's social worker but so had Jakob. Just the day before, Angie had attended court to be available to the sheriff if he wanted to ask questions. The doctor did the main application but it gave Angie such a buzz to hear the solicitor say, 'The family's social worker of some years, Mr Jacob Goldberg, is present should you wish to ask him any questions.' Yes! That was the business. The sheriff hadn't bothered to ask for Angie, of course. These affairs were fitted in between the normal day-to-day business of the courts.

The hearing took less than five minutes and, from what Angie could hear, most of that was spent shuffling paper. Angie had spent the time reading the doctor's formal report. Ten lines of barely legible handwritten pap. Angie reckoned he could do better with a hangover and a dose of the piles. But the sheriff didn't seem to notice, he just read the report – the beak's lips moving as he read – then asked a question Angie couldn't hear. The doctor mumbled something back and that was it. No big pronouncement, no declaration, justice was dealt with a mumble. So, fine, let's lock the old couple up. An old couple that the sheriff didn't even bother seeing. In fact, Jakob and Ruth didn't even know the application had been made. That was the law. All above board.

'This is my social worker,' old Jakob protested to the doctor, 'he knows. Listen to Mr Goldberg, please.'

Angie preened himself, took a deep breath and started: 'Mr and Mrs Wise are coping well under the circumstances. Mrs Wise, unfortunately, suffers from advanced senile dementia resulting in a loss of short-term memory and extreme chronological displacement. Given the unfortunate circumstances of Mrs Wise's early life, some of her time displacement can be distressing but, equally, can be full of joy, depending entirely on the impact of the disorder. Mrs Wise is, therefore, quite incapable of caring for herself. Mr Wise is her full-time carer and has recently abandoned his business to ensure his wife's safety and well-being . . .'

'See,' said Jakob Wise, 'see, you listen to Mr Goldberg. He knows. He knows everything.'

'. . . while Mrs Wise is occasionally eneuretic it needs to be said that she does not suffer from the double incontinence often associated with her condition. On the contrary, she remains extremely regular, perhaps too regular, in her bowel movements, being required to visit the toilet at two-hourly intervals from awakening, which she always does at 6.13 a.m. precisely every morning. Now, while this might indicate a sign of . . .'

'Shut up, you bloody prat,' said the doctor, his fists rose to strike Angie but paused in mid air as if held back by invisible restraints.

'You listen,' pleaded Jakob Wise.

'. . . extreme neurosis, it is, I suspect, more indicative of the privations suffered during the early years of her . . .' continued Angie, not stopping to draw breath.

'Such work,' muttered Ruth Wise, 'too much work, must finish before Papa comes home. Go to the dance with my Jakob . . .' Ruth Wise spoke to herself and stood folding carrier bags into neat rectangles.

'FUUUUCK, THAT'S IT,' howled the doctor, his fists gripped and his face turned to the ceiling. 'Get them out of here, NOW!' he ordered the two paramedics, whose ambulance had been reversed with their rear door right up to the close mouth.

'High fucking time as well,' said the female ambulance driver, 'Ah've no had ma tea. Look at the fucking time.' She cocked her wrist, showing her wristwatch, jabbing at it with the index finger of her other hand. Her colleague nodded and grabbed Ruth Wise by one arm. He wasn't sure about all of this but he had already been shown the court order by the doctor with the bad dose of the shakes. If he didn't do it somebody else would and he'd find himself on a discipline charge. He couldn't risk that, not with a wife in a wheelchair and two kids still at primary school.

'Come oan, love,' he said, 'take ye some place nice.'

'Dancing with my Jakob,' said Ruth Wise, 'he's so handsome, so dapper.'

'Aye, no worries, babe,' said the male paramedic, 'yer Jakob's coming as well.'

'Work, must work, or Papa won't allow me to the dance,' Ruth Wise looked up at the male paramedic with unseeing navy-blue eyes. The paramedic grabbed a handful of carrier bags and stuffed them into Ruth Wise's hands.

'Sure, love, you work away. Now, let's just take a wee drive in ma motor,' he looked down and smiled at Ruth. 'Take ye tae the dancing, sugar?' She smiled, a sweet girl's smile and nodded. 'Madame, yer carriage awaits,' he announced, offering her his arm and walking her out of the house for the last time.

On the wasteground across from Jakob and Ruth's house the old jakie poked at his campfire with a length of copper pipe. He'd hoped to earn a few bob from that pipe but the scrap merchant said there wasn't enough and, besides, the price of scrap metal had gone down so much. So the jakie had told the scrappie to fuck off and brought the pipe home, an ideal poker if ever he saw one. The jakie looked up from his embers and watched the charade across the road.

'Listen to Mr Goldberg,' old Jakob Wise pleaded.

'Mr and Mrs Wise have a perfectly complementary relationship,' Angie obliged. 'Finely balanced and easily disturbed by external pressures, yet somehow . . .' Angie kept gabbing as he helped old Jakob into the back of the ambulance and then turned to Mrs Wise.

'Have to work,' she gibbered. 'Papa home soon . . .' Angie helped her up the steps and slipped into the ambulance behind her. The male paramedic was last to enter, checking right and left and then slamming the doors shut.

The old jakie watched the ambulance rev and drive slowly out of the scheme, then turned to watch the doctor sitting in his Audi estate. Hurriedly opening the glove compartment he brought out a small brown bottle. Checking for voyeurs and seeing no one, he unscrewed the top and drunk deep. Hit delivered home, he could face the world again.

The old jakie watched the doctor drive off down the street. He had a feeling that he wouldn't be seeing his neighbours again. With the old couple gone, all he had to keep him company were the rats, stray dogs and the demolition men. The machines and the men were getting closer. The big track machines he couldn't stand with their rattle and exhaust fumes. But the men he was hopeful of. They could speak, spare a second and that's all he wanted, some company. But they all seemed to be too preoccupied and they all looked the same. Small men dressed in red boiler suits. Grimes insisted that the squad wore red so that the gaffers could more easily spot them if they were skiving off. The old jakie wouldn't have understood those values if they were ever explained to him. All he knew was that the men all looked the same and he didn't like it.

The old jakie dug into the pile of rubble and pulled out his bottle of Buckfast, already two-thirds down and him with no money. It was going to be a sleepless night and a rough morning. Unscrewing the top he looked at the bottle in admiration, licked his lips and lifted the neck to his mouth. Two big swallows is all he could afford but, ah, they tasted sweet. As he lowered his bottle a stranger came into sight. A small, young-looking guy he thought, but how would he know since the guy was dressed in that red boiler suit like everyone else and a baseball cap on his napper to boot. The stranger walked quickly though, as quickly as the others dragged their limbs. He walked straight up to Jakob and Ruth Wise's close, obviously knowing where he was headed. Five minutes later he came out with a bundle wrapped in newspaper under his arm, walking just as jauntily, no quicker or slower. Halfway along the pavement the man in the boiler suit turned and threw the jakie a cheery salute and kept walking. The old jakie saluted back – it was manners to do so – but he didn't know the man and wondered why he of all the workies should be friendly.

'Filthy rotten bastard,' muttered the jakie, 'robbing folk's hooses when they've hardly left.'

Halfway across the city the ambulance was stopped at red lights. The woman driver wished she had an excuse to turn on the flashing lights and siren and speed across the junction. She had a heavy date with a childminder and her two young kids to pick up. If she was late again the childminder would quit and then there would be trouble finding another one before her next shift. She hated these time-consuming, oldies jobs. Give her an emergency, something important any time.

In the back of the ambulance, Angie had stopped speaking to take a breath. Then he thought, then he realised. He wasn't meant to be in the back of the ambulance. He was meant to be in the old couple's house nabbing the Bearer Bonds. If anything had gone wrong while he was away, Grimes would eat his guts while he was still alive and kicking. Angie the Gopher was in serious trouble and he wanted to pee again.

SEEN IT ALL BEFORE

The sound of the oars dipped quietly into the water, easy in an even rhythm. All else he could hear was his own regular breathing and somewhere in the distance a lonely steam hammer belting at metal.

Then he heard the shouts.

'Here, hey, over here, pal.'

A dozen or so men were standing on the far bank, waving and jumping – overgrown, muscle-bound excited children. It wasn't the first time he'd received a call-out from a rowing club. You'd think the new members would be told when they signed up. But no, the rowing clubs seemed to want to keep the prospect of these events a little secret. He supposed he understood why but, still, a little forewarning might make his job easier. Save him having to deal with quite as many hysterical young people. Let him get on with his real work.

'Over here,' the shouts were rising in frequency as he got closer. 'Down there, mate, beside the jetty.' Half a dozen young men in what looked like identical, gaudy Lycra suits were standing on the bank, pointing into the water. For athletes, their faces looked wan and drawn. He wondered how many would tell a different version of the story in the west-end pubs that night. A smaller young man, an emaciated midget standing among the others, was watching him and the rowing boat thoughtfully. Probably surprised that it's not a fancy speed launch, crewed by tanned men in uniforms and an officious-looking flag fluttering from the bow. Too much TV these days. People thought the world was like Hollywood's version and didn't take the time to check out what was really happening right under their noses. In the corners of their own city.

He eased the rowing boat's speed, holding it back with the oars till it moved gently towards the indicated point. He could tell what it was even before he got close. Years of this work had given him a fine eye. Too often corpses would bob up and down the Clyde, close to busy pedestrian walkways, totally ignored by the passers-by. When the bodies bloated and the faces changed to a dark hue, they look like just another piece of flotsam. Waste floating on the grey water – nothing remarkable there. But this was a body all right and it had been in the water for weeks.

As the rowing boat moved up close he could see it was a big man, dressed in a suit. Suicide clothes are all types and those were his usual customers. Poor souls who'd lost all hope and jumped in from King George IV Bridge. The height wasn't great and most survived the fall only to wave and struggle, dance the drowning man's dance. Women and the kids upset him most, still reaching him after all these years. But this was a man, middle aged by the look of his hair. Reaching out his hook to steady the corpse, the body bobbed up and down, turning round with the movement of the water.

'Get to a phone will you, someone?' he shouted from the rowing boat. The small, thin man held up his thumb in recognition that he was up to the task. 'Dial 999, ask for the police. Tell them we've got a suspicious body in the water.'

He knew this was trouble. Too often they had injuries like this one – the top of his skull smashed in. Sometimes it was as a result of the fall, sometimes it caused the fall. But not often had he picked up a corpse wearing a gun holster.

The Yank would be leaving Glasgow and going home.

THE SMART MOVE

'Whit ye bloody mean the tin's empty?' Grimes paced the floor of his office, arms tense, face close to purple with rage. Angie the Gopher stood in front of him, his head bowed and his wig in his hands. Grimes had knocked it off with his first punch, leaving Angie with a red abrasion on his skull where he should have had hair. If Grimes' knuckles didn't hurt so much, Angie would have received more punishment.

'Boss, Ah checked as soon as the quack left wi Jakob and Rose . . . eh, wi the old couple,' Angie whimpered and looked up, tears welling in his eyes, 'Nothing, boss. Nothing.' Maggie Small watched from the far end of the room. She was wary of Grimes' temper, likely to flare up to lethal violence at any time. Murdering Angie would solve nothing and bring a great deal of grief to their door, trouble that not even Birse could make disappear. She was ready to intervene at any minute.

When Angie had realised that he had got carried away with his bogus role, he had banged on the side of the ambulance till the driver pulled in and let him out. The fracas had left Ruth Wise crying, hysterical. Angie was sorry about that but he had more pressing priorities.

Breaking a habit of a frugal lifestyle, Angie had stood in the centre of Shawlands Cross and hailed a cab as four lanes of cars and buses sped past him on either side. A quick recce at the Wise house revealed the empty box in exactly the same position he had last seen it, when he had stolen the one Bearer Bond. Angie had gone frantic searching everywhere, throwing the piles of sodden newspapers over the floor, ripping open the dripping black bin bags, scattering food, lifting the lid of the toilet cistern. Nothing. He had run out into the street, sticking his wig in his pocket, and hired another taxi to take him straight to Leverndale Hospital where Jakob and Ruth were to be admitted.

Locating the ward with some difficulty, Angie sprinted in, his chest heaving with the effort and the panic, to a greeting from Jakob,

'My friend, you have come to rescue us.' Turning to his wife, 'See,

I said Mr Goldberg would not allow this . . . such a good man.' Ruth Wise smiled and nodded her head, she was too busy folding carrier bags into neat little rectangles. Jakob continued to thank the bogus social worker. Angie ignored him, going immediately to the locker. Finding it bare he'd moved on to the one small bag of possessions the couple had brought with them. Spilling the few items out on the floor, Angie could see it was some bread, a bottle of water and an old, mildewed photograph of the couple. No bonds. Next he started searching old Jakob's pockets, ignoring the old man's protestations. Finally it was Ruth's turn, searching between her layers of woollen cardigans, raking through her supply of carrier bags and then Angie stopped.

'Take us away, please, Jacob,' pleaded old Mr Wise. 'They are cruel to us in here . . .' Angie gulped and took a deep breath. The thought of what he was about to do made him feel sick, repulsed, dirty. But it was an extreme situation. One final deep breath and he leaned over hiking up old Ruth Wise's skirt. 'NO! NO!' screamed Jakob Wise. 'What you doing. Leave my Ruthie, leave her . . .' Angie rifled through the material of the woman's skirt, trying hard not to look at her varicose-veined legs. And he found nothing.

There was only one place left to look and he wasn't going there. Ruth Wise's underwear. No, he wasn't going there. With Jakob's upset complaining fading in his ears, Angie walked slowly out of the ward, a defeated man. At the door he stopped and looked back. Jakob was fussing about his wife, straightening her dress, chattering non-stop. Ruth Wise sat on the edge of the hospital bed and smiled with the sparkling eyes of the fifteen-year-old girl she sometimes thought she still was. A crafty smile, a smile of secrets. Was that a smirk? Angie wondered what she knew. But search her underwear? No, that was too much to ask.

'Mr Goldberg,' cried Jakob Wise after Angie. 'Please help. Our things. We need our things.' Angie spun round, alert to what was coming next. 'Some clothes maybe and the radio and there's a tin I need. In the cupboard. Second shelf on the left. Picture of the young Queen.' Angie looked at the old man's face, now suddenly pleading even more than before. His eyes begged Angie to fetch the tin. The tin Angie knew was empty. Angie the Gopher ignored the old man's cries and slinked to the door saying a silent farewell to Jakob and Ruth Wise and hello to a dread of the next few hours.

'I'm gonnae murder you, ye cunt,' screamed Grimes still rubbing at his fist. 'Fucking maulicate yese, ye wee slimy bastard.' Angie the Gopher wanted to pee badly.

'Andy,' Maggie Small's hand reached out gently for Grimes' arm. She knew the trick was to stop him before he reached boiling point. After that it would be too late. 'Andy, come on, let's talk.'

'IN FACT AH'M GONNAE KILL YESE RIGHT NOO,' Grimes shrugged Maggie off and took a step towards Angie the Gopher, cowering and waiting. He knew from experience that to run only made it worse. The first slap made Angie cower and shudder. But it was the noise of a slap, just the noise not the pain. He peered up in time to see Maggie Small standing between him and Andy Grimes, her arm swung out wide and came round for a second time into the big man's face. And again and again. Maggie said nothing as she slapped Grimes. He cringed and shied back with every blow, moving further and further away from Angie.

'Now listen,' Maggie finally said, breathing heavily from the effort of the assault. 'Just fucking listen, Andy, before you go and spoil everything.' She held Grimes' forearms with her hands, standing close to him, eye to eye, as she spoke. 'We are winning, Andy. Winning. Don't go and lose just because you're angry with Angie.' Grimes went to move but Maggie held on to him, standing closer. 'You've got the council contract for Dalmeny Street in the bag in just a few weeks time.' Maggie raised her eyes in a question, seeking confirmation. Grimes just nodded his head, his fat bottom lip overlapping his top lip, some spoiled child in the middle of a tantrum. 'You've got Deadeye and The Arse Bandit in prison. All right, I guess you wanted a worse fate for them but, Andy, YOU have got James Addison off the street.' Grimes nodded more enthusiastically, his lips curling a little into the hint of a smile. 'And best of all, you've got one bond, Andy. Three hundred grand for nothing.' Grimes grinned wide, the murderous look being replaced in his eyes by what passed for pleasure on his face. 'And who have you to thank for that? Hmm, Andy, think? Angie's too frightened of you ever to cheat you. Ever, Andy.' Grimes looking more serious now. 'You have the Bearer Bond, Andy, that was a gift from Angie.'

Grimes knew that Maggie was making sense, she always did. The only person in the world that he ever listened to and he was glad of their partnership. Maggie Small was right.

'Andy Grimes, ye've come out of this well,' he thought. 'Very well indeed.'

As Grimes walked slowly and calmly across the floor of the office, Angie gripped his wig tighter and tensed his whole body.

'Hrrmph,' Grimes cleared his voice, 'Angie, eh . . . well done an that.' Grimes was struggling with the sentiment and the words were stuck in his gullet. 'Eh, aye, well done. Now away an have a drink – oan me. Tell the barmen, right?' Angie the Gopher didn't hesitate. The words and free booze passed as the closest Grimes would ever get to a compliment. Besides, Angie the Gopher wanted to pee again.

'See,' said Maggie Small once Angie had gone, 'that didn't hurt. That was a very smart move you made there, Andy.'

'Aye, aye. Thanks,' replied Grimes. 'Ah was thinking, soon be New Year, eh? Maybe a good time for yese tae recruit another couple o lassies?'

'I'm on top of it, Andy,' smiled Maggie Small. 'Have a couple in mind.'

Out in the Gents, Angie the Gopher stood at the urinal and winced as one pitiful and painful dribble ran against the white ceramic. Things were getting too much for him around The Cat's Whiskers. Lately he had been thinking of a change. Time to move on. Things just weren't the same anymore.

THE OLD, THE NEW AND THE SAME

BEGINNINGS

Cathy Brodie wasn't surprised by the caller at her door. Joe Murphy
kissed her cheek, chucked Tim under the chin and walked into her flat
with the ease of a regular and welcome guest. The flat had been tidied
up since the police raid and a few extra items of furniture brought in.
Like the two easy chairs Cathy and Joe sat in, across from each other,
their knees almost touching.

'You look helluva pleased with yourself,' Cathy said, smiling.

'Aye, an so Ah should be,' Joe smiled back.

'It's the first time Ah've seen you look properly relaxed since . . .
well,' Cathy hesitated, 'that business wi Fergie.' Joe's face turned
solemn and Cathy bit her lip, wishing she hadn't mentioned Fergie's
name.

'Aye, aye Ah know, but that's the way it goes.'

'Have ye heard anything o him lately?' Cathy knew Joe needed to
talk about his friend even though it hurt.

'Naw, no since that night in the pub,' replied Joe. 'He's shot the
craw, disappeared, and no bloody wonder.'

'Ye dinnae think he grassed ye up?'

'Me? No, elsewise Ah'd be in custody right now. But Deadeye's inside
and been charged with the job.' One of the many things Joe liked about
Cathy was her background, her understanding of his business. He could
tell her anything and it was safe with her. Hadn't she proven that by
refusing to help Birse identify James Addison? An issue she hadn't
mentioned to him as they had grown closer, more trusting. Whatever she
saw, if she saw anything, had not happened as far as Cathy Brodie was
concerned. That was the old street way, the right way, the way that helped
Joe Murphy feel as close to her as he did. 'An if Ah hadnae warned Beano
that very night . . . well, who knows?'

'Think Fergie is under the polis protection scheme?'

'Aye, maybe,' sighed Joe, 'or jist lying low or something. Just as well
or Ah'd have tae see tae him. Be seen to be making him prove to me
that he's no a grass. An if he didnae – make an example o him. Might

still have tae.' Joe had explained to Cathy before that Fergie being noted as a police informant had repercussions on Joe as his former best friend. If Fergie ever showed his face again, Joe would have to assault him, seriously and in public. Joe believed in the old ways. A person took responsibility for what they did and had to live – or die – by their actions. Being a grass was an either/or, a straightforward decision. Fergie was a grass and Joe wasn't – simple – and it was up to Fergie to prove otherwise. 'Just shows ye, ye cannae trust some people even when ye think ye know them.'

'Aye, but ye can trust me, Joe,' Cathy eased Tim gently up her shoulder and leaned over, stroking Joe's hand.

'Aye, listen, whit are we so gloomy for? It's Hogmanay, eh?' Joe suddenly enthused, smiling, enervated.

'Aye, almost New Year,' Cathy giggled.

'Well, Ah have an early present.'

'Oooh, hear that, Timmy, Joe's brought ye a present an for Hogmanay no jist Christmas.' Cathy was so used to Joe bringing gifts for her baby son. It was as if Joe was already his father, cramming in all the missed moments, making up for them, taking pleasure in the baby's ways.

'For both of ye this time,' Joe smiled. 'Shut yer eyes and hold out yer hand.' Cathy giggled and obliged. She felt cold metal weight. Opening her eyes again she saw a set of heavy mortice keys.

'Whit?' she didn't understand, her pretty face perplexed and wrinkled.

'They're for a hoose,' Joe said, as if that was enough explanation. 'It's a new hoose Ah've bought. Up at Robroyston. A new home for you and Timmy.'

'Joe, it's too . . .'

'No strings, it's just for the two of you. Get ye oot o this dump.'

'But . . .'

'And Ah mean no strings,' Joe was talking too fast, gibbering. 'Ye know how Ah feel aboot ye and Timmy, eh? But we'll let that take its time. Tae we're ready, eh? The hoose is yours. Happy New Beginnings, Cathy.'

'Joe, how could ye afford this?' Cathy worried, overwhelmed.

'Aw, Ah've got ma secrets, Cathy, even frae you. Though the most important ones we share, eh?' The two started laughing, Cathy leaned over and kissed Joe on the mouth, ruffling his hair.

Joe was happy, the dilemma had plagued him for ages. What to do with Fergie's money? He was never going to return it to him that's for sure. It was handy as a contribution to the costs of the house.

'At least some good had come out of Fergie's betrayal,' thought Joe. 'If he is a grass, serve the wee bastard right.'

BUSINESS AS USUAL

The Cat's Whiskers was packed. Up on the dance floor the sloe-eyed brunette gyrated naked to 'Let's Party' by Jive Bunny and the Mastermixers as if it was her party and she could take her clothes off if she wanted. Other young women moved among the packed tables, wearing thongs with ten pound notes stuffed into the side straps and little more. The rules had been lifted. It was New Year's Eve, every pub and club in the city centre was heaving. No one cared about the minor by-laws tonight. For a tenner the girls would rub themselves on any customer's lap. For another tenner their thongs would be discarded and they'd wrap their legs round his or her waist, his or her neck. There were a lot of twenty-pound payers that night. It was New Year after all.

In the office, Andy Grimes was having a brandy and a chat with DCI Alex Birse and Maggie Small.

'It's been a fucking good year,' toasted Grimes.

'Ah'll drink tae that, Andy,' saluted Birse, raising his glass.

'Next year will be even better,' smiled Maggie Small, sipping at her glass of chilled Chardonnay.

'Aye, think yer right there, Maggie,' said Grimes, delivering an exaggerated, conspiratorial wink with his words. Birse hadn't been told about the bond, of course, no one knew apart from Grimes and Maggie and Angie, of course. The Bearer Bond was due to be lodged with the Deutsche Bank in the first week of the new year. The delay had been deemed sensible to ensure that no one was going to come looking for it. 'Did that guy frae the Licensing Committee turn up?' asked Grimes.

'Oh, yes,' Maggie laughed, 'and his friends. The last I saw of him he had a girl on each knee.'

'Good,' said Grimes, 'first class. Well done, Maggie.' The free night for the councillor and officials was a reward for The Cat's Whiskers having its late-night licence extended. 'What about your boys, Alex?'

'Aw their having a rerr time oot there,' replied Birse. 'They're aw here apart from one, but she's a lassie. So, Ah suppose . . .'

'Aye, if we'd known, Maggie could've fixed up a coupla young boys, eh?' laughed Grimes, accompanied by Birse and Maggie most enthusiastic of all. She wondered if Jeannie would enjoy the strip show that was going on right now, remembering the night of her blushes as Maggie fixed one of the girl's costumes.

'Listen, thanks for the drink,' said Birse, 'but Ah better head oot an join ma team.'

'Aye, good for morale annat, eh?' Grimes laughed.

'Is that wee lassie . . . what's it . . . eh, Suzie, oan the night?' asked Birse.

'No, we had to let her go,' replied Maggie, 'unreliable, but don't worry, we have some real young crackers out there.'

Maggie had sacked Suzie because of her moonlighting at other jobs and cheating on the payments by punters. The final straw had been that American's corpse being pulled from the Clyde. Maggie had recognised the newspapers' description from the passport and correspondence she'd handled. She had remembered those documents because a Yank on the streets of Glasgow, her streets, was most unusual. Bad enough that Suzie had been working on her own, but to then pass on a dead man's goods to Maggie was to pass on the contamination of the murder. To Maggie Small that was an infringement way off the scale. Suzie had left in a fury promising all sorts of revenge. In a way, Maggie recognised some of herself in the young woman, ambitious, hard headed, eager for money. Suzie would turn up again, of that Maggie was certain.

'At's a shame,' continued Birse, 'Ah liked her.' Birse downed his drink and left the office.

'You going so soon?' asked Grimes.

'Yes, if you don't mind, I have to meet someone,' replied Maggie.

'No problem, place can manage without you for a few hours, eh?'

'Remember you have that new girl to vet,' said Maggie with a grin.

'How could Ah forget,' laughed Grimes, 'send her in oan yer way oot.'

'Sure,' said Maggie walking towards the door.

'Oh, and, Maggie,' Grimes called after her. Maggie turned and looked at him, 'Happy New Year when it comes, eh?'

'Yeah, Happy New Year to you too, Andy.'

By the time Maggie was heading up to Sauchiehall Street in the back of a taxi, Grimes had started his interview.

'So, yese want tae work here, eh?' The fifteen-year-old girl from the Tuxedo Princess smiled, nodded and, without being asked, yanked her dress over her head revealing her small-breasted, naked body. Strutting behind the desk, the girl sat down on Grimes' large leather captain's chair and hooked her legs over the arms at either side. Grimes filled his glass and looked down at the young girl,

'Aw, you'll fit in here dandy. Just dandy.'

ENDS?

Jeannie Stirk was sitting at a table, a drink in her hand and another ready and waiting for Maggie by the time she arrived. Nico's Bar was packed but somehow Jeannie had managed to secure a table with the two seats crammed close together.

'Thanks for coming, Maggie,' said Jeannie reaching up to kiss her on the cheek.

'Always a pleasure to see you, Jeannie,' Maggie smiled a sly grin.

'Don't tease.'

'I'm not, you know that,' Maggie stroked the back of Jeannie's hand.

'It's just a quick drink,' Jeannie continued, 'on duty as usual,' rolling her eyes in her head.

'No change there then,' Maggie teased.

'It's a celebration,' Jeannie continued quietly. 'Just been told that I'm promoted to sergeant.'

'Well done,' Maggie reached across and hugged her friend. 'Ha, what's Birse going to think about that then, eh?'

Jeannie joined in the humour then added, 'Apparently he recommended me.'

'Oh, be careful, Jeannie.'

'I know,' smiled Jeannie, 'I will, don't worry.' The music flared up on the opening riffs of Bruce Springstein's 'Dancing in the Dark', ruling out conversation till someone behind the bar turned the volume down a shade. 'It's also to say thank you,' continued Jeannie.

'Whatever for?'

'Well, look at me.'

'Gorgeous as ever.' Jeannie smiled, it still gave her a thrill to hear Maggie say those kind of things.

'Noooo, I'm sitting here, in public, holding a beautiful woman's hand, kissing her. In public.' Jeannie leaned over and pecked Maggie's cheek. Just then her radio sounded and Jeannie scrambled to answer it.

'And while on duty even,' said Maggie, 'who's been taking brave pills?' When Jeannie eventually managed to understand the message on the radio she looked at Maggie and shrugged. 'Don't tell me . . .' said Maggie

'I'm sorry, Maggie, got to go . . . as usual.'

'Don't worry, I've someone else to meet anyway,' said Maggie then, seeing the hurt look on Jeannie's face, added immediately, 'Nothing like that. Honest. For a start it's a man.'

The two women left the bar together. Out on Sauchiehall Street, the late-night revellers were noisy and good-humoured as they warmed up towards midnight. Maggie and Jeannie stood facing each other, holding each other's hands.

'Have a good new year when it comes,' said Jeannie.

'I will, and you.'

'Yeah, sure,' Jeannie said quietly. 'I meant what I said in there.'

'I know, but I'm grateful too,' whispered Maggie.

'It was good.'

'The best.' The women kissed, their arms wrapped around each other, deaf to the comments from passing drunks, a car horn peeping. 'I meant what I said, Jeannie, you take great care.'

'I will, Maggie, and you too.' Maggie and Jeannie smiled. They were at opposite ends of the fence and the risks were the same.

'At least we'll be seeing each other from time to time.'

'That's for sure.'

The two women parted. Jeannie off to a serious assault in Gorbals, Maggie to a meeting. An important meeting. Maggie knew that they'd be seeing each other again. Maybe more often than either could guess.

31 DECEMBER 1989

The letter changed my mind, proving once and for all the value of information and of words. One minute I was guarding the two of them from afar, feeling helpless and contemplating breaking my cover. The next, well, she handed me the letter . . .

It was addressed to a Melvyn Wiseman of New York, dated June 1988, from his father. Let me spare you the full letter. Much of it was a personal farewell from an old dying man to his only son. Bad enough that you catch slivers of me in these chronicles but Mel Wiseman's father didn't write to be read by anyone other than his son. Let's respect that.

The old man was in a hospice some place out in Queens. While I'm not familiar with that part of the States, any part of the States beyond what I've gleaned from films and news reports, I believe that father and son were only an hour or so apart. The letter indicates that Mel was a regular visitor, 'a blessing to have such a son', still the old guy needed to write some thoughts down and put pen to paper.

Mel Wiseman's father was born and raised in Berlin, part of a large family, well settled for years and prosperous, owning three factories and a sweatshop. The Wisemans were Jewish and when the Nazis came to power trouble visited their door very quickly. Within a couple of years their father had suffered a stroke and was an invalid, unable to rise out of bed. The old man could talk and think, though, and he understood what was happening around them. He begged his children to flee Germany. At first they all refused. Their father was too ill to travel and their mother wouldn't leave his side. There was no way the children, all young adults by that time, would leave their parents.

One day, Mel's father discovered that his own brother had fled Berlin along with his wife without saying a word. Then the family discovered that certain valuable items were missing. Gold jewellery, diamond rings belonging to their mother and her great-grandmother before her. Small, light objects of high value, and the Bearer Bonds were missing from the family's safety deposit box: a family box and all had keys, 'Why would we not trust each other?' I can almost hear the old, dying man's wail in his words. The family had invested heavily in the bonds in the economic recession of the 1930s. They were good value investments and they thought the German government would see their actions as patriotic – a fine and futile aim of Jews in those days, in those places.

Before the start of the war, Mel's grandmother and grandfather were taken away one night. The SS came and flashed papers saying all frail people over a certain age were to have the benefit of new convalescent homes in the Black Forest. Mel's father asked why the papers were marked with the Star of David. He never got an answer and he never saw his parents again or heard from them or of them.

Mel's father and his brothers and sisters ended up in concentration camps. Of them all, he was the only one to survive. 'I look at the mark of the camp, that wretched number on my arm, and see the faces of your lost aunts and uncles.' He carried the guilt of his survival to his deathbed.

When he was liberated, his health built up, he decided to get as far away from Germany, from the nightmares as he could. Poor man, he thought that distance would help dispel his horrors but found that they clung to his back. He met and married and Mel was born. The old man seems to have been a reasonably successful journalist. 'When you were young and I was not there, Mama told you I was abroad working. She was telling you the truth but not in the way you have always thought.'

The old man went on expeditions to Europe in search of his brother, Jakob, and his sister-in-law, Ruth. He wasn't a journalist for nothing. Research showed him part of their trail and their arrival in Britain where they were dumped in a detention centre for almost all of the war. So he started there in the Channel Islands. Moved back to Amsterdam and even to Marseilles where they had been known to travel through en route to safety.

All along the way he met some who remembered Jakob and Ruth Wiseman and recognised them from one of the few family photographs that had survived the war. All spoke of what a loving couple Jakob and Ruth had been, then, with some embarrassment, raised less complimentary memories.

Wherever they travelled, Jakob and Ruth Wiseman had made a habit of swindling the very people who risked their lives to shelter them. Family jewellery, money, even clothes and food. 'They had left a trail of shame on our family.'

Finally, the old man received a phone call saying that Jakob and Ruth now called themselves Wise and had moved to Glasgow. By that time his health was ruined and he was unable to travel. Now he was dying and was passing on a duty of honour to his only son.

'Go find them. Take from them what is not theirs to have. Do not harm them but beware, they may harm you. Please, Melvyn, finish my task in my memory and for the honour of your family.'

The old man attached copious details to his letter. Every name and address of every person he'd met who claimed Jakob and Ruth Wise had cheated them, and every item listed. All were to be repaid. Then a list of the Bearer Bonds, with serial numbers, and pencilled against them the names of the family members who owned the bonds. Young Mel was to return the bonds to the original owners' relatives where there were such distant survivors. For those with no survivors the money was to go to charities, a different one for each family member, I guess reflecting something of what moved them.

Finally, the old man's calculations of how much

the bonds were likely to be worth. Five of the bonds
were to be inherited by Mel himself. He was going
to be well off and had two motivations: honour and
gain, a dangerous combination.

Then she handed me the letter and papers along
with Mel Wiseman's passport and later I learned he
had been fished out of the Clyde. That's when I
decided to redeem the bonds. As I did so I almost
felt sorry for Angie the Gopher – almost but not
quite. He made the job easier for me by floating
away in that ambulance. I hope Grimes doesn't treat
him too badly, that bastard has a long evil memory.

Now my task is to follow Mel's father's wishes.
Why not? It's a debt caused by real crime against
citizens of the world. I don't mean Jakob and Ruth,
they were just greedy like so many others. I mean
the treatment of the Jews, the death camps. If that
hadn't happened maybe Jakob and Ruth Wise would
still be called Wiseman, living in the bosom of
their family in the heart of Berlin. Maybe.

Now all I need is for her to agree to my plan. As
for the bonds that were Mel's inheritance, well, they
are ours to split but I have plans about . . .

'James Addison, put that gun down. And another thing, if you keep
typing every night you'll hurt your eyesight.'

'And if you keep using yer key without buzzing up first, maybe one
day ye'll end up being shot.' Addie laid the pistol flat on the table
between the typewriter and his glass of white wine.

'Help me with a problem.' Maggie Small took off her coat and laid
it on the back of a chair.

'If Ah can.'

'When we meet in here are you always James Addison . . .' she pulled
cigarettes out of her handbag, selected one by the tips of her fine nails,
tapped the tobacco end on the side of the packet then lit it, exhaling a
luxurious thick plume of blue smoke, '. . . or are you occasionally Sean
Ferguson?'

'Whit's this?' smiled Fergie. 'A bit late at night for philosophical
conundrums.'

'Mmm,' smiled Maggie, 'it's New Year, that time between the old and the new, separating past from future, the real from the spectres.'

'Pheew, ye've been with Jeannie.'

'How do you know?'

'You always get either deep or dreamy afterwards.' Maggie nodded her head, thinking what Fergie had said was probably accurate. 'Besides, ye've got her shade of red lipstick smeared over your cheek.'

'Well, it isn't just anybody gets snogged by a detective sergeant, I'll have you know,' Maggie said giggling, hoping it was game, set and match, pulling a mirror out, fixing her make-up. Fergie just smiled and conceded while Maggie continued, 'You're not watching that, are you?'

'Whit?'

'The TV, there's some boring political programme on,' grumbled Maggie, 'it's New Year's Eve, for Christ's sake.'

'Ach, it's oan for the Bells,' said Fergie.

'Addie the traditionalist,' she smirked, 'who would've thought?'

'Aye, aye take the piss, go ahead.'

'Heard from Joe lately?' Maggie asked, knowing the question would hurt but believing Fergie needed to talk about it.

'Naw, don't think Ah gave him this address,' replied Fergie with a sickly grin, 'just as well, eh?'

'Charing Cross Mansions – don't think he'd expect Fergie to have a pad up here.' Maggie spread her arms to indicate the pristine, modern, penthouse flat. Everything about it was trendy, middle-class professional – not Fergie at all but certainly Addie.

'One of my wee secrets,' he grinned.

'One of many,' she countered with a simper.

'It was an accident,' his face turned sombre.

'Mmmmm,' she teased, showing a mouthful of even white teeth. He shook his head sadly and continued.

'Addie was invented when Ah was a teenager,' he paused, hoping against hope that no further explanation was necessary.

'Yeah,' she smiled, 'I invented a few fantasies myself back then. But you . . . you seem real to me. Could be mistaken though . . .'

'Whit Ah mean,' he blustered on, 'is that Fergie got stuck. Stranded in a world of cheap hash, bottled lager and women that's his for a fifty quid night on the razzle. Being Fergie,' he insisted, 'was an accident.

The timing was not of my choosing. I hate Fergie BUUUT I can be him – the dirty stopout, feckless fuckwit that's always broke – on spare change.' She eyed him sceptically from the other side of the room. 'Look,' he persisted, 'Ah get pissed, rent the council flat in Balornock, throw away dough at the bookies and still have the best part of my stash.'

'You should give lessons to pimply adolescents,' she grinned.

'Naw. Joe Murphy should.' He was in the mood for elegy not jests.

'Joe again,' she sighed.

'Aye,' a reasonable sweet, indignant tone to his voice. 'Joe Murphy. Thank Joe for this,' he spread his arms out indicating the flat. 'And thank Joe Murphy for Addie. James Addison.'

'Think he'd approve if he knew?' she asked, serious and curious.

'Bet yer wages oan it he would,' he answered, conviction raising his voice. Maggie looked at Fergie across the room and slowly nodded her head. In business she made partnerships reluctantly, so warily that this was her first. All the others were shams, part of her game plan. But she was gently acknowledging that she would consider Joe Murphy. After all, if James Addison trusted in him what higher recommendation did she need?

'High time you got a computer, by the way,' she grinned and changed the subject, 'that old typewriter just doesn't suit this place.' Fergie seemed not to hear her, his head slumping forward, eyes looking blindly at his feet. Maggie noticed, 'I'm sorry about that, about Joe, the way it happened.'

'Aye, well it was necessary, and sometimes things have tae go back before they can go forward, eh?'

'Still . . .'

'Ah'll sort it. New Year's resolution,' Fergie replied winking, 'you can bet yer bottom dollar oan it.' Maggie would have if she'd found anyone daft enough to give her odds. Fergie and Joe were as close as she'd found any two people and all the others in her top ten were women. There was something special about Joe and no one knew that better than Fergie.

'You sure you're going to have that long to sort it out?' asked Maggie, her face masked with softness, concern.

'Whit ye mean?'

'Are you not wanted for a bank robbery?'

'Aye but . . .'

'So why have they not arrested you?' she shrilled, showing more emotion than she cared to. 'Are they waiting to see if somebody else takes you out . . . suspecting you as an informant?' Fergie looked at her worried face, all wrinkled brow and wide eyes, and smiled.

'Aye,' he grinned, 'of course they are. It's standard practice.'

'Aren't you . . .'

'It's just Birse. Holding the paperwork up.' He shrugged and smirked as he watched her take a double draw on her cigarette. 'But tell me,' he went on, catching her attention, 'how's your Jeannie Stirk?'

'Fine . . .' she hesitated, 'I mean, why?'

'Can Ah rely oan her? Ah mean really rely oan her like ma life depended oan it?'

'Of cou . . . yes . . . mean absolutely.'

'Good,' he nodded and smiled. 'Good. In which case it's just a matter of time afore Ah'm lifted.' She frowned, still not understanding. 'Look,' he went on, 'never believe what you read in the papers or see in the movies. Suspects are lifted at all sorts of different times. Ma people know that – it's part o the life we lead.' She nodded slowly. 'If Jeannie's okay – and Ah think she is – Ah'm going to jail.'

'Oh, you're going to jail then, Sean Ferguson,' Maggie nodded her head.

'Good.' For a second, just a second, Maggie Small wondered what kind of upside-down world she'd fallen into. But if she had any doubts about who her ally really was, that act of sacrificing his one close friendship told her all. Jack the lad Fergie, who couldn't keep a secret. Always looking for a good time, quick with a knife, his heart ruling his head – he would have wept for Scotland and killed anyone who mocked while proclaiming that Joe Murphy was the best thing since screw-tops. Addie, now he'd take the pain, lose his mate for a while and find him again as if the water had not been disturbed – smooth, effortless, uncomplaining. It was Addie she knew.

'Listen,' said Maggie, changing the topic away from Joe, 'I agree.'

'So ye think that Aberdeen will win the football league again this year in spite of both gods willing otherwise?' Fergie butted in.

'Nooo,' Maggie shook her head, wondering who it was talking to her, the daftie Fergie or the spectre Addie. 'I agree with your plan on the bonds. Follow the old man's instructions and what's left is ours.' Fergie looked at Maggie with troubled eyes but inside he was feeling amazement and gratitude.

'Ye know, you're aw right, Maggie Small,' he said warmly. 'Ye must've had a helluva set of parents. Lots o early nourishing annat, eh?' Maggie didn't answer. Fergie continued, 'Ye must be really bloody angry with Grimes. To be doing all this, teaming up with me like.'

'So, this is the traditional Hogmanay approach is it, Fergie?' said Maggie. ' A New Year's Eve of bringing out the emotions, touching on the past, all the better to move forward, stronger.'

'Aye,' smiled Fergie, 'well, you started it.'

'No, I don't hate Grimes. I'm indifferent about Grimes,' replied Maggie. 'But somebody just like him, so like him . . .'

'If ye don't want tae speak aboot it it's okay,' Fergie hadn't ever seen Maggie show signs of vulnerability but it was shining through now.

'Somebody like Grimes hurt my father, badly hurt my father and didn't even notice. Nobody noticed unless you were his son . . . or his daughter. Then you knew you had lost him, forever. Men like Grimes did that.' Maggie recalled the night she'd blurted it all out to Jeannie Stirk – the bland details. Then she hadn't said what it all meant. Just gave her the historical summary. Who was she telling most to – Jeannie or Fergie or Addie? She took a deep breath, 'I'm going to help Andy Grimes achieve his goals. Build him up till he has everything he has ever wanted and then . . .'

'Aye, then what?' asked Addie. Maggie pulled a long, thin cigarette from her packet, tapped the tip rapidly on the coffee table, put the fag in her mouth and lifted her lighter. 'I'm going to ruin him.' She lit her cigarette. 'Take it all away. Then I'm taking a bunch of red roses to a cemetery in Coatbridge.' She puffed nervously on her smoke for a while, the tip growing red and angry. 'After? I'm going to live MY life.' Maggie hushed then, enough had been said, New Year or no New Year. She just picked up the bottle of wine from the coffee table and poured herself a drink. Then words from the television caught her attention,

'*Deutsche Bank . . . Bearer Bonds . . . serial numbers . . . valid . . . invalid . . . later announcement . . .*'

'What the hell was that about?' asked Maggie, but Fergie was already scribbling notes, the volume of the TV turned up. Fergie had beaten her to it. On his feet and across the room. She hadn't known about the safe covered by the carpet under the TV. Was his carelessness in going to it now a mark of his trust in her or his desperate worry?

Fergie back on his seat, bonds on his lap, working through each thick sheet of paper one by one. The TV item went on.

'. . . *the Deutsche Bank has announced that many of the Bearer Bonds bought in the early 1930s have already been redeemed through special negotiation . . . given the likely imminent reunification of Germany, the Bank expect many more Bearer Bonds to be brought forward. Many may be forged or copied . . . high value interest . . . drain on resources . . . the Bank has released details of redeemed bonds . . .*'

The TV anchorman kept talking as the screen filled with lists of serial numbers of Bearer Bonds which had already been cashed in. Maggie watched with horror as Fergie noted and wrote fast. As the programme moved to another topic, Fergie remained quiet, working through the list of bonds, checking his thumb across the serial numbers.

'Well?' Maggie had waited long enough to ask the question.

'Well, well,' replied Fergie looking up, smiling. 'Ye want the good news or the bad news?'

'Come on, Fergie,' Maggie pleaded, 'just tell me.'

'The bad news is that most of these bonds are worthless.' As it had said in the letter, the bonds ran consecutively, the Wiseman family having bought many bonds at the one time. 'And the good news is, if the bond that Grimes has is this one here, a missing number in the sequence . . .' Fergie paused, looking at Maggie. It didn't take her long to work it out and she finished his sentence,

'Grimes' bond is worthless too . . . show me the number,' Maggie was on her feet. Fergie wrote out the missing number in the sequence and circled it. Fergie stared at her and she smiled. The two looked at each other, trying to work out how the other was feeling about the loss, the sudden change in the situation.

'Dae ye think,' started Fergie, 'that Grimes is watching the TV right now?'

'Mmm, let's see,' Maggie answered, a smile creeping on to her lips, 'mmm, No.'

In The Cat's Whiskers Club, Grimes was sitting in his large desk chair, the naked fifteen-year-old girl on his lap feeding him sips of his favourite brandy by dipping her finger into the amber fluid and lifting it to his lips. In the background, a large TV set threw ghostly shadows over the dark room – a silent and ignored screen – while Grimes explained to the girl how the next year was going to be a very big year for him.

'He's going to be a wee bit angry, eh?' said Fergie, a laugh breaking through his voice.

'Bloody furious,' said Maggie laughing loudly.

When their laughter had died away, slowly and painfully, still hanging on to their spirits, Fergie added, 'Ah forgot the really good news.'

'You holding out on me?' Maggie retorted. 'That's more Fergie than Addie. Or is it more . . .'

'One of our bonds wasn't on the list,' he added finally. Serious expression now, holding the bond up.

'One bond,' mused Maggie, the dreamy look returning to her face, 'what will we do with one bond?'

'Campaign funds, Ah reckon,' smiled Fergie, 'for next year.'

Maggie shook her head and smiled across at her friend, 'You've come over all James Addison on me again.'

THE BELLS

Maggie Small and Fergie stood in the middle of the room at Charing Cross Mansions, full glasses of whisky in their hands, the way the New Year should be welcomed. They were watching the TV screen, waiting for a change of scene to London.

'Do you never tire of playing the fool?' she asked.

'Aye and no. The trouble is I started too young. Then I was the boy with the blade, fast on his feet, slow in his noggin, obsessed with flashy fanny, bevvy, loud music . . . candy-floss shite. Ah forgot tae let him grow up but Ah moved oan. Pain in the ass sometimes but it can be a laugh,' he answered, cradling his drink in both hands.

'A laugh but not a joke,' she offered.

'Oh, naw,' he replied, 'never a joke.'

'You could use the money to get out of here,' she suggested, 'end this game, leave, go abroad.'

'Naw, don't think so,' he replied, 'James Addison has some unfinished business.'

The midnight chimes of Big Ben rang out, weighty and solemn, bringing an end to their conversation.

As the last stroke of midnight rung out, 'Happy New Year,' she said.

'Happy New Year,' he smiled. They drank and kissed.

'And here's to James Addison,' she raised her glass and toasted.

'Aye,' he said, 'a good year coming tae James Addison. That's for sure.'

DEADLY DIVISIONS